WYRD

WHITE HAVEN WITCHES (BOOK 11)

MAGIC

TJ GREEN

Wyrd Magic

Mountolive Publishing

Copyright © 2023 TJ Green

All rights reserved

ISBN eBook: 978-1-99-004756-5

ISBN Paperback: 978-1-99-004757-2

Cover design by Fiona Jayde Media

Editing by Missed Period Editing

www.tjgreenauthor.com

Contents

Chapter One

Briar Ashworth threw another pile of golden leaves onto the garden fire, and then dusted the debris from her hands.

She smiled with satisfaction as she looked at her surroundings. She was working in one of Stormcrossed Manor's larger courtyards, this one with a potting shed on one side, and finally, after weeks of work, the grounds were looking much tidier. However, there was no doubt they still required a lot more work. *No matter.* She was enjoying every minute of it.

It was Sunday afternoon near the end of October, and the sun was sinking low on the horizon. She was wrapped up in boots, scarf, and thick layers of clothes to keep out the autumnal chill. It was one of her favourite times of year. She enjoyed the feeling of putting the garden to bed, knowing that everything would be ready to emerge again in the spring.

The gardens were now a skeletal framework of branches. Perennials were dying, some had been cut back, and only the hardiest of flowers now remained. Tamsyn, her grandmother—even now saying that word brought a smile to Briar's lips—had given her permission to come and go as she pleased. It meant that with every day that Briar spent there, she'd been able to spend time with her newfound family, too. It was strange to think that only three months earlier she hadn't even known they existed.

The squeaking of the wheelbarrow as it came down the path heralded the return of Max, Briar's twelve-year old nephew. His excited chatter had accompanied many of her hours there. After the events in July in which the family banshee had almost killed Tamsyn and Briar, Max seemed to have recovered well. Back then he'd been quiet and withdrawn. Now, he never stopped talking. He was keeping a running commentary at present, as he appeared with Tamsyn next to him.

"Granny! You've come to see us!" Briar said to her in greeting, kissing her cheek. "I thought you were baking."

"I've baked enough to see us through until Yuletide. Well, I would have if this small man didn't eat three times his body weight every day." Tamsyn narrowed her beetle-dark eyes at Max, who was almost taller than she was, but her smile was genuine.

"I can't help it, I'm always hungry," he grumbled as he forked the leaves out of the wheelbarrow and into the big pile ready for burning. Briar had organised a compost heap for the leaves to rot down and create leaf mould, but there was so many of them that they added them to the piles of dead and pruned branches that needed burning, too.

"That's all right," Tamsyn reassured him. "It's a sign my cakes and biscuits are good."

Max grinned, wheeled his barrow around, and headed off again. "I'll go and fetch some more."

Briar laughed. "I think you know that your baking is good, Gran. My friends never stop asking for it."

"Good. Take some home with you. Although, you know this could be your home."

This was a familiar discussion, and one that Briar refused to back down on. "As lovely as this place is—or will be—I need my space, Gran. And I like being in White Haven, close to my shop, and my friend's pub. I won't lie."

"And that nice Newton man."

"He's a friend! I've told you, I'm seeing Hunter." Briar hadn't told her that Hunter was a wolf shifter. Tamsyn had accepted witches and banshees, and there was no doubt she was open minded to the old ways and the paranormal, but a shifter? *Maybe not so much*. And she hadn't told her about the Nephilim, either.

"You are so not seeing Hunter," Tamsyn said. "He's miles away. He's been here once since I've known you. That's no way to have a relationship."

Briar fell quiet, staring into the flames. She was right. Cumbria was a long way away, and Hunter was busy with his family and his pack. She was busy with her own circle of friends and family. As much as Briar had fantasised about Hunter moving to White Haven, or her moving to Cumbria, she knew it would never happen. Especially now that she had family here.

Tamsyn cleared her throat, and Briar felt the weight of her stare. She turned to her. "Yes, I know. I need to end it. But I don't want to."

"Why not?"

"Because I like him! He makes me feel loved and safe."

"With abs to die for, too." Tamsyn cackled with glee as Briar's mouth dropped open. "Oh yes, I remember abs. I'm old, not an idiot. But a nice chest does you no good so far away. You need someone close. Maybe that big man who helps here sometimes. That Zee. I bet he has abs, and then some. If I was fifty years younger..."

Tamsyn had met Zee when he had helped with some of the bigger gardening jobs, and was impressed with his size. *The Goddess help her if Tamsyn ever met Eli*. Briar was determined to keep them apart, or she'd never hear the last of it. Briar shook her head, unable to believe the change in her grandmother. Now that she had shed the weight of carrying the banshee's grief, her sense of humour had emerged, and it was wicked. She was observant, teased them all mercilessly, baked endlessly, and helped in the garden where she could. And, with Rosa's help, she was cleaning the house, which was no mean feat. The place had years of accumulated dirt and everything was dilapidated, but she scrubbed what she could manage. Her kitchen now gleamed.

Briar huffed. "Gran, please stop trying to fix my love life. I'll work it out."

"Well, just make sure you do. And let Hunter down gently. It will be hard for him, too."

Briar felt her eyes prick with tears just at the thought, and she brushed them aside with the back of her hand. She needed to change the subject. "How's Beth doing?"

Tamsyn heaved a forkful of leaves onto the fire, and then prodded the burning branches, watching embers drift skyward. "It's slow going. She's gifted, but too young to control the Sight well. It doesn't help that her power is so raw."

"Do you think the lapis lazuli and obsidian necklace is helping her?" El had fashioned a necklace with two small gemstones and spells woven into it, designed to protect Beth and help strengthen her response to visions.

Tamsyn shrugged. "Perhaps. It has been a while since she's had a vision. It could be the necklace, but more likely that things are stable right now. She's happier, too. The fact that Rosa is calmer is also helping."

Tamsyn's lips tightened at this statement. She and Rosa did not always see eye to eye. Briar understood why. Rosa had a flair for the dramatic, and had clashed with Tamsyn over the family's ability with the Sight. She was furious that Beth had the gift, but it was hardly Tamsyn's fault. She had known it was a possibility, but had tried to forget about it. Briar found her cousin's attitude frustrating, too.

"What about Alex's help?" Briar asked. Alex Bonneville had been a regular visitor to the manor. His own psychic abilities were strong, but trying to teach a child was not Alex's specialty.

"When she's older he will help, no doubt about it. His strength is in calming his mind and his ability to focus, but she's too young to grasp that right now. And of course, the fact that he can walk paths that few can." Tamsyn cocked her head at her like a bird. "A great skill, and a scary one. Hopefully a skill Beth will never have. I certainly haven't got it."

"I agree. It's not something I would like," Briar confessed. She shuddered at the thought of entering the spirit realm. "But the thing is, Gran, it will soon be Samhain. The time when the veils between worlds will be thinner. I'm not joking when I say that in White Haven it can be very strong. Could that affect Beth? Or you?"

Tamsyn drew her shawl around her shoulders and stared into the flames. "Since the banshee has gone, I have felt my own abilities stir. Last night, I saw a stag. A white stag. It was on a rise on the moor, wrapped in mists. Its eyes glowed a bright blue and it seemed to stare right through me. It was...odd."

"A white stag? That means something, doesn't it? Doesn't it signify that something important it about to happen? Something good?"

"It offers support for what will come. Emotional and spiritual support." She turned to Briar. "The stag is positive, a good thing—I felt it. But what it portends, I don't know. Perhaps it is to do with Samhain. Time will tell."

"Have you ever seen one before?"

"Never. That's why I'm confused. Normally, I see snatches of the future. This felt different. A totem spirit perhaps, come to guide me."

Briar was unfamiliar with the concept, although she had heard of it. "A spirit guide! Is that yours?"

"I never knew I had one, but maybe it is. I'm not a spirit-worker, Briar. It doesn't make sense to me. Not yet."

Briar was going to ask more, but Tamsyn had fallen silent as she stared into the flames.

The sun had almost vanished below the horizon now and ground mist was rising and mixing with the smoke from the fire. It was so cold that Briar could see her breath pluming in front of her. A shadowy stillness had fallen over them, broken only by the crackle of the branches in the fire. Briar pulled her thick cardigan around her and held her hands to the flames, comforted by their warmth.

The branches shifted as the fire consumed them, and just for a moment they looked like huge, tined antlers mounted above a face covered in swirling symbols, from which two intense eyes stared back at her.

Not a stag, but a young man.

"Here you go, Avery," Alex said, thrusting a glass of mulled wine into her hands. "That will warm you up. It's a good one."

Avery Hamilton smiled at him. She was wrapped in a voluminous green scarf that brought out the colour of her eyes and deepened the red of her hair. "Your mulled wine is always good. Too good." She sipped it and shuddered with delight. "Lovely."

"Excellent." He leaned forward and kissed her cheek, taking in the scent that was all Avery. A hint of musk and roses, with extra hints of woodsmoke rolled in. "Smoky. Sexy!"

They were in their walled garden, celebrating the end of a hard day's gardening. They had collected herbs, plants, and roots for spell work, as well as raked up leaves and cut plants back. A fire burned on the turned soil beyond the small lawn, and twilight was already thickening, although it was only late afternoon.

"I think I prefer autumn to any other season," Alex confessed after sipping his own spiced drink. "Although maybe it's because of Samhain, my favourite festival. This year should be fun. Are we at Rasmus's again?"

"Yes, and he's excited, too. He's providing mulled wine and cider, toffee apples, cinnamon buns, and all sorts of other delicious treats. It's all he could talk about at the last Witches Council meeting." She looked over her steaming glass at Alex. "We need a good celebration. Something that doesn't involve being attacked or having to bind other coven members."

"And we need a Samhain that doesn't involve us tackling the Wild Hunt."

"It did deliver us Shadow. That was a blessing."

Alex laughed. "That's one way of putting it. At least we've had a few quiet months." He rested his arm around her shoulders and pulled her to his side. "I've enjoyed that. It's been good to spend time with Briar's new family, too. I just wish I could help Beth more."

"She's too young to really understand what's happening."

"I suppose so." Alex thought of Beth's intense stare and far-seeing gaze. "She's uncanny, though. An old soul."

"Is she?" Avery twisted to look up at him. "You haven't said that before."

"Don't you think so? Maybe it's because I've spent more time with her. I've been trying to get her to understand she needs to relax when the visions come. At the moment, it freaks her out so much she tenses up." He laughed. "Maybe she isn't an old soul, or you'd think she'd be more comfortable with all this. Maybe it's the Sight that makes her seem that way. Tamsyn calls it raw power, and she's right. It certainly is."

"I believe in that, though," Avery said thoughtfully. "The old soul thing. Some people are new to the world, as if they have only just arrived. They're naïve, see everything at face value. Others, like us, we've been around a few times, wouldn't you say? I sometimes feel the weight of previous lives, especially when I'm reading the tarot. It's as if other eyes are seeing through mine, and passing their knowledge on to me."

"Your fugue state, you sometimes call it," Alex said, nodding. The cards always transported Avery to another place. It was her way of accessing the unseen things of the world, like the visions and spirit-walking worked for him. "Of course I believe it, but this is a strange topic for mulled wine and fires."

"I think it's the perfect time. Twilight, smoke, and flames, at the end of a day spent collecting herbs and plants for spell-making. Magic is spinning around us tonight. I feel it."

That's why he loved Avery. Her ability to feel magic in everything. It wasn't just her capabilities as a witch and her strength with air; it went beyond that. He stilled his mind, casting his worry for Beth away, and opened his senses to the garden. She was right. "It's a liminal time, though, isn't it? When the veils between worlds become thin, especially at Samhain. But there's more." He sent his magical awareness out further into the gathering twilight that was cloaked with mist and whispers. "It's like something is watching us, just beyond our normal sight."

Avery wriggled into him, her arm around his waist under his jacket. "Our ancestors are gathering, ready for Samhain. Helena is stronger than usual. I see her every day now. I wonder if Gil will return. I hope he does. I miss him."

"Me too. Although, I hope he's at rest, too. But I feel more than just a vague sense of spirits. It's something else." Alex closed his eyes and focussed. "A strong presence seems to be predominant. A male, I think. I sense that he's old—both in time and place. As if he's reaching out from the past." The longer Alex stood with his eyes closed, the stronger the presence felt. The garden and the fire fell away, but the scent of smoke remained. In fact, it was getting stronger. He took a sharp intake of breath and his eyes flew open, and immediately the sensation vanished. The fire still burned low in front of them, the smoke idling towards the sky. "That was odd. I thought the smoke had blown my way, it smelled so strong."

Avery pulled away from his arms and faced him. "I sensed something, too. I'm not sure if it was a presence, but I had the feeling of being watched, and the distance of time. How old, do you think?"

"Hard to say from that brief interaction, and now it's gone. Damn it. I should have just focussed a bit longer."

"While I hate to say this, it's likely we'll feel it again. Especially as we get closer to Samhain. Perhaps it's an ancestor reaching out. I like that idea. I think." She grimaced. "As long as he just wants to say hello."

Alex's phone buzzed in his pocket, dragging him back to the present. A text message from the tone. When he saw it, he couldn't quite believe his eyes. "Bloody hell, Avery. Something weird *is* happening."

"Why?" She looked alarmed. "Is everyone okay?"

"Hard to say. My dad is coming to visit. All the way from bonny Scotland."

Chapter Two

A very surveyed Happenstance Books with a sigh of delight. It was mid-morning on Monday, and she and Sally were behind the counter, drinking coffee and chatting.

Sally had once again worked her own kind of magic over the previous few days, decorating the shop for Samhain, and it looked fabulous. Lights twinkled, Briar's candles emitted bewitching scents, incense smoked around the books, and strings of paper pumpkins, ghosts, and bats were suspended over the bookcases. Sally had also set up display tables stacked with witchcraft books, diaries, tarot cards, and other witch-themed goodies.

"You look happy," Sally told her, dunking a shortbread biscuit into her coffee. "You had a good weekend?"

"The best. But it's your decorating that has really made me happy! Seeing it again this morning has given me the warm fuzzies."

Sally blushed. "Thanks. Let's hope you're still as happy when your costume arrives in a couple of days. Dan picked it."

Avery's good mood instantly evaporated. She had forgotten all about Halloween costumes. "Dan! Why couldn't *I* pick it? Or you?"

"Avery! You know why you didn't. You made a face. The very face that you are making now. As if we'd shut up and it would go away. Well, it hasn't. You're wearing a costume, whether you like it not. It's good for business. And Dan beat me to it." Sally had the grace to look guilty. "We tossed for it, and he won."

Avery tried not to scowl, especially as one of her regulars sniggered and then scooted further into the shop. Sally had asked her the question a couple of months ago. "You asked me when I was preparing for Mabon. I was distracted."

"You put it off." Sally grinned. "Actually, I think it's cool. It will be so much fun!"

"What is it?"

"I'll let Dan tell you." She swept her arm to the front window, decorated with swags of dried leaves and pumpkins. "And here he is!"

The morning had a nip of frost in the air, and Dan was wrapped in a scarf and thick coat. He swept through the front door with a jingle of bells and carrying a bag of cakes. He grinned as he greeted them. "Ladies! Thanks for that extra time off, Avery. It was a crazy busy weekend, but the podcast is all done!"

"No problem. Well, there wasn't one, until I heard you've picked a weird costume for me to wear for Samhain."

Dan huffed, ruffling his hair as he pulled his woolly hat off. "Sally is telling porky pies. It's really fun! Playful! You want to be playful, don't you?"

"Playful! That sounds ominous. I'm not sure I do." By now, Avery was fairly seething with curiosity. "Well?"

"You're going to be a fortune teller—Gypsy Rose! Fun, right?"

"You have got to be kidding me. Gypsy Rose?" All sorts of images flashed through her mind. "Don't you dare make me tell fortunes!"

Dan sighed dramatically. "Just a pretend one! The customers will love it!"

"Told you," Sally said, grabbing a pastry after finishing her biscuit. "You were nearly a slinky black cat in a rubber costume. I saved you from that. You're welcome!"

Avery took a deep breath and kept her voice low, knowing her customers had very big ears. "And how long do I have to wear if for?"

"You know the drill, Ave!" Dan shrugged his coat off, revealing a seasonal t-shirt saying, "*Trick or Read*" with a ghost and books on it. "All of Samhain week. Maybe earlier. We'll all be wearing them. I shall be Edgar Allen Poe, complete with a raven on my shoulder, and Sally will be the Queen of Hearts. See? Fun! And literary."

Avery considered complaining, and then decided just to suck it up. She'd had a fantastic Sunday, all cosied up with Alex, and she didn't want to sour it. "Fine. I shall wear it with grace and dignity. Will you be running the reading corner, Dan?"

"Of course. I will think of some suitably spooky books for the kids. We're going to have a great Samhain!" He nudged her arm playfully. "You can thank me later."

Sally rolled her eyes. "Both of us! Who will be doing the baking?"

"Ah, yes. You will, and thank the Gods for that. Biscuits?"

"Of course, and Halloween muffins with appropriately gruesome toppings. I've had some great ideas! And," her eyes widened with delight, "I'll set up tables stacked with Edgar Allen Poe's books, *Alice in Wonderland*, clairvoyancy books, and..." She shot Avery a guilty look. "A little corner for you. It's going to be so much fun!"

"A corner for me to do what?"

Sally actually squeaked. "Tell fortunes! We can use tarot cards, a crystal ball, pots of tea, palmistry... They can pay you a few pennies, and we'll give it all to charity." As Avery glared, speechless, she added, "Of your choosing, obviously!"

"*We*? There is no we, there is only *I*!" Resigning herself to her fate, Avery sighed. "I must admit, I'm impressed. Promoting books with the costumes we're wearing is brilliant. I will do my best—but I will only perform for *one* hour a day! Anyway, I have weird news. Alex's dad, Finn, is coming to visit."

"Love that name!" Sally said. "So gorgeous."

"But that's good news, right?" Dan asked as he eased behind the counter and started to search through their music selection.

"Well, yes, but it's unusual. He hasn't lived here for years. I mean, they get on well enough, but we just don't know why he wants to come back."

Sally frowned. "He didn't say?"

"No. It was just a text. Actually, I feel a bit nervous about it, which is silly, I know," Avery confessed. She reached for a cinnamon bun. The sugar would help calm her nerves. "I haven't met him before. I feel I need to get his approval because I'm seeing Alex."

"Living with Alex! Not just seeing him," Sally corrected her. "And does it even matter? You and Alex have been together now for over a year. Alex won't give a monkey's arse what his dad thinks!"

"I know! But you know what I mean. Dan, have you met Caro's parents yet?"

Dan adjusted the volume of the blues album he'd put on, and then leaned against the wall. "I've met her mum, and that went well, but yes, I was nervous. I don't know when I'll meet her dad. They're separated, and he doesn't live around here. But that's good for me. Men always worry about meeting their girlfriend's dad and that stare of disapproval."

"Exactly! What if he thinks I'm not good enough for Alex?"

"Of course he'll think you're good enough. Why wouldn't he?" Sally sounded exasperated. "You're lovely. Just make sure you clean up your flat if he comes around!" She gave Avery a cheeky grin. It was well known that she accumulated things in her eclectic flat.

"Alex is very tidy. He's constantly moving my stuff. I never know where anything is anymore. I had a perfectly good system going that he ignores."

Dan laughed. "The system where you leave stuff everywhere in a heap of crazy? Yes, that's not so helpful."

Avery bristled and decided to bring the conversation back to Alex's dad. "Anyway, at least he won't be staying with us. He'll stay in Alex's old flat. It's still furnished. He's getting it ready to rent, actually."

Sally nodded. "I noticed the construction work the other day. Is he putting in a new entrance?"

"Yes. He's boxing off the stairs so that it's separate from the pub. It's a good idea. At the moment, it doesn't get used for anything." Avery mulled over Finn's arrival. "He must have some kind of news, or why come all this way?"

"Families do visit sometimes, Ave. It's normal," Sally said, finishing her pastry and sweeping crumbs off the counter and into the bin. "Ours come and go all the time."

"Not for us. You know most of our families left Cornwall a long time ago. All that history and our old issues with the council weighs on them."

"Yes, but it's Samhain," Dan said. "It's a time for people to remember and honour their ancestors. Maybe he wants to reconnect with the living and the dead—before it's too late."

"I suppose so." Avery stared at her friends' baffled expressions and tried to shrug off her concerns. It was a nice thing. It didn't have to mean anything. However, it did prompt feelings of guilt about her own family. "I should go and see my gran. It's been a few weeks since my last visit. I put it off because she can never remember me. Maybe I'll call my mum, too."

"And your sister, maybe?" Sally asked.

"Let's not go mad!" Avery did not have a good relationship with her sister, and Sally and Dan both knew that. "Distance suits us."

Sally was strongly family-orientated, and struggled with Avery's odd familial relationships. "At least call your mum, Avery, before she calls you. It will make her happy. I'm a mum. I know that to be true! Anyway," she collected the mugs and the bag that the cakes had been in, "I need to do some ordering for Samhain. I have books I need to stock, and a few other themed goodies, so I'll do it now."

"She's right, you know," Dan said as Sally headed to the back room. "Things are different in White Haven now. She might want to visit. You can tell her about the council and the coven you've formed. I think she'll be pleased."

"I'm not sure I want her to, actually, but maybe there is something to the time of the year. Alex and I had a strange experience in the garden last night. I put it down to the twilight, the silence, and the fire. It was so still, so calm. I felt...peaceful. At one with nature."

"Aren't you always? Isn't that," Dan lowered his voice, "a witchy thing?"

"Well, yes, but I *really* felt it last night. This strong connection to the land. It felt like a spirit was watching, one with a real presence. And no, it wasn't Helena."

"Really? Interesting. Any idea who it may have been?"

"No. Alex was sure it was male. One thing we agreed on was that it seemed to reach from the distant past—I don't know how far back, though."

Dan sat on the stool vacated by Sally and leaned on the counter. "That's odd, surely. Don't ghosts manifest in the present? I mean, you know. They're dead, but when they cross over from their plane to ours, that puts them in our time. *If* they cross planes. Perhaps some have never *crossed* at all."

Avery sank her chin into her palm, her elbow on the counter. "That's sort of a good point. But spirits are odd. If they died a long time ago, they might feel old. As if they were in the past."

"Is that how it's felt to you before? I mean, I can't say. I've only experienced Helena, and she feels very much in the present. Well, apart from the smoke smell she brings with her. That's definitely from the past! But...well, you know what I mean."

"I do, actually. She's very much in the here and now." Avery considered how the ghosts in White Haven Castle had felt the night they first met Ghost OPS. They were violent, and were incredibly corporeal, as were the spirits of the pirates who'd attacked them. "The ones we've fought were really physical, so yes, they felt very much in the present. There was no sense of *time* at all. They were just there." She sat up, perplexed. "I'll have to talk to Alex about that. Ghost OPS, too."

Dan glanced around the shop to make sure no one was close enough to hear. "But you didn't see a ghost last night?"

"No. Just felt a presence." Avery tried to recapture the feeling, but in the busy shop it was impossible.

"Maybe it's just a Samhain thing." Dan jumped to his feet as a customer headed towards them with a selection of books, tarot cards, and candles. "Keep me posted, Avery. I'm intrigued."

"Will do. I'll go and tidy some shelves." She threaded her way between the bookshelves, hoping for time to think. Something was off, she just knew it.

"Well, it's definitely started," Ben said with satisfaction as he listened to the whine of his EMF meter. "There are stronger frequencies here than we've had before. It's the Samhain effect!" He gave a little happy jig, even though he knew he looked ridiculous.

"Oh goodie!" Cassie clapped her hands. "The temperature has dropped over here, too. There's a distinct cold patch."

"I can see something in the thermal imaging," Dylan confirmed. "Yep. This place has a spirit."

Ghost OPS had returned to Old Haven Church on the hill above White Haven, all wrapped in thick, down jackets and scarves. The place had become a bit of an obsession with them after the events of Samhain the year before. But they weren't in the grounds tonight. They were in the church itself, after James the vicar had given them permission to be there. He, like them, had brooding feelings about the place, even though it had been thoroughly cleansed by the Cornwall Coven after the Wild Hunt had broken through the veil, as Ben liked to call it. It had cool overtones that spoke of shadowy places beyond their realm.

Ben considered the feeling the place gave him. "Nothing sinister, though. Just a restless ghost who has been made more so by Samhain."

"But it's almost two weeks away," Cassie reminded him as she stamped her feet to keep warm. "Surely it's too soon for that to start happening."

"Long, dark nights lend a quickening to Samhain, though, don't you think? Everything feels expectant." Dylan lowered his camera. "No point recording anymore. It's a regular spirit, and not even a haunting, really. Nothing malevolent. Do we leave it, or exorcise it?"

"We should do as James asked," Ben said, grimacing with distaste. He had grown to think of spirits as fellow humans who for the most part did no harm. They had just become stuck, and he liked them to be able to do what they wanted to. Exorcising them felt mean. "He has a service up here and he doesn't want his parishioners freaked out."

James was holding a service to honour the dead buried in Old Haven graveyard. The church would be decorated with seasonal fare such as pumpkins, gourds, and cut branches closer to the time. James had explained it all to them. It was his way of repairing things after last year's events. He was doing the same in All Souls', the main church in White Haven. Although, obviously the blessing would be on All Saints' Day, the day after Samhain.

"Me and Dylan can manage it, if you don't want to," Cassie told him. "I know you hate it."

"Don't you?"

"I see it as sending them to rest. It's for the best."

"I'm with Cassie," Dylan agreed. "Head outside, and we'll catch up with you soon. And take my camera. I don't need it now."

Ben smiled at them. "Cheers, guys. See you soon." He shouldered his bag with his equipment in it, and headed to the weak sunshine in the graveyard, shutting the huge wooden doors behind him.

The graveyard was bathed in muted sunshine that gave absolutely no warmth whatsoever. His breath plumed in front of him, and he realised it was actually fractionally warmer outside the church than in it. He strolled through the well-maintained graves. Someone had been up here, tidying up. The grass was trimmed, the gravel paths had been raked and weeded, and the whole place had a feeling of calm introspection that was radically different from the year before.

He ended up in front of the Jackson Mausoleum. Out of sheer curiosity he turned his EMF meter on again and nearly jumped out of his skin when the whine resonated around him. He blinked. The readings were sky high. That had never happened before. The mausoleum was always quiet. They'd scanned it on many occasions.

Curious, he tried the handle. Surprisingly it was unlocked, but the door was stiff, and as Ben leaned his weight against it, it creaked open, releasing a damp, musty odour, and a billowing swathe of mist. *Mist?* For a second, he hesitated. *There shouldn't be mist inside anywhere*! Pulling himself together, and with his EMF meter held before him like a weapon, he stepped inside, and immediately felt the press of spirits around him. His skin prickled as he heard the murmurs of the dead. *What was happening?* It was as if something had upset them.

His skin, damp from the thickening mist, erupted in goose bumps and he felt their intense stares, even though he couldn't see them. He was used to spirits, but so many of them pressing close made his mouth dry. Then he realised he could use Dylan's camera. He fumbled for it, his back to the wall closest to the door where a stripe of light pierced the gloom.

As soon as the camera was on, he saw them. Well over a dozen bodies, pressed close together. He couldn't make out features, but the fact that they weren't moving suggested some kind of shock. It was odd, but it was as if they seemed scared, wary even. *No wonder.* They'd been having a happy rest, and now they were kicked out of the spirit world and had ended up here. *But why? What would cause so many spirits in one mausoleum to rise?* Perhaps he should call Reuben.

And then something shouldered its way through the spirits. He saw them shuffling aside, as if they had real bodies. *Weird.*

Ben edged back, pressing against the cold wall, half an eye on the open doorway. He wanted to run, but then he cursed himself. *Calm down. You're used to this.*

Then he felt it. Something unbelievably old. He felt it in the core of his being. Something primal was in there. The shape emerged from the bodies, and with slow deliberation passed right through him, and despite all of his experience, Ben blacked out.

Chapter Three

Reuben Jackson settled himself on a stool in front of The Wayward Son's bar and caught the end of Zee's conversation.

He was talking to one of the regulars as he polished a glass, shaking his head with concern. "No, mate. You need to give her space. Don't pester her yet. You'll drive her away."

Reuben fiddled with his phone and pretended not to listen as Evan, one of the locals, said, "Yeah, but she might never talk to me again!"

"You had an argument! And honestly, you were a bit of a dick. Give her space, and then make a *genuine* apology. No crappy flowers. Do it right. A very expensive meal in a place she likes!"

Evan picked up his beer. "Cheers, Zee. I suppose you're right." He spotted Reuben and nodded in greeting. "Woman trouble." With a sigh, he headed to his table.

Reuben grinned at Zee. "Well! I didn't take you to be an agony aunt."

"You'd be surprised. I listen well, always have done. I'm fascinated by why people do what they do. And people chat a lot, especially when we're quiet." He shrugged. "With a bit of luck, he'll salvage his relationship, poor bugger. Anyway, you want a pint?"

"Of course. Cornish Knocker, please, and a burger. The special." Reuben glanced around him at the half full pub. "Not too busy today. I guess it is only Monday lunchtime."

"Good." Zee slid the pint over, and raked his hands through his thick, black, wavy hair. "The weekend was crazy busy. It's all ramping up for Samhain."

"Your scar has finally gone." Zee had been injured by a fey's blade when the Wild Hunt attacked White Haven the previous year. Normally Nephilim healed quickly, but the cut had taken longer than usual.

Zee rubbed his cheek where it had been. "Yeah. Dragonium blade, according to Shadow." He lowered his voice. "Made from dead dragons, which is pretty gross. Potent metal, apparently. Her blade is Dragonium, too. Deadly stuff."

"Like Shadow. How're her driving lessons going?" Reuben had heard all about how Ash was teaching her to drive. It had been...hazardous.

Zee sniggered. "It's finally over. She passed her test, which is fortunate, because I think Ash, as patient as he is, was ready to kill her."

"So, she'll actually be driving? On the road. In a car."

"Yep. Worried?"

Reuben didn't want to think about encountering Shadow on a narrow country lane. "Yes. I can't believe she passed."

"Neither could we. At least we won't have to run her around anymore."

"What about your newfound wealth?" The Nephilim had been involved with a major treasure discovery a couple of months earlier, and were entitled to a portion of the trove's value—and it was a lot of money.

"Haven't got the cash yet. It takes a while for it all to go through." He grinned. "Will be great when it happens, though."

"But does it mean you'll leave? I like you guys being around," Reuben confessed. "You're handy in a fight, and well, you're mates now."

"Cheers. We feel the same about you guys, so, we're staying put. Don't know what it means for where we may live around here. Gabe is talking about buying the farmhouse and some of the land, if we can. We're only renting it now. I mean, we've made a few changes, but it would mean we can renovate properly, and spread out. We could convert some of the barn, and the room next to Shadow's place."

Relief swept through Reuben. "Great. I thought you might all move abroad or something."

"No." Zee shook his head. "This place is a fresh start for us. A chance to leave our past behind. We'll travel, of course. We already do, but everyone is keen to stay."

While they chatted, Alex emerged from the kitchen and headed to their side. "Hey, Reu."

"Just heard Zee and the others are staying. Good news!"

"Very."

Alex looked distracted, and Reuben wasn't sure if it was about pub business. "Everything okay?"

"Yeah. I think the season is getting to me. I had the weirdest feeling in the garden with Avery yesterday. We both did. It felt like something was watching us." He shrugged. "It was probably nothing. What's weirder is the fact that my dad is coming to visit."

"Is he?" Reuben asked, surprised.

Zee frowned. "What's weird about that?"

"He doesn't like White Haven. Moved to Scotland to get away from here. That's a lot of distance!"

Reuben sipped his pint and leaned on the counter. "Did he say why he's coming?"

"No." Alex grabbed a cloth and wiped the counter down, even though it was perfectly clean. "Maybe it's nothing. Maybe it's Samhain. Anyway, it will be good to see him—I think. At least he can meet Avery."

Reuben's phone rang, and he moved away from the bar to take the call. "Hey Dylan..."

Dylan launched into the conversation, almost tripping over his words. "Ben has vanished! We think he was in your family's mausoleum. I think you should get here."

"Are you kidding? *Vanished*! Is it Gil?" His heart was already thudding in his chest just at the thought of it.

"No. Not Gil. Look, just come. We're freaking out up here!"

Reuben's thoughts were reeling. *Ben had vanished?* "Er, yes, coming right now."

El Robinson finished packaging her customer's jewellery with the special Samhain bags, and said her goodbyes as the young woman left, a satisfied smile on her face.

Zoe arrived from the back room with two coffees and handed one to El. "That looks like another new, very happy customer."

"She was thrilled!" El sat on the stool behind the counter and sipped her drink. There were other customers in the shop, but they were still browsing. "I needed this, thank you. Yes, she's very happy. She's here with some friends, and she's going to bring them here."

"I guess that's the payoff for White Haven being so busy. Lots more business. It's not so much fun though when you have to battle your way through the town." Zoe settled on to her stool with an air of gossip. "I tried to get a table in the Thai restaurant on Friday, and it was fully booked! So was the bistro. We're having Indian instead."

El gave a rueful smile. "I know what you mean. White Haven seems permanently busy now, regardless of seasonal celebrations. We shouldn't complain. It's better than living in a dying town. And we're never bored!"

"Sometimes, I crave boredom. I just shut my door and pretend nothing is happening here at all."

Before El could answer, Stan, the town's pseudo-Druid, swept through the door in his ceremonial robes, his cheeks flushed from the cold. El frowned. "Hi, Stan! Aren't the clothes a bit premature?"

He grinned. "Not at all. Everyone is here for the Walk of the Spirits! The town is decorated beautifully, as is your shop, by the way." He gave a nod of appreciation. "I feel underdressed if I don't wear this. I think it keeps the excitement levels high!"

Seeing as her current customers were giggling and eyeing Stan with excitement, El had to agree. "I think we all admire your enthusiasm, Stan."

Zoe added, "And it's great for business."

"Exactly!" He clapped with glee and bounced on his feet. A very characteristic Stan gesture, which reminded El of how fond she was of his endless enthusiasm.

El reached under the counter and extracted a packet of hobnobs. "Have a biscuit, and keep your strength up."

"Thank you, I think I shall. So, have you heard the latest?"

"About what?" Zoe asked.

"The walk, of course! We were going to end at the harbour, where it all finished last year—if you remember?"

Zoe rolled her eyes. "No one is likely to forget that. It got half the town out of bed."

And had dragged El and the rest of her coven from Old Haven Church to the town, thinking they needed to do something to stop it. As it turned out, Helena had it all in hand, and they just had to let it play out. Instead, El lied. "Including me!"

Stan carried on, regardless. "Well, as much I would like to emulate that, the harbour is really too small for the crowds, so there's been a change of plan. We've decided to stick with the castle as our end point. It's very atmospheric, so it should work out well."

"I think that's a good idea," El agreed. "No one wants to accidentally fall into the harbour. That would be a disaster."

"Exactly, and we can have a fire and offer libations to the Gods!" He grinned at them. "I just wanted to make sure that you knew and will be there. Obviously, we'll be updating all of our fliers, and Sarah will interview me for the news." He took another biscuit. "If I may?"

"Of course." El smiled. "I can make you a drink, if you want."

"No. Must get on. I need to head up to the castle and finalise some plans. I have so much to do!"

Their customers clustered around Stan to ask a few questions, and at the same time the bell rang above the door, announcing another visitor. El frowned as a woman wearing a voluminous coat and woollen hat that looked remarkably like a witch's hat swept inside. For a moment, El couldn't see her face as she shut the door, but her figure looked strangely familiar.

She turned and beamed at El. "Darling! You look marvellous!" She regally crossed the shop, arms outstretched for a hug. "And look at your beautiful shop!"

"Aunt Olympia!" El was momentarily frozen in shock, before hurriedly lifting the countertop and hugging her. Her scent of tuberose brought back so many memories, El could barely think straight. "I can't believe you're here!"

They each stepped back a pace, studying the other, Olympia's hands clutching El's shoulders. Olympia was an imposing woman, as tall as El, still slim built, and wearing skilfully-applied makeup. Her blonde hair was now white, but most was hidden by her hat. However, she had more wrinkles than when El had last seen her, and El immediately felt guilty for not visiting her more often.

"Look at you!" Olympia declared. "This place suits you. You look happy."

"I am happy." El was suddenly aware that everyone was looking at them, and she turned, flustered. "This is my aunt, Olympia."

Stan's eyes lit up. "Madam! May I say how fantastic you look, and what an honour it is to meet you. Stan, at your service." He kissed her offered hand and bowed over it.

El could barely believe her eyes, and neither could Zoe, by the look on her face. She grinned and shook Olympia's hand. "Lovely to meet you. I'm Zoe."

Olympia took it all in her stride. "Delightful to meet you both, too. And you are?" She turned to the customers.

El rushed in to rescue them as they looked on, wide-eyed with amusement. Olympia had that effect. "Our lovely customers. Come on through to the back room and I can make you a drink. Are you just visiting?"

"Depends what you mean by visiting, dear. I'm here for Samhain!"

Chapter Four

Cassie paced outside Reuben's family mausoleum with their second EMF meter, sweeping it backwards and forwards, desperate to find anything that would reveal what had happened to Ben.

Panic was seated deep within her, but she forced herself to keep calm. *There had to be a rational explanation for his disappearance. Any minute now he would appear with a goofy grin on his face.*

"Still nothing?" Dylan asked.

"Very slightly elevated energy readings, but that's all. Not enough to indicate a ghost. You?"

"No." Dylan straightened up from where he'd been examining the ground, hands on hips as he stared at the mausoleum and then the graveyard. "This is ridiculous. He has to be around here somewhere. With my camera!"

"Are you sure he isn't hiding in the mausoleum?"

"I've searched it from top to bottom! No!"

"There's no need to shout!"

Dylan rubbed his face, eyes closed, and then stared at her. "Sorry. I'm worried. People don't just vanish."

They had completed the exorcism in the church. That had been easy, and both were feeling accomplished as they locked the main doors and wandered the grounds, looking for Ben. That feeling had swiftly vanished when all they found was his scarf on the floor inside the open mausoleum, and the ribboned remnants of fading mist. They had shouted for him, searched amongst the graves, ventured into the wood, and then called Reuben.

Cassie wrestled her emotions under control. "I'm worried, too. But why leave his scarf? And what's taking Reuben so long?"

The squeal of tyres and pounding feet answered that question, and Cassie whirled around, relieved to see not just Reuben running down the path, but Alex, too. It was a sign the weather was colder, because Reuben, like Alex, was wearing jeans rather than his customary board shorts and t-shirt.

Cassie sighed with relief. "Thank the Gods you're here!"

"Has he appeared yet?" Reuben asked. "You're having us on, right?"

Dylan shook his head. "No. I wish we were. His scarf is here, but he isn't."

Alex was already climbing the mausoleum steps as he said, "Take us through it. I don't get why you're here in the first place."

Dylan explained how they'd exorcised the ghost from the church. "James wants to make sure nothing interrupts his All Saints' Day service. I think this place still spooks him. Now I know why."

"Did you have the key to the mausoleum?" Reuben asked, frowning as he followed Alex. "It should be locked."

Cassie shook her head, deciding to stay on the path and keep an eye on their surroundings. She'd already been inside, and its musty dampness was unpleasant. "No. When we exited the church, it was already open. Ben must have opened it, because it was shut when we first arrived." She looked at Dylan. "But he didn't have the key either, right?"

"No. So it must have been unlocked." Dylan followed the witches to the door of the building. "Hey look, guys, we don't know what happened, so be careful in there."

Reuben's voice echoed from inside. "So, you actually saw Ben vanish?"

"No. He was out here on his own." He pointed to Ben's scarf that was still on the floor. "That's all we found. He has my camera, so I can't do any thermal imaging. Cassie's got the other EMF, but is getting nothing. Well, just a low whine that's neither here nor there."

Alex stuck his head out of the door. "Come and test it again, Cassie."

Reluctantly she mounted the steps and went inside, the gloom enveloping her. As her eyes adjusted to the light, she saw the rows of stone coffins lined up, and Reuben standing next to Gil's. His hand rested on it, as if for comfort.

"Gil would never hurt anyone," he said, almost aggressively.

"Of course he wouldn't. We know that!" Cassie told him as she turned the meter on again. "He helped save us from the pirate spirits. That's not what we're saying."

Alex squeezed Reuben's shoulder. "I can't feel anything remotely spirit-like in here." He looked around, frowning. "There is a kind of odd energy displacement, though. Can you feel it, Reu?"

"I don't know. I'm not as good at that kind of thing as you are." He finally stepped away from Gil's tomb. "You don't think Ben would have triggered the opening to the underground room, do you? And got stuck in there?"

"What room?" Cassie asked, the meter in her hand forgotten.

"Ah!" Reuben's handsome face was wrinkled with concern. "I'd forgotten you didn't know about that. My ancestors' hall of doom."

Cassie expected Alex to laugh and call Reuben out for exaggerating, but he didn't. Instead, he shuddered. "I hate it down there. It's seriously creepy, but we'd better open it up, just in case."

Dylan stared at them. "You've been holding stuff back? Show us!"

Reuben strode past him and headed into a small side room, the others trailing behind. "It's been used for blood sacrifice in the past. Shadow ended up trapped down there a few months ago. It's got bad vibes, so prepare yourselves."

While Reuben fiddled with a hidden mechanism, Cassie once again scanned the room using the EMF meter, desperately hoping nothing would suddenly spike. She had a horrible feeling that something had taken Ben. They had been searching for over an hour now, and still had found nothing of any use. *Perhaps he would be downstairs.* She crossed her fingers.

"Cassie?" Alex asked, standing next to her. "I can hear a whine. Is that significant?"

"Not really. If there were spirits around, or something else paranormal, we'd definitely get a stronger read out. And it's not cold, either—well, not in specific spots. We were in the church and I felt *distinct* cold spots, and the EMF was strong." She shrugged, feeling helpless. "Where is he?"

"I don't know, but I promise we'll find out." Alex was always so kind and reassuring. He placed his hand in the small of her back, guiding her through to the next room. "Come down with us. I don't want to leave you alone."

With horror, she saw steps leading down into darkness, revealed by a tomb that had moved to the side. A bobbing witch-light and Dylan's voice reassured her. She was a ghost hunter. She shouldn't be creeped out by this.

"After you. I'm not letting you out of my sight," Alex insisted.

Taking a deep breath, she headed down the steps, halting at the bottom to study the chamber. They were right. It *was* creepy. The witch-light showed sigils carved onto the floors and walls, and in seconds, candles flickered to life as Reuben lit them with a spell. She could smell the metallic tang of blood, and saw dark splashes on the floor and walls.

"They're new," Alex said, pointing at them. "A result of Shadow's imprisonment by the necromancer."

"But no Ben," Dylan said.

Cassie scanned the room with the EMF meter, but there was no change in frequencies. "Nothing. Nothing at all! It's like he's vanished into thin air!"

Reuben stared beyond her to Alex. "Any ideas? Because I haven't. I think we should call Newton. And we need to tell James, too."

The room beneath the mausoleum stank of blood, and Detective Inspector Mathias Newton studied it with barely-concealed revulsion. It reeked of violence. Fortunately, Detective Sergeant Kendall paced around unperturbed, exploring every nook and cranny. He'd left DS Moore upstairs with Alex.

Newton glared at Reuben, Cassie, and Dylan. "I don't like this at all! Has he been sacrificed to something?"

Cassie smacked him on the arm. Hard. "Don't say that!"

"Me saying it doesn't make it more or less likely to have happened! Are you sure there are no readings down here?"

"Nothing," Dylan answered. "And no sign of Ben even being down here."

"He's right," Reuben said. He looked bleak. "The mechanism hasn't been used in ages, and no one has been here in months. We only left it open because we knew you'd want to see it."

Kendall finally spoke, obviously fascinated with the place. She was dressed in smart dark trousers, a plain shirt, and flat shoes, her short hair neat and tidy. "Reuben, this place is grim. I can't believe your family owns it! Is that a devil's trap?"

"Unfortunately, yes. I can only assume that they had a very good reason for it. One I don't want to dwell on."

"Me neither," Newton declared. "I've seen enough. Let's go."

He walked up the steps, eager to get into the weak autumnal sunshine and the cold, fresh air. The room made him feel sullied. Within minutes, the place was sealed and they all stood outside the mausoleum, six expectant faces looking at him as if he knew exactly what to do. He didn't. He stared at the woods bordering the graveyard and felt for the scar on his neck left by Susannah's long, sharp blade, Avery's revenge-filled ancestor. He hated being there. Not surprising. He'd almost died.

Newton took a deep breath and faced the others. "People don't just vanish! Have you searched the woods?"

Alex nodded. "We did, while we waited for you, and I searched again with Moore while you were inside. He's not there, either."

Moore's red hair glinted in the light as he agreed with Alex. "Nothing. Could he have slipped between worlds? It is almost Samhain, after all."

Newton tried not to roll his eyes. Moore and his bloody fey borderlands. He was obsessed with them. "That sounds unlikely."

"But a portal did open here before!"

"Yes, but that took an immense amount of magic!" Newton swept his hand out, almost whacking Reuben in the process. "Is there any evidence of that here?"

Moore jutted his chin out. "No, but you don't need that in Ravens' Wood."

"This isn't Raven's Wood, though!"

"Forget Ravens' Wood," Reuben interjected. "It has its own special magic. This place does not. There's no sign that any magic has been worked here, although..." He hesitated and looked at Alex. "We agree that something feels different."

"You do?" Cassie asked, eyes wide. "You didn't say so!"

Alex wiggled his hand. "It's tenuous. It's similar to a feeling I had with Avery in our garden last night. As if something from the past was watching us." He laughed. "I guess we were waxing lyrical on a glass of mulled wine, but time felt suspended. Different."

"You believe it, though, don't you?" Newton said, studying his friend's face. "Even though you're trying to laugh it off."

"I do, yes. Even more so now that I'm feeling the same thing here." He shook his head. "It's faint, but it's there. I'll chat to Avery, see if there's a spell that might help. She's good at working out new spells, or mixing together old ones. In the meantime, me and Reuben wondered if a finding spell might work. We could bring our gear here. We just need something personal of his to use."

"Easy," Dylan said straight away. He held up Ben's scarf. "You could use this, or there'll be stuff in the van. Anything in particular?"

"Hair would be best, but the scarf should be fine, if not."

"We need a few ingredients," Reuben said. "Herbs and stuff. I can drive to mine and get them now. I guess the question is, though, is this place safe? We don't know what happened, but Ben has gone. What if it happens again?"

Good question. Newton had been mulling on it ever since he arrived. "There's only one option right now. This place is now out of bounds until we work out what happened. We need to leave a couple of people here at all times. I'm hoping Ben will come back, somehow."

"We've already talked about that," Dylan said, nodding at Cassie. "We'll ask James if we can hang out in the church, and maybe we'll set a tent up, too."

Newton was flooded with misgivings, but they were the best people to be here, given their experience. "Okay, but one of us will be here, too. I'll stay tonight."

Kendall leapt in immediately. "Let me!"

"No! You can take over tomorrow. Well work out some shifts. Fair enough?"

"No problem, Guv," Moore answered.

Alex shook his head. "I don't think that's a good idea. Whatever's happening could be worse at night."

Cassie huffed. "Don't care. If Ben comes back, we need to be here. Or," she paused and took a deep breath, "if it happens again, it means one of us goes to him—wherever that is."

"And if he's dead?" Newton asked, scowling.

Cassie almost snarled at him. "He won't be! Don't you dare suggest that."

"We need to be realistic, Cassie, although obviously I'm hoping he'll be fine."

"In which case, maybe a witch should be here, too," Reuben suggested.

"You're right," Alex said reluctantly as he met Reuben's questioning look. "One of us should be."

Reuben nodded. "Good. In that case, I'll head home now. I have a tent somewhere, and a portable barbeque. I'll bring the spell ingredients and a few other things with me. Blankets and stuff. Alex can stay here and provide magical protection—just in case. And when I return, you better all be here!"

Ben blinked and tried to focus, but everything was dark, and smoke choked the air, further obscuring his vision.

For a second, he thought he was locked in the mausoleum and that it was on fire. He was going to burn to death. His eyes widened with horror and shock, and he sat up abruptly. Immediately, a grizzled face thrust itself into his own and he recoiled in shock. It was a man, his face a map of wrinkles, surrounding dark, cunning eyes, topped off with a tangled mass of hair. He stank of stale sweat, and his breath was rancid. Ben scooted back and hit a wall.

He wasn't in the mausoleum. He was in a stone hut, with packed earth and animal skins beneath him, and a banked fire in the middle of the room. The smoke eddied around before idling through a hole in the thatched roof.

Where the hell was he?

The man launched an unintelligible stream of guttural noises, thrusting his face back in Ben's own. He looked pleased, triumphant.

Ben shook his head. "I don't understand! Where am I?"

The man continued to speak, over and over again, but Ben kept shaking his head to indicate his lack of understanding. With a frustrated howl, the man slapped Ben with such force that his head bounced off the wall. The man grabbed something from a pot next to him and blew it in Ben's face, and for the second time, everything went black.

Chapter Five

E l handed Aunt Oly, her preferred name to the more grandiose
Olympia, her cup of tea. El was very pleased to see her, but for
two weeks? She was already starting to feel crowded.

"Auntie, this is lovely to see you, but what's prompted the visit, and
why didn't you call first?"

Oly put her tea on the bench so she could examine El's jewellery
better. "By the Goddess! You are so good at this." She beamed at her.
"I always knew you'd make an excellent witch! I can feel the magic
in these. They're so powerful, and yet so subtle. And your shop is
so lovely!" Once again, she hugged El. "How dare your father try to
pretend magic wasn't in you."

"Auntie! You're avoiding the question." El extricated herself from
her aunt's arms. She was actually her great-aunt, but Oly didn't like to
be reminded of that. "What's going on?"

Oly sighed, picked up her tea, and inhaled deeply. "Lavender and
chamomile, just lovely." She sipped before she answered. "I can't explain why. I woke up yesterday knowing I had to be here to see you. I
mean, I think of you often, of course, but this feeling was overwhelming! So, I settled the house—you know how it hates to be left empty,
asked Marmaduke to look after Florence, and drove here today."

El had forgotten how Oly's house had a life of its own. Her aunt had
made it that way by using some powerful spells. The house was several

hundred years old; the doors and floors creaked, cabinets shut and opened of their own accord, lamps turned on all on their own. It was unnerving, but somehow comforting. Oly's husband had died years before, and now she lived on her own. The house gave her company. Marmaduke was her eccentric neighbour who lived down the lane, and El was shocked to hear that he was still alive. Florence was Oly's beloved cat. It was a miracle she was still alive, too.

"You drove?" Of all of the pressing questions that El had, that was the most important. El didn't add *at your age*. Oly's driving was reckless when she was younger, and probably worse now.

"Yes, I drove. I'm not taking public transport!" She shuddered. "Ugh. Grubby and smelly. I managed to park down by the harbour." She winked. "Courtesy of a little spell."

"Well, I'm glad you arrived safe and sound. I presume you need a bed?"

"Oh, darling, yes please. White Haven is positively heaving with people. It's so popular here! All of these people craving a little bit of magic in their lives. It almost makes me want to move here, but I won't." She lowered her voice. "Who's the strange Druid man?"

"He's not a real Druid. He's a councillor, but he officiates all of our Wheel of the Year events." El was very fond of him. "He actually does a great job. But look, to get back to your bed. I only have one bedroom. You could either stay in my flat on your own, and I'll move in with Reuben, or we could both stay at Reuben's place. That way I get to see more of you. But it's your choice."

"Is this the Jackson boy?"

El nodded. She'd talked about Reuben on the phone, and she knew her aunt remained up to date with White Haven news. "He lives at Greenlane Manor."

Oly's eyes lit up. "There! Oh, yes. That would be fabulous. I've always wanted to see it. Would he mind?"

"Absolutely not. He's very generous, and he'd love to meet you." El reached for her phone. "I'll call him now. In the meantime, do you want to see my place?"

"In a couple of hours." Oly patted her arm. "I'll leave you to finish work, and I'll meander the streets. So much to see and soak up. All these marvellous decorations."

"If you're sure? I don't mind taking time off."

"I wouldn't dream of it." Oly downed her tea and picked up her voluminous leather bag. Her fondness for bags was something she had in common with El. "Besides, I need to see what drew me here. For me to wake up one morning and just need to be here is odd. We both know that. I need to investigate."

El experienced an uneasy feeling at Oly's words, and as soon as she'd left, she called Reuben.

"Hey babe," he answered. "This is timely. I was going to call you. Weird shit is happening at Old Haven Church." For the next few minutes El listened, stunned, while he outlined the news and his plans. "We need a meeting later, and I suggest my house, as it's closest to the mausoleum. I'll be at the church, but the rest of you can meet at my place with the others. Alex can update you."

"Hold on, Reu! What you're doing could be really dangerous!"

"Ben is gone. We have to do what we can. Call Briar and Avery for me?"

Knowing she was fighting a losing battle, and still trying to digest the news, she sighed. "Of course. But look, I have news, too. My aunt is here. She felt compelled to visit White Haven—also weird. Can we both stay at yours?"

"You don't even have to ask that. Of course you can. Interesting, though. Things are afoot, El. See you later—and be careful!" And with that, he hung up.

Briar was the last of the witches to arrive at Reuben's house. She found Avery, El, and Alex clustered in the cosy snug next to the kitchen.

Alex was standing with his back to the blazing fire, while Avery and El were seated in the armchairs on either side. The house was warm and welcoming, especially after the chilly weather outside. It was close to six in the evening, and it was already dark. Mist was rising, and frost carpeted the ground.

Briar put her coat over the back of a chair before she sat down, noting their worried expressions. "I'd hoped that maybe they would have found Ben by now, but clearly not. Any other news?"

Alex huffed with disappointment. He looked dishevelled and dispirited, which was unusual. He may have long hair and wear old rock t-shirts with well-worn jeans, but he always looked groomed. Now, his hair looked wild, and his face was twisted with concern as he looked at Briar. "Our finding spell didn't work. We tried a few varieties, and the smoke just drifted in the air. Unless something is blocking our spell, or Ben is in some kind of protection circle, he's not *here*."

"By which you mean..."

"Not our Earthly plane," Avery answered.

"The spirit realm? How can that be possible?"

"I don't think we should leap to conclusions," El said, her legs curled under her with catlike grace. "There could be other explanations."

Alex cocked his head at her. "Like what? Another realm? There was no evidence of a portal."

"He's not a spirit-walker or a witch," El countered. "He couldn't go to the spirit world! Not physically vanish, at least. It's impossible."

"I'm inclined to agree with El," Briar said. "I can understand his mind being trapped there, but not his body. Ever since you called me, Avery, I've been thinking about our options, but to be honest, I'm a bit flummoxed. I've never encountered anything like this before."

"None of us have, but," Avery leaned forward, elbows on knees, "we have a Witches Council meeting on Wednesday. I can bring it up there. It was really a planning meeting for Samhain, but that doesn't matter. With luck, one of the other witches will have an idea of what to do."

Briar was horrified. "Wednesday! That's two days away." A dozen different scenarios filled her mind, none of them good.

"He might even be back by then," El suggested hopefully.

"Let's hope so," Alex said. "If not, the council is a good idea, Ave. There's a lot of collective magical knowledge in that group."

"By the way, Briar," El said, "I need to warn you that my Great Aunt Olympia has arrived, and she's upstairs at the moment, in her bedroom. Just prepare yourself. She's a force of nature, and I'm not sure whether it's a good thing or not that she's here, as yet."

"The aunt who taught you magic? That's great!"

"I guess so." El looked uneasy. "She said she was drawn here and doesn't know why. Maybe it's for this very problem! She has years of spell work behind her. The Fates move in mysterious ways sometimes."

"Interesting suggestion," Alex said, staring at El. "My dad is on his way, too. Maybe he's been drawn here for the same thing."

Knowing Alex's dad's aversion to White Haven, Briar's unease intensified. "Your dad is coming?"

Alex nodded. "He phoned yesterday. Should be here in a day or two. He'll be staying in my flat."

"I don't like it. Two of our relatives are coming, older than us, with years of experience and powerful magic, drawn by something they don't understand. Is Ben's disappearance a lure?"

All three witches stared at her, but it was Avery who broke the silence. "A lure? No, that can't be right. Alex's dad phoned yesterday, before Ben had disappeared."

"My aunt had the same urge to travel yesterday morning," El added.

"You have to admit that the timing is uncanny," Briar pointed out. "And we all know that there's no such thing as coincidence."

"So where does that leave my mother, or sister?" Avery asked. "Or Alex's brother? Or any of Reu's relatives? They're not coming."

"Yet!" El said ominously. "Anyway, I'm not happy just sitting here. I want to go to the church and see what's happening. I'm worried about Reu. About all of them, actually."

"I think I should share my experience first," Briar said, recollecting her strange fireside apparition with her gran. "And Gran's vision. Since we banished the banshee, she says her seer powers have rallied, and she saw a white stag on the moors the other night. It was looking right at her. She said it felt like a spirit animal."

Alex sat on the sofa next to her. "She saw it on the moor, or in a vision?"

"It sounded like a vision." She hesitated, trying to recall her words. "I'm sure it was. We were talking about Beth and her progress. Anyway, she said she felt connected to it—hence feeling it was a spirit animal. Although, she also confessed she'd never had one before, and it wasn't really her thing." She shrugged. "I don't know what to think."

"Okay. Something to bear in mind. What happened to you?"

"I saw a face in the fire, just after we were talking about the stag, actually. It was yesterday evening while we were outside burning some garden rubbish." Briar hesitated, partly out of the wish to make sure she was describing it properly, but also wondering whether she'd just let the moment influence her. *No, she knew what she'd seen.* "It was a man's face, topped with huge antlers. And I think there were markings on his face, but that could have just been the flames. I felt his power through the intensity of his eyes." She laughed, trying to make light of it. "Odd, I know. It's probably just the fire playing tricks on me."

"But you haven't dismissed it," El said. "Not even now, hours later. How did it make you feel?"

Briar didn't need to think on that one. "Very young and inexperienced, as if my power was minute compared to his. He felt so ancient. And yet, I also felt *seen*! Do you know what I mean?" She stared at her friends. "Like he really understood me. Could see right in here." Briar tapped her chest. "Then, that was it. The fire shifted, branches collapsed, and he vanished. I felt a little bereft, actually."

"What about the Green Man?" Avery asked. "Did he stir at his presence?"

"No. Not at all, but he's been quiet lately. He's sleeping, I guess—like the season."

Alex exchanged a worried glance with Avery. "You said he felt ancient?"

"Very. It was sort of like time had shifted for a moment."

"Bollocks. Because that's exactly the kind of feeling I had last night, about the same time, I reckon. Twilight, while we had a garden fire going. We were talking about old souls and how I think Beth is one."

"Do you?" Briar looked at him, surprised, and with a measure of relief that she wasn't the only one. "You've never mentioned that before. I do, too. She's uncanny, isn't she?"

"Yeah." Alex rolled his eyes. "Especially as she's so young, but she's still a child, too, so it's doubly weird."

Avery laughed. "Now that Alex has brought it to my attention, I can't *not* see it in Beth."

"I see it in her," El agreed. "But like you say, it's tempered with her being so young. I get a real sense of dislocation when I see her. How is she managing with her seer abilities, Alex?"

"She's wide open to it, and too young to control it, but I'm trying to teach her some coping strategies." He waved his hand as if to brush it away. "But that doesn't solve this problem. However, she certainly hasn't seen anything about this event, yet."

"Maybe," Briar tentatively suggested, "the banshee triggered particularly strongly with her because she was part of the family."

Alex nodded. "I wondered that. She's makes odd little predictions lately, just day to day family stuff. I guess that's good."

El stood up. "I'm restless, which may be because I'm hungry, however, I need to see what's going on at the church. Try to get my head around all this. I'm going to check on Oly first, and then I'm going to see Reuben. Anyone else want to come?"

"Me!" Avery said immediately.

"Of course," Briar said. "I'm so worried about all of them."

"Me too," Alex said, standing too. "Let's hope that things haven't got weirder in the dark."

Chapter Six

For one heart-stopping moment, as Alex approached the church from the carpark, he thought everyone had vanished. It was eerily quiet. The only sign of life was a golden light that flamed in the mausoleum, visible through the partially open doorway. A beacon for the missing Ben.

However, as he rounded the corner of the church, he saw lights through the windows and smelled smoke from the barbeque outside the door.

"They must all be inside," he told the others.

Briar hesitated on the path, looking at the mausoleum. "The light is a nice touch. Something to welcome him home."

Avery put an arm around her shoulder and hugged her. "He's clever! He'll be okay."

Briar shook her head. "You don't know that, but I hope you're right."

"Maybe someone took him deliberately," Oly suggested as she adjusted her thick woollen cape. Her eyes narrowed as she studied the mausoleum. "For his connections, or what he knew. Once we've said hello to the others, we need to go in there. See what we can feel."

Alex felt strangely comforted by El's stridently loud and eccentric aunt. She had insisted on accompanying them after greeting them all with great enthusiasm, and Alex found that he liked her a lot. It was how he imagined El would be in another few decades.

"Come on," she continued, flapping her arms like she was herding chickens. "Inside, all of you. It's freezing out here!"

Alex was only too glad to oblige. The sky was clear, the temperature was plummeting, and frost was thickening by the second. He pushed opened the heavy wooden door of the church, passed through the vestibule, and entered the nave. Reuben, Cassie, Dylan, and Newton were clustered at the front by the altar, sitting on a spread of blankets or in deckchairs, surrounded by candles, lanterns, and heaters, all wearing layers of winter clothing. A couple of small tents had been erected at the side. Fortunately, the temperature was much higher than it had been a few hours earlier, and Alex suspected a spell played a large part in that, too.

"Welcome, witches!" Reuben boomed from the front. "Are you here for the night?"

"I'm not sure about that," Avery said, looking around with curiosity. "I like your camp, though."

Olympia clapped her hands. "So do I! Let's hope the old God brings us some luck, that misogynistic old devil!"

El rolled her eyes and made the introductions. Alex watched amused as Reuben charmed the old lady, but he noticed Cassie and Dylan were finding it hard to summon any enthusiasm. Newton tried to appear cheerful, but failed.

Alex sat on a cushion next to Cassie while the others made themselves comfortable. "No luck at all, I take it?"

She shook her head. "No, and I'm horribly worried. What if he was spirited away somewhere *here* and is lost outside? He'll freeze to death!"

"You mean like he's been kidnapped?" Avery asked. "I hadn't even considered that!"

"Cassie," Dylan gently remonstrated, "we'd have surely heard something. Someone wanting a ransom, most likely. And what could they possibly get from us that's so special? We've got no bloody money."

"Maybe they think we know something paranormal that would benefit them?"

"We post too much stuff online for anyone to think we're hiding anything. I just don't buy it!" He nodded at the two small screens that were plugged into the mains via a long extension cord. "We'll have more luck with those, I hope."

"You've set cameras up?" Briar sounded surprised. "That's a great idea. One's thermal, by the look of it."

Dylan nodded. "I thought both would be useful. So far, though, we've got diddly fucking squat." He shot a panic-stricken look at Oly. "Oops, sorry!"

"Language does not bother me," Oly declared, waving her hand airily. "Missing friends do. So, other than watching and waiting, what else are we doing?"

"We did a finding spell, earlier, and found nothing," Reuben told her before staring at Avery with a hopeful expression. "We were hoping Avery would think of something. She's very inventive with spells."

Avery blushed. "No more so than any of us!"

"Not true," El said. "Any suggestions?"

"Not yet, but I will spend a few hours tonight looking through spells and maybe chatting to Helena. I'll ask the Witches Council for advice, too."

"Helena?" Oly shot forward in her deckchair. "Your ghost ancestor who was burned at the stake?"

"Yes, why?"

"You *speak* with her?"

Avery looked baffled at the question, but Alex realised that they were all so used to it, they forgot that many people, including witches, would find it odd. Avery finally answered. "On occasions, when she blesses me with her presence. Which is quite a lot, at the moment. But our communication is not always easy. She doesn't exactly *speak*."

Oly tapped her lip thoughtfully. "If she would consent to joining a circle here, she may lend our endeavours extra strength."

"Let's leave her out of it, for now," Avery said, casting an unease glance at Alex.

"We can't do a circle in the church!" El looked horrified. "If James ever found out, he'd be furious. I know he's accepted you, Avery and Alex, but he's still wary of the whole magic thing."

"Not here!" Oly huffed. "In the mausoleum, where he went missing."

"By the way, James arrived here earlier," Reuben added. "He was very upset to learn of Ben's disappearance. Kept muttering about his parishioners and the service. I think he's planning to chat to you, Ave. And I think he's guessed I'm a witch—not that I said anything, obviously."

Avery nodded, looking resigned. "That's fine. I'm used to my chats with James."

Dylan turned to Oly, going back to the previous subject. "We're not one hundred percent sure that Ben vanished in the mausoleum. We just found his scarf there. He could have left it and walked elsewhere."

"But that's the most likely place," she insisted, rising to her feet. "Hopefully there will be residual energies there. I'm going to go and see, and then I'll decide on the best spell. If nothing happens, then we'll try other things. Maybe your council will be useful." She sniffed with a hint of derision, which indicated to Alex that she had very little faith in them. "Any other witches close by that could help?"

"Caspian," Reuben said immediately. "He's close, practical, and powerful. And he'll be really pissed we didn't tell him about Ben going missing, so we'd better rectify that."

Alex inwardly groaned but said nothing. He'd accepted the fact that Caspian Faversham was now a permanent fixture in their circle.

"Excellent. I like him already," Olympia said, heading to the door.

Briar, El, and Avery hurried after her, and then after a moment's hesitation, so did Cassie. El called out, "Slow down! You're not twenty anymore!"

"And thank the Gods for that," Oly grunted. "I was young and stupid. Age is a blessing! And tell your friend to be here before midnight! Let's do this the right way."

Once the door had slammed shut behind them, the energy seemed to seep out of the room, and Alex studied the remaining men. Reuben was stretched out on an outdoor recliner, looking like he was poolside in a resort, but his earlier cheerful countenance had vanished. Newton stared into a candle flame and sipped a cup of tea, and Dylan studied his camera feeds.

"Herne's horns. You three look grim."

Dylan flopped back in his chair. "I *feel* grim. Ben has vanished without a trace, and I haven't got a bloody clue what to do. I mean, seriously, where the fuck is he?" He angled away from the screens to stare at Alex. "People don't just vanish! What if he never comes back? I can't cope with that. What the fuck do I tell his family?"

"It won't be you telling his family," Newton said, his shoulders dropping. "It will be me."

"Fuck off!" Dylan was clearly riled up and cranky. "I'm his friend, I know them. I won't have a stranger telling them that!"

"Will you both chill out!" Reuben sat up, planting his long legs on either side of his lounger. "This is a bit early to say he's never coming back."

"The first few hours," Newton said, "are the most important in any missing persons case, and we know nothing."

"But," Alex reminded them, "this is no ordinary missing person, is it? This is paranormal weirdness." He nodded at Dylan's spread of equipment. "We need to be logical. What have you observed with all your stuff?"

"Slightly heightened energy readings, but nothing especially concrete. No cold spots, no extreme temperature variations, and there aren't any spirits anywhere! Me and Cassie have scanned around the graveyard several times, walked through the wood, and again found nothing unusual. We spent a lot of time by the huge yew where the portal was last year, but again, nothing weird happening there, either." He clutched his short dreads and pulled at them, exasperated. "I'm running out of ideas!" And then he froze. "We were doing a banishing spell when Ben vanished. Could we have somehow included him in that?"

"No way," Alex said at the same time as Reuben. Alex continued, "Was it one of our spells you used?"

"Yes. It was simple. An incantation and a circle with candles, in here. I told you we found a spirit in here, right? It was harmless. Everything seemed to go off without a hitch."

"Then no," Reuben repeated after exchanging a confirmatory glance with Alex. "You can't banish a human that way."

Newton was fully focussed on them. "What if another spirit got caught in it, and it was close to Ben?"

Alex shook his head. "No. That's still not how that works. Or you'd risk banishing yourself saying the spell. It's designed only for spirits, and that's all."

Reuben fidgeted, playing with the hem of his sweatshirt before looking at Alex. "Perhaps you should enter the spirit world to see if you can detect anything odd. Maybe even try to find Gil. He'd help us if he could."

Alex couldn't quite believe his ears. "But Reu, we said that was something we'd never do. I don't want to unsettle Gil's spirit!"

"Ben is missing. We—I—can't afford to be squeamish about this. He's our inside man. He'd tell us if anything weird was happening."

Alex had considered doing that, but dismissed it straight away. *But now...* "Only if you're absolutely sure."

"I am."

Alex nodded. "Okay. I won't do it here. I need to be in a quiet space, at home. The other thing I'd considered was spirit-walking and scrying." He shrugged. "I'm not sure of the efficacy of the last two in this situation, but hell, why not?"

"Thanks, both of you," Dylan said, a mix of worry and gratitude on his face. "I really appreciate it. But please, don't do anything that might endanger you. I'd hate for anything to happen, and I know Ben would, too."

"Don't give it a second's thought," Alex reassured him.

"What's worrying me," Newton said, "is whether this is the start of something bigger. What if more people disappear? How do I even start to investigate it?"

"We do exactly what we're doing now," Reuben said, reaching for his phone. "Just on a larger scale. I'll call Caspian and see if he can help us."

Avery shivered in the cold mausoleum, rearranged her scarf, and tucked it into her wool coat. Her breath misted in front of her. Casting a circle in there was going to be a nightmare.

She looked around the mausoleum, opening her senses to the elements to try to detect what might have happened there. "Something feels off, but I can't work out what."

Oly fixed her with sharp blue eyes that were so like El's. Avery felt like she was under a spotlight. "Really? Because the distinct lack of spirits in here is very odd to me."

El frowned at her aunt. "What do you mean? Just because it's a mausoleum in a graveyard, doesn't mean that spirits will be roaming in a pack. They could be at rest!"

To Avery's utmost relief, Oly turned and fixed El with the same stare. "Darling, there are always the presence of spirits in a place like this, even if they are at rest. This place feels like a void!"

"You're right," Cassie said, breaking her uncharacteristic silence. "I've been here lots of times. It's one of our favourite places to seek out spirits and check our instruments. Other graveyards are the same. We might not see active spirits, but there's always a feeling of presences." She nodded to herself as she prowled around. "Yes, the more I think on it, the more I realise this is utterly odd. I don't know why I didn't notice it before!"

Briar shrugged. "It's because you're in shock, and worried about Ben. But that is an interesting observation. What does it mean?"

"Too soon to say," Oly said. "But I'm surer than ever now that we should cast a circle here."

Avery was annoyed with herself. She should have noticed the strange emptiness, too. It *was* weird. However, she hated woolly, ill-defined plans, and while she didn't want to insult Oly, she wasn't happy with the suggestion. "But to do what? Are we trying to summon something? Cast protection? Do some kind of spell?"

"We are going to contact my spirit guide using my Ouija board. He and I commune regularly. He has never let me down."

Avery's mouth dropped open. "You're a psychic?"

"Oh, no!" Oly widened her eyes dramatically. "Not at all. But I met Egberk years ago in my youth, through the use of the board. I had a hazardous time because I summoned a demon quite accidentally, and I've been respectful of it ever since. We've kept in touch. With Egberk, obviously, not the demon. When I need advice for what is happening beyond our spiritual realm, I turn to him."

El explained, "Aunt Oly is a fire witch, like me, but has also dab—" She stopped herself as Oly pursed her lips. "*Experimented* with the beyond in an attempt to broaden her powers."

"So," Briar said, "this is a summoning. It's a powerful place and time to be doing such a thing."

"Exactly! This place holds great promise. Midnight is several hours away yet. I need to go home to prepare, and so should you. Cleanse yourselves, and open your minds. El! Take me to Reuben's!"

She swept out of the door, but El lingered. "I'd almost forgotten how eccentric Oly is. I'd certainly pushed Egberk to the back of my mind."

Cassie looked horrified and excited all at the same time. "I've never used a Ouija board. I've always been too scared, thinking it's too powerful for the uninitiated."

"Hence my aunt summoning a demon," El said dryly. "I've never used one, but spirit work is not my thing. What about you two?" She looked at Briar and Avery.

The both shook their heads, Avery adding, "But Alex may have. Like you said, if spirit work isn't your thing, why bother? I wonder if Caspian has?"

"Well, we're all about to get a crash course," El said, heading out of the mausoleum, "so I suggest you do as Oly says. Prepare yourself."

When Ben woke up again, his head ached and his mouth was dry. He swallowed a few times in an attempt to alleviate the dryness, but soon wished he hadn't. He had a strange, bitter taste in his mouth that he was sure was caused by whatever the man had blown in his face.

He'd been drugged.

Rather than sit up straight away, he opened his eyes to slits so that he could see his surroundings.

He was in the same stone hut, lying on pungent animal skins. The fire was a few feet away, and around it were rudimentary cooking tools, pots, and animal skin bags. The man was on the other side of the fire, his attention on grinding something into a pot. He could see his pack and the thermal imaging camera on the ground not far away; it looked undamaged. He'd been holding it when he...what? *Crossed? But to where?*

The place felt real enough. This was no spirit realm. It was potent and earthy, with strong scents and tangible objects. He was still wearing his puffer jacket over his jeans and sweatshirt, and he was glad he was wearing his sturdy leather boots, too. They weren't quite enough to insulate him from the chill, though. The low fire gave off a steady heat that didn't repel the rising cold from the bare earth.

With a horrible certainty, unless someone was playing a terrible joke on him, he was sure he'd moved through time. Everything was ancient, different, raw; no hint of modernity at all. Panic started to rise, but he forced it away. Fear would achieve nothing here. He was a scientist. He needed to be objective, and see this as an opportunity to learn.

He shifted his cramped limbs, and with surprising swiftness, the man darted to his side, his rough, calloused fingers prodding him.

"Woah! Enough!" Ben brushed the man's hand away and edged backwards. *Time for some boundaries.* He gestured to his mouth and stomach. "I need water and food."

The man examined him, his eyes roving over his face and body. With a satisfied nod, he picked up a pot filled with clear water and passed it to Ben. With a cautious sniff, he decided it seemed safe enough and sipped it. It was pure stream water, icy cold and crisp, and he drank greedily. The man then passed him strips of dried meat and dried berries from another pot, and Ben chewed. *Good enough. At least he wasn't going to starve to death.*

Ben gestured to the hut and shrugged. "Why am I here? Where am I?"

The man smiled, revealing crooked, broken, and yellowed teeth, the remnants of food still in them. He tapped his chest and pointed to Ben, uttering something completely unintelligible.

Ben shrugged again. "I don't understand."

Abruptly the man stood and headed to the single wooden door, and he gestured Ben to follow him. Ben grabbed his pack and camera and quickly followed.

It was dark outside, and a bitterly cold wind carried the scent of the sea, buffeting another, bigger fire that burned brightly. Surrounding the hut was a spiked wooden palisade, clearly designed to keep something out. *Wild animals, perhaps.* The man was standing by the fence, his thick, coarse woollen cloak billowing around him, his finger outstretched as he pointed down the slope of land. As his eyes adjusted to the light, Ben realised there was a valley below, edged with a shallow bay.

Ben moved to his side, spotting the flare of flames below and the shapes of other buildings close to the sea. *A village, maybe?* The man patted his shoulder, indicating he should stay there, and gave him a feral, cunning smile. He gestured to his eyes and back to the village.

Watch.

Chapter Seven

Zee was looking forward to finishing his shift at The Wayward Son. He'd worked longer than normal, as one of the new bar staff had phoned in sick. One of the hazards of the season, and something he was glad he was immune to. Nephilim rarely ever caught colds or became sick.

Something to thank his father for.

The early quiet of the day had continued into the evening, which meant it had dragged. On the flip side, he caught up with jobs, chatted to the flirtatious and funny Marie, and participated in White Haven gossip with the regulars. It was now just past nine, and the more he looked at the clock, the more time seemed to slow.

Feeling a blast of cold air, he turned to the door, and saw Kendall, Newton's sergeant, walk in. She caught his eye and smiled as she took a seat at the bar, drawing a few admiring glances while she did so. Kendall was very pretty with her pixie cut hair, minimal makeup, and tall, slim figure; something she seemed unaware of.

"I'm glad you're here," she said, shrugging off her jacket. "I wanted to pick your brain."

Zee reached for a glass. "Over a pint, I presume."

"Just a *half* a Guinness, please. Tempting though a pint is." While she chatted, she glanced around the room, taking everything in. Like Moore and Newton, she was very observant. Part of police training, he presumed. "Anything odd happening in here? Or out there?" She nodded towards the window and the streets of White Haven.

"Not so far, unless you count bored gossip about Samhain and whether Stan is having an affair with the mayor."

Kendall looked intrigued. "Is he?"

Zee laughed. "Do you really care?"

"Not really, but they are of a similar age and do get on very well." She winked. "I wouldn't be surprised."

He considered the twinkle in Stan's eye earlier that day. "I suppose he did look a bit more cheerful than usual, but his *events* tend to do that." He leaned forward while he waited for her Guinness to settle. "Word is that they're going at it like teenagers."

She giggled. "Lucky Stan."

Zee grinned but didn't comment. He was not about to get into talk about Stan's sex life or his lack thereof with Kendall. She was pretty and single, but he was not about to muddy his own back door. *Not like Eli and the ever-adoring ladies of White Haven.*

"Anyway," she continued, "that wasn't what I was really interested in. You've heard about Ben?"

Zee topped up the rest of her drink and placed it in front of her. "I have. Is he back yet?"

"No. I've just heard from Newton that El's great aunt, Oly, who he described as an elegant but crazy old bat, is about to perform some kind of séance in the mausoleum."

"Intriguing. For what purpose?"

"To summon her spirit guide to see if he knows what's going on."

"Okay!" Zee had a sudden urge to be there. It sounded like fun. "I hope she finds out. I like Ben. He's a good guy. Is there anything we can do? Join the summoning, perhaps?"

Kendall laughed as she brushed foam from her lip. "I asked if I could, but Newton said if he ended up dying at the hand of an out-of-control demon, me and Moore would need to complete the investigation."

"Ah. Not much faith in Aunt Oly, then?"

"No. But he's grumpy because he's worried about Ben, and the potential for more disappearances. Which is why I'm here. If there's anything remotely odd happening, including your customers talking about weird experiences, we need to know about it."

"Of course. Nothing so far, though."

Then, as if Zee had tempted fate, the entrance door burst open, and Roger, who ran the garage at the top of White Haven, burst in, banging the door against the wall. He was in his fifties, and usually a calm, chatty man who was always dressed in a smart jumper and casual trousers. Now, however, his thinning hair was dishevelled, and his coat was askew.

He yelled at everyone, "Something is happening at the harbour! Half of it has vanished! Come and see!"

For a moment, no one moved, as everyone looked at Roger and then at each other in disbelief, then the scraping of chairs heralded a mass exodus as they followed Roger out of the pub.

Kendall slammed her pint on the bar and took off after them.

Zee yelled at Marie, "Stay here! I'm going to see what's happening."

Marie nodded, shouting after him, "Be careful!"

Zee raced after the others, quickly catching up with Kendall and the customers. The harbour was only a few minutes' walk from the pub, and Zee fervently hoped that Roger was having some kind of episode. *Too much alcohol, perhaps? A mini-stroke?*

Zee was desperate to get ahead of the group, but everyone was tightly packed into the narrow lane as they herded around the corner and onto the road overlooking the harbour. With a horrified gasp, they came to a dead stop.

The converted warehouse building where El lived was still there, but the harbour beyond it with its strong and seemingly impenetrable sea wall had vanished, as had a portion of the road that bordered it. The fish and chip shop and the row of seaside shops had been replaced with a stretch of beach edged with huge rocks, draped in mist, onto which a winter sea pounded remorselessly.

Kendall forced her way to the front of the group, and Zee forged forward with her, as she said, "No one move! We don't know what's happening here."

"Love," one old man muttered, "I'm not going anywhere near that. Don't worry about me!"

Kendall looked up at Zee, her voice low. "What could be causing this?"

"I have no idea!" He stared at the scene again, trying to focus his whirling thoughts.

"Could this be a portal of sorts?"

"It doesn't feel like one. And it's too big!"

Kendall spun around, searching the crowd, and spotting Roger close by, talking to a group of men, interrupted his conversation. "Roger. When did you first see this?"

"Just now, of course. I walked down from the square to have a pint before bed."

"You didn't see it happen?"

"No." He shrugged, looking baffled, and to be honest, slightly excited. "It was just there...or rather, it wasn't."

"You didn't go near it?"

"God, no! Do I look like an idiot?" He turned back to his friends, seemingly unconcerned that he'd just insulted a police officer.

By now, others were gathering as they exited other pubs and restaurants around the harbour, and mounting panic and excitement were filling the air. Fortunately, everyone seemed to be keeping a wary distance.

Kendall pulled her phone from her pocket. "I need to call in a team to cordon this off. No one goes in there."

Zee didn't answer, focussing only on the wild beach and the coast beyond it. Not only had part of the town vanished, but the castle as well. The rocky headland was lost in a squall of water and wind. He squinted, trying to discern details. There was something on the clifftop. A light, and what looked like a rustic, squat, stone building. The smell of smoke drifted towards him, mixing with the sharp wind and scent of salty sea. But the more he tried to focus, the more it seemed to shimmer in the growing mist. For the briefest moment he saw a figure draped in a long cloak who seemed to be looking right at him, and then suddenly, it all vanished. The mist rose like a wall, hiding everything from sight, but lasted seconds only. When it cleared, the harbour and the road beyond it had returned, along with the bobbing boats and a few pedestrians on the street.

Whatever it was, was over.

As soon as Newton received Kendall's call, he left Old Haven Church, deciding he had more important places to be than participating in a séance. After a moment's indecision, Dylan had left with him, especially when Cassie argued that they should split up for maximum effect.

Now, Newton looked on in grim satisfaction, pleased that the area encompassing the harbour, the road, the shops that ran alongside it, and the buildings just beyond, was being cordoned off so quickly. For good measure, they'd included the converted warehouse where El lived. A couple of PCs who were part of White Haven's Community Policing Team were just finishing setting it up, whilst herding everyone to safety. Dylan was walking the perimeter with his EMF meter and his normal camera.

He shifted to look at Kendall standing next to him. "Well done. What's happening with the residents of the warehouse?"

"I went in there myself, basically door knocking and telling everyone to go elsewhere overnight. A couple refused, and on their head be it, but the others have left." She nodded behind her towards The Wayward Son. "Zee offered to let everyone gather in the pub so we can question who we need to. He's keeping an eye on them and making sure they don't leave." She shrugged, looking a little sheepish. "I sort of co-opted him into the response."

He nodded, pleased with her decisions. Kendall was an excellent addition to the team. "Good. Zee is empathetic, large, and extremely trustworthy. I've noticed the customers like him. Does the group include those who'd been caught up in the anomaly?"

"Yep." Her lips tightened. "I haven't had a chance to question them yet. I wanted to make sure this was organised first, but it's clear that they could tell they were somewhere else..." She trailed off, looking Newton squarely in the eye. "There are a lot of very spooked people in the pub."

"Then we better get in there and start questioning them. Moore?"

"On his way."

Newton surveyed the crowd of onlookers, noting a few of them heading to The Wayward Son as if they knew exactly where to go for information. *News travelled fast.* "I take it these have all come to gawk."

"Unfortunately, but they're not hanging around. Let's face it—there's not much to see anymore. I'm just relieved it's all over. I can't help but feel, though, that it might happen again."

"I have a horrible suspicion that you're right, Kendall," he said, turning towards The Wayward Son. "Do me a favour and grab one of the PCs to help us do the interviews. And Dylan. I want him to listen, too. Whatever *this* is, it's just beginning. I'll see you in the pub."

Victims seemed an odd word choice for those caught in the event, but as far as Newton was concerned, they were. They had been abducted somewhere by an unknown someone. He just hoped he could get a coherent statement from them. However, the noise coming from Alex's pub suggested a general level of hysteria he could do without, and once he was through the door, the noise level rocketed.

The pub was heaving, and Zee, Marie, and young Jake who'd been drafted in from the kitchen to help, were busy serving the customers. Newton pushed through them until he reached Zee. "Any idea who was part of the abduction?"

Zee finished serving a customer and nodded towards a knot of a dozen people in the corner. One woman was crying, another man was shouting and red-faced, but most looked shell-shocked. "They're all there, clinging to each other like they're survivors of a shipwreck. I've given them a drink on the house. They needed it."

"Anywhere I can take them for some peace and quiet? Alex's place, perhaps?"

Zee smiled and handed him a key. "Thought you'd want it. Just watch the stairs. Workmen have started boxing it off, and it's a bit hazardous. The lights are on up there, and the heating is on, so it's warm. Anything I can do?"

"You've already done more than enough. Thank you. But, ring the bell, will you? I want to address them all."

"Sure, but I need to let you know that I saw a man on the cliff top, where the castle is—but wasn't, if you know what I mean."

"You saw a man?" Newton wasn't sure what was more astonishing...or worrying. "And the castle had gone?"

"Oh, yeah. It was just rugged cliff top, and a fierce storm was rolling in. A man, wrapped in a cloak, was on the top, and it seemed as if he was looking right at me. At us."

"You're sure it was a man?"

"Pretty sure, although he was a distance away. It was the way he held himself. He was wearing a cloak, and he had long, wild hair. But then the mist rose like a wall, he vanished, and then everything returned to normal."

Newton leaned across the bar, searching Zee's face for answers. "What do you think happened?"

"Honestly, I don't know, but I don't think I was seeing something from somewhere *else*. I think it was here, White Haven, but in another time."

"That's not funny, Zee."

"I'm not trying to be. The coast was virtually the same, except for the fact that it was ancient land. I even saw a kind of stone bothy on the hill. Time felt raw, old. Almost as old as I am, perhaps." Zee shrugged, perplexed. "I could be wrong. They were my first impressions, and they were fleeting."

"Fuck! That's all I need. Some nutjob who's trying to disrupt time." He spotted Kendall entering the pub, followed by Moore and one of the PCs. "You'd better ring that bell so I can get started."

Zee rang the bell for last orders, and a collective groan ran around the room, with a few complaints thrown in.

"Chill out!" Zee said, raising his hands for calm. "It's not last orders. Detective Inspector Newton wants to speak to you, so shut up and listen."

Newton suppressed a grin at Zee's easy authority and faced the rapt group. "Thanks, Zee. Right. I need you all to stay here until DS Moore and the Police Constable have taken your details. Anything you saw or experienced is vitally important, so please tell us. *Anything!*" He eyed them all, wondering what scattered ramblings would come of this. "The victims of this...experience will come with me and DS Kendall upstairs. I ask you to bear with us. This is going to take some time."

As he finished speaking, the excited chatter rose again. He'd speak to Moore and the PC and then leave them to it. This was going to be a long night.

Chapter Eight

"**W**ell," Caspian Faversham said, staring at his adopted coven's unusual surroundings, "this is different."

"You know us," Reuben joked, semi reclining on a sun lounger. "We always like to keep life interesting."

The White Haven Coven—everyone except for El, plus Cassie—were gathered in Old Haven Church in their makeshift camp, wrapped in winter layers. Candlelight gleamed off the polished wooden pews, but it wasn't a comforting place. Not to Caspian, anyway. The white walls and stone columns were cold and forbidding. It was an alien environment, this stark edifice to an old God. Caspian, as a rule, did not follow any God or Goddess. He made his offerings to the elements—Air, Earth, Fire and Water.

Briar rose and kissed his cheek. "Thanks so much for coming. This is such a weird thing to have happened. We're worried sick about Ben!"

"I'm not surprised. I'm glad you called me. I like Ben, and am happy to help in any way." He sat on a deckchair, their air of desperation only too apparent. "Does James know you're here?" He'd met James once or twice in Avery's bookshop, and he struck him as an earnest, devout man who'd be uncomfortable with this set up.

Cassie answered for the group. "Yes, we arranged it with him earlier. He's okay with it. He's planning on having an All Saints' Day service here, and he needs to know the church is safe."

"Which it clearly isn't, at the moment." Avery's expression was wary as she glanced around the church. Unlike Reuben who looked like he was about to drink a cocktail, Avery leaned forward in her chair, elbows on knees. "Well, the mausoleum at least."

Caspian nodded. "The scene of the crime. I saw a light on in there. Is that where we're forming the circle?"

"For a séance, yes." There was a gleam of mischief in Alex's eyes. "I'm not convinced that this is the way to go at all, but El's aunt, Oly, is eager to help, so why not?"

"I must admit, it does seem like an odd suggestion. What would you rather do?"

"Well, that's the problem. This whole thing seems so bizarre, it's hard to know what to do. I plan on doing some spirit-walking later. Maybe my astral body will see something of use—unusual energies, perhaps. I'll also talk to the spirit realm—in my way, not using a Ouija board." He shot a look of concern at Reuben. "To try to talk to Gil. But I'd put money on the fact that spirits have nothing to do with this."

Briar, seated next to him, touched Caspian's arm to draw his attention. "Have you had any thoughts on what we can do?"

"I spent a couple of hours searching my grimoire before coming here, but nothing has struck me so far. I need to know more about what's happening."

"Don't we all." Avery sounded despondent, and not her usual positive self at all. "Have you heard about White Haven's vanishing harbour?"

"*What*?" Caspian thought he misheard. "Vanishing harbour? What are you on about? I used witch-flight to get here, so haven't even driven through there."

Reuben gave a short, dry laugh, and then updated him on the latest news. "Newton's team and Dylan are there now trying to make sense of it all. Zee thought it seemed as if he was seeing the coast as it would have looked years ago."

"You're describing a sort of time slip." Caspian's thoughts whirled with uneasy possibilities. "If someone has caused this to happen, they're wielding extremely powerful magic."

"Perhaps the man that Zee saw," Alex suggested.

Avery straightened in her chair. "If it is magic, that means there's a solution."

"You said *if*," Cassie noted, her brow wrinkling. "What could the alternative be? If it is a time slip—whatever *that* is—they don't just happen! And if Ben has been taken somewhere in time, how do we get him back?" She looked sick. "This just gets worse!"

Before Caspian could comment further, the main door creaked open and El joined them, her booted footsteps loud in the echoing church. "Caspian! Thank you for coming." Like Briar, she leaned in and kissed his cheek, a waft of her familiar scent, Chypre, floating over him. "We're ready. Please don't judge my aunt for what's about to happen. Well, not too badly. She's very eager to help. She thinks this is what she's been summoned here for."

As they stood, Caspian repeated, "Summoned? Here? Who by?"

El's hand flew to her forehead, and she pressed it as if seeking guidance. "Great question. Weird things are happening, and I have no idea what. I'll tell you while we walk."

In a few minutes' time, and with Caspian even more confused by El's news, they were all seated in their designated places in Oly's circle. El had introduced him to her aunt, and he studied her surreptitiously, while taking in the set up in the mausoleum. The scent of burning herbs hung on the air, a black cloth was spread on the floor, and around it was a collection of cushions for them all to sit on. In front of each of them was a white candle, and groups of other candles had been placed around the mausoleum, their flames flickering in the still, stale air of the tomb. A ring of thick salt encompassed an inner circle beyond the candles, in which Oly sat, dressed in a voluminous purple and black gown. If El hadn't vouched for her, Caspian would have sworn she was a circus act. The Ouija board was placed in front of her, her eyes were closed, and her hands rested on her knees as if she was about to do yoga.

"Join hands," she instructed them, her eyes fluttering open. "I shall call Egberk within the circle. He is a powerful being. You are without, for your own safety."

Egberk? They all exchanged worried glances but did as she asked. Caspian was seated between Cassie and Briar, and clasped their cold hands within his own. He kept his distance from Avery. Holding her hand and feeling her magic still affected him more than he wished to admit.

Oly began, "I call upon the spirits of Air, Water, Fire and Earth." As she said their names, Oly wafted incense, sprinkled water, conjured a flame, and cast salt to the cardinal directions. "Watch over us as we venture forth into the spirit realm. Protect us from those that would do us harm. I open myself up to your guidance and wisdom." She said an incantation that they all repeated after her, and within moments, Caspian felt the flare of magic around the salt circle, sealing Oly and the Ouija board inside. She leaned forward and placed her hands on the board, her head dropping onto her chest as she began another incantation in a low voice.

Caspian had never used a Ouija board, although he was familiar with their design. For one thing he didn't work with spirits, and secondly, he thought them crude tools for the uninitiated. He was surprised that Oly used one, considering the strength of her magic. Like El's, it was considerable.

She must have her reasons.

He focussed on the board, and with a shock, he saw that extra sigils were carved onto its surface. In fact, that wasn't all that was different. It was bigger than usual, the dark wood at least an inch thick. The letters and symbols were highlighted in white. *Another wood, perhaps.* And they were runes, not the traditional alphabet. The moon and sun designs were ornate, and other tarot symbols were woven into the design, too. The dial that was already swinging back and forth was of an aged metal.

Caspian looked at El, but she focussed only on her aunt. Instead, he caught Alex's attention, and narrowed his eyes at the board, a silent question. Alex nodded his acknowledgement, his eyes tightening with worry. Caspian summoned his magic to his fingertips. He felt he needed to be prepared, sensing anything could happen. He would prefer if Oly were outside the circle with them. This was no ordinary way of working with Ouija, and he hoped she knew what she was doing.

Oly continued her incantation, and the louder she spoke in some incomprehensible language, the faster the dial moved. The symbols and runes flared into flames one at a time, seeming to impart knowledge from Oly to someone else. Caspian frowned. Normally the letters were for receiving a message, not sending one. Unexpectedly, she keened, and the hairs on Caspian's arm stood up. Cassie's hand gripped his so tightly, he could feel her nails digging into his skin. Briar, however, remained calm, her magic grounded deep within the earth. The dial flew around more swiftly, and this time all of the runes ignited into flames, and the air crackled with power.

Throwing her head back, Oly bellowed, "Egberk Hæd! Come to me, my friend, and share your wisdom. The old Gods interfere with our path. Worlds are colliding. Tell me what you see!" Her language changed again as she plunged back into what Caspian realised was Old English, as was the name of her guide.

The light within the centre of the circle darkened and became a gateway from which escaped the murmuring of voices, all overlapping one another. Mixed languages, ancient and modern, tumbled over one another as the darkness in the centre of the circle grew. Mist started to ooze out of it.

What the hell was Oly doing? It looked as if she were opening a portal into the realm of the dead. She wasn't aiming to just speak to the disembodied voice of her guide, Egberk Hæd, but to actually summon him. The only thing that consoled Caspian was the presence of Alex, who was skilled with spirits, and the powerful circle of protection that encompassed it.

Cassie's hand was now like a vice on his own, her eyes wide as she leaned back, away from the expanding darkness and swirling mist. He stared at her and mouthed, '*Don't let go!*'

She shook her head, plainly terrified.

His gaze swept over the other witches, not sure whether to be alarmed or relieved that they looked as shocked as him. Alex actually looked furious. He stared intensely at Oly, as if to draw her attention, but she focussed only on the thickening mist as she continued to call her guide. Magic was intensifying now, and time seemed to expand and shrink all at once.

A flash of light erupted from within the mist, and a huge figure stepped into the centre of the circle with an almighty bellow that made the building shake. He was dressed in skins and coarse cloth, his lower legs clad in boots made of leather. His hair was long and matted, plaited with beads and feathers, and his beard was thick, down to his chest. He gripped a huge, wooden stave carved with symbols, a large stone on top of it. As he turned to survey his surroundings, Caspian caught sight of a long leather necklace on which tiny skulls and more feathers were attached. *A shaman, then, this Egberk Hæd.* And even though a spirit, he resonated with, ancient, primal power. Now this made a little more sense. *Who better to ask than a powerful shaman, now a spirit guide, in the other realm?*

Egberk swung his staff in a wide arc, and the wind that whooshed in its wake seemed real enough. Caspian could feel his already cold skin cool even further. Where the staff connected with the circle of protection, it sparked with blue fire, and the man snarled like a wild animal.

Oly, however, seemed unconcerned. No. That was wrong. She seemed positively delighted. She murmured his name, followed by something incomprehensible as she stood to greet him, but she kept on her side of the board, Caspian noticed. The man's hard eyes softened as he saw her, and he bobbed his head as he said her name. It sounded strange in his tongue. Thick and unwieldly.

This time, Oly responded in English. "Let us speak so everyone can understand us, Egberk Hæd. I know you speak many languages in the spirit world. Thank you for joining us."

"As if I had a choice, Olympia. You drag me from my rest as if I am a plaything to you. Pulled through time, leaving my grave cold behind me. The earth mourns my loss and yearns for my return."

"Your body has long been earth, Egberk, son of Wulfnoth!" Oly seemed to be teasing him. "You're part of time now, woven deeply in its fabric in the spirit world."

"There is no time in the spirit world. It is all one. There is no beginning and no end." He gazed around him with glittering, black eyes. "You have summoned me to a place of the dead. Hard stone is no place to rest. And you have a circle of magic. We are not alone."

"Do you blame me, after the last time?"

His crooked smile was like that of a naughty child, except it revealed broken, yellow teeth. "You asked much. I was annoyed."

"You tried to break free." Oly drew herself upright. "Fortunately, I was stronger than you. But today I take no chances."

Egberk cackled. "We shall see. Tell me why I am here."

"You see much with your Second Sight." She gestured to her own two eyes and then the centre of the forehead, the place where the Third Eye was. "Two things happened today. A young man was taken, and we don't know where to. Could he have passed into your realm?"

He laughed. "No *body* could survive our world. Only spirits may pass here."

"But if he was wrapped in magic, would it be possible then?"

He shook his head, rattling his bones and beads. "No. It is impossible. This is no place for flesh and bone. His arrival would herald a storm and his body would be picked clean by vulture spirits. That has not happened. I would know."

Caspian recoiled at the words, but it was at least good to confirm what they suspected. As Egberk spoke, pressure increased on the circle that contained him, as if the shaman was testing his boundaries. He redoubled his magic to strengthen the protection, and felt the other witches do the same.

Oly continued, but now sweat was beading on her brow, despite the cold mausoleum. She was struggling to control Egberk, no doubt. "No one has passed through. You are sure?"

"I am sure. Do not doubt the words of Egberk Hæd."

"I do not doubt. I merely confirm." Oly bowed her head briefly. "Let us speak of the second problem. A part of our world today disappeared, as if taken somewhere else. I want to know if there is talk in the spirit world. If someone is manipulating time."

Egberk frowned. "Your question makes no sense. Time is one and the same here. I died as if yesterday, my body broken with age. I was buried with my trove as was fitting, beneath my cairn of stone."

"So, if someone is manipulating time, then it is not a spirit? Is that what you're saying?"

"What would be the purpose? A spirit has no need to change time. There is no tomorrow or yesterday. There is only now."

Oly changed tack. "You would be familiar with many magics, mighty Egberk. Do you know what magic could take a place and move it? Or could take a man? This person is dear to us. We need him to return. Whoever has done this, has also taken the spirits from here. There are no murmurs, no sense of rest or unrest. Only a void."

Egberk fell silent, his staff tapping on the ground, his bones and beads rattling. The circle of protection shuddered with every strike of the staff. It was terrifying. He seemed corporeal. He made sounds, and even emitted an animalistic, earthy scent. He finally spoke.

"What time of year is it in your world?"

"We approach Samhain. The time of ancestors. The Witches' New Year. The wheel is turning to darkness."

"I know of this time. It is a time of darkness indeed. Someone is calling upon the sisters, or perhaps just one. *Wyrd*." The name floated in the air, the intonations strange on his tongue. The single word seemed to carry a magic of its own. "They play with the ancestors, but for what purpose, I do not know."

Oly's voice was sharp. "Wyrd? One of the Fates?"

He nodded, and his beads rattled again. "Someone seeks to change personal destiny, perhaps. Why else move time? Why else," his fist clenched at the air, "snatch someone and take him?" He wagged a bent, gnarled finger at her. "To change their fate. All fate. All time."

The witches and Cassie exchanged nervous glances. *To change fate! That was enormous. Terrifying. Cataclysmic.*

But why?

"Who could do this?" Oly demanded, her commanding voice booming around the tombs.

"I know not. But this person would be powerful. To use Wyrd and cross time requires great sacrifice. And knowledge. *Intimate* knowledge." His gaze fell on them all, one by one. "Your fates are bound now, for good or ill. If you fail to unravel Wyrd's plans, all will fall. Time will fragment." He looked at Oly. "That is all I can offer. I have heard nothing, and I know nothing. Only this. *A cumendlicness.* A possibility."

The strain on Oly's face was unmistakable. "Thank you, dear friend. You have helped beyond measure. I will close this path between us now. Return to your rightful place, and rest."

Egberk Hæd, ancient shaman from the depths of time, stared once more at each one of them around the circle, and Caspian again felt pressure on the circle of protection. For a second, he wondered if the shaman would challenge the instruction, but then he bowed his head, rattled his staff, and stepped back into the void. With a crack like thunder, the darkness was banished and Oly collapsed, unconscious, on the ground.

Chapter Nine

"Well, that was something different," Reuben declared, sipping his whiskey. He shuddered with pleasure as the fiery drink warmed his throat. He took another sip, then passed the hip flask to El. She looked like she needed it, too. *They all did.*

He wasn't ashamed to admit that the encounter with the shaman had rattled him. Even though they were all back in the relative warmth and golden candlelight of the church, he still felt cold deep inside. A cold more from Egberk's unexpected suggestion than the mausoleum.

Cassie huffed, retreating further into her enormous puffer down jacket. "I can honestly say that for all I like to experience the paranormal and different magical rites, I really would not like to repeat that again. Although," she shot a look at Alex, "at least it wasn't a demon, like in the House of Spirits."

Alex glared at her, his tone abrupt. "I didn't actually summon it—it invited itself. And it remained firmly in the spirit world, unlike Egberk!" He now directed his glare at Oly. "You're mad for dragging him into our world. He was testing his boundaries constantly. It was dangerous!"

Oly at least had the grace to look embarrassed. She had recovered from her faint, and now looked horribly pale, a sheen of sweat on her brow. "I'm sorry. He is strong, isn't he? But I can't speak to him properly otherwise!"

"I suggest you don't do it again!" Alex shook his head, incredulous. "Why were you even in the circle with him? You should have been with us!"

"If I'm outside the circle, he won't come. And," she drew herself upright in her deckchair, "he didn't attack me. I surround myself with protection, too."

"But he did once, you said so yourself. And probably will again."

"He's right," El said, taking Oly's hand. "He was constantly testing the circle, and then you fainted! What if you had done that with him there? It doesn't bear thinking about."

"At least," Avery interjected, "he had a suggestion for what is happening. I hate it, but it's something to work on."

Avery never changed, and Reuben was glad of it. She always liked having a puzzle to chew over.

"What about Wyrd?" Caspian asked, looking bleak. He had been silent for a while, and now he accepted the hip flask that was being passed around the group. "I can't understand why one of the Fates would want to be involved in this. Or how someone could make her."

"*If* Egberk was right," Alex pointed out. "It was a suggestion! A pretty out there one."

"Other than being one of the Fates," Cassie asked, "what exactly is she, and what does she do?"

"Great question," El said. "I know only the barest facts. Anyone else?"

Everyone shook their heads, but Avery said, "I can look into her, and ask Dan to help, too. He's great at research projects."

"Thank you, Avery." Oly lifted her chin, and her eyes flashed with annoyance as she stared at Alex, clearly still riled at his earlier criticism. "Egberk has offered me many useful insights over the years. His magic is deeply rooted in the elements, and from a time when we didn't have all this modern paraphernalia dulling our senses. I always feel that his connection to the land, and the old Gods and Goddesses, is far more powerful than ours."

Briar played with her hair as she listened, wrapping strands around her fingers. "I think you're right there, Oly. I could feel his connection to the earth, despite the fact that he was a spirit. His staff resonated with the elements. The Green Man stirred at his presence, too."

Reuben sifted through the possibilities. "Perhaps, if this event is rooted in the past, the person perpetrating all this could be a shaman, too, or an ancient witch."

Caspian shrugged. "It's a possibility. But why? What's the end game? And why is Wyrd involved?"

"Maybe," Reuben suggested, "she's been offered a deal she can't refuse. Although, I have no idea what that could be."

Avery sagged back in her chair. "I'm honestly too tired to work it out now. I need to sleep on it."

"Ben's disappearance has to be connected to what happened tonight in White Haven," Caspian said. "We need to meet tomorrow and hear what happened from Newton and Dylan. Are you okay with me being there?"

"Of course we are, you tit," Reuben said, glad to see Caspian laugh. "Let's either meet at my place, or at Alex's pub. Or here. I guess we'll see what happens tonight." He looked at Cassie. "Ben might return."

She turned away, her eyes filling with tears. "I hope so, but I doubt it."

Alex rose to his feet. "I'll do as I planned tomorrow, but now I'm knackered." He pulled Avery to her feet, and turned to Reuben. "Are you sure you don't want me to stay tonight?"

Reuben gestured to his blankets next to the sun lounger. "I'm all set up. This is where I need to be. Go home, and I'll call you tomorrow."

He addressed that to all of them. "I'm happy to keep watch." He hoped Gil might make an appearance, even though he knew it was unlikely.

El nudged him. "You're not staying alone. I'll stay, too. Oly, you're going home to rest. Alex or Briar will drop you off."

"And me," Cassie said. "I'm not moving until Ben is back."

Reuben nodded, trying to remain cheerful for Cassie. "That's settled, then. We'll see the rest of you tomorrow."

"Then so be it." Caspian looked tired, too, as he stood. "Good luck. I'll consult my grimoire in the meantime."

With a whirl of air, and a flurry of activity, their friends left, and Reuben, El, and Cassie settled in for the night.

The only subject anyone was talking to Avery about in Happenstance Books on Tuesday morning was the disappearance of the harbour the night before.

As soon as she opened the shop, the main counter became a hub of gossip, and Sally and Dan were trapped behind it with her. Some of her regulars were there to exchange news, while others eyed Avery, and she knew that sooner or later she'd be asked a weird question.

"I saw it!" Mary, one of Avery's regulars, declared to her. It looked like she wasn't buying anything, but had only come to gossip. She crossed her arms over her ample bosom, and pursed her lips. "It was unearthly, but beautiful. Nothing was there except sea and sky!"

"Proper wild, it was," old Billy agreed, his eyes wide as he joined in the discussion. "I thought I'd had one too many pints when I left the pub. All that mizzle."

"My friend, Elsie, was one of them that got taken," added another woman, whose face Avery knew, but not her name. "Said it was the most terrifying moment of her life. Thought she was stranded there forever."

Dan leaned over the counter. "Would Elsie speak to me, do you think? I'd like to interview her for our podcast. And anyone else you know who was involved."

The woman, who looked to be in her fifties, shrugged. "I'll tell her to pop in and talk to you. Proper scared she was at the time, but now...well, she said it were magical!" She tapped her head. "I think it's affected her."

"Sounds terrifying," Sally said, eyes darting between Avery and Dan. "It doesn't seem magical to me. What if they got stuck there?" She didn't add, *Like Ben*, but Avery knew she was thinking it. They had agreed not to talk about that in front of anyone else.

"But what do you think, my lover?" Mary asked, turning to Avery and addressing her in old Cornish fashion. "You know the old ways. What's going on? Are we in danger?"

The half a dozen or so people gathered around the counter, and the ones lurking in the stacks to listen, all stared at Avery, including Dan and Sally. She took in their expectant faces that exhibited a mixture of worry and excitement, and knew she had to be honest.

"I really don't know what's going on, but it seems to me that there's a lot of magic in White Haven right now. And yes, I think it *is* dangerous. Unfortunately, I can't give you any advice yet. All I can suggest is that you keep well away from any pockets of mist that you see."

Billy nodded like a wise, old sage. "The mist is the trouble, then. Well, that will be proper tricky. October is full of mizzle. Can't tell magical mizzle from plain old weather, aye?" He elbowed Mary in the ribs as murmurings accompanied Avery's warning.

Maybe she had been a bit too honest. She raised her voice and appealed to her customers. "Look! This might turn out to be a one-off event. It's probably too soon to be making predictions, so just stay calm. I'm sure the police will have some advice for everyone later."

Avery sighed with relief when the crowd dispersed, and picked up her now cold coffee. "Ugh. I need a fresh cup. What a morning! It's barely ten o'clock!"

Sally turned her back to the shop, resting her hip against the counter as she lowered her voice. "There's still no news on Ben?"

"No, but I have other news, unfortunately." She hadn't had time to tell them about Oly's séance and Egberk's ominous suggestion, but keeping it brief, she updated them.

Predictably, Dan became very excited. "Wyrd? One of the Fates? Fascinating!"

Sally whacked his arm. "Not fascinating! Changing destiny? Messing with the future—or past? That's horrific."

"Well," he looked sheepish, "I was speaking from a research point of view on myths, and thinking of a future podcast episode."

"Well, try thinking of it from a 'let's not destroy our entire existence' point of view!"

Dan held his hands up in surrender. "Yes, sorry. Fair point." His eyes widened meaningfully at Avery. "Perhaps we should discuss this in the back room, and make more coffee?"

"Yes! You go do that!" Sally was riled, and Avery knew what was coming next. It was Sally's comfort blanket. "I will arrange our seasonal displays. Make my coffee strong and with a biscuit."

Without another word, Dan and Avery headed to the back room-come-kitchen and general staff area of the shop.

Avery sank into a chair at the table and reached for a chocolate biscuit while Dan prepared more coffee. "This is really bad, Dan. It's huge. We don't even know where to start!"

"Start with Wyrd. That's as good a place as any. I just wish I'd seen it happen last night—or even better, was caught up in it!"

"*Really*? Even though Ben has vanished? I'm scared we'll never see him again."

"Okay, maybe just witnessed it." He sat at the table with her while the coffee machine gurgled.

"You know, Dylan was there. He was filming and doing his paranormal stuff while Cassie was with us. He might well have discovered something useful. I gather Newton and his team interviewed everyone. And Zee saw everything, too," she added, knowing any insight he had would be valuable.

Dan perked up. "Brilliant. I'll speak to both of them."

"We're meeting later, not sure where yet, but I'll let you know. So, do you know anything about Wyrd? I know the word means uncanny, and it's got something to do with Norse myth, but that's all."

"I know the definition of the *original* word and the basic myth, but I'll find out more. Essentially, Wyrd with a 'y' predates the word weird, and it meant far more than just uncanny. It's an Anglo-Saxon concept, relating to fate and personal destiny. It's deeply rooted in who we are and what we do in the world. How our decisions shape our destiny, and the destiny of others. It's a weighty word, full of import. It featured heavily in Beowulf. And," Dan grinned at her, "the three witches in Macbeth were the Wyrd Sisters. The three Fates."

Avery groaned. *This was getting worse.* "There are three of them?"

"Yep. All related to personal destiny." Dan frowned as he crunched his biscuit. "I'm not sure of the names of the others, but I'll check it out, and see if they have differing roles and responsibilities."

"So, they're a variation of the Greek Fates?"

"Absolutely, but Wyrd is most definitely an Anglo-Saxon concept."

"Interesting. You know Oly's spirit guide was a shaman, possibly Anglo-Saxon, maybe earlier, even. He knew all about Wyrd. It was the first thing he suggested."

"I wish I'd seen that, too. You do all the fun stuff, Ave."

"You wouldn't have thought that if you'd been there." She came to a decision and stood up. "I have to consult my grimoires. There must be something in them."

Dan stood, too, and walked to the coffee machine to pour the drinks. "Okay, but bear in mind that Wyrd's concept of fate and destiny is linked to our ancestors, and we all know what Samhain is about. The veils are thin, Avery. What better time than now to mess with fate?"

Chapter Ten

D ylan studied the photos of the harbour and surrounding area that he'd taken the night before for what felt like the millionth time, and confirmed he had virtually nothing of any use that would indicate what had happened there.

"Bollocking fuck bucket!" He pushed away from his computer screen and paced around the office, full of energy he didn't know what to do with. "Just bits of mist and bugger all else!"

He was talking to no one but himself as Cassie was still at the church, a place he was planning to visit very soon. He had been tempted to go straight there after he'd finished investigating the harbour's disappearance, but knew he needed to study the photos and EMF readings properly. The only thing of use he had detected was a higher than usual level of electromagnetic energy. Not high enough to indicate ghosts, but it did match the frequency they had found in the mausoleum. That at least was progress. It backed up their theory that the harbour event and Ben's disappearance were connected.

He was missing something that his overtired brain wasn't focussing on. He returned to his desk and the messy notes that he'd made of the interviews the night before. He couldn't believe Newton had allowed him to be there, which was a sign of how desperate he was. *And perhaps*, Dylan admitted with a feeling of pride, *how well-respected their work was.* He'd also recorded some of the interviews, but not many. Most people didn't want to be recorded, for fear of it leaking out and making them sound ridiculous.

The overall impression from all of them, mixed within their complete shock, was the feeling of displacement. That they weren't in their own time or place. When they had pressed them further on this, no one could really explain why. They had just said that everything felt different. Untamed. One man actually thought he'd been abducted by aliens, until he reluctantly admitted that he probably was on Earth and not another planet. None of them had seen anyone, though. What they had seen beyond their own transplanted harbour was a wild and windy coastline barely touched by man, and a rugged valley. A couple had thought they had seen a light in the near distance that was possibly a fire, but they couldn't be sure.

Dylan skimmed the notes he'd made of Zee's observations. He had seen a man in a cloak on the clifftop, and strangely, Zee was the only one to see him. Perhaps it was something only the Nephilim could see. Or maybe he had just thought to look around more. The jumble of observations from those who had seen it happen were varied and confusing, but again, there was a common theme and belief that they were seeing ancient land. Was that where Ben was? Stuck in the past?

There was one place that Dylan hadn't explored fully yet, and that was where Zee had seen the man. Intriguingly, Zee thought he'd seen a wild tangle of forest up there. The predecessor of Ravens' Wood, perhaps.

Dylan grabbed the second thermal imaging camera he kept for back-up, and all of his recording devices.

Time to see what he could find on the clifftop.

Briar nodded with satisfaction as she added the final herbs to her spell bundles. She'd been working on them for hours in the back room of her shop, desperate to be doing something of use, and sick of hearing the many stories of Monday night's event.

She needed to clear her head, and this was her way of doing it. She felt heartsick, and she knew it was an old-fashioned term, but it described exactly how she was feeling. She mourned Ben's disappearance, and the threat that hung over her friends and White Haven. Her herb room, filled with delicious scents and all of her familiar magical paraphernalia, was a healing place for her. She looked around at her organised shelving and bottles of tinctures, creams, herbs, and potions. She couldn't imagine doing anything else or being anywhere else. White Haven, her friends, and Charming Balms Apothecary, a business she had built up from nothing, sustained her. Unfortunately, that also made her think of Hunter.

Briar sat at her sturdy wooden table in the middle of the room, even more depressed. She couldn't put it off anymore. She had to call him and end their relationship. It had been weeks since she had seen him, and this was no way to be together. Phone calls weren't enough any longer. In fact, the last time she had spoken to him, she sensed he was holding back, too, perhaps thinking the same thing. What a mess. Both of them knew it wasn't working, but both were unwilling to end it. If she called him today, that would be one less thing to worry about.

There was a knock at the door, and Eli came in. "Everything okay in here? You've been gone a while."

"I'm fine! Sorry. Time got away from me." She brushed away the herbs that were still on her hands and lifted her fingers to her nose. Rosemary and lavender mixed with other scents, all dried over the summer. "I'm making protection amulets."

"So I see." Eli smiled, dazzling her with his easy good looks and gentle eyes. He picked up one of the muslin bags. "You put small gems in here, too?"

"I'm about to spell them all, but essentially, they offer protection from spirits and, well...negative energy. But how do I protect the people I love from something we don't even understand?"

"Looks like you're doing a good job to me. Perhaps they need some kind of detection spell, too."

"A detection spell? I confess, I'm baffled!"

He sat next to her. "From what I've gathered from Zee after his chat to Dylan last night, the weird mist that preceded the event had slightly heightened energy levels. He detected it around the harbour where a few remnants of mist remained."

"Really? That's like what they detected in the mausoleum."

"Exactly, suggesting the events are linked. Maybe you could weave a spell that would take advantage of that, and give a warning? Or maybe you could put a bell on the bags?" He laughed. "Sorry. That's probably an insane suggestion. I was up late talking to Zee last night, and I think my brain must be addled."

Briar didn't laugh; she was buzzing with ideas. "Herne's horns, Eli. That's a brilliant suggestion. An early warning system triggered by raised energy levels! I have no idea of the spell I could use for that, but..." She trailed off, already considering her options, and reached for her grimoires.

"Glad I could be of help. I'm going to make you my special restorative tea. I can feel your energy is low, which is not good, Briar. You need to look after yourself." Eli headed to the kettle in the tiny kitchen area. "Don't worry about the shop. I've closed up for lunch."

Briar looked at the time, alarmed. "I'm so sorry. I had no idea I'd been in here all morning. You've been putting up with everything all on your own."

"I can cope with garrulous customers. I've actually learned quite a lot from them." He organised the cups and teapot while he talked. "It seems that the people who witnessed the event last night are already starting to forget it. I heard that first hand from a couple of witnesses this morning. They described it as dreamlike. One actually thought it *was* a dream, until they saw it on the morning news."

"Really? That's odd. A side-effect, perhaps, of the spell that was used."

"Or a *deliberate* effect," Eli countered. He leaned against the cupboard while the kettle boiled. "It's intriguing that Ben has vanished without a trace, and yet no one disappeared last night. Everyone returned. Well, we think they did."

"That's true. Someone on their own could have disappeared, and that might take days before they're reported missing."

"We can't worry about that until it happens. Let's assume the best. Perhaps our unknown perpetrator, possibly the man Zee saw, is looking for someone? When he doesn't find them, they all get sent back. And then as an added measure, no one can remember the details, presumably to protect himself. Fortunately, Zee isn't just anyone. He's remembering details just fine."

"You think he's looking for someone? Who?"

Eli poured the water onto the tea and then carried the pot to the table, sitting down next to her. He studied her for a moment. "I think he's looking for one of your coven—or all of you. Zee does, too."

For a moment, she thought he was joking, but he looked deadly serious. "Why?"

"Ben knows you, really well. Perhaps this person thinks Ben can give him information about you. Earlier, you told me about the shaman's theory about Wyrd and her involvement. Maybe this is about changing the balance of power between magical beings." He poured the tea and handed her a cup of the aromatic brew. "It sounds mad, and to be honest, pretty vague right now."

"It's an interesting idea, and very disturbing. You think this balance would need to be addressed years ago?"

"It seems that way, but why interfere in the present? Why not just change things then? All supposing this *is* happening in the past. This is just mad conjecture based on the sighting of a wild coastline." Eli sipped his tea, his eyes distant as he continued to muse on possibilities. "What does meddling here achieve? That's what we need to work out. Of course, my earlier suggestion that the perpetrator of this is looking for someone who knows your coven well does assume that all of you have been in this area for generations, which is a big leap."

"Unless it just affects one of us." Briar sipped her tea, aware that Eli was studying her with his calm, appraising gaze. "But how would someone know where to find Ben? Especially someone all the way from the past? That really is nuts. Unless..." A horrible thought occurred to her. "Unless they targeted the mausoleum—not Ben. That has been in Reuben's family for generations. Maybe, somehow, this perpetrator found a magical energy that suggested witchcraft and magic."

Eli grinned. "Great suggestion! They found a magical signature, honed in on it, and found Ben. He was taken by mistake."

"Which could put him in even more danger!" Briar dropped her head in her hands and groaned. "This is all so awful."

"We could be completely wrong." She lifted her head and looked at Eli's sympathetic smile as he continued, "I hope we are."

"I don't. It's a theory, a good one, and it's better than nothing. I don't think I told you about my experience with my grandmother at the manor. I saw an ancient figure in the garden fire. A man with a huge, antlered headdress and a painted face."

"Another kind of shaman?"

"I think so. And Gran saw a white stag on the moor. She said he felt like a totem animal. They must be related to what's happening." The tea started to work its magic on her, and her cloudy, worried thoughts began to clear, bringing with it a strange certainty. "What if my ancestors from way back are reaching out to help with all this?"

Eli nodded. "I think it sounds like a very interesting possibility. Have the other witches experienced anything like that?"

"I don't think so. Not yet, at least. But we're all meeting later, so I can ask them then. I don't know where yet."

"Sounds like a good idea. If there's anything we can do to help, just say so. There's just me and Zee around here at the moment. The rest are off chasing treasures and Black Cronos."

"You two are more than enough, thank you."

Eli squeezed her hand. "Now I'm going to fix you some lunch, too. You've got a lot on your mind. Are you going to end it with Hunter?"

She froze. "Why are you asking that?"

"Because I know you. Rip the plaster off, Briar. It's the only way."

"But I'll miss him."

"And he'll miss you. But when one door closes, another one opens. You need to make room for new things in your life."

"Is that your philosophy with your girlfriends?"

He winked. "I like lots of doors opening and closing. Stops life from getting dull." He pointed at her phone. "Do it now, in the privacy of the shop. Lunch will be ready by then."

Before she lost her courage, she was in the shop, calling Hunter.

Newton finished reviewing the transcripts of the interviews that his sergeants had entered into the computer, and then leaned back in his chair.

He felt like he'd been reading some drug-addled group hallucination event, but he knew that it had really happened. Kendall had witnessed it, and so had Zee, and he trusted both of them. He also hoped that the town's security cameras had recorded something of use. He shouted for Kendall and Moore, and in seconds they were both in his office.

"How have you got on with the CCTV footage?" he asked Moore.

"Should be with us very soon. The PCs are organising it now. I don't think we'll get much, though. Large spikes of electromagnetic energy tend to white-out camera footage." He grinned, looking pleased with himself. "I've been chatting with Dylan."

Newton inwardly groaned. The more paranormal things they experienced, the more enthusiastic his sergeant became. He shouldn't complain about that; it was a good thing. Enthusiastic staff worked twice as hard. "I thought Dylan said there was only a low EMF reading?"

"Yeah, but he reckons that it would have been higher at the time. With a huge event like that, he said it was inevitable."

"I suppose that makes sense, but I hope he's wrong. I would like to witness it for myself."

"There's a camera not far from The Wayward Son, so it should catch at least part of it."

"I hope so," Kendall said, ruffling her short hair so that it stuck up on her head. "I'm beginning to think it was a dream. Everything's so vague and insubstantial."

Moore nodded. "I've had a couple of witnesses contact me this morning saying they think they've imagined it. It's some weird after-effect."

"In that case, let's contact all of them again," Newton said. "I'd like to know if everyone is thinking the same."

Kendall looked horrified. "*All* of them? There were over fifty sightings! What would that achieve?"

"I don't know what it will achieve yet, but it could turn out to be important. It might demonstrate a pattern that means nothing right now, but could make all the difference later." He stared at her, perplexed. "It's called policing, you know that! Get the PCs to help you."

Moore also looked surprised, and he shifted his position to look at Kendall. "That's a weird question for you to ask. Are you okay?"

"I'm not sure I am, actually. I feel kind of hungover, but all I drank was half a pint of Guinness last night. Maybe I'm just tired."

"And maybe it's the spell," Newton said, deciding not to pretend it could be anything else. "Have we actually taken your statement?"

"Not formally, but Dylan interviewed me."

"Maybe I should recruit him." Newton made a mental note to get a copy. "Moore, do it now, and also record Kendall's aftereffects." He waved his finger around his head. "Any other symptoms?"

"I had a troubled night's sleep. You know, lots of dreams that made no sense. It was not a restful night, that's for sure."

"Tell Moore everything, no matter how odd. Dream imagery, characters, the works, and then tell the PCs to ask the witnesses the same questions."

Newton watched them leave, wondering not if, but when this would happen again. *And where?* Part of the town had disappeared for minutes last night, but what if that turned into hours? And what would the aftereffects of that be? He just hoped the witches would have some answers.

Chapter Eleven

I t was almost lunchtime, and Avery was about to go upstairs to her
flat, when James, the vicar of the Church of All Souls in the centre
of White Haven, entered the shop and joined her at the counter.

James was wearing casual clothes, the white collar just visible under
his thick jumper. He tried to smile, but failed. "Hi Avery, I'm really
pleased to see you."

"It's good to see you, too." James had dark circles beneath his eyes,
and looked like he'd barely slept. "I think I know why you're here.
Come and have a cup of tea." She led him to the back room, letting
Dan know she was leaving when she passed him stacking shelves.

As soon as they were alone, James said, "You know about Ben?"

"I do. It's awful. Have a seat, please. Tea?"

"Yes, thanks, and make it strong."

She turned the kettle on and prepared the pot, watching him look
through the books stacked on the table, and endeavoured to make
small talk. "That's our Samhain stock. Dan is running a reading corner
again. He's reading Edgar Allen Poe, while dressed as him!"

That provoked a laugh. "You're dressing up again?"

"Unfortunately. I'm Gypsy Rose, the fortune teller."

James's smile broadened. "That sounds like fun. We need it right
now." The smile slid from his face as he sagged into a chair. "I presume
Ben hasn't returned."

"Not that I've heard. It reinforces our belief that he hasn't just wandered off."

"Of course not. Ben is a sensible man, not an idiot." He stared at her, a flash of regret crossing his face. "Is there some force of evil in the mausoleum? I didn't feel I could ask Reuben. After all, his ancestors are in there."

Avery carried a tray to the table, loaded with the teapot, mugs, and biscuits, and sat down next to him. "No, absolutely not. This is something else. Something bigger than just the church and mausoleum."

"Something to do with last night's event? The vanishing harbour?"

"We think so. Did you see it?"

"No, I was at home. Of course, it's all I'm hearing this morning. My phone hasn't stopped ringing."

"Your parishioners?" Avery passed him a cup of tea and pushed the biscuits towards him.

"A few, yes, seeking guidance, and also my superiors." He sipped his tea, his shoulders visibly dropping. "I needed that. I don't think I've stopped all morning. They want to know what's being done to stop it from happening again."

"The parishioners or your superiors?"

"Both. I had no idea what to say."

Avery sipped her own tea, wondering how much to tell him. She certainly wasn't going to mention anything about Wyrd. "To be honest, I don't know what we're going to do, or what caused the event. It was only just last night, after all."

"But you're looking into it?"

"Of course we are. We have a few ideas, but nothing I want to expand upon until we're sure."

"Do you think it could happen again?"

"I sincerely hope not, but I'm sure it could—and probably will." Hope seemed to drain from his eyes, so she added, "I promise that we are doing everything we can."

"I know. I trust you, Avery, I do. It's odd, isn't it, that we should sit here chatting about such things? You with your old-world pagan beliefs, and me, a vicar in the church."

"A sign of our open-mindedness, and our ability to let others find their path, as long as they harm none."

"Your friend, Reuben. Is he a witch? One of your coven?"

"He is. He has a good heart."

"Another old family, the Jacksons. Were they all?"

"Some of them, yes. His family, like Helena's family, my ancestor who was burned at the stake, have been part of White Haven's magical community for years. As you know, we protect this place. It's part of our job."

"Which offers me a great deal of comfort—strange though it may seem." He changed tack. "Will this be over by All Hallows' Eve?"

She noticed James never referred to Samhain by the old pagan name. "Again, I hope so, but I don't know. However, I promise you, we'll do everything we can to stop this."

James shuffled in his seat, his eyes hooded. He looked uncomfortable. Nervous. "There's talk about sending an exorcism team to White Haven."

"To exorcise what?"

"Whatever's causing this."

"It's not spirits. Not ones that can be exorcised, anyway." *Well, probably not.*

"So, you do know what's behind it!"

"A suspicion, that's all. I'll tell you when we know more."

"All right, Avery. But be aware, if you don't sort this out, a delegation will be heading here, and they are not as open-minded as me."

Alex made the final adjustments to his circle of protection, ready to communicate with the spirit world, and perhaps Gil.

"I'm not sure I should be doing this," he said to Avery, who was studying their grimoires at the attic table. "We said we wouldn't."

She turned to look at him, her green eyes dark in the candlelit room. It was the middle of Tuesday afternoon, and dark clouds had raced in, promising rain. They had drawn the blinds in the attic, and lit the fire and incense. Alex had decided he wanted to speak to Gil earlier than he had originally planned, hoping there would be news to take to their meeting later that day.

"Gil came to you last time," Avery pointed out, "and Reuben asked you to. Who else would you trust in the spirit world?" She gave an impish grin. "Egberk?"

"Don't start!" He'd only just calmed down after the debacle from last night. "I still can't believe she did that. Amateur spirit work."

"Oly did say it wasn't her strength."

"Then don't mess with such things! He fixed on me, you know. I could feel him trying to probe my mind."

"Really?" He had Avery's full attention now, and she pushed her books away. "He knew of your abilities, then. I wonder how she found him?"

"How he found her, more like! He doesn't seem to be a particularly benevolent spirit. She's playing with fire."

"You made that very clear. I don't think that will stop her, though. And he had some very useful intel."

"Which could all be bullshit."

"It rang true, though."

Reluctantly, Alex said, "Yes, it did. It makes a horrible sort of sense. But maybe he's a skilled liar." He wasn't about to celebrate Egberk's input just yet. "Say I can't find Gil, or anyone. How do we try to corroborate his story?"

Avery worried her bottom lip with her finger. "I don't know. Yet."

He smiled, despite their situation. "I like *yet*. Okay, you know the drill. My circle is prepared, I have gemstones and herbs to support my journey. I could be gone a while."

"What are you using? A scrying bowl? A mirror?"

"A crystal ball, my ancestor's old one that I found in the rune box. It feels the right thing to use now."

"Good luck, and be careful!"

Alex nodded and turned to the fire. He was surrounded by a salt circle and a ring of white and black candles. He lit his herb bowl and once it was burning well, inhaled deeply. He was well practiced now, and he slipped into the necessary state quickly. He started his incantation, his words strengthening with every iteration, and he stared into the heart of the old crystal ball, the flames visible through the thick glass.

Within a few moments the flickering flames were replaced by a black void, and Alex plunged into it. He opened his mind and called to Gil. The darkness shifted and eddied, and he felt the press of spirits around him. He waited, a harmless observer, making sure not to press ahead like he had before. He had no intention of being lost again.

He repeated his request. "*Gil. It's Alex. Where are you, old friend? I need help. Reuben needs your help.*" Alex tried to discern his friend's unique presence. His strong but gentle personality, his water magic mixed with earth. For endless moments, Alex waited while the murmur of spirits ebbed and flowed. They sensed him, but didn't know what to do with him. Then, with relief, he recognised Gil, and a clear image of his face swam into his mind.

"Gil! It's Alex. Can you hear me?"

"Of course. Your voice carried far, Alex. You've grown stronger. Are you and the rest of the coven well?"

"We are. Reuben sends his love. I'm sorry for disturbing your rest. I vowed never to call on you again."

"You can call on me whenever you need me. You must have a problem."

"We do." Alex summarised the situation. *"Have you heard anything? Do you even see any of our ancestors in there?"*

"There are many spirits here. I see Helena because I know her, but no one else is familiar. What was the name of your spirit guide again?"

"Not mine! Egberk Hæd. A shaman."

Oddly, it felt as though Gil nodded. *"An ancient spirit who carries the old magic. Such spirits are powerful in here—especially if they choose to exert their power on others. But no, I haven't come across him. I will, however, investigate."*

"Not if it endangers you."

"Do not fear for me. But I think he is right. I doubt that the events you describe, including Ben's disappearance, arose in here."

Alex's hope dropped, but he always knew it was unlikely. *"Thank you. I'll visit again in a few days."*

"Days have no meaning here, but I feel the veil thinning. Is it Samhain?"

"Yes! You can tell?"

"I see glimmers of your world, and watch spirits passing through. I have seen it—felt it."

Alex was confused. *"You didn't need that before, when we were attacked. You were able to pass through then to help us. How did that happen?"*

"Helena happened." Gil sounded amused. *"She does not need the veil to lift. She makes her own way. She is still in your house?"*

"Too often."

"Then you should speak to her. She might know more."

"But she can't speak!"

"Not there, perhaps, but surely here. You can speak to her as you do to me."

"I suppose I could." Alex hadn't really considered that. Helena appeared so often in the house, he hadn't considered speaking to her in the spirit world. He presumed she was rarely there, given her regular presence in the apartment. *"I'll discuss it with Avery, and return soon to see what you have found. Thank you."*

"Any time, old friend."

The darkness faded and was replaced by the fire in the attic, the flames dancing and twisting through the distortion of the crystal ball. Alex was still in a dream-state, his mind not yet fully returned to his body. He stared into the flames, enjoying their warmth and light after the darkness of the spirit world.

Suddenly, two eyes manifested, along with the shape of a jaw and snapping teeth. But the image was odd, misshapen. Patterns writhed on skin, and a howl rose from the depths. Alex's skin prickled, but he held firm. What was he seeing? It was no demon, he was sure of that.

A voice replaced the howl, a young woman's voice, and strongly accented. *"Alex, son of witches, child of Kernow, bringer of magic, spir-*

it-walker, you are in danger. Tiernan seeks to change your path. You must stop him."

For a moment, Alex was too stunned to answer, stumbling over his words. "*What? Who are you?*"

"*Follow me.*"

The flames consumed Alex, dragging him from his own fireside to another. For what felt like endless moments, the fire writhed around him, and then he was spat out. He sprawled on bare earth in darkness, a fire burning within a stone pit a few feet away.

He sat up, his hair falling around his eyes, and brushed it impatiently away. Dirt was on his hands and in his hair. The ground was hard, a cold wind was on his skin, and the feeling of space stretched around him. For a moment, his breath caught in his chest. *Where was he?* It felt very real.

Breathe. He inhaled and let it out slowly. If there was one thing he'd learned, it was that panic never helped him.

He squinted, trying to see into the darkness, and with a shock saw a figure on the other side of the fire, beast-like and hunched, with dark eyes that glinted with flame. As his eyes adjusted, he realised the figure was not a beast but a woman, wrapped in an animal pelt, a huge wolf's head settled above her own.

The woman gave a wolfish smile. "*Well met, Alex, son of Finn. Forgive my intrusion, but time is running out.*"

"*Who are you?*"

"*I am you, of course, from many years before your own time.*"

"*I don't understand.*"

"*You do. You are unwilling to see it. I am your ancestor, here to guide you. Protect you.*"

With these words, Alex felt dizzy, and the landscape seemed to spin around him before settling again. "*My spirit guide?*"

"Your ancestor. My soul to yours." The woman tapped her chest. *"We are at a time of crossing, and you are in great danger. I have passed through many lifetimes to reach you, just as our enemy has. You must listen. Pay attention."*

"Wait! I'm not ready." Alex's thoughts were reeling. *"I can't focus. I need to...orientate. What is this place?"*

"It is the same place, just a long time before."

"I've gone back in time? This is Cornwall?" Alex tried to discern his surroundings through the intense darkness. Beyond the firelight he could make out the rise and fall of land, what appeared to be standing stones. Above him was a star-filled sky, far more visible than in his own time. The place felt desolate, eerie and lonely.

His ancestor said, *"You call it Cornwall, we call it Cornovii. Land of the horn. But that is not important."*

"It is to me! How am I here?"

"Because I called you, as my circle calls to the others in yours."

"The others?" Alex felt like a parrot, and wished he was sounding more intelligent. This was so surreal; it was hard to focus. The spirit world he was used to; this felt so different. *"My coven? The other witches?"*

"Yes. We are here to guide you. But it is hard. Our links are weak. You and I have spirit strength. You must help them to connect."

"I can do that." He hoped. *"Why are we in danger? Is this to do with our land vanishing?"*

The woman sighed. *"So, it has started. Yes. He searches for you. He will kill you to have his revenge on us."*

"Who?"

"Tiernan. A powerful man with a dark soul who seeks to twist the future to his own ends. That cannot be. We stopped him once. Now he tries a different way." The woman eased her pelt from one arm and banged

her staff on the ground, a staff similar to that which Egberk carried. It was carved with symbols and imagery, and bones and feathers rattled on it. *"He commands Wyrd to do his bidding. I know not how, yet. He steps between times."*

"He has taken our friend."

"Then it is already too late."

"No! We must get him back!" Alex stared into the darkness of what had to be iron age or Celtic Cornwall. Ben here? He must be terrified. *"You are here. You must find him."*

"Fate is already playing her part."

"This has barely begun. We have time. Find him. If you want to help us, this is part of it. We will find a way to bring him home."

Alex stared into the woman's glittering eyes, and the wolf's eyes glittered, too. Some kind of polished stone, perhaps. Now Alex was angry, and it helped him focus. A stack of skins lay next to the woman, along with a bag and a pile of stones that were some kind of early rune stone, plus a small skin drum. Magic was thick in the air. He could feel it now. All four elements felt super-charged. The earth hummed beneath him, the cold wind seared his skin, the fire danced and seemed to respond to him like a living thing, and water... Alex looked around. It was close by. He could hear the trickle of a stream and smell the moisture on the air. Raw, elemental power was everywhere, and he was sure that this woman, his ancestor, had enhanced the natural powers. Unless this was nature, without the distractions of the modern world. Something to consider later, not now.

Alex stared at his ancestor, refusing to back down.

Eventually, she nodded. *"I will try."*

"What is your name, and how is it that I can understand you?"

"My name is Kendra. We understand each other because we speak in our minds. This," her hand gestured around her, *"is not real. I sum-*

moned you with magic because the time of great darkness approaches. The veils between worlds are thinning. Help the other magic-wielders find their guides. They are in their totem animal. Then we will talk again. We have much to do."

"*And my totem?*" Even as Alex was asking it, he knew the answer.

His ancestor dropped her head forward onto her chest and the wolf stared at him, and with an unearthly reality, it was the wolf that spoke, a growl that resonated in Alex's chest. *"The wolf, of course. Find me, quickly. You need my strength."*

Alex fell into the fire again, the flames licking around him like a cage, and suddenly he was back in his own time, the crystal ball in his hands, the fire snapping and crackling beyond it.

Alex slipped sideways onto the rug, and immediately passed out.

Chapter Twelve

For once, Ben was alone, and he shivered despite the thick furs wrapped around him and the bright fire in the centre of the rudimentary stone hut. He threw more wood on it, and then held his hands close to the flames.

It wasn't just the bitter cold that made him shiver, though; it was his situation. His energy was ebbing, but he was still hopeful that he would get out of here. He had to be. The alternative, that he was stuck in ancient Cornwall, was too hard to bear. At least he thought he was in ancient Cornwall, especially after the events of the previous night.

His captor, after a strange, complex ritual that allowed him to perform a powerful spell, had summoned White Haven's harbour into view.

Ben had stood in the darkness watching the air shift and eddy, wondering if he was making a portal that would send him home. However, his hopes were dashed when the dazzle of the harbour shimmered into view, transforming the coast. His own cry of amazement had been dwarfed by the shouts and screams below.

People had been brought there, too. Desperate, terrified people.

Ben still wasn't sure how the man had achieved such a gargantuan feat, but he seemed to have created a window in time. It had lasted for a couple of minutes, and the man had looked on with a greedy, gleeful expression. Unbelievably, Ben was sure he could see the tall figure of Zee looking up at them, towering over everyone else.

And then it was over. His captor had cocked his head at him, seeming to say, *"See what I can do."* The only good thing about it was that it seemed to have exhausted the man, because his body trembled so badly, he almost collapsed on the ground. However, the man hadn't performed the magic alone. A woman had materialised out of the darkness, her white dress fluttering in the wind, power radiating from her lithe form. She was no ordinary woman; that was obvious. It was bitterly cold, and she didn't shiver once. Long, blonde hair framed a pale, ageless face, and she looked at Ben with a hard stare that made him feel as insignificant as a blade of grass. They communicated in low voices for a while, and then she vanished again.

The man had staggered back to the palisade, hustled Ben into the hut, and in seconds drugged Ben with the strange, powdered substance before he could resist.

Ben had no idea how long he had slept for, but it was a relief to wake alone, free from the man's probing stare and impatient tuts. He expected his captor to reappear at any moment, but the longer he waited, the more he realised this was a great opportunity to look around. He hated to risk the man's wrath, but equally felt he couldn't just sit there doing nothing.

Quickly making a decision, Ben drank more of the stream water, pulled a thick fur over his own coat, and stepped outside into grey, overcast light. His heart sank. In daylight, the true isolation of the hut was clear. It was remote, bleak, and cold.

Not far from the hut was a steep cliff that tumbled down to the sea, the surf crashing and booming against it. Behind him was thick, tangled forest. Remembering the fires from the night before, he headed to the edge of the palisade and was able to see into the valley below. He groaned with disappointment. There wasn't a village. It was another couple of stone buildings, but that was all. Beyond the valley, to his left, he could see rolling moorland, dotted with huge stones that jutted out of the earth like a wild herd of boar, however, there were also a few cultivated fields. His spirits lifted. That meant farmers and some kind of society.

Unfortunately, there were also wild animals. Ben swallowed and stepped back, glad of the thick, spiked palisade that protected the hut. He could clearly see wolves. And...he squinted, doubting his eyes. *Was that a bear?*

Herne's horns. How far back in time was he?

Then, something else caught his eye. It looked like a hillfort high on the moors. Its outer perimeter blended with the landscape so well, he'd barely noticed it. *If he ventured there, would he be in more trouble than he was now?* Besides, he wanted to get home, and there was only one man who could do that. The man who had brought him here.

How would Ben describe him? *A madman seemed most apt.* But he was powerful too, wielding plenty of magic. Ben hesitated to call him a shaman. *Wizard* seemed the most suitable word, and that felt faintly ridiculous. Like he was in a fantasy book. He was old, his face a map of endless creases surrounding dark, cunning eyes that were filled with malevolence, topped by a tangled mass of hair.

It was clear that he wanted something from Ben. He had made strange, guttural noises that were impossible to understand, and their inability to communicate was clearly frustrating.

Checking his camera again, Ben saw he only a little battery time left, and he didn't have spare batteries. They were in Dylan's pack. Perhaps thermal images would reveal something useful in the short time he had to use it. He turned it on and panned it around. Immediately, he saw an orange band of light around the hut. Ben groaned. He recognised that. It was caused by magic. The man had sealed him in somehow. *Damn it.*

Okay. Time to collate as much evidence as he could while he had the chance. He was determined to find something that would help him return home.

Perhaps something to bargain with, too.

El brushed away the sweat from her forehead with the back of her hand. Despite the bitter cold outside, her forge that was situated behind her shop was hot.

She had retreated there in the mid-afternoon to work on some of her bigger designs, particularly her Green Man wall hanging made from beaten copper. So far it was a basic design, but it would be elaborate by the time she finished it. It was part of a series that she was making for Reuben to sell in Greenlane Nurseries, and she was relishing the challenge.

Today it was also a welcome distraction. She didn't intend to forget about their current predicament—she couldn't, anyway—but this type of work allowed her mind to churn over possible solutions while she worked on something else. She also wondered what to do about Oly, her more batty than usual great aunt.

El pulled the goggles over her face, thrust her design into the fire, and then placed it on the anvil to hammer it out, her thoughts drifting as she did so. Oly had always been a force of nature. Indomitable, kind, generous, and a skilled witch. El had never worried about her—until now. Yes, of course she had controlled Egberk's appearance, but it had been risky. Perhaps she was being ageist. There was no reason to think anything bad would happen. Oly had clearly been doing her Ouija board magic for years.

But what did his prediction mean? Why would anyone want to interfere in her fate? Their fate. What had they done that deserved such retribution?

Leaving the wall art on the anvil, she turned her attention to the fire again, and thrust another log on it. El liked fire, it was her strongest element, and she started to play with it. She held her hands in front of the flames and manipulated them. Within seconds, the flames danced to the pattern she wove. With another whispered spell the flames changed colour, and she introduced reds, blues, and greens into the orange and yellows.

She smiled with pleasure as she plaited the flames like ribbons then released them, and then changed the pattern again so that they rolled like the surf, ebbing and flowing. So calming and relaxing. A balm for her senses. The more the flames danced, the more her shoulders dropped and her mind drifted. Within seconds, the flames encompassed her whole vision, and the room beyond vanished.

In the centre of the fire, a column of flames rose, twisting like a tornado—and it wasn't of her doing. She had enough wit about her to raise her hands, magic poised in defence, but El was more curious than scared.

The column continued to rise until the top was at El's eye level, and then it morphed into the shape of a slender woman with long, flowing hair that wrapped around her figure like a cloak. An arm extended out of the flames in a gesture of greeting. The details of her face revealed delicate-features, with high cheekbones, a sharp chin, and wide-set eyes.

Sparks spluttered at the end of her outstretched hand, and tendrils of light ribboned towards El. She wondered if she should erect a protective shield, but there was something about the woman that she trusted. El extended her hand, and as soon as the light connected to her fingertips, images raced into her mind.

She was on a hill above a wild, windswept valley, the sea visible a short distance away. A fast-flowing stream wound down to the beach, its chattering carrying to her. The beautiful landscape of moors and rolling hills was strangely familiar. She lifted her head and inhaled the scent of the sea that was carried on the blustery wind, so real that she shivered with cold as her hair lifted from her shoulders. If this was an illusion, it was a powerful one.

But where was the woman who had summoned her?

The keening cry of a bird made her turn, and with surprise she saw a low, stone building behind her, and an old woman with long, grey hair stood in the doorway, watching her.

El stepped back, shocked, stumbling on the uneven ground. "Who are you?"

The woman didn't speak, instead raising her hands and conjuring a fireball within her palms. El raised her own hands, ready to retaliate, if her magic would even work wherever she was now. However, it seemed the woman had no intention of harming El. Instead, she weaved a complicated dance with her hand, transforming the fire into a sign. As the flames settled into shape, a blaze of intersecting straight lines that took great skill to maintain, El realised that it was a rune.

It grew so large that it filled her vision, and the next thing she knew, she was back in her smithy, and the house and ancient landscape had vanished.

Cassie paced around Old Haven Church graveyard in an effort to keep herself warm as she took some more EMF readings.

She was shattered after an almost sleepless night. Staying in Old Haven Church had felt weird, despite the fact that Reuben and El had been with her. Now only she and Reuben remained after El had left for work that morning. No one had joined them. Dylan was exploring the clifftop, Newton was following up on last night, and the witches were investigating their own theories.

The mausoleum seemed to mock her. The door was propped open in case Ben returned, but the longer he was away, the more unlikely that seemed. She marched over to it and took readings there, too, but even the faint energy signature had now vanished.

Tears welled, and frustrated, Cassie wiped them away. She was a fool. She should be focussing on getting Ben back, not being maudlin. They had powerful witches on their side, so she had no reason to feel such despair so early on. It was barely even twenty-four hours since he'd vanished.

The weather echoed her mood. As rain started to fall, she sheltered under the broad porch of the mausoleum, hoping Reuben had found shelter in the woodland behind the church where he was exploring around the old yew tree. Last year that site had a become a portal to the Otherworld, and Reuben wanted to check for any magical vibrations there, alone, so that he could focus.

As she leaned against a stone column, she heard the rumble of an engine, quickly followed by the sound of running, and within moments, Dylan rounded the corner of the church. She called to him, and he sprinted down the gravel path.

"You here on your own?" he asked, looking perplexed. Water beaded on his face and dreads, and his coat was soaked, but he seemed unconcerned about that. "Where's Reuben?"

"In the wood. Don't worry, everything's okay. Sort of. Except that Ben still isn't here."

"Anything useful from the EMF readings?"

"Nothing. This place is dead. Excuse the pun. Did you find anything useful in the footage?"

He wiggled his hand. "Sort of. The interviews were fascinating, but unfortunately the whole event was over by the time me and Newton arrived. The EMF meter did pick up higher than normal energy readings in the harbour, very similar to what we found here last night. That indicates these events are connected, so that's good. But I had more luck at the castle."

"Where Zee saw the cloaked man."

"Yeah. I wondered if there was any residual energy there." He pulled his camera out of his bag and retreated further into the mausoleum where the gusts of rain couldn't penetrate, and Cassie followed. "I detected a bit of a glow, which is unusual so many hours after the event. It's an indication of how much magic was used last night."

She leaned in to study the small video screen. "I see it. Just a general glow by the cliff edge."

"Hopefully I'll see more once I put it on the bigger screen. Raised EMF readings, too."

"Do you think that's where this man is based?"

"Hard to say, Cass. But I did have another thought." He looked around at the mausoleum and then back at her with a resigned expression. "Just because Ben vanished from here, doesn't mean he'll return here. I think our vigil is pointless. That bloke just made the whole harbour vanish! He could do anything, anywhere!"

Cassie didn't think her mood could get any worse, and yet it did. "But we can't just leave! He's out there, somewhere."

"I know, and we will find him. I just think sitting out here for hours is wasting productive time. We'll talk to Reuben and James about leaving the mausoleum unlocked, and we'll check it regularly. Leave him a note, even. But we have to broaden our investigation."

Cassie sagged against the doorframe. "This is a nightmare."

"We'll work it out. We're smart. So is Ben."

"What do you think the point of the harbour stunt was?"

Dylan shrugged. "An exhibition of power, perhaps? A way to search for the witches? Or someone else?"

"Why doesn't he take the whole place? All of us." Even as she was asking it, she knew the answer. "Because it's too big!"

"I think so. Maybe that spell weakened him, but that's pure speculation. If Wyrd is helping him, who knows what he could do. Let's round up Reuben, head back to the church, and close up. I'm wet and cold and starving, and I just want to get out of here."

She hesitated, looking around the mausoleum and graveyard. Everything was wet and dreary. "But if he returns alone, here, in this..."

"He'll be ecstatic to be back, and I promise we'll check in regularly." He nudged her gently out of the door. "Time to plan phase two, Cass."

Chapter Thirteen

A very handed Alex a strong, reviving cup of tea, and watched him grimace with the first mouthful.

"Yuck. Why does something so good for you have to taste so horrible?"

"You sound like Reuben. You'll be asking for whiskey next."

"Can I?" He looked at her with big, puppy dog eyes, his hair falling over his face in a way that made her want to run her fingers through it.

"You are adorable. But no. Tea first. Now I know how Briar feels."

"You're both mean!"

"You just passed out on the rug!"

"Can you make it sound more manly? I haven't had a fit of the vapours."

She laughed, relieved to see that Alex seemed to have recovered from his strange experience, although she wasn't as worried as she would have been months earlier. She was used to the aftereffects now. "So, what happened this time?"

"Well, it wasn't my chat with Gil that affected me. I ended up meeting one of my ancestors." His eyes sparkled with mischief. "It seems I have to help you all meet your totem animal."

"My *what*?"

"Your totem animal. It will strengthen you. Act as your guide and support you in what we have to do. A sort of liaison between us and our ancestors."

Avery searched his face, but his humour had vanished, and he regarded her steadily. She released her breath slowly. "By the Goddess. You're serious."

"I know a little bit about what we're facing, but I must admit, I'm confused. It seems that our ancestors once thwarted someone who was trying to... Shit, what were her words? She said something about them stopping a powerful man who was trying to change the future. They'd stopped him once, and now he is trying again. My ancestor, Kendra, said that our enemy was 'stepping between times.'"

"That's an odd phrase."

"I know. She also confirmed that he was manipulating Wyrd somehow."

"So, Egberk was right." Avery could barely comprehend what he was saying. "How did this even happen? How could you be talking to Gil, and then your ancestor? How did it work?"

Avery liked to fully understand the workings of magic. Not knowing made her frustrated. If she was to make a new spell to be able to do something similar, she had to understand what was at play.

Alex finished his tea and sat cross-legged. "I don't know. *She* made it happen. She contacted me through the fire. All of a sudden, I was sitting around another fire, in another time. It was utterly surreal. But she did say that we weren't actually together. It was a powerful mental connection."

Avery mirrored his actions, sitting cross-legged so that they were knee to knee. "Through time."

"Perhaps. I need to think on it, Avery. Try and really understand what just happened. I do know what my spirit animal is, though." He looked at her expectantly.

"Go on."

"A wolf. It was so cool. Now I need to understand how that works, too."

"She didn't implant you with the knowledge?"

"No. It wasn't *The Matrix*!"

She sniggered. "I shouldn't laugh. This is weird. And Wyrd!"

He rolled his eyes. "Terrible. Do you know anything about finding your totem animal?"

"I'm aware of such a thing, obviously, but it's not something I've ever looked into. I think this is on you. I'll try and help, of course. Didn't your ancestor give you any pointers at all?"

"Nope. I suspect it will involve drugs and a fire. Maybe naked chanting. Not peyote or LSD or anything, just in case you were going to ask." He grinned at her, prompting a stir of desire. "I quite like the idea of naked chanting around a fire."

"There will be no naked chanting! Unless it's just us two."

He gave a raucous laugh. "Oh, Ave. That sounds fun!"

Avery giggled and then stifled it. This was taking her out of her comfort zone, and while she loved to be challenged, this was...odd. "Just don't mention naked chanting to Reuben! As far as everything else goes, I trust you. What about Caspian? How does he fit into this? I presume he can still help us."

"Good question." Alex's eyes darkened. "Let's hope it isn't his ancestor that's causing all this."

"I'm not entertaining that idea. And Caspian would be devastated, you know he would."

He considered her for a long moment, and Avery willed him to be generous. Finally, he nodded. "I know. He's been a good friend recently, but I think we have to consider the possibility. What if he is contacted by his malevolent ancestor to take us on? He might not have a choice."

"*We* do. We're not being possessed by our ancestors."

"Yet," Alex interjected.

She pressed on, ignoring—*no*, choosing not to believe that. "We are *not* being possessed by our ancestors, and neither will he. We're still free to choose our actions. Besides, that would be too easy, and we're not ever that lucky. Caspian is our friend, and after putting up with his father's crap for years, he's hardly likely to buy into that again," she said with conviction. She leaned forward to kiss Alex, and then rose to her feet. "Whoever is after us will be trickier than that. I'm going back to the spell books and let you think things through. At least I have something to really focus on now."

"His name is Tiernan."

"What?" Avery was halfway across the attic, but she turned back to him. "That's his name? Our enemy?"

Alex nodded. "I'm not sure it helps, but it's good to know."

Tiernan.

"It sounds Celtic. Old. That's a lot of years between us." She shivered with the weight of it all as she headed to her books.

"I'm going to spirit-walk now, check the energy over White Haven. Will you update the others?" Alex called after her. "Let's arrange to meet somewhere. I'd rather not go to the church in this crappy weather, but see what they want to do."

"But what if Ben returns?"

"My ancestor said it was already too late for him. I disagreed."

For a moment, Avery couldn't speak, horrified by the possibility. She looked out at the thickening twilight and heavy rain, and imagined how it would be without shelter, in a time far from her own. It brought back memories of her own experience at the crossroads when she had been pulled away against her will. It had been terrifying and lonely. To think she might have been trapped there, died there... She still had nightmares about it sometimes.

Avery hurried to her books. *Ben would not suffer that fate.* She would find a way to bring him back.

Newton stared at Alex. "You have got to be kidding me!"

Alex grinned and raised his beer glass in response. "No. Despite the oddity of it all, I'm quite excited at the prospect of bonding with my totem animal!"

Newton didn't know what to say. Of all the strange rituals and spells he had seen the witches do, this sounded like the weirdest yet. Looking around the room, he was pleased to see a mixture of doubt and excitement on his friends' faces.

The five White Haven witches, plus Caspian, Oly, Cassie, Dylan, and Newton, were gathered in Alex and Avery's open-plan living and dining room. The fire was blazing, rain was lashing against the windows, and only candles and lamps illuminated the room. They had all arrived an hour or so earlier, and after eating a wide variety of curries, had settled in front of the fire with drinks. The occasion felt very civilised, considering the circumstances. Too civilised.

So far, Alex had just related his conversation with Gil, and then his ancestor.

"I'm intrigued," Caspian confessed.

"Yeah! Naked chanting!" Reuben said, performing a comedic dance in front of the fireplace. "I love it."

El threw a cushion that hit him in the stomach. "Behave! There is no need for naked chanting."

"Exactly what I said," Avery said, rolling her eyes. "Men are so predictable."

"I was going to ask if I could film it, but I guess that's a no?" Dylan said, cocking his head at them.

Avery shot him a quelling glance. "A very big no!"

"I think it all sounds fascinating. Whatever gets the job done, in my opinion," Oly said, a gleam in her eyes that shocked Reuben into silence.

Briar, however, was subdued. She sat quietly, curled up in the corner of the sofa, not even laughing at Reuben's antics. She said, "I think my spirit animal will be a stag. I just feel it."

"Because of what you saw in the fire?" Cassie asked. She was sitting next to her, pale and preoccupied. She'd taken Ben's disappearance harder than anyone.

Briar nodded. "Yes. Especially after what Tamsyn saw." Newton noticed she often flipped between calling her Gran and Tamsyn, as though she still wasn't quite used to the idea of her new family. "Nothing from Beth so far, though."

"That's a good thing, though, right?" Newton asked. Beth's visions had freaked them all out.

"Yes and no. You would expect that with so much going on, she would have sensed something."

Alex frowned. "I agree, especially considering she has what I consider to be an old soul. I would have thought that our ancestors' attempts to contact us, and the time slips, would have triggered some-thing."

"I'm going to see them again tomorrow, so I'll check." Briar shook off her preoccupation and said, "So, spirit animals. What's yours, Alex?"

"A wolf. It was odd—powerful, actually. My ancestor was wrapped in a wolf pelt, the head over her own. Her voice came through the wolf." He tapped his chest. "I felt it, right here."

"That isn't something you've felt before?" Newton asked, noticing that Briar had flinched at the word *wolf*, and wondered what that meant.

Alex ran his fingers across his lower lip. "No. My dad is due to arrive tomorrow though, so I can ask him about it. My ancestor seemed to think I could help the rest of us find our spirit animals, but I can't. Not yet, anyway. It's going to need a lot more work on my behalf. By the way, I also spirit-walked this morning, but I didn't see any strange energy over White Haven. I guess that's a good thing, but I had hoped to see something that might give us some insight." He sighed, disappointed.

"I've been searching our grimoires, specifically looking for anything about Wyrd or totem animals," Avery added. "There are references to both, but not much. There are certainly no spells to invoke Wyrd or use her, or the concept, in any way. However, there are spells that describe how to connect to your animal totem. Well, less spells than rituals. They're also personal rituals, not group ones. And guess what? No nakedness required."

Reuben huffed. "Spoilsport."

"I think," Alex said thoughtfully, "that I can modify those rituals so we can do them—or one of them—together. I'm going to try one on my own first. I need to connect with my spirit animal again, so I'm familiar with the process. Feel confident in it."

Oly was sitting in the armchair closest to the fire, swirling red wine in a large glass. She nodded in approval. "Excellent plan. Of course, I wish to be involved. I'm here, so why not. Your father should be, too. The more witches involved, the more powerful we will be."

"Which brings me to the Cornwall Coven," Avery said with a nod to include Caspian. "We're meeting tomorrow. I'm sure someone there will have experience with their totem animal. It's not uncommon, just to us. We need to discover not just what they are, but learn how to use them. The coven offers a wealth of knowledge to draw on."

"I'm afraid," Caspian added, "that I cannot offer any advice. It's a type of magic that I am utterly unfamiliar with. My father deemed it too pagan and wild. He liked to keep his power tightly reigned." He smiled. "If I'd had a rebellious streak, I would have probably experimented with it just to annoy him."

"Well, better late than never," Reuben told him with a wicked grin. "I can't wait. I want to be a bear."

"I think you'll be a pig," El shot back. "Oink, oink, oink."

Newton shuffled in his seat, ignoring Reuben's one fingered salute to El. He was glad some of them thought it sounded fun, and then he realised how old he sounded. And felt. However, there was too much at stake for frivolity. "This sounds like it could take a long time. Time we don't have. Something could be happening out there, right now! Maybe someone else is being kidnapped by some bloody, crazed Gandalf character!"

"We have to be patient!" Briar said, her brown eyes sparking with a ring of green, a flash of warning from the Green Man. "There are no shortcuts in magic. To act too soon and get it wrong would be a disaster. Besides, we *have* time. I think our adversary is waiting for Samhain. That's over a week away."

Newton scowled, knowing he was being grumpy, but unable to control himself. "Waiting to do what? He's already started causing havoc. Do you want more people to vanish? More parts of the town to disappear into the mists of time?"

"Newton!" Briar snapped, and then she took a deep breath to calm herself down. "Newton, we are in the dark as much as you, and we are working as quickly as we can. I hate that Ben has vanished, and that someone appears to have a vendetta against us. I don't understand any of this! However, I have made something that I think will help us. Eli suggested some of it." Briar leaned forward and rummaged in the bag at her feet, and then pulled a handful of small muslin bags out, the scent of herbs filling the room as she did so. "I have made protection bags—with bells."

Reuben looked appalled, commenting before anyone else could speak. "Bells! I'm supposed to wear that? Like a bloody cow?"

"If you'd just give me a moment to explain!" Briar's eyes blazed again. Her temper was short this evening, much like Newton's, and everyone sat back as if to give her space, including Newton. "Eli pointed out that mist seemed to herald the two events. Two isn't many, I know, but it could be pertinent. He also pointed out that raised energy levels were present. So, after literally spending all my afternoon experimenting with spells, I have enchanted these bells to react to a certain level of magic." She passed them around the room. "They're basic, I know. It's all I could do in the time I had."

Newton examined the fine muslin cloth filled with aromatic herbs and tied with white ribbon, the initials 'CBA' embroidered on them. Two tiny bells were attached at the neck of the bag where it had been pulled tight. Without question, he unwound the thin leather strip that was in place of a chain, slipped it over his head, and tucked it under his shirt and against his heart. Immediately he felt her warm, calming magic start to settle his anxiety.

Clearing his throat, he said, "Thank you, Briar. How do the bells work? Won't me just moving about make them jingle?"

"No. They didn't make a sound just then, did they?"

Cassie gasped. "No, they didn't! How did you do that?"

"A muffling spell that will be undone by magic. Of course, *we* could set it off if we use our own magic," she gestured to her coven and Oly, "but you three shouldn't. Be alert for rising mist, too. Again, difficult to do in October. There's so much of it about."

"Wow, Briar," Avery said, settling her bag into position, too. "That's clever. Thank you. I also suggest that at the slightest sound of tinkling bells and thickening mist, we all get away from the area as quickly as possible. The parameters of the last event were huge, though, so that could be tricky..."

"We think," Dylan said, glancing at Cassie for confirmation, "that Ben won't necessarily return to the mausoleum. He could come back anywhere. *Will* come back anywhere. Although we should keep monitoring the place, camping out there for days on end will achieve nothing. I'm going to set up cameras in certain key places—just not sure where, yet."

"That's a good idea," Caspian said, nodding. "It will be interesting to hear what the council has to say on this. So far these events are centred on White Haven, but what if they are also happening further afield? That would suggest that it concerns more than just the White Haven Coven. Have you had any reports from elsewhere, Newton?"

He shook his head. "No, thank the Gods, but I suppose it's early days yet. Or the time slips, or whatever we should call them, might have been so small before now that no one has noticed them." He had so many thoughts swirling around his head, so many things to follow up on, he wished he'd brought a white board with him. Instead, he whipped his notebook out of his pocket and jotted a few things down. "By the way, I suppose you've heard that the disappearing experience has left people with a loss of memory? Must be a side effect of the spell."

"Loss of memory?" El asked. "Like a blackout?"

"No, more like progressive memory loss. The event was vivid at the time, but the details are now slipping away. Even Kendall described the experience as feeling dreamlike. She was quite odd today. I sent out the PCs to re-interview the victims again, to catalogue the changes."

Dylan leaned forward in his chair, a wrinkle of annoyance on his face. "It would be useful to stick some electrodes on a few people's heads and monitor them in our office, but I doubt anyone would consent. Most people didn't even want their interview to be recorded."

"Electrodes?" Images of Frankenstein's lab leapt into Newton's mind. "Sounds barbaric!"

"It really isn't. They just monitor brain waves." Dylan shrugged. "The only thing is, with no baselines, there's nothing to compare them to."

"But," Cassie interjected with excitement, "we know basic brain function. We could try. I'm sure Zee and Kendall would consent, if no one else does."

Newton groaned, and pointedly ignored Cassie and Dylan's glares of resentment. "That's all very well for your research, but it won't help us stop this! I want practical suggestions, not fancy experiments." He stared at the witches, especially Alex. "Your ancestor says that Tiernan wants revenge on you, for past wrongs. *How*? What's his end game?"

"Aren't you a detective?" Oly asked, with silky sarcasm.

Newton shot forward in his chair, glaring at the elegant, but eccentric, old woman, and not caring that she was El's aunt. Her cool arrogance and risky behaviour the other night was infuriating. "I know my bloody job, thank you. Unfortunately, I haven't got a hotline to the bloody ancestors! Also, madam, you do not have the entire safety of White Haven and its population resting on your shoulders. Nor," he continued, his voice rising with anger, "are you answerable to my superiors! You just like to play with Ouija boards and summon crazy shamans!"

Oly drew herself upright, fixing Newton with her steely glare. "My shaman gave us the first insight about Wyrd, which by the way," now she shot Alex a withering glance, too, "was confirmed by Alex's ancestor, despite aspersions cast about my abilities. Nice to see that ageism is rife amongst witches and not just the general population."

El gasped. "Aunt Oly! No one is ageist here!"

"Really? Could have fooled me."

General murmurs of denial rumbled around the room as Avery leapt in. "Please, Oly, we are very grateful for your help! Thank you. You did, indeed, set us on the right path. A long, winding path, it seems..."

Newton didn't give a crap about the rising tension in the room. Reuben giggling about naked chanting didn't help his mood either, or Briar's simmering silence that felt like it was directed at him. Obviously, he had done something to set her off. *Again.* "Just to remind you all that Ben has vanished, to who knows where. Sitting around until Samhain doesn't seem like the best plan."

"*Newton!*" Alex was just about keeping his temper in check, too. "As Briar has just explained, we don't know what's really going on yet! Chatting with millennia-old ancestors about past magic is not something I'm used to! For now, we just have to feel our way through this."

"Actually," El said tentatively, into the sudden silence, "I had a strange experience that I'd like to share."

Everyone twisted around to look at her, and alarm swept across Oly's face. "What happened, my dear?"

"I was in my smithy making my latest Green Man decoration, and someone who I presume to be my ancestor contacted me through the fire. Just like you two." She nodded at Alex and Briar. "A common medium, it seems. Anyway, like Alex, I was pulled through the fire to another place. Mentally, that is. Somewhere that existed a long, long time ago. It felt so real." Her eyes looked haunted, her gaze in the middle distance. "I could feel the wind, and smell the sea. The landscape seemed familiar, and I think that's because I was on the moor above White Haven. Anyway, an old woman stood in front of a small stone building, conjuring a fire ball. She turned it into a shape of interlocking lines. A rune, I later found out, that symbolises Wyrd." She shrugged. "And that was it. I was back in my smithy, and it was all over." She reached into the pocket of her slim fitting jeans, pulled out a piece of paper, and passed it to Avery, who was sitting next to her. "It looked like this."

Avery frowned and passed the image on. "Another confirmation of her involvement."

El continued, "The other name for that design is Skuld's Net. It's a Norse expression, and Skuld is one of the Fates in Norse Mythology. Essentially, the sign denotes the weaving of past, present, and future. But more than that, it symbolises the connectedness of all life."

"A very pagan concept," Caspian said thoughtfully. "A concept that we witches believe in, obviously. Connections between all things.

Wyrd, I presume, is the Anglo-Saxon version of the Norns. The three
Fates in Norse mythology. The Shapers of Destiny."

"You've been reading up on it, too," Avery said.

"I might not know much about totem animals, but I'm familiar
with some mythologies. I read a lot as a child," he explained to everyone.

When El's image arrived in his hands, Newton leaned back in his
chair, examining it closely. "Skuld's Net, hmm? And we're caught up
in it. Trapped just like a fish in a net."

"That's a very interesting way of putting it, Newton," Briar said
softly. She looked him in the eye, her expression chastened after her
earlier shortness. There was a hint of regret, maybe sadness in her gaze;
something he couldn't quite fathom. "Skuld's Net. Wyrd weaving our
fate. You're right. It's nothing to joke about. It's actually terrifying."
Her phone began to ring from deep inside her bag, and she dug it
out, frowning as she answered it. "Gran? Is everything—" She listened
while everyone watched, the tension in the room spiking again. "No,
I'll come right now." She ended the call and stood up. "It's Beth. I
spoke too soon. She's having a vision."

There was a flurry of movement as everyone stood, but Briar waved
them away. "No, it's okay. I don't want everyone coming. It's too
much. Just me and Alex. Would you mind?" she asked him.

"Of course not! Avery, we could use witch-flight. Get there straight
away."

Caspian eased his way to Briar's side. "I'll take Briar. I don't have to
stay. I can just drop you off and come back later."

"Please! Yes, speed is good!"

In seconds, all four had vanished in a whirl of air, leaving Newton
staring at the remaining group, wondering what would happen next.

Caspian delivered Briar safely to Stormcrossed Manor's hallway, and as soon as he made sure she was okay, he went to leave.

"No, stay. Please," she said, her hand on his arm, her dark eyes full of worry. "I just didn't want *everyone* here. You can stay, if you want."

"Thanks, Briar. I'd love to, actually. I promise to keep out of the way." Not only was he worried about Beth's health, he was also curious to know what she had seen. Plus, things were tense at Avery's place, and he was pleased to get out of there.

"You're never in the way." She smiled briefly, and then hurried along the hall, shouting, "Tamsyn! Rosa! Where are you?"

Before he could follow her, another swirl of air announced the arrival of Alex and Avery. As usual, Alex reacted badly to witch-flight. He rested his hands on his knees for several seconds, heaving, and then finally straightened. "I fucking hate that. Where's Briar?"

Caspian pointed. "That way."

"Why the bloody hell isn't she sick?" he grumbled as he headed up the hall. "Bloody witch-flight."

Avery rolled her eyes at Caspian, and called after Alex, "At least you're here quickly."

Before he could respond, Max, Beth's twelve-year old brother ran down the hall, grabbed Alex's arm, and pulled him along. It was obvious he was comfortable with him. "Uncle Alex, we're upstairs."

Caspian turned to Avery, amused. "Uncle?"

She grinned. "I know. I'm Auntie Avery, and if you come here often enough, you'll be Uncle Caspian, too."

Caspian wasn't sure what he thought about that. He never saw his cousin's kids, and he doubted that Estelle would ever have any. *As for him?* Well, he had never entertained the idea.

Max led the way up twisting stairs and along narrow passageways until they reached Beth's bedroom. Caspian noticed how much cleaner the whole house looked since he'd last been here. Floors had been scrubbed, walls repainted, and the feeling of doom that had filled the house had vanished, replaced by warmth and light. It was good to know that he'd helped achieve this when they banished the banshee. Despite being worried about Beth, it lightened his step.

Rosa was in the doorway, arms folded across her chest, lips tight, watching Tamsyn tend to Beth, who was lying on the bed. Briar was already kneeling next to her gran, and Alex joined them.

Caspian hung back by Rosa and Avery, drawing Rosa into the corridor. "When did it start, Rosa?"

"Just minutes ago." She was flushed, tendrils of her hair stuck onto her forehead. "She'd just had her evening bath, and then her eyes rolled back and she was out! I carried her in here."

"Has she said anything?" Avery asked.

Rosa shook her head, eyes on Beth. "Nothing audible, just murmurings. She was doing so well, too. I thought that all the work Alex and Tamsyn had done with her had made progress."

Caspian exchanged a worried look with Avery. "Rosa, this isn't something that will ever go away."

"I know. I thought maybe it would just go away for now! She's a child!"

Caspian inwardly sighed. Here she was, still in denial. Briar had told him about her cousin's unrealistic expectations, and Avery's tight-lipped expression revealed her annoyance about it, too. "What about Tamsyn? Has she seen the stag again?"

"Not that I know of."

"She did," Max said, unexpectedly at their side. He was looking important, like the man of the house. "The stag was on the moor again this morning. At dawn, she said. It comes every morning now."

"Have you seen it?" Caspian asked him.

"No. I was with her this morning, but it was invisible to me. Tamsyn said it's *her* stag, that's why." Max seemed to accept that fact without question.

Caspian exchanged a puzzled glance with Avery before looking at Tamsyn's tiny figure, bent over her granddaughter. He wondered if she had a touch of witchcraft in her blood, and wasn't just a seer.

Beth's shout shattered their conversation. She sat upright on the bed, her white-eyed gaze fixed on the wall. For a moment, her words were unintelligible, and then, like tuning in a radio station, her words became crystal clear.

"The Twister of Fates is upon us. He tears the threads that bind." She cocked her head as if she was straining to hear him. "Unseen, he lays his traps. I see the dark sky. I see the stones fall. I hear the crash of surf." She paused, and her childish voice made the prediction all the more chilling. "The ancient ones gather. Wings beat, teeth tear, hooves stamp, claws scratch. The stag holds the moon."

Beth took a shuddering, deep breath and fell back on the bed, her vision over.

Chapter Fourteen

It was dawn when Reuben wriggled into his wetsuit and plunged into the sea for his early-morning surf.

The weather was bracingly cold, the sea frigid, but he didn't care. It would chase away the shadows of the night before.

He paddled out into deeper water where the swells were lifting a line of his fellow surfers. A few shouts broke the morning silence, but for the most part, his companions were quiet. It was sacred time at this hour. The call of the seagulls, the crash of the waves, the sky thick with low clouds, as if it was trying to touch the sea.

Reuben mulled over the fragments of Beth's prediction. The phrase that his brain wouldn't let go: *The Twister of Fates is upon us.* Reuben knew all about fate, but he liked to make his own. He didn't believe that his whole life was laid out before he was even born. That would suggest that, even now, his every movement was foreseen. The way the wave crashed, the path his surfboard would follow. He made his own path. Chose his own destiny.

The waves lifted and he mounted his surfboard, steadied his position, and crouching low, allowed the wave to carry him forward. For a while, the rush of the wind and the power of the sea chased it all away. He wasn't sure how long he was out there. He never was. Time lost all meaning on the water. Over and over again he surfed in, then paddled back out, his magic instinctively wrapping around him.

Eventually, he lay on his board, catching his breath. From his position, the beach was a bedraggled line of seaweed and rocks beyond the crashing surf. The sea was wild today, like an animal tugging at him. He laughed from the pure joy of it, and leaping on his board again, rode the pounding waves to the shore, following the break to his left. It curled into a tube around him, the world sparkling in cold blues and greens; a wall of glassy brilliance.

However, something was different. The curl of the breaking waves, their frothy whiteness as he shot through and emerged on the other side; they looked like hooves. He could swear he heard horses whinnying around him.

Reuben turned, startled, and lost his balance. He fell into the water, and when he lifted his head clear of the sea, a thundering wall of galloping, white, surf horses were bearing down on him. They tossed their manes, and blew water from their nostrils. He froze, wide-eyed, sure he was seeing things. But they were too real. They reached him, hooves pounding over and through him. He floundered underwater, the sheer force of them pushing him down. His face hit the sand. The board pulled on his leg. His lungs screamed for air.

He couldn't surface. He was washed towards the shore like flotsam and jetsam.

And then it was over. He was thrown onto the beach, breathless, aching, and convinced he was hallucinating. Deep down, however, he knew he wasn't. The raw, visceral feeling he always experienced when he was surfing was now accompanied by so much more. He felt ancient power and a connection to the sea he had never experienced before—and that was saying something, because he lived to surf.

He'd just met his spirit animal.

Alex related Beth's vision to Zee at just after ten on Wednesday morning, as they were getting the pub ready to open.

They were alone, a time when Alex liked to gather his thoughts. Chatting to Zee was one of the perks. He was a good listener, and he valued their time together. It was odd. This time last year, Alex barely knew him; now, he couldn't imagine the bar without him.

"The stag holds the moon?" Zee asked. "What does that mean?"

"Fuck knows," Alex said, grumpy. His head pounded from a night spent tossing and turning. "At least she's broken her silence. I must admit, with the events going on around here, it was odd for her *not* to have a vision."

"You can't pick and choose, can you? Uncanny, though."

"Very." Alex shuddered, goose bumps rising on his arms at the memory. "Hearing anyone's predictions would be odd. That flat-toned, hollowed-out voice seems to come out of nowhere. But in a little girl's voice. Herne's horns. It's chilling."

Zee balled up the towel he was using to wipe the bar down, and leaned across the shiny surface, watching Alex. "Can you imagine, though, what it must be like to be her? To experience that?"

"She can't remember it, and then sleeps immediately. That may not happen as she gets older. This morning Briar said Beth couldn't remember a thing."

"Briar stayed there?"

"Yes. Something is wrong with her, too. She's preoccupied. And she was a bit abrupt last night. Very unlike Briar."

Zee's face twisted into a grimace. "She ended her relationship with Hunter yesterday. Pretend you don't know, though."

"*What*?" Alex felt like Zee had punched him. "Really? She said nothing!"

"It's been coming for a while, Alex. Eli saw it. She knew she had to. She was putting it off."

Alex sagged onto a bar stool. "I feel like shit. I had no idea. She's one of my best friends. I should have known!"

"He hasn't visited for a while. You must have suspected!"

Alex groaned, rubbing his face. "I noticed, but I thought it suited them. I bet Avery knows—or at least suspects. Women do, don't they?"

"I have a feeling she's kept it quiet from everyone."

Alex reviewed Briar's behaviour in the light of this new knowledge, and her reactions started to make sense. Especially her clipped tone with Newton. "Is this about Newton? Do you think she'll get back with him?"

"Were they ever really together? Doesn't sound like it to me." He shrugged. "Anyway, what do I know?" Zee started emptying the dishwasher. "Tell me about Beth's prediction. Does it help you?"

"No. Yes. Oh, I don't know. Skuld's Net, that's what El saw. Beth talked about the Twister of Fates tearing the threads that bind. She said he's laying a trap. She must be referring to Tiernan. My ancestor said something about him changing the future to suit his own ends. All that sounds hideous! We're in the dark, and I feel that all I'm seeing is glimpses of things."

"Interesting. Laying a trap sounds ominous. Maybe you should lay your own trap."

Alex regarded Zee's calm expression. "That's...interesting."

"You need to even the playing field. Sounds like your opponent is playing dirty. You should, too."

Alex smiled. He could always rely on a Nephilim to spell it out. "I'll think on that. How are you feeling? I gather that anyone witnessing the event the other night is losing their memory."

"Not me. I remember it as clear as I see you now. The old man was standing where the castle is. Windswept, wrapped in a cloak, looking down on his work. Gloating. Ravens' Wood was there, though. I suspect it's the same wood as then."

Alex laughed. "Even though it only came into existence this year?"

"Maybe the Green Man brought back the forest that was always there. That's a link! A big one. I might go up myself. Look around. See if I can feel him."

"You're sure he wasn't some innocent bystander?"

Zee grunted with disdain. "No! I know he was in the distance, but I have good eyesight. I saw his expression. He wasn't shocked, or scared. He was pleased with what he'd done. He saw me, too. I know it. I felt it."

"Really?" Alex had tried to imagine how the scene must have looked. "I wish I could have witnessed it."

"Maybe it's best you didn't, if he's searching for you."

"Why now, though? Why us, of all the generations of witches?"

"Because it's the first time in years—hundreds of years—that your coven has been complete. That's right, isn't it? Everyone split up after Helena died at the stake."

Alex fell silent, mulling over Zee's words. "I guess you're right. I actually hadn't considered that. But why not attack us before all that happened? Say, back in the thirteenth century?"

"Maybe he did, and you just don't know it."

"Interesting. That suggests they would have beaten him some-how—if it happened." He nodded to himself, seeing his grimoire in his mind, turning the pages. "We need to look. See if there are annotations in the old grimoires. Me and Avery have been looking for spells and rituals, but perhaps we're looking for the wrong thing. And those spells are hard to read. The writing is spidery, and the words are almost like another language. I'll call her. She might have time to look this morning."

Zee gave him a wry smile. "Do you need to go? Marie will be here soon, and then Simon, in an hour."

"No." Alex stood up, energised. "I'm stopping here today. I have things to think on, and my dad could turn up at any point. Plus, I want to listen to the town's gossip. If anything else happens here, I want to witness it."

On Wednesday at lunchtime, Briar found Gran, Rosa, and Beth in Tamsyn's ancient kitchen at Stormcrossed Manor. Max was at school.

She'd left Eli minding the shop, anxious to check in on Beth after the events of the night before. It was only with great reluctance that she'd gone to work at all, but Tamsyn had shooed her off, saying there was nothing that she could do, and Rosa had kindly driven her to her shop. Beth had slept deeply all night with no further visions.

Briar wished she had slept so well. Instead, she had kept watch, taking it in turns with Tamsyn after she had sent Alex home. When she did manage to sleep, her dreams were vivid. She was surrounded by beating wings, unable to see beyond the dark feathers. She heard the thunder of hooves against frost-hardened ground, and caught a glimpse of a man with a painted face and antlered head. He was elusive, though, slipping away like a wraith.

The scent of baking bread and biscuits, a familiar scent in Tamsyn's kitchen, brought Briar back to the present. Tamsyn was at the counter, kneading yet more dough, while Beth and Rosa sat at the scrubbed oak table. The scene of calm domesticity settled Briar's anxiety.

"Hi! Everything okay?" She looked meaningfully at Beth.

Tamsyn nodded and smiled, continuing to knead. "We're all fine. I think Beth has enjoyed her morning off from school. She's been drawing."

"So I can see." Briar took her coat off and placed it on the back of the chair before sitting next to her niece.

The kitchen table was covered in paper and scattered crayons, the pages vivid with a variety of images. Rosa was sifting through them, preoccupied, but she glanced over at Briar.

"Beth has drawn some interesting things, haven't you, darling? Animals, the sea, a house..." she trailed off, pushing some of the images in front of Briar. "Say hello to Auntie Briar, Beth!"

Beth paused from her task, looked up briefly with a preoccupied smile, her eyes solemn before returning to drawing. Her dark hair fell over her face, while her lips pursed in concentration. A piskie child. Briar was struck again by Alex's words. An old soul. *Yes, she was.* Beth was self-sufficient, and wise beyond years for such a young child. She was mostly untroubled by her visions, as if they had happened to someone else.

Briar kept her voice light as she studied the images. "You're drawing some lovely things, Beth. There are a lot of birds." Feathers, drawn with a thick black crayon, were all over some pages. They appeared to have been drawn hurriedly, carelessly. "She's been drawing all morning?"

"Hasn't stopped since breakfast. She's drawn a stag, too. And a few odd shapes that I don't understand."

Briar gasped when she saw them. "The Wyrd rune. The image that El saw." There were lots of them, some small, while others filled the whole page. There were images of a woman, too. The images were simplistic, of course, but were more than just the stick images that Briar expected. It was as if Beth was being guided by another hand. "Have you seen these, Tamsyn?"

Tamsyn dried her hands on her apron, and then sat next to them. "I have. They're clever, aren't they? Skilful." She raised her eyebrows above her beetle-dark eyes that Briar had come to love and respect. "Unusually so."

Briar shivered, despite the warmth in the kitchen. Outside, the heavy, cloud-laden grey skies threatened rain; maybe even snow. She stared at the trees in the garden, bare branches rattling in the brisk wind, and wondered if the wizard was causing any problems in White Haven. "Beth, you talked about a man last night. The Twister of Fates. Do you remember?"

Beth nodded. "He's very quiet. He's trying to break things that shouldn't be broken."

Briar's breath caught in her throat. "Can you see him?"

"Sometimes. He is cloaked in cloud, like a bird."

Rosa froze, staring at Briar with wide-eyed horror, but Briar ignored her. "Have you seen him this morning?"

"No. He's busy. So are the others."

"The others?"

"The old ones. They're trying to get in. You have to help them, Auntie. They can't do it on their own."

Briar felt dizzy, the world tipping around her, but forced herself to remember that she was talking to a child. "Who are *they*? Are they nice? I don't want nasty people to get in."

"They aren't nasty! They want to help you. I like them. Especially the wolf, like Uncle Alex."

By the great Goddess. She was talking about their totems...their ancestors. "How do I do that, Beth? Do you know?"

"Feathers and fur." Beth looked up at her, smiling broadly. "And a fire. They like fire. But so does he."

Chapter Fifteen

Dylan paced around White Haven Castle, trying not to stumble over the stone footings of long-since collapsed rooms, as he stared at his thermal imaging camera. Desperate to do something, he had suggested returning to the castle grounds to run tests again, thinking that because Zee had seen the man there, it could be an important place.

"I can see red, Cassie! It's faint, but here!"

Cassie hurried to his side, the EMF meter whining at low pitch in her hands. "I'm detecting raised energy levels, too. Yesterday wasn't an anomaly after all."

"I'm not sure whether that's a good or a bad thing, though." He thrust the screen in front of her as he panned it around again. "See, a red glow in certain places, but I can't detect a pattern."

"Nor me."

He lowered the camera as they both stared at the ruins. They were at the edge of the castle grounds, where the outer wall ended, and the grass ran down to the cliff edge. The main complex of the castle was behind them, and behind that was Ravens' Wood.

"I wonder if he crossed again?" Dylan walked across the grounds and stood on the rise to look at White Haven in the valley below. "Perhaps he stood looking over it, just like we're doing now, thinking on what to do."

"I still don't understand how he's doing it, though. Is he actually here? Actually time traveling?" A gust of wind caught Cassie's hair, and she pinned it behind her ear with her hand. "If he can do that, why isn't he here all the time?"

"Because it's like we said yesterday. It's too big to manage. I think he has a small window in which to do things. Bastard," he added, viciously kicking at a rock. "I think I'm going to set up cameras here. We might find nothing, but it's worth trying."

Cassie nodded, turning her back on the wind. "It's freezing here. Let's get in the shelter of the wood. We may as well explore the perimeter of that, too, while we're here."

She hurried ahead of him, eager to escape the cold wind, but Dylan trekked slowly behind her, lost in his thoughts. The past felt very close in the castle, the ruins a stark reminder of the passing of time. With Ravens' Wood up ahead, which always felt timeless and ancient, Dylan felt he might step into the past himself.

Then, out of nowhere, he heard the faintest ringing of a bell. For a second, he thought it was his phone, and then he realised it was coming from under his jacket. "Shit! Cassie! My bells are ringing! Something is happening!"

Cassie didn't stop, and he realised she hadn't heard him over the crashing surf. Then he saw patchy mist rising among the castle ruins, thickening by the second. It encompassed the outer walls and seeped towards him.

He ran. "Cassie! Run to the wood!"

She seemed to turn in slow motion, her hand at her chest as she stared at Briar's amulet, and her eyes widened with horror. He reached her side, grabbed her arm, and pulled her with him.

"The mist, Cassie! It's surrounding us. We have to get to the wood."

"What if it follows us?"

"We keep running until it stops!"

They leapt over low walls and zigzagged round the large ones, and he risked a glance behind him. The thick mist was advancing over the ruins, swallowing everything into its murky interior.

"Bollocks! I don't think we're going to make it!"

By now, their bells were ringing louder and louder, their clear peal a note of odd joy in the horror of their circumstances.

Breathless, Cassie said, "Don't forget, the amulets are spelled for protection, too!"

"Do you want to risk testing that?"

"Not really, no!"

The mist was on their heels by the time they reached the edge of the wood, and Dylan hurtled past the first trees, sure he would feel the mist tug on his ankle and drag him backwards. He glanced behind them, and finally slowed. "It's stopped."

He leaned against a tree trunk to catch his breath, but remained alert, ready to sprint at a moment's notice. The mist had halted at the wood's perimeter.

Hands on her knees, bent double, Cassie took huge breaths. "Why has it stopped there?"

"I don't know. It's like the trees have made a barrier." He risked taking a step towards the edge of the wood, aware that the ringing of his amulet's bells had quieted. However, as he moved closer, the noise rose in volume again. *Impressive*. He could feel heat from the amulet too, like a mini hot water bottle against his skin. Steadying his camera, he filmed the mist, fingers fumbling on the mechanism. "Cassie, you need to see this."

She was at his side in seconds. "What? Oh!"

Visible only through the thermal imaging, was a face in the mist, and it was staring right at them.

Avery was in the backroom of her shop at just after midday, her lips curling with frustration. "I cannot believe that I have to wear this!"

"Where's your sense of humour, Ave? You'll look great." Dan sniggered, clearly overjoyed with Avery's Halloween costume.

"I will look ridiculous!"

"But that's the point. It's fun!" He sighed, his grin fading. "I know you're worried about what's going on, but so is everyone. We need to reassure the town. Provide some light relief. If you're carrying on as normal, it will reassure everyone else."

She snorted. "As if that's your real reason for this monstrosity! You'd already chosen it."

"Because *you* didn't! This is your own fault."

Avery groaned, knowing he was right. Her Gypsy Rose fortune-telling costume was made of garish purples and greens, with several layers of flounced skirts, a tight waist, and a low-cut bodice. Striped tights and black-heeled ankle boots with laces in dark purple completed the outfit. "Good grief. Look at that top! There's hardly anything to it!"

Dan winked. "That'll pull the punters in. Alex might want you to wear it in the bedroom."

"If you make one more joke about this..."

"You're going to bewitch me? I don't think so. I have plenty more jokes to share." He popped a Halloween sweet in his mouth, blithely ignoring her glare to examine his own costume, which was a severe black suit with coattails and a stuffed bird to fix to his shoulder. "This is fantastic! I can't wait. Let's start tomorrow!"

"You said next week!"

"The town is stressed. We need levity. *I* need levity. Come on, it's Halloween! The best time of year. The shop looks great, White Haven is groaning under pumpkin decorations, and Stan is doing his rounds. It's time!" He batted his eyes at her, looking ridiculous.

She finally laughed. "All right. Let's do it tomorrow. I must admit, I do need cheering up. All this talk of ancestors, and Wyrd, and the Twister of Fates. Which brings me to my question. What do you know about Skuld's Net?"

"Ah, the Norse equivalent of Wyrd."

"You've heard of her?"

"Of course! The Fates are represented in many cultures. Greek, Norse, Anglo-Saxon and others. Their role was essentially the same, and actually the root of the word 'Wyrd' is the same in Norse and Anglo-Saxon languages. The root word actually means 'to become'. As we already talked about, the three sisters are in control of destiny. I've been reading up on it to refresh my memory, and I came across Skuld's name. Wyrd's name in Norse mythology is Urd as well as Skuld. It's confusing."

"It always is. I guess for it to be such a popular concept, it's also a powerful one."

Dan nodded, settling in his seat. "Wyrd as a concept, though—that is interesting! It's huge. One of those meaty topics that have real depth." He pulled his phone out of his pocket and scrolled. "I made a few notes. The article I read talked about the Norns, who are the Norse Fates, weaving a web across the world—AKA Skuld's Net. The core concept is that we are connected to our past actions, our surroundings, and other people, as well as the present and future. All of our actions cause this web, or matrix, as it's also called, to shift constantly. It underpinned our pagan ancestors' actions and beliefs. Made them consider their choices."

"Like Karma. If you do something wrong, it will catch up with you in another life."

"Sort of." He reached for a biscuit, eyebrows drawing together as he frowned at Avery. "What made you ask about Skuld's Net?

"El had a strange vision yesterday, through fire." She related her experience, and Dan straightened, his full attention on Avery.

"She saw her ancestor?"

"We think it was her ancestor. They didn't actually communicate, but neither was she aggressive. It was a mental connection, and a strong one. El did her own research and found that the pattern was Skuld's Net."

"Wow. How would you even go about doing that? Reach across the years?"

"Honestly, I have no idea." Avery had mulled over it all night, but was still baffled by how it had been achieved. Preoccupied, she reached for a biscuit, too. "Alex had an even stronger vision—if that's even the right word!" She quickly summarised that, too.

Dan's biscuit was now half-eaten on the table, a sign of his fascination. He never abandoned food. "So, he also had a sensory experience?"

"Both of them did." She laughed in disbelief. "I can't believe that we have to find our spirit animals in order to connect to our ancestors. Well, I think that's the point of it. Herne's horns! Who am I kidding? I have no idea what's going on! Stags on the moor by Stormcrossed Manor, visions in fires. Crazy wizards and mists. All these things are happening, and I have no idea where to start."

"But you'll figure it out, Avery. I have faith in you." Dan leaned forward and squeezed her hand. "What about you? Have you seen anything?"

"Not a thing. By the way, Briar saw the antlered figure in a fire, too. A common medium for contact, it seems." She shrugged, perplexed, and feeling a bit put out. "So, just Reuben and me to go."

"What about Helena? Doesn't she have anything to say on the matter?"

"Not so far. I see her regularly these days, but she hasn't indicated that she knows anything about this. Gil suggested that Alex should summon her spirit, like he does Gil's. He thinks that Alex could talk to her that way."

"You and Helena still don't actually talk?"

"She's a ghost. No! She gestures and conjures spectral winds to flick the pages of my grimoire. No chatting at all. Not even in my head."

"Maybe Alex should try, then. She was a clever witch."

Avery wasn't really sure she wanted Alex chatting to Helena. She had a gleam of desire in her eyes whenever she looked at him. The thought of her ancestor flirting with Alex was just weird. Brushing aside her ridiculous concerns, she said, "All this talk of weaving and nets is making me feel trapped. I don't like it. Nor do I like feeling my fate is being determined by someone else."

"There are many paths in our fate, young Padawan," Dan said, invoking his Jedi side with a sly grin. "You choose which path to take. It's a weaving, not a straight line. You still have options, and don't let anyone make you think otherwise."

Chapter Sixteen

El was enjoying her customary mid-afternoon coffee with Zoe when Stan entered the shop, resplendent in his Druid's cloak. Under it was a long, dark, belted robe she hadn't seen before, and he clasped a wooden staff in his hand.

He glanced around the shop, and satisfied they were alone, joined Zoe and El at the counter. He was not the bright-eyed Stan of only a few days before. Instead, he looked as if he'd sucked on a sour lemon. "Well, ladies, DI Newton has contacted me and suggested we cancel our Samhain celebrations."

"Has he?" El almost spilled her coffee in shock. "I saw him last night, and he didn't mention a thing."

Stan sniffed imperiously. "I refused, of course. Too much time has been spent on this, and money, and the hotels and B and Bs are jam-packed. I can't cancel it now! He's a madman!"

"He's very worried about recent events. Surely, you have to admit that the harbour's temporary disappearance is very concerning."

Stan waved his hands about, vaguely gesturing at nothing. "I think that it was highly overrated. A bit of Samhain high jinks."

El was stunned into silence, especially when Zoe unexpectedly supported him. "I agree, Stan. It was probably a pocket of really thick sea mist that hid the harbour." She leaned forward, conspiratorially. "My friend saw it happen. He thinks he got caught up in the hype afterwards. He said that everyone was so freaked out, it was hard not to be. Now, everyone's just okay with it."

El floundered for words, looking at both of them. "Really, Zoe? You didn't mention this earlier. And Stan, I know Newton has been reviewing the video cameras from around the town. It really happened! This is serious."

"*Did* it happen?" Stan swept his arm outwards. "Please, explain how, but you'll have to be convincing. It's too outlandish!"

A great question, and one Stan wouldn't like the answer to. *A mad wizard is using Wyrd and magic to change the present as revenge for something our ancestors did in the past.* "I don't know how it happened, but I know it did. Zee who works in The Wayward Son witnessed it, and so did DS Kendall. She's a police officer, and very trustworthy. I think you should consider Newton's request."

"Absolutely not! One little incident, and everyone goes mad. I came here, Elspeth, to see if you would talk to him. I know you're friends. He's getting agitated, and upsetting the council. Just get him to see reason."

"Stan! He *is* being reasonable. He's thinking of the safety of this town. As am I."

He looked down his nose at her. Well, he actually looked up at her, while looking down his nose. El was taller than he was. "I'm disappointed in you, El. I thought you would see sense. I shall speak to Briar. She might be more amenable."

El drew herself upright, her magic swelling, too. Immediately the flames in the candles placed around the shop flared higher, and Stan stepped back in alarm. "Do *not* bother Briar. She has lots to deal with right now. Besides, I can assure you that Newton won't listen to her, either. It's your choice as to whether to go ahead with the celebrations, but can you handle the criticism if something terrible happens?"

Zoe didn't say a word, and El was grateful she didn't make things worse. Stan, however, huffed out of the door, saying, "I shall see you in a few days, and you will see how wrong you are!" The door slammed behind him, her shop bells clanging dramatically.

El groaned. "Well, that went badly." She stared at Zoe. "Do you really believe that? You're a Wiccan. You understand magic. You know that what happened on Monday night was real. And you know that my friend, Ben, has vanished!"

"I know what I thought had happened, but now I'm not sure." A frown marred her perfectly made-up face. "I am genuinely confused. It feels like a dream. Especially because I wasn't there." She shrugged apologetically. "I'll wash the cups up; you can stay here."

Maybe, El reflected as she watched Zoe head to the back of the shop, *this was the true genius of the spell. The fact that no one could really remember it. A forgotten thread in the tapestry.*

The bell clanged again, and Reuben strode inside. Before she could even say hello, he strode over, reached over the counter, and kissed her, leaving her breathless. He smelled of the sea and wide-open spaces. "Hello, gorgeous."

"Hello gorgeous, yourself." She drew back, noting his blue eyes gleamed with intrigue and excitement. "What's going on? Something has happened."

"Oh, yeah, something has happened. No Zoe?"

"In the back. We had a bit of a disagreement. And I argued with Stan." She outlined their conversation.

Reuben whistled. "Wow. Newton isn't wasting any time."

"No, and neither should we. I just wish I knew what to do next."

"Well, I had an interesting experience this morning. A good one." He took a deep breath before plunging on. "I met my sprit animal. Totem animal, whatever you call it."

"How?"

"I was surfing, and I was trampled by sea horses."

"What? Little seahorses? I'm confused."

"No. Sea *horses*. Two words. Big horses with hooves and tossing manes galloping out of the surf."

She studied him for a moment, wondering if he was pulling her leg. He loved to tease her. "You're very funny, but this isn't a joke. You're as bad as Stan."

He leaned across the counter and took her hand. "I'm serious. You know how I enter this sort of Zen state when I surf? That's when it happened." He tapped his broad chest and then his head. "I felt it here and here. I have spent the entire morning surfing with them. I'm shattered, but exhilarated."

El sank on to the stool behind the counter, momentarily speechless as she tried to envisage it. "Did anyone else see them?"

"Of course not! They were visible to just me. Or *it* was. After the initial charge with a herd of them, I just had one riding the waves with me. It was like nothing I've experienced before."

El could believe that. For a moment, Reuben's gaze was distant, as if he had trouble grounding himself in the here and now. "Did you speak to it? Is it male or female?"

"Male. A stallion." He winked. "Like me. And no, we didn't speak. Not as such. I just felt his energy and power."

"I don't know what to think about it. If our ancestors are behind this—and I say *if*, because I'm really not convinced yet—then they must be very powerful."

"Or just desperate. Desperation is a big driving force."

El felt lost. Out of her depth. Everything was shifting and changing in ways she couldn't predict, but Reuben was excited, and she needed to support him. She squeezed his hand. "It's very cool, and I'm really pleased for you. I confess, I'm very curious as to what my spirit animal could be. If I've even got one." Before she could comment any further, El felt her amulet tremble against her chest, and heard the faint tingling of bells. Her hand flew to where the amulet rested beneath her top. "Reuben..."

"I feel it. Briar's warning."

A quick glance around her shop confirmed that everything was fine in there. Reuben headed to the shop door while El looked into the back room where Zoe was listening to music as she tidied. Rather than disturb her, and seeing as there was no sign of mist, El left her to it and joined Reuben on the lane. There, the amulet bells sounded even louder.

The far end of the lane that fed onto the main road had vanished into a thick wall of mist. A few people were milling between shops, unaware of the threat. Her fellow shop owners were inside, oblivious to the risks, too. Golden light spilled onto the cobbled lane from the decorated shop windows, illuminating the pumpkin and Halloween displays. Everything looked charming in the late afternoon light. Except that the mist was still advancing, swallowing up the lane, shop by shop.

Instinctively, El raised her hands, summoning magic to her fingertips, and she felt Reuben do the same. "Do you think the main road has vanished, like the harbour?"

"Hard to say, seeing as we can't see a damn thing through it. I don't know how it happened last time. I mean, does the mist just vanish at some point, leaving us with a window into a different place?"

"I don't know, but it's getting closer. We have to stop it!"

Frustration was written across Reuben's face. "What if we make it worse, and whoever's in there is harmed?"

"Well, what if they haven't vanished yet, and we can still save them?"

Reuben took a deep breath and rolled his shoulders back as he faced the oncoming mist. "Suggestions?"

"Something not too showy that doesn't alarm anyone. I'll try a protection spell."

The charmed bells were ringing furiously, as if worn by demonic piskies, but ignoring them, she advanced down the lane and cast her favourite protection spell. She drew wards into the air with swift, precise movements, repeating the spell as she worked. The magical lines formed a barrier, through which the mist shouldn't pass. The spell complete, she retreated to Reuben's side.

However, the mist continued to advance, and with horror, she watched her spell dissolve within it. "Damn it!"

"My turn."

Reuben must have used some kind of water spell, because the edge of the mist shimmered as if it was about to break apart. Unfortunately, it didn't last, quickly solidifying and advancing again, like a living, breathing thing. Between them, increasingly frantic, they cast spell after spell, retreating all the time as nothing worked. By now they had attracted a few curious glances, even though they were keeping their magic as lowkey as possible.

Then she heard a faint whinnying sound, as if a horse had joined them on the lane, and looking around, saw a wicked gleam in Reuben's eyes. "Time to invoke my spirit animal. Shelter in the shop, El."

There was no time to question him. She ran to the doorway, watching Reuben retreat, as if to give himself space. The air shimmered around him, and a silvery horse manifested next to him so quickly that El could barely take it in. It pawed the ground, tossed its mane, and then galloped down the lane, punching a hole through the wall of mist. Flashes of darkness and lightning erupted as the horse vanished.

Then, as if a strong wind had whipped down the alley, the mist vanished, and Reuben turned to her with a massive grin on his face.

Ben and the wizard were outside the stone bothy, and Ben was restrained by some kind of magic. He was sitting close to the fire, trying not to shiver in the bitter cold. Overhead the blue sky was clear, promising a frosty night.

The wizard, however, was outside the palisade on a stretch of tufted grass, performing his complicated ritual that Ben now knew heralded another attack on White Haven. He'd seen him perform it a few times now. The wizard liked to make him watch, deeming it a kind of torture. He wasn't wrong. Ben ached to stop him, but so far he didn't have much ammunition. He had the spells he'd brought with him in his backpack, but he didn't want to use them until the most opportune moment.

There was also the small matter of the restraining spell.

He felt useless, and he was sure the old man was getting tired of him. He still hadn't worked out a way to communicate with him, despite numerous attempts at what Ben called his Vulcan mind meld. The wizard had clasped Ben's head between strong hands as if he could read his thoughts. So far, he'd failed.

Ben's thoughts returned to the present, and while the man continued his preparations, he scanned the landscape. Their position was isolated, and he presumed the man had chosen that for a reason. Or perhaps it was just that the population was so low, there was hardly anyone around anyway. He twisted to look behind him at the section of wild moorland he could see. He was now surer than ever that he was where White Haven would eventually be. There was definitely a kind of hillfort in the distance. On a clear day it was easier to see. Probably only a couple of miles away. If he could escape, perhaps they could help him.

The screech of a bird call drew his attention to a huge raven on the edge of the forest. It stared at him, unblinking, and for a horrible moment, Ben thought it might dive at him, like he was food, but then it flew away, heading straight for the settlement before wheeling back again. It stared down at Ben, and then just disappeared. Ben blinked, wondering where it had gone, but there was no sign of it in the clear blue sky above. He had the most uncanny feeling that he'd been given a message.

A shout made him turn back to the old man, a gathering darkness growing like a storm cloud in front of him. A thick mist bloomed and swelled, revealing a glimpse of a cobbled street. Ben had often wondered why the man could not pass through, but had decided it must be too hard. Perhaps he was scared he would never get back again. Perhaps he just liked to create havoc from afar.

However, Ben knew something had gone horribly wrong from the look of sheer rage he could see on the wizard's face.

With a boom that shook the ground and banished the window onto White Haven, a strange horse arrived out of literally nowhere and charged around the wizard. The animal was utterly silent and appeared to be made of nothing but mist and water, but it was so animated it seemed real, especially when it shook its mane, spraying Ben with water. He watched, mesmerised, as it struck the wizard in the chest, knocked him to the ground, and pounded over him and away.

It vanished as quickly as it had arrived, and Ben felt a moment of triumph. *Who had sent it? Was it something to do with the bird?*

However, in seconds, his euphoria also vanished, because a crumpled heap lay on the ground, moaning. With horror, Ben recognised the bald head and distinctive cloak, and as the man struggled to sit up, Ben's worst fears were realised.

Stan, the town's pseudo-Druid, had been pulled through the mist.

Chapter Seventeen

Z ee soared on the air currents that gusted up from the cliffs below White Haven Castle, feeling exhilarated despite the cold and rain. Actually, because of the wind and rain.

He always loved flying, and while good weather offered obvious pleasures, wrestling with strong winds and the full force of winter had its own merits. Below him, heavy swells crashed into the rocks, sending plumes of water high into the air.

He took a deep breath, filling his lungs with fresh, cold air, driven in from the ocean. Glancing to his left, he saw Eli soar further out to sea before sweeping around, and he smiled. Being outside on nights like this made you feel truly alive.

Zee plummeted downwards, wings close to his body, diving to the maelstrom of waves that crashed against the base of the cliff. Drenched in spray, his heart pounding, he pulled up just as he was about to hit the water, and headed out to sea, flying only feet above the waves. He grinned, unable to stop himself.

There was no moon tonight. The heavy cloud cover obliterated all light, and that made it perfect flying weather. Much further out, he saw the lights of fishing boats, also no doubt wrestling with the weather for their catch, and turning, the lights of White Haven twinkled behind him, just visible through the sea spray.

But he and Eli weren't out here just for pleasure. They had come to hunt the wizard—as they had all taken to calling him.

Zee flapped his huge wings, fighting the air currents that tore at his feathers, and banked to the shore again. The dark ruins of the castle sprawled below him, and Zee dropped to the ground and wrapped his wings around himself to shield him from the worst of the wind. This was where he'd seen the wizard, wrapped in his dark cloak. He stared down at White Haven, only a portion of the town visible from here. The harbour's lights blurred in the mizzle, as the locals liked to say. Further on was The Wayward Son, and the corner where Zee had previously stood.

This was definitely the spot.

Soon Eli was at his side. His hair was wet, plastered to his head, and like Zee, he was grinning with exhilaration. "This is something, brother. What a night! I feel more alive than I have in months."

"Even better than seeing your girlfriends?"

His smile broadened. "There's time tonight for both." He turned to survey the headland between the castle and the cliff. "So, this was where you saw him? Our conjuror of mists?"

"Right here. He was staring directly at me, the malevolent bastard, pleased with his work."

"Could you see anything else behind him?"

"Just the wood. Maybe the precursor of Ravens' Wood." Zee stared at its rippling mass. The branches were twisting and groaning in the wind, its interior dark and forbidding. "I think the Green Man pulled it from the ground because it has always stood here."

"You're probably right. But how does this help us work out how to find him?"

"I don't know. I just thought I needed to come here, to see if I felt anything. I'm afraid to say that I don't." He walked away from the cliff's edge, soon passing into the ruins of the castle that partially sheltered them from the wind. Eli kept pace with him. "I thought that maybe I would feel his energy. His magic."

"I confess that I feel absolutely nothing except the raw, elemental power of the weather," Eli said, his voice heavy with disappointment. "But, say Ravens' Wood was the wood that was here all those years ago. Would the dryads carry memories of that time?"

"The dryads and the other creatures are from Shadow's world. A gift from the Green Man and the Raven King."

Eli shrugged. "Some places are always magical, especially ancient woodland. As we know, the Gods and spirits were not always so shy as to hide themselves from mortals. We also know that once the borders between worlds were thin, and fey and humans crossed back and forth all the time."

"True. However, I'm not sure the dryads will speak to us. Not without Shadow."

"Not much we can do about that. She's abroad and won't be home for ages," Eli pointed out. "We have to manage on our own. Besides, we helped rescue them only weeks ago from those hunters. Well, I did." Eli smirked. "You were trapped with them."

Zee laughed. "Fair point. Let's try our luck then, shall we?"

Ben took in Stan's stricken expression, and gestured for him to calm down while the old man's back was turned. The wizard had been transfixed by Stan's appearance. His eyes had widened at his long cloak and cape, and he eyed him with a mixture of suspicion and admiration.

Ben suspected he couldn't work out whether he was a threat or not.

When the wizard had recovered from being knocked over by the horse, he had dragged Stan to his feet, still shocked, and pulled him into the palisade. After sealing the perimeter with a spell, he hustled them all inside the hut and confiscated Stan's staff. It was now propped against the far wall.

Initially, Stan had been mute with shock, but as he'd recovered, he stared at Ben. "It's you! Is this a joke?"

Ben shook his head. "You must pretend you don't know me! I'll explain later."

"But..."

"No! *Later*."

Stan fell silent while the old man paced, vibrating with fury. He yelled at Stan, almost spitting with anger. Ben watched, powerless, not wanting to reveal he knew Stan, but also anxious that he shouldn't be hurt.

From what Ben could discern, the wizard wasn't sure if Stan had created the horse that had trampled him, or was just a victim. The longer Stan looked terrified, the more the wizard calmed down. He searched Stan's cloak, pulling out a wallet from an inner pocket, sweets, and scraps of receipts, and eventually, when he found nothing remotely magical, he sat back on his haunches, glaring at them.

Ben held his breath, hoping they weren't about to be split up. Then he hoped he wasn't about to have the horrible, powdered drug blown in his face, either. But the wizard did neither. Instead, he used another spell to secure them both in place on opposite sides of the room, slammed the door, and left them alone.

Ben gestured silence to Stan, and when he was sure the man had left, he whispered, "Stan, I think he thinks you might actually be a wizard, too."

"What do you mean, *too*? What is going on? Is this a trick or treat? I can tell you right now, this is not funny!"

"No, it's not. You need to calm down while I explain what's happening, and then it's your turn. If we're going to get out of here, we need to work together."

Stan's normal curiosity was winning over, and his eyes darted around the small room. "But where are we? What do we need to get out of? I was walking down the street in White Haven, and then *poof*!"

"Was there mist around you? I've seen the old man use it before. I watched him bring the harbour here."

"Ah. You saw that?"

"Yes! It was very impressive. It exhausted him, though. He didn't do much after that for a good twenty-four hours." Stan looked shifty, and Ben asked, "Did you see it happen? It must have shocked everyone! Was my team there?" He felt horribly homesick at the thought of his friends doing their usual investigations without him.

"No, I didn't see it. In fact, it's left everyone who saw it doubting it ever happened. I, er, thought it was a Halloween joke."

"A joke! What about the wit..." He caught himself in time. "What about Avery and El? Or Briar?"

"Oh, El told me off. That Newton man told me to cancel the Walk of Spirits, and I refused. I actually had an argument with El about it. Oh, God! Have I got it wrong? It's real?"

Ben's frustration boiled over. "Look around, Stan! Does it look real?"

Stan studied the smoking fire, the rudimentary stone-built room, the basic bedding, cooking utensils, and particularly the magical paraphernalia in one corner of the room. "It could be one of those themed..."

"No! It's real. We are the prisoners of a madman, and I think we have gone back in time. The only thing is, I have no idea what he actually wants! I think he brought me here deliberately, but you are an accident. I think. Fuck!" Ben yelled into the air, furious with his lack of answers. He took a deep breath to calm himself down. He shouldn't be angry. At least he wasn't alone anymore. "Look, I've been biding my time, trying to work out what he's doing and find a way to stop him. Plus, I've sort of been incapacitated by magic. But I am determined to get out of here and return home. Will you help?"

"Will it be dangerous?"

"Oh, yes. It could get us killed. But think, Stan. You are the town's Druid. The leader of our celebrations. Right now, you are in the middle of a mystery. You could help save White Haven! Think of how good that would be!"

Stan's eyes gleamed. "That's an excellent point. I'm in."

Chapter Eighteen

When Caspian entered Oswald's drawing room, he felt like he'd gone back in time. The heavy, damask curtains had been drawn, blocking out the cold night, and the blazing fire illuminated Oswald's heavy oak furniture and rich fabrics.

Most of the witches looked to be in attendance, and the eccentric clothing of the older members added another layer of the past. It felt to Caspian that time seemed to be slipping even more frequently this Samhain, and it would only get worse as the day itself approached.

Oswald intercepted him, and he accepted the offered glass of gin and tonic with pleasure. The joy of witch-flight was that you could drink and fly. "Thanks, Oswald. I need this."

"Everything all right?" Oswald asked as he sipped his own drink. "You look a bit peaky."

"I'm helping Avery and her coven with a new issue," he explained, glancing over at Avery who was talking to Eve. "We'll explain it more later, but do you know much about spirit animals?"

"My father was a great believer, but I confess it is not something I am familiar with." He narrowed his eyes. "I presume your current predicament has something to do with them?"

"Well, we hope they will be there to help us. It seems the White Haven witches' ancestors are trying to contact them...by any means necessary."

He rocked on his heels. "Interesting. Is this to do with the incident at the harbour? I saw it on the news. Although, am I right in saying there is now some doubt about the veracity of the incident?"

"There is no doubt, I can assure you. The issue is that the magic appears to cause amnesia after the event. Now, those involved are doubting it ever happened."

"Not entirely surprising. Shock itself can cause memory loss and a distortion of events. You know who is behind it?"

"An ancient enemy of the witches' ancestors—very ancient, by the glimpses we have had of them so far. Well, I say *we*, but I haven't seen a thing."

His expression must have said everything, because Oswald asked, "Are you feeling left out?"

Caspian wasn't sure how to respond to that. He always kept so much of himself hidden away that his instinct was to do the same now. However, the firelight and candles, the excellent gin and tonic, and the murmur of conversation around them seemed to invite confidences. "I suppose I am, a little. Despite our early enmity, I have become good friends with the White Haven witches, and they in turn have been generous in extending their friendship to me. Every single one of them." *Even Alex*, he thought, but kept that to himself. "And yet..."

He fell silent, but Oswald finished his sentence. "You still feel left out."

"I do, and yet I have no reason to." Caspian gave a dry laugh. "I'm on *Team White Haven* now. An honorary coven member. I suppose in all the times that I've helped them, and they have helped me, we have had a common goal. Now, however, this is about *their* ancestors. *Their* coven. They have been a coven, it seems, for hundreds of years, in one form or another." The thought was dizzying. "That's an unbreakable connection. I'm not a part of that. And I certainly don't have that bond with my own coven, despite my improving relationship with Estelle."

"Well, that's hardly surprising. Your father was a divisive man. He lived off breeding discontent. He sowed the seeds of discord among us, too, the fruit of which was finally crushed at the solstice." Oswald's face wrinkled with distaste. "Odious man. Sorry."

"Don't apologise. He was."

Oswald's expression softened. "But I think you do yourself a disservice. They are not only clearly fond of you, but respect you, too. As they should. You are an excellent, powerful witch, and have shown yourself to have a strong moral compass. I have watched you, as have the other elder council members, after your father's demise. You could have taken a different route. One of darkness and revenge. Instead, you have moved on. Reinvented yourself. Or maybe, just found the man you really were all along."

Caspian found he couldn't speak. His chest felt full and tight. Fighting for control, he finally said, "Thank you, Oswald. That's a very generous comment. Although, knowing I have been watched is a little unnerving."

Oswald laughed. "Don't worry. We don't stalk you. But you know, you have another opportunity here. You can reinvent your own coven, just as you want it to be. No doubt your cousins and uncle all had their issues with your father. You said your sister did."

"Oh, my sister is reinventing herself all right. She works with the Nephilim now."

"Excellent. I would imagine she would probably appreciate your support. Your advice and knowledge. Your coven, too, has an impressive history of its own. Talk to them. A fractured coven is no good to anyone. Not that I'm suggesting you should abandon 'Team White

Haven', of course." Oswald's eyes sparkled with mischief. "Does your coven meet regularly?"

Guilt ripped through Caspian as he realised that they only really met at the big sabbats with the Cornwall Coven. He'd neglected them. Rejected them. "No. I think it would be fair to say that it's hanging together by a thread."

Oswald extended his hands, almost sloshing his gin. "This is the perfect moment. Samhain. A time when our ancestors look on through the thinning veil. It is also the Witches' New Year. A time to give thanks for what has gone before and plan anew. Summon your coven, Caspian. I suspect what you feel now is the lack of *them*. You're not separated from your White Haven friends. They clearly need you. However, you crave your own group, too. Make it happen." Oswald nodded beyond Caspian, to where the witches had started to enter the long room where they held their meetings. "It's time to join the others."

Caspian allowed himself to be led to the next room, Oswald's hand under his elbow, and pondered how insightful Oswald was. That was exactly what he needed to do. Strengthen his coven, and find an anchor in the dark.

Before he could mull on it further, the meeting was underway. Genevieve started with their regular business, discussing plans for Samhain at Rasmus's house. All the covens were attending, and it promised to be a night of reflection and celebration. After that there was a roundup of news from across Cornwall.

Hemani reported an abnormal level of spirit activity in Launceston, but reassured everyone that it was all in hand. Claudia reported her coven had stabilised after the loss of Cornell in the summer. Many towns were having their own Samhain celebrations, and everyone was looking forward to them. When the discussion turned to White

Haven, Avery updated everyone with their news. Their group had met in Alex's pub before the meeting, so they had all the latest information, but it seemed that no one else was having issues with aggressive, magical mist and vanishing townspeople.

Avery concluded, "So our biggest question is, who understands or uses animal spirits? It's something we are utterly unfamiliar with, but need to understand—really quickly!"

Eve laughed. "It sounds like Reuben is adapting to his well."

"I think it's fair to say," Caspian said, "that Reuben never ceases to surprise us."

"Well, unfortunately," Eve continued ruefully, "as much as I would like to help, I can't with this. It sounds fascinating, though."

Jasper leaned forward, hands clasped together under his chin. "I know the theory, but have never tried to find my own. Many people think that spirit animals belonged solely to the indigenous American Indian culture, but that's far from true. Other indigenous peoples connect strongly to animal totems. The Aboriginal people of Australia, for example. Their dream-weaving is deeply embedded in spirit animals. Ancient cave paintings across the world often depict animals, including in Europe, which means Celtic cultures also incorporated spirit animals into their spiritual beliefs. Of course, European witchcraft has its own version." He smiled as his gaze ran around the table. "We call them familiars."

Genevieve laughed. "Of course! How could I have forgotten that familiars and spirit animals are the same! Unfortunately, I always feel that *familiar* is a term that seems to belittle the experience of our connection to animals. Totem animals sound so much more..."

"Powerful?" Jasper suggested. "Less twee. And certainly, during the witch hunts of the fifteenth and sixteenth centuries, familiars were demonized. Literally."

Claudia nodded, and her huge earrings swung like chandeliers. "Said to be the work of the devil by those ridiculous men."

"Who also," Rasmus said next to her, his voice rasping as usual, "simultaneously undermined the familiar, while demonising it. Reduced the concept to cats and owls. A spirit animal is so much more than that."

Caspian heard the resentment in Rasmus's voice, and asked, "You've had experience of it, Rasmus?"

"A long time ago, after my wife was killed by vampires. It was something she embraced, and wanting to be close to her, I tried to find mine." He looked at Caspian before his eyes took on a faraway gaze. "I stared into the fire on long, dark evenings several times, taking the necessary steps to put myself into the right frame of mind. Only once did I have a fleeting connection to an animal, but it didn't last. It felt contrived, strange. I certainly didn't feel guided or protected. Maybe I wasn't in the right mindset to begin with."

Avery shuffled in her seat, framing her next question. "I wonder if it's because we're disconnected to the landscape more than we used to be."

Gray, the lead witch from Bude Coven with a wild mass of red hair, frowned. "But we're witches. I don't know about you, but I strongly connect with the landscape and the elements. Surely, we all do?"

"Of course we do," Caspian said immediately. "As an air witch, I feel elemental wind strongly. The way it carries scents to me, and even changes in the weather. I suppose I do it so subconsciously now, it doesn't even register. But, to reach out and find a spirit guide requires an extra step." He hesitated, feeling he'd explained it badly.

Oswald jumped in to support him. "I agree, Caspian. Connecting to the elements is one thing, but a totem animal, or a familiar to put it into European language, is quite something else."

"It has fallen out of fashion, for years," Hemani added. "Only now, with the Wiccan movement, has it become more popular."

Rasmus snorted. "Popular! Witchcraft is *not* popular. It is always and forever here, whether you choose to see it or not."

"Or are born with gifts or not," Genevieve reminded him. "And Hemani is right. It has fallen out of fashion to a certain degree, you know it has. Things do. In our modern world, things that are uncool are dismissed. Familiars are associated with the witch hunts, and with Medieval magic. When familiars are inserted into literature and films, they become twee, exactly as Jasper said. Familiars are—or should be—so much more than that." She addressed Avery and Caspian. "I may not be able to offer you advice, but I am certainly interested in the outcome."

"I should also add," Jasper said, "that the familiar was not always an animal."

Caspian smiled. As usual, Jasper was a wealth of knowledge.

He continued, "They could present as humanoid in form, and were said to be vivid in their appearance. Not a wishy-washy ghost figure. They assisted with magic, as well as offered protection." He laughed. "I'm now wondering why I have never sought out my own. I should add, by the way, that you don't always need to search for one. Sometimes they come to you, unbidden. They offer advice depending on your need. Plus, each animal means different things—has their own power."

"You have certainly helped flesh out the concept," Caspian told them. "At least for me. Calling it a familiar helps ground it. Roots it in my own culture." He glanced over at Avery. "I suppose unless anyone else has any more insights, we should move on to our next question. Shall I?" She nodded, her red hair falling forward to frame her face, and in the candlelight her skin glowed. Caspian turned away hurriedly as his familiar heartache surfaced again. "Skuld's Net, and Wyrd, the weaver of worlds. It seems that White Haven's enemy is using her to help his cause."

"The Fates!" Eve exclaimed. "That's a powerful enemy."

"*Three* powerful enemies," Rasmus growled. "It is rare they work alone."

Caspian exchanged a startled look with Avery. "You think all three are involved?"

"Just a thought." He shrugged his shoulders, rounded with age. "However, whenever they are referred to in myths across cultures, they are always together."

Jasper nodded. "I'm afraid he's right. Depending on what you read, the three Fates represent past, present, and future. The weave of time is always enmeshed. If you pull one thread, another will pull, too."

Avery paled. "So, that's three Goddesses we might face, and a wizard. Fantastic."

"I'm not so sure," Gray said with a frown. "The past, present, and future is one interpretation of their roles, but for the Morai, the Fates from Greek myth, their actions were more specific. The youngest determined birth, the middle sister determined your path or destiny, and the third determined your death. The weaver, therefore, is the middle sister."

"Not according to Norse myth," Jasper pointed out. "The Norns, to whom Skuld belongs, is the weaver, but all three sisters work together. Wyrd is more of a concept, although is seen as a Goddess, too. Loosely."

Caspian leaned back in his chair, feeling overwhelmed. The discussion was animated now. Small conversations started around the table, buzzing with the excited back and forth exchanging of ideas. *At least everyone was as confused as they were.* Somehow, that made him feel better.

He felt a prickle that suggested someone was staring at him, and turning, he found Avery looking at him, full of sorrow and despondency. Like him, she was overwhelmed. He gave her a weak smile meant to convey reassurance.

If they had expected answers from the coven, they were going to leave sorely disappointed.

Chapter Nineteen

I t was close to last orders on Wednesday night when Alex saw the familiar figure of his father enter the pub. Like Alex, he was tall with a lean, muscular build, but his dark hair, still thick despite his age, was now streaked with grey. Unlike Alex's hair, it was short and swept back from his forehead, revealing a firm jawline.

For a moment, he stood just inside the entrance to the pub, taking in the room and the quiet murmur of conversation, and then he saw Alex and smiled. In a few long strides, he reached the bar and dropped his overnight bag on the floor, but Alex had already walked around it to hug his father.

"Good to see you, Dad. Has it been a long journey?"

"Too long." He stood back, clasping Alex's shoulders. "You look good. Happy. Life here is suiting you. The pub looks good, too." He dropped his hands and turned to study the room again. "You've revamped it. Spruced it up. I like it."

"Thanks. It's hard work, but I love it. Do you want me to take you up to the flat? It's ready for you."

His dad shook his head and sat on a barstool at the place where his friends usually sat. "Not before I've had a drink. A single malt should do it."

Alex's coven and friends had all gone home after their meeting. He should be home too, with Avery. He knew the council meeting had ended, and he was eager to hear about what happened. His shift had long finished, but knowing his father was arriving soon, he was killing time by helping behind the bar. After pouring them both a shot, he sat on the barstool next to him.

Rather than plunge straight into their issues, Alex said, "It must be strange for you to be back here."

"Strange, but not unpleasant. White Haven is busier than it used to be."

"Courtesy of some very odd magical events, and our resident pseudo-Druid endlessly promoting our pagan festivals."

Finn laughed. "Stan! I remember you telling me about him. The town certainly looks festive at the moment. I haven't seen so many pumpkins in one place in years."

"We take our celebrations very seriously! Not only do they tie us to our pagan roots, they bring in a lot of money for our businesses. We are even often featured on the news...for good or ill."

"I'm afraid I don't get to see your local news reports in Scotland."

Alex hadn't seen his father in a long time, but he looked relaxed. "It must suit you there. Does it really make a difference to your psychic experiences?"

He sipped his whiskey and nodded. "It does, and I can't really explain it. Maybe the pull of our ancestors here really does exaggerate our magic. Well, for me at least."

"Ah! Our ancestors." Alex leaned on the counter and sighed. "Before I get to that, don't you miss it? The feeling that wells up inside you as your magic responds to things? I know it's hard. It certainly has been for me. The feeling that I'm not in control sometimes when I experience visions or communicate with spirits. Fortunately, that doesn't happen that often anymore."

"Which is down to your hard work and talent, I'm sure," Finn said. "I think you work harder at it than I do."

"I put in a lot of hours, that's for sure. Whether it's more than you? I don't know."

"I guarantee you do. I always found it more of a burden than a gift. But neither would I wish to lose it. It's a double-edged sword for me. I know that if I stay here, I would regress to the old ways. I can't do that again."

"And yet, you're here."

Finn sighed as he looked around the bar. "Yes, I am. I was called."

"Who by?"

"I don't know. I just woke up a couple of days ago, and knew I had to come back. That's when I phoned you. I needed to make sure that you were okay. When you were, it just opened up more questions that I have no answers to. Do you know why I'm here?"

"I didn't before, but I do now. I'll explain in a minute. Avery, who by the way, I can't wait for you to meet, has been to the Witches Council meeting tonight. We're hoping they have some information that can help us."

Finn smiled. "Your girlfriend is Avery Hamilton, from one of the old families."

"An original, like us."

"I knew her mother, Diana, and grandmother, Clea. Are they around?"

"Her mother moved away years ago, like you. Her grandmother is in care in a place close by. She has Alzheimer's. Avery visits her regularly."

"How tragic." Finn swirled his drink before taking another sip. "She was a good witch. Diana was, too. However, she was always...different. Didn't she have two daughters?"

"Bryony. Avery and her sister aren't close. She also moved away, and has little to do with the craft. It seems that although some of our families are feeling a compulsion to return here, others are not. You wouldn't know the other woman who has returned. Olympia, El Robinson's great aunt."

"One of the families who left the town. It's good that El has returned."

"El and Briar both followed that pull to their roots. Our coven is now complete. Five old families reunited. Except that someone wants to destroy that. Destroy *us*. Over something we did in our past. Our very distant past."

Finn downed his drink and held out his glass. "Let's have another, son. I want you to tell me everything."

Eli plunged through the pitch blackness of Ravens' Wood, thrusting aside branches and bushes that crowded close to the narrow path.

He and Zee were aiming for the heart of Ravens' Wood, or as close to it as they could get. The paths to it changed, and despite their superior abilities, Eli still found himself turned around and disorientated. Trying to fly to it was impossible, too. The canopy of branches was so tightly enmeshed, it repelled all attempts to drop in from above. *That in itself was odd*. Eli knew there were clearings where the sunlight and moonlight could penetrate; he'd been in them. However, finding them from above was impossible. In the dark, it would be so much worse.

Zee swore loudly behind him. "These damn branches keep whacking me in the face! I have a feeling they don't want us in here."

"The more you swear at them, the more they'll hit you. These trees are very receptive."

"Not all the trees have dryads."

"No, but they all have an Otherworldly sentience." As if to prove his point, a huge branch seemed to swing out of nowhere at Eli's face, and his arm shot up to stop it. "All right! Calm down," he said, addressing the trees. "I come in peace!"

Zee sniggered. "This isn't Star Trek."

"Do you want to lead?"

"Nope."

After trudging on for a few more moments, Eli paused in the crossroad of two paths. The trunks were spread apart, giving them breathing space. "I recognise this place. It's close to where the hunters trapped you."

"Close to the centre, then?"

"Close enough." Eli peered into the dark, rustling depths of the forest. His eyes had adjusted to the light, and he discerned twisting shadows that skulked behind tree trunks, and the soft flit of the dryads with their shade-dappled skin. "I see them. I'll speak to them in fey."

All of the Nephilim could speak Shadow's language. When she felt homesick, it cheered her up to use it. He hoped it would prove useful now. He called softly and politely.

With startling speed, a dryad emerged from a birch tree only feet away. "You are not fey? How is it you wield our ancient language?"

Eli nodded to Zee. "We are Nephilim, Shadow's friends, and we have come to seek your guidance."

The wood nymph stepped closer, her huge eyes like dark pools, her mottled green and brown skin mimicking the knots in tree bark. Her diaphanous clothes revealed her slender, long limbs and the soft curves of her body, and despite the situation, Eli felt his desire stirring.

The windy weather still raged outside of the wood, tossing the high branches, but it was sheltered within, and the thought of a wild coupling on the mossy ground filled his vision.

She knew it, too. Her hand pressed against his broad chest, still bare after flying. Her lips curved in a smile. "I hear your quickening blood, Nephilim." She gazed at Zee. "And yours. I remember you, now. You helped defeat the hunters." Her eyes fixed on Eli again. "I think you desire more than just our flesh. It is something else, yes?"

Eli realised that in the long moments he'd been transfixed, other nymphs now formed a circle around them, all swaying gently to their own music. He cleared his throat, carefully removing her cool hand from his skin. "We need to know how long Ravens' Wood has been here, and if you, the dryads and other Otherworldly creatures, were here then?"

"A curious question. Ravens' Wood has existed for always and forever. It is as old as time itself. As are we."

"But this wood only appeared here a few months ago." He gestured around him. "Until then, this place was just fields."

She shook her head, puzzled. "It has always been here. As have I."

"Not in this world. The Green Man pulled it from the earth."

Her confusion vanished. "You talk of the great magic that brought this forest from the Otherworld to here. The magic that allows the humans and you to walk in our woods."

"Your woods?" Eli hadn't considered them quite that way before. "Yes, I suppose they are. But does that mean that these woods *aren't* the ancient woods that once stood on this land?"

"Not at all. Our wood and the ancient wood are the same. Like it is now."

Zee groaned. "I'm really confused."

The dryad turned to him. "At one time, all of this woodland was felled, and only pockets remained. It happened over a long time, and we were powerless to stop it. It was the same with many ancient woodlands in *this* world. However, they were always in *our* world. Now, our magic crosses into this world only occasionally."

"It's not occasional here," Eli pointed out. "You seem to be here all of the time."

"Because the great Green Man made it so when he pulled the wood from the ghost of its roots. A marriage." She knitted her fingers together. "Our forest and yours, together once more. But, as you know, we keep to the remote places, and make sure the paths are purposely misleading."

Zee's voice quickened with excitement. "So, part of this wood did exist then! Were you here? Because something happened in the past, a very long time ago, before the wood was chopped down. A battle between witches. It's happening again now. The past is reaching into the present. If you can remember anything at all that could help us, we'd be very grateful."

The dryad didn't answer, instead turning to her companions, and small, murmured conversations started flowing around them.

Eli pulled Zee aside. "I'm not sure they know anything. It was such a long time ago."

"To us. It might seem like yesterday to them. What I'm worried about is that Shadow says that fey information always comes with a price. She also warns to be wary of striking deals with the fey. We can fight our way out of most things, but tangling with dryad magic could be beyond both of us."

Eli felt uneasy as he considered Zee's words. The gnarled and knotted trees were leaning in as if listening, and the sibilant whispers of the swaying dryads mixed with the wind. He was used to the supernatural.

He *was* supernatural. But at night, this place, with its wild, untamed beauty that you could lose yourself in, was something darker and more dangerous. You could not only lose your way, but also yourself.

The dryad stepped close to them again. "Some of us were here then. Our trees' roots run deep. But there are others we must talk to. Come back again tomorrow, and bring a gift."

"A gift?" Eli's senses sharpened as he considered the dark-eyed stares of the dryads. "What kind of gift?"

"Something worthy of the weight of our information. Your choice. If it is deemed sufficient, we will share what we know. If it's not, then you will leave knowing nothing." She placed her cool hand once again on his chest, and Eli's skin prickled. Not with desire this time, but fear. "Until tomorrow."

The dryads vanished, and the storm returned with a vengeance. Eli realised he couldn't wait to leave Ravens' Wood.

Chapter Twenty

A very decided to take advantage of her evening alone, and focussed on finding out more about Wyrd and her weaving.

The council meeting had put her on edge, as well as making her despondent. There were two things that her coven had to follow up on, each intwined in the other—Wyrd and her weaving, and finding their totem spirits, which would connect them to their ancestors. Or *familiars*, as Jasper had put it. While the council had provided useful insights, it wasn't nearly enough to form a plan to stop their adversary. *Tiernan*.

She settled in the attic spell room, shut the blinds on the wild weather raging outside, used magic to light the fire and plenty of candles, and chose an appropriate incense to set the right tone. Her small altar was dressed for the season with pumpkins, dried leaves, and early winter berries, and she made sure to light a candle there, too. Once she was seated at her table with a glass of red wine, she started to calm down, and the room responded to her mood. She always felt centred in the attic.

At her side was a collection of books from those she'd found on her attic shelves, including one on witches' familiars that she wished she'd thought to look for sooner. Unfortunately, because she had a tendency to keep her books stacked haphazardly, it was hidden behind the others. Plus, like Caspian, she had failed to connect totem animals and familiars, in what she decided was a juvenile error. She also had her grimoires, her own book of shadows that she made notes in, and her cards. She picked them up, shuffling as she mused on her problems. She thought about the sigil that El's ancestor had shown her. The intersection of the long, straight strokes that comprised Skuld's Net. Nine lines all intersecting.

Of course.

The Nine of Wands.

She shuffled the cards, keeping the image of the suit in her mind. The cards, soft with use, slipped over each other easily, and at a certain point she placed the deck on the table and turned over the top card. The Nine of Wands stared back at her.

The common image on all of the Nine of Wands cards, her own included, was of a man carrying a staff—a wand—as tall as he was. To either side were eight more wands, towering over him like a forest. However, he wasn't lost, and he didn't look scared. He wielded the wand like a weapon, and the wands looked like a fence behind him. If she had drawn this card in a reading, the traditional meaning suggested someone defending their territory after a period of adversity. It signified success. A job well done. But what it suggested to her now was that she faced a greater fate. She was *defending* her territory, White Haven, against Fate herself and whatever she had planned. She saw herself in the card, holding her wand, refusing to be driven from somewhere she loved.

Avery lifted the card and held it up to the light, seeing the man's resolve. It was a powerful card.

A rush of conviction and insight flashed through her. *There were five in the coven. Six with Caspian. Seven with Olympia. Eight with Finn.* She needed one more. *A coven of nine to fight Wyrd, to match the lines in the rune.*

The ancestors were sending more witches to help them.

As if she'd been summoned, Helena appeared on the other side of the table, her pale face framed by long, dark hair, her black dress with the tight bodice cinched at her tiny waist. Her eyes bore into Avery's as she seated herself at the table—as if she were flesh and blood. The scent of violets and smoke wafted from her, a smell that now invoked loss and sadness. A life ended too soon.

Avery turned the card towards her. "I need you, Helena. A coven of nine to fight Wyrd and Tiernan."

Helena nodded, and gestured at the cards. The rest of the pack sat on the table.

Avery turned another card over, and The Magician stared at her. *Their adversary.* His tools, the four tools of the tarot, were on a table at his side. Wand, chalice, athame, and pentagram. She leaned back in her chair, considering the many meanings of the card. Knowing what they faced, however, the card could not be more apt. The Magician was not a threatening card by any means, but the character wielded all the tools of magic to manipulate the world to align with his desires. Right now, his desire was to end them, or change their existence in some way. Neither fate sounded desirable to her.

"I refuse to let him win, Helena. What we have here, now, is a good thing. White Haven is a special place. The people who live here are special. I just wish I knew what we'd done to earn such enmity. Context is useful."

Helena gestured at the cards again, holding up one finger. *One more card.* A turn of three. Past, present and future, at its simplest reading.

Avery took a deep breath and turned the top card. The Hermit, card number nine of the Major Arcana. She gave a short, dry laugh. "Oh, that's prescient. Nine again."

The Hermit card was not what it seemed. He was an old man, bearded, draped in a cloak, holding a lantern and a staff. A lantern to light the way. The Hermit was actually a teacher and spiritual guide, and he looked out of frame to the future. *Their future*. The appearance of this card basically suggested to the querent that they should find a guide to help them with their current issues, or even connect to their personal spirit guide. Earlier, she would have called this her totem animal; now, she used the term more common to her culture. She needed to find her familiar. Everything was pointing to it. But it was a journey she didn't know how to start.

Helena smiled, a mischievous glint to her eye.

"Are you my guide? *Our* guide?" At the quick shake of Helena's head, Avery said, "No, that would be too easy. I don't know how to find mine, but Alex will find a way. Did you have a familiar?"

Helena shook her head again and tapped her grimoire, then pointed at the tarot cards. At a flick of her wrist, the front page of her grimoire flipped over, and a magical wind ruffled through the pages. Every now and then, they stopped, and Avery quickly marked the page with scraps of paper at hand. By now the ancient book had many pages highlighted for future use with scraps of paper, old and new, as well as proper bookmarks throughout.

By the time Helena had finished, at least a dozen pages warranted her attention. She pulled the book towards her, and studied the selected spells. There was a common theme.

"Spells using tarot cards?" Avery asked her, startled. "Did you find them effective?"

Helena shrugged and wiggled her hand. Avery took that to mean *sometimes*.

"I must admit that for all I use the tarot, I have rarely tried spells with them. But maybe you're right. I could incorporate these three cards into a spell. Maybe more."

Avery stared at the three cards. The Nine of Wands that signified a coven to battle Wyrd. The Magician, the source of their problems. The Hermit, their spiritual guide. She couldn't help but feel there was another meaning to these three cards she couldn't quite discern yet.

For now, she would focus on spells and see where that took her.

Ben could barely focus, the pain in his head was so intense.

He yelled, "Stop it! You're killing me!"

The old man relaxed his grip, and the pain dulled, but he didn't release him. The old man had clasped Ben's head within his hands, and they sat knee to knee, the man's piercing gaze feeling like it was burning a hole through Ben's soul.

After the horse had charged around the camp earlier, the man had redoubled his efforts to speak to Ben, but he'd kept a wary, respectful distance from Stan, seemingly unsure of what to do with him.

He had used magic again to subdue Ben, and had this time succeeded with the weird mind meld. Communication by normal means was impossible. The language was far too different. It didn't help that Ben's thought processes were slowed because of the wizard's magic and drugs. The fortunate thing was, though, that because he was so dismissive of Ben, he didn't even examine his pack. Ben still had the spells the witches had made for him. It was just a matter of when and how to use them.

Ben wrestled to control his thoughts, but the old man was dredging through his memories, dragging images of people and situations to the forefront. He sifted through them, pausing when he found the witches. Unfortunately, Ben had spent too much time with them using their magic for there to be any doubt as to who they were.

The man's grip relaxed as he focussed on the White Haven Coven, one by one. Ben felt sick with fear when he realised what the old man wanted. *Now that he knew what they looked like, what did it mean for their safety?* He filtered through the situations, seeing their homes and businesses, their laughter and frustration. More importantly, Ben felt him assessing their magic.

However, the more he focussed on them, the less attention he paid to Ben, and he realised that he now had some control over his body. Tucked into the pockets of his padded coat were the bottled spells. A couple of shadow spells, a sunlight spell, one containing pure power, one of fire, and one to immobilise.

Ben knew he couldn't wait any longer. Now that the man had managed to penetrate his mind, it was far too dangerous to stay there. He might even decide that Ben was no longer needed. Ben had no clear idea of where he could go, but he'd talked to Stan about the distant buildings he'd seen on the moor. That had to be their destination, after hopefully losing him in the wood.

He slid his hand into his pocket, his fingers running over the familiar bottles, all slightly different shapes and textures, until he found the one he needed.

The man was so focussed on Ben's memories, he was oblivious to his plans. But Ben had to act fast, or it would be a disaster. The only thing was, he risked injuring himself, too. He forced himself to be patient, but the man continued to greedily search his memories. With a sinking feeling, Ben realised this could go on all night. He might never recover.

Earlier, he had told Stan that he would take action at the first opportunity, and he hoped Stan was paying attention on the other side
of the room. He closed his eyes tightly, and grasped the sunlight bottle
with his left hand, instead of the fireball bottle he'd originally chosen.
He eased it free of his pocket and slammed it into the ground between
them, simultaneously jerking backwards.

The man cried out, dazzled. But he didn't let go as Ben thought he
would. Instead, he gripped his head even tighter as he roared with fury.
Ben brought his right fist between them, eyes still closed against the
blinding light, and punched the man again and again.

The man might wield great magic, but physically, he was weak. He
released Ben and fell backwards, and Ben managed to get one final,
huge punch in before he scooted away. The last remnants of magic
that had restrained him vanished.

Stan shouted, "I'm free!"

"Stay back! I'm going to blow the wall."

Ben's eyes were still closed, but aiming for the wall to his left, the
one least likely to inflict damage on him and Stan, he threw the bottle
containing the ball of pure power. The glass shattered and the wall
exploded, stone flying in all directions. He dived to the floor, shielding
his head, as bitter cold air filled the room.

The fake sunlight was fading now, and opening his eyes, Ben saw
he'd obliterated half the bothy. The dark night beckoned, and he
staggered to his feet. The man was groaning on the floor, showered
in debris, hand pressed over his eyes. Beyond him, curled up with his
cloak over his head, was Stan.

"Time to go, Stan!"

While Stan staggered to his feet, Ben lunged for his backpack,
grabbed a heavy pelt, and ran outside. Within seconds, Stan was next

to him, blinking as he tried to focus. "Impressive, Ben! That's quite a trick."

"You could call it that."

The palisade that ringed the bothy had also been partly demolished, and hoping that the protection spell had been broken, too, Ben kicked a heavy wooden beam aside, grabbed Stan's arm, and ran.

Chapter Twenty-One

On Thursday morning, Moore stood next to Kendall at the edge of White Haven Castle. He frowned at the strange patch of thick clouds and mist that hovered over the headland, unmoved by the strong wind that blew in from the sea. The cliff's edge had completely disappeared.

"Who called this in?"

Kendall pointed to a man wearing jeans and thick jacket who was organising the fencing for the upcoming Samhain celebrations a short distance away with his colleagues. "Mr Kevin Harrison arrived early this morning, and after an hour of arranging cones and organising the path for the Samhain celebrations, realised the odd cloud wasn't moving. Remembering all the chatter about mists and the disappearing harbour, he called it in. Very apologetic about it, too."

"He shouldn't be. He's right. It is odd." Moore studied the clear edges of the mass. "It's too specific, and you can't even see into the middle of it."

Kendall looked nervous, shuffling backwards and forwards on her feet. She hadn't looked like herself since Monday night. "Are we overacting?"

"No. We're being cautious. We need to cordon it off. Not that it should be an issue. No bugger will come up here today. Not with this weather." He glanced around at the thickening clouds that seemed to press closer and closer to the ground, almost scraping across the top of Ravens' Wood. It wasn't raining yet, but it looked imminent. "This is the spot, isn't it? The place where Zee saw the man?"

Kendall looked distracted, but she seemed to force herself to focus. "Yes. Do you think he's trying the mist-thing again?"

"Maybe. It's hard to know what the hell is happening. We need to tell Newton. And I think we should get Ghost OPS back, and maybe one of the witches." He studied the mist again, noting how it was poised on the cliff, ready to roll into town. "I don't like it. At all. So far, this lunatic has just been chipping away at us, but maybe he's preparing for a big offensive. And this is the place where Dylan and Cassie were chased yesterday. Into *that*." He pointed to the brooding tangle of Ravens' Wood.

"Chipping away? He's taken Ben!"

"We don't know *who's* taken Ben, actually. We're making some massive assumptions."

Moore narrowed his eyes as he studied the castle and surrounding lands, especially the moors above White Haven. He tried to imagine how it would look in the distant past—primitive, raw, wild. *Was this what the man wanted? To return them all to the past? Wipe White Haven and modern Cornwall from the map?* That would have far-reaching consequences for much more than just Cornwall.

The man that Kendall had pointed to finished a conversation with his crew, and strode across the grass toward them, a wary eye on the mist beyond them. He looked agitated, and Moore braced himself for more bad news. "Everything all right, Mr Harrison?"

"No. At least, I don't think so. I presume you know Stan Rogers? The councillor who organises Samhain."

"The Druid. Well, pretend Druid," Kendall said, nodding. "Yes, of course."

"Well, he should be here. We arranged to meet this morning. We're finalising the plans for Samhain, and he always likes to have the final say. Unfortunately, he's not at work, nor at home, and no one has seen him since yesterday afternoon."

"Why hasn't anyone reported this before?" Moore asked, incredulous.

Harrison huffed, apologetic. "He often heads home after he's rallied the locals. Judy, the mayor, was expecting him to pop in at the end of the afternoon, but wasn't too worried when he didn't. This morning, however... That *is* unusual. He's not answering his phone. They just realised that his car is still on the council carpark, too."

Moore had spoken to Newton earlier that morning, and knew that Reuben and El had encountered the mist near El's shop. "Thank you. Leave it with us. And I think you should all head home. This is not a safe place to be."

He watched Harrison nod and walk away, then reached for his phone, and braced himself for Newton's annoyance. The way things were going, they'd have to evacuate the town, and that didn't bear thinking about at all.

Briar could barely take in Eli's news. "Please don't tell me you made a deal with the dryads!"

"Not yet. I have no idea what I could even offer them. Well, apart from me, of course." He tried to laugh, and failed. "Or maybe not."

"That's not even funny."

It was mid-morning, and they were in Briar's shop, having elevenses behind the counter. Briar, in an effort to take her mind off their issues—and her recent split with Hunter—had spent the previous evening with her gran after she'd left the pub, baking cakes and cookies. She'd kept an eye on Beth, but fortunately there was no return of her seer state, and no unnerving predictions.

Eli chewed his cake thoughtfully. "I know. But I do need to think of something. They could offer some valuable help. If we're right, and Ben has gone back in time, they might have seen him!"

"I can't believe that's even possibly true."

"They admitted that it's the same wood, Briar! Plus, they live ridiculously long lives. It's worth a shot, surely, to save Ben and stop all this! Our mysterious wizard could launch another attack today. Yesterday, Reuben was able to stop it. Today we might not be so lucky."

"Regardless, you cannot put yourself in danger. You shouldn't make deals with fey creatures."

"Let me worry about that. What about *you*? Have you figured out how to find your spirit animal?"

"No. I'm hoping Avery and Caspian gathered some tips at the meeting. Alex phoned to say we're reconvening at Reuben's tonight. Perhaps he has news, too. His dad has arrived."

"What about your grandmother, or your cousin? Could they play a part in this?"

"I'm not sure. My grandmother keeps seeing a stag on the moor, but I haven't figured out what that means yet. Beth seems to be seeing what our ancestors are up to. And Wyrd." She shivered as she considered Beth's unnervingly far-sighted gaze. "She's such an odd child, though I hate myself for saying that."

"It's a huge burden for her."

"It is, but I'm not sure she even knows it yet."

"And how are *you*, Briar? Feeling better after ending things with Hunter?"

Briar forced herself to meet Eli's gaze, hard though it was. She'd avoided talking about it to everyone except her gran. "Yes and no. It was the right thing to do, but I felt horrible for doing it."

"How did he take it?"

"He went very quiet, and then said that unfortunately, I was right. He said he'd miss me."

"Of course he will. As much as you'll miss him, I'm sure. What do Avery and El think about it all?"

"I haven't told them yet."

Eli frowned. "They're your closest friends!"

"I know. They'll be so nice about it that I'll probably cry. I don't want that. Or their pity."

"They won't pity you! You're the one who ended it!"

Briar idly played with the crumbs on her plate. "It will make it more real if I tell them. I'm in a bubble right now. I quite like it. It's been a year, you know, since he arrived in White Haven with his bloody wounds and his cocky swagger."

"I remember. Alex and Reuben will miss him, too. But, that's how it is. You're still friends."

"Is this why you refuse to have serious relationships? Because it's too hard?"

"No. It's because I like sleeping with lots of women." He grinned, relieving the solemn mood. "Besides, it adds to my allure."

She laughed. "You're impossible."

He glanced to the window. "Speaking of old lovers, guess who's here?"

Newton was on the phone outside her shop, face creased with worry. He nodded at them both in greeting while finishing his call.

Briar felt herself flush. "He's not an old lover!"

"Not for want of trying, though." Eli stood and collected the cups, still grinning. "I'll give you some privacy and put the kettle on again."

Before she could complain further, Newton entered, and Eli headed to the back room, shouting, "I'll bring you a coffee, Newton."

"No time for that," he called back, looking regretful. "I need to steal Briar, if possible. There's something I want to show you on the cliff. Another patch of cloudy, misty weirdness."

Flustered, she said, "I can't leave Eli alone. We've been busy."

Eli, annoyingly, hung around at the door. "I'll manage. This is obviously important."

"But, can't one of the others go with you?"

Newton frowned. "I haven't asked them, yet, but if you really can't help..."

"She can. It's fine," Eli insisted.

Feeling she'd be making a really big fuss to refuse, Briar gave him a huge glare that promised retribution, and said, "I'll get my coat."

Avery glared at Billy, one of her regulars, as he eyed her Gypsy Rose costume appreciatively.

"Well, that's quite the outfit, Avery. I think you should wear it more often."

"Excuse my language, but you can piss off!"

He threw back his head and guffawed. "Ha! That's the spirit. Your Alex is a lucky man. Has he seen it yet?"

Avery started to blush at the thought of his response that morning. She'd ended up having to get dressed twice. "Yes, actually. He approved."

"I bet he did." Billy winked before moving swiftly on. "Now, can I cross your palm with silver?"

"I can tell you exactly what will happen in your future. If you don't stop teasing me right now, I'm going to…" she floundered for threats, and then noticed him reaching for one of Sally's Halloween cupcakes on the counter. "I'll ban you from eating Sally's cakes!"

His eyes widened in mock horror. "You are a very devious wench!"

"I know."

He smirked. "Fair enough. I won't push it, but I think you should prepare yourself for a week of compliments." He took his cupcake and returned to perusing the bookshelves, ignoring Avery's scowl.

Avery took a deep breath and pasted a smile on her face. This was going to be the nature of her week, and she was just going to have to get used to it. In the far corner of the shop, next to the occult section, was the table where she would offer "readings". As usual, Sally had surpassed herself. The corner was draped in gauzy fabrics and twinkling fairy lights, and on the table were a selection of tarot cards, a crystal ball, and books on palm reading—just in case the customers wanted to buy some after having their fortunes read.

Dan was putting the finishing touches to his reading area in the children's section. He suited his costume nicely. The severely-cut frock coat complimented his lean, tall frame, and the stuffed raven on his shoulder completed the look. Sally emerged from the stacks with a twinkle in her eye, resplendent in her costume. It was a long dress with a tight bodice on which a huge, red heart took centre place. The sleeves were capped, and the full skirt was layered with red and white fabric, with more red hearts on the centre panel. Her hair was twisted up on her head, and she wore a crown.

At the sight of Avery, Sally yelled, "Off with her head!"

Avery's grumpiness vanished in seconds as she laughed. "Funny! You look awesome!"

"So do you."

"Sorry if I'm grumpy. I'm worried about...stuff."

"Then you should enjoy the distraction!"

Avery, for the millionth time, wondered what she'd do without Sally. "I know. I feel ridiculous, but it is fun." She glanced around at the customers browsing the books in her festive shop. "And everything looks so lovely. I just wish all this stuff wasn't happening. And I wish I knew where Ben was! I'm so worried about him."

Sally looked around furtively, leaned over the counter, and said, "Haven't you heard the latest rumour?"

"No. What is it?"

"Stan has vanished, too. No one's seen him since yesterday afternoon."

Avery's hand flew to her mouth. "Are you sure he's not sick, at home?"

"Apparently not. Do you think he's in the same place as Ben?"

"I have no idea." Avery sank onto the stool, picked up a cupcake with icing in the shape of a ghost on it, and took a large bite. *Bollocks to the calories*. "That settles it. We have to try and find our familiars tonight. We can't wait for them." She quickly explained what had happened at the Witches Council meeting.

"Familiars? Of course. That's a term I know better. Totem animals seems so foreign."

"That's because it is, sort of. Familiar is an old term that became popular in Medieval times. I was reading up on the whole thing last night, and it seems our Celtic ancestors had strong connections to animals, so they probably called them animal spirits." She shrugged. "Whatever they called them, it's the same thing. The problem is, I'm not sure I want a familiar. They were seen as servants. I don't need a servant!"

"Surely they were also helpers and guides?"

"Well, yes. And they weren't always animals, either. Helena visited last night. I wondered if she could be mine. She laughed."

"So, that's a no, then. I think that's for the best, though, don't you?"

"I guess so." Avery was about to explain her theory about needing nine members in the coven to tackle Wyrd when she saw Reuben enter the shop. He took one look at her and his mouth dropped open. "Reuben, don't you start," she warned him.

"Oh, Ave!" He walked to the counter and leaned over it, his eyes travelling from her head to her toes and back again. Then he turned to Sally and did the same. "Ladies! Aren't you both looking fabulous. My loins are stirring at the sight."

Sally giggled like a schoolgirl and smacked his arm. "Reuben! You're so naughty."

"Yes, I am. I have some *very* naughty thoughts running through my head right now. And look! Cupcakes, too. This is my lucky day."

Avery tried not to laugh at his ridiculous expression, although the glint in his eyes was enough to give anyone a shiver. "I doubt El would be pleased to hear of your naughty thoughts."

"Oh, there's room for her there, too. Perhaps when you two have finished with your costumes..."

"You hire your own costumes for your bedroom antics, Reuben Jackson!" Avery remonstrated. "Are you here to stare at us, or is there a purpose to your visit?"

"I have been summoned by Alex, actually. Seeing as I," he blew on his fingernails and puffed out his chest, "have found my animal spirit—a *stallion*, by the way, Sally, in case you wondered. I have come to help Alex find his, and then formulate a way for the rest of us."

Sally was only too happy to stoke Reuben's ego. "A stallion! Well, what else could it be!"

"I know, right! Anyway, as much as I would like to stand here all day and admire your costumes, duty calls. Any messages for Alex, Avery?"

Her humour vanished and she lowered her voice. "Unfortunately, yes. It seems Stan has vanished, too. We all need to find our familiars tonight."

"Stan? Damn it!"

"And we need a coven of nine. I need Oly, Finn, and Helena to join us."

"Nine?"

"I'll explain later. Alex knows. But essentially it means—I think—that they need familiars, too. You're going to be busy."

"It's what I was born, for, Ave." With a final wink, he kissed Sally's hand, and headed out to see Alex.

Chapter Twenty-Two

Newton knew something was wrong with Briar. She was more guarded than normal, and that was saying something, because she always liked to keep her thoughts and emotions private. In general, he tried to respect that, but he wondered if he had done something wrong. Maybe it was just the situation. Cornish mizzle and magic was not a great combination.

"So, what do you think?" he asked her. "Could Stan be with Ben?"

She was sitting in his passenger seat, watching the lanes whizz by as he drove them up to White Haven Castle, but she turned to him, her lips tight. "I'd like to think so. They can support each other if they're together. But that makes me even more worried. Now we have to get two of them back from wherever they are!"

"Perhaps we're wrong. Although, the alternative is that he could be lying unconscious in a ditch somewhere, and that's worse, surely."

"Newton!"

"I'm just saying! I like Stan. Stubborn old mule that he is," he grumbled.

The last time he'd spoken to Stan, only yesterday morning, they'd had a very uncomfortable conversation about cancelling the Samhain celebrations. Newton was too long in the tooth to feel guilty about it, but he was still worried.

Briar bristled silently next to him, and he sighed. "Have I upset you somehow? If I have, I'm really sorry!"

"No. Of course you haven't. Why?"

"You seem sort of cranky with me. Preoccupied."

"Oh, that." She sank down into her seat, her shoulders dropping. "I'm worried about the weird mist, vanishing harbours, and old wizards with vendettas."

"That's fair enough. So am I. You just usually seem to handle it better than me. You're less sweary and grumpy. Although, to be honest, I like being sweary and grumpy." He grinned at her, glad to see her smile.

"You do it very well."

"Thanks."

"I'm worried about Eli and Zee now, too. They're going to see the dryads in Ravens' Wood tonight." She outlined their plans, and Newton's heart sank.

"That's a terrible idea."

"I agree, but they do know what they're doing. We have to trust them."

Despite their rocky beginnings, Newton liked the Nephilim, and did not want anything happening to them. White Haven seemed safer for having them around. "I'll chat to them later. See if I can talk some sense into them."

Briar fell silent for a beat, and then said, "I have a confession, too. You may as well hear it now." She was staring at the view now, rather than him.

"Shit! You're not ill, are you?"

"No, nothing like that. I've spilt up with Hunter. That's adding to my bad mood. Although I know it's the right decision, I just feel shit about it."

Newton whipped his head around to stare at her, and almost veered into a hedge. "You've done *what*? Why?"

"He's so far away, and so busy. So am I. I've only been to see him a handful of times, which seems mean. He came to see me more often. But lately, well...it's tailed off. We both knew it wasn't working."

"Briar, I'm so sorry."

"No, you're not. You hated him."

A variety of emotions raced through Newton's mind, the primary one being guilt, swiftly followed by relief and an inkling of hope. "No, of course I didn't hate him. He was a good bloke. Cocky, but decent." Reluctantly he added, "He seemed to make you happy."

"He did, so I feel pretty bad about it."

Newton glanced at her again, but she'd turned away, her shoulders rounded as if to protect herself. Rather than risk crashing again, he fell silent as he negotiated up the final lane to the castle's carpark, and then pulled into a parking spot next to his sergeants' cars. He turned the engine off, and silence enveloped them.

He turned in his seat, deciding that Moore and Kendall could wait. "Briar, I mean it. I really am sorry. Relationships are hard enough without distance coming into it. I must admit, I was worried you might move to Cumbria. I'm glad you didn't."

She finally turned to look at him. "I couldn't possibly leave White Haven and my coven, nor all my friends, especially now that I've found my grandmother and cousin. And I suppose I'd miss you, too."

"Thanks," he said, deadpan. "That's nice to know."

She gave a short laugh. "Of course I would miss you. I just feel upside down right now. I thought I'd feel relieved, but I don't. Well, I feel a little bit of relief, I suppose. It's done now, and I don't need to worry about what to do. Eli was right."

"Eli?" Newton felt a stab of resentment that Eli had been the one to offer her advice, and then felt annoyed with himself for the thought. This was Briar's life, not some bloody playground competition. "Well, I'm glad you could talk to him. I must admit, I thought it would have been Avery or El."

"They don't know yet, actually. I'll tell them later. So, don't say anything," she added, staring at the sea again.

"No, of course not." Newton followed her gaze.

The waves were high and wild, their crests white, and a sudden image of Reuben's wild horses came to him. All that churning water and wild power. It was such an alien environment to Newton, it suddenly felt terrifying. Here, however, in the warm cocoon of the car with Briar, life felt safe, and anything seemed possible—despite the looming mist and Wyrd magic. Not that he would presume anything, of course. If all they did was remain friends, that would be all right with him. For a long moment, neither of them spoke, and then a splatter of wind-driven rain and the arrival of the Ghost OPS van broke the mood.

Newton reached for the door. "We'd better go and check the patch of mist, then. Hopefully Dylan's cameras will have recorded something useful."

Briar nodded. "I've also had another thought about my amulet spell. If this mist is going to keep returning, we need a bigger warning system. Something that will benefit the whole town."

"Like what?"

"Like the bell in the Church of All Souls."

"*What*? Are you for real?"

"Yes. How can we keep people safe if the mist keeps swallowing things up?"

"But what you're proposing would be crazy. Do you mean they should evacuate the town?"

She rolled her eyes. "No. They should retreat inside and lock the doors."

"But the mist took buildings, too!"

"It's better than nothing! Have you got a better suggestion?"

"Other than stopping the mad bastard? No."

"There you go, then. I'll get Avery to liaise with James."

She exited the car, leaving Newton to scramble out too, wondering just what he'd agreed to.

Ben was exhausted. He hadn't slept all night, had a pounding headache, and he was cold. Stan was veering between being grumpy and delighted.

They were lost in the wood and it was the morning after their escape. Ben was pretty sure they were going in circles. He was also increasingly convinced that they were in Ravens' Wood, or at least an earlier version of it. Every now and again he came upon clearings he thought he knew, and then he would just become disorientated again.

One thing was certain, however. They had lost the wizard.

Ben stopped to get his bearings, trying to discern the best place to exit the wood and head inland to where he thought he'd seen a settlement. The previous night, he hadn't wanted to run across open land so close to the bothy, fearing it would be too easy for the wizard to see them and catch them. He'd plunged into the wood, instead.

"This is splendid," Stan said, wheezing slightly from the exertion. "I can't believe we're escaping on foot from a mad wizard! I feel like I'm in *Lord of the Rings*."

"I'm glad you're excited, Stan. I'd be more excited if I didn't think he was hiding behind every tree, or that we'll be stuck in here forever. Last night, in case you've forgotten, was freaky. And very cold!"

The long run through the forest had left them covered in scratches, but at least they'd worked up a sweat. They'd managed to find shelter in a huge, hollowed out tree trunk, after virtually falling into it after stumbling over a log. There were bugs, damp leaves, and slime, but at least it was sheltered from the bitter cold. It had also protected them from the strange noises of the wood, like the cracking of branches that could have been the wizard, or could have been animals. *Or something else entirely*.

Every now and again, Ben thought he heard whispers and giggles through the moan of the wind and the rattle of leaves. Although it was winter, some trees retained their greenery, giving the place a feeling of timelessness. Tiredness was making him paranoid, as were his old memories of Ravens' Wood. This was a different place, and a different time.

"Come on, Stan. I think we need to head that way." He pointed to the right. "I'm pretty sure the moor to rear of the valley is in that direction."

"But what if there's nothing there?"

"I saw lights and buildings, I'm sure of it. Hopefully someone will help us."

"What if they're working with him?" Stan jerked his head over his shoulder. "We don't know who to trust."

"What's the alternative? We live in the wood forever?" Ben shook his head. "I am determined to get us home. And find out what that lunatic wants, and stop him. It has to have something to do with our future."

A howl suddenly broke the forest's silence, and goose bumps erupted along Ben's skin. The howls quickly multiplied, and with horror, Ben realised they were all around them.

"Er, are those wolves?" Stan asked, staring around with wide, horrified, eyes.

"Shit! Get up the tree. Now!"

Ben leaped for the lowest branch, managed to grab it, and quickly swung himself up. Stan, however, was jumping up and down and getting nowhere, and the howls were growing closer and closer. Through a break in the trees, Ben saw a silver streak slide through the undergrowth.

Ben dropped to the ground again, ready to give Stan a leg up.

Unfortunately, he wasn't quick enough. A wolf edged into view, low to the ground and hackles raised. Another emerged to his right, then more and more, until they were completely surrounded.

Ben stepped back, feeling the trunk of the tree behind him, and pulled Stan to his side. The beasts were huge, with thick, shaggy grey fur and yellow eyes. His heart was pounding so hard he thought it would leap out of his chest. There was no way he could scramble up the tree without them attacking, and he certainly couldn't get Stan up there, too.

"Didn't you have some of those spells left?" Stan asked.

"Shit, yes!" Ben fumbled in his pocket, trying to remember in his panicked state what he had left.

But it was too late.

The lead wolf lunged at them with a snarl that turned his blood to ice.

"Ah! I see you've cast a bloody huge circle!" Reuben noted approvingly when he arrived in Alex's attic spell room. The circle took up one half of the room in front of the fire. "I do love a ring of candles and salt!"

Alex laughed. "You have a bounce to your step today."

"I've just been teasing your missus!" Reuben whistled. "That dress, wow! I think I upset her."

"You keep your eyes off that dress, and what's in it!"

"It's hard when things are on show. Besides, I'm being polite!" He grinned as his oldest friend wrestled with his emotions, and then finally flipped him off. "Nice."

"You're a dick."

"Piss off. Do you want my help or not?"

"I suppose so. Although, I warn you. I am not absolutely sure how this will go."

Reuben glanced around the room. "Where's your dad? I thought you said he'd arrived."

"He has. He's gone to see Avery's gran." He looked slightly put out as he brushed his hair back from his eyes. "He hasn't even met Avery yet."

"Probably for the best, until she's out of that dress."

"I doubt my dad will make a move on my girlfriend."

"Just saying!" At the sight of Alex's eyeroll, he decided to change the subject. "Anyway. What do you want me to do?"

"After looking at a few rituals, I decided to fashion my own. Something I hope will work for all of us later." He sat on the floor, inside the circle, and gestured for Reuben to sit opposite him. "I'll raise a protection circle around us, and then I'll focus on the flame. But I need to hold your hands."

Reuben sniggered as he settled into position. "You're so romantic. But how will that help? I was surfing when I found my spirit animal. The sea is where I feel most at home. Plus, I'm a water witch. Where are you most at home?"

"Well, I figured that seeing as I spend a lot of time staring into flames for my spirit to travel, and that's the way my ancestor contacted me, that's the place I'm most comfortable. Plus, El and Briar found that fire was their strongest medium."

"So, why do you need me?"

Alex frowned. "I'm hoping your spirit animal can help you to guide me. Can you feel your horse now?"

"Sort of." Reuben considered the wild restlessness of the horse, its unbridled strength, and how he'd managed to summon it the day before, just by sheer need and panic as the mist closed in. He closed his eyes, looking inward, and quickly felt his presence. He opened his eyes and found Alex watching him. "Yes. It's odd. I can feel him when I focus, but otherwise I just feel normal."

"How did you summon it yesterday?"

"I needed it, plain and simple."

Alex rubbed his hands over his face. "This is so strange. I'm trying to imagine how it will feel. How it will work. I figure that if I know that, it will help me."

"I think you're overthinking it. You need to do exactly the opposite. I wasn't thinking at all. I was surfing." Reuben always felt he was the last one to catch on to things, and was the least powerful witch, so to be one step ahead of everyone was a very good feeling, for a change. The only downside was that he was crap at teaching. "You need to empty your mind. The good thing is, I think our ancestors have in some way triggered our spirit animals." He fell silent again as he once more summoned the spirit of his horse from deep within him. The instant flare of recognition was uncanny. "Yeah. It's old."

"Old?"

"You know. Like we were talking about old souls. It carries this ancient wisdom."

Alex groaned. "But that's the problem! Spirit guides should be unique to us. To *me*! It shouldn't be the same as that of my ancestors."

"Maybe it's the same guide, but in a different animal? Something unique to you. Perhaps you saw your ancestor's wolf and thought it was yours, but it's not. Plus, the spirit animal is a way for them to communicate with us—apparently. So maybe it *is* theirs, not yours." He shrugged. "Then again, I'm just spit balling. Maybe Circe is your spirit animal." He pointed to the cat, who sat watching them with lidded eyes from beside the fire. "*Meow!*"

Alex ignored the jibe. "Summon your horse now, you gigantic oaf."

"Now? In your attic? He's big."

"He?"

"Of course. My stallion. Don't make me go there."

"I want to see it, Reu. Impress me."

Not entirely sure that this would be a good thing, but equally keen to impress his friend and prove to himself he could do it while not under duress, he said, "Sure. Sit tight."

Reuben closed his eyes again, placing his hands on his knees, cross-legged. He summoned an image of his spirit guide, especially the water it was created from. For some reason, he didn't imagine it as flesh and blood. Instead, its watery birth commanded its appearance. He imagined himself in the ocean, the bracing coldness and the powerful undercurrents pulling deep within him. Then he heard his whinny, and saw the toss of his head.

Feeling foolish, he spoke to his stallion. *Can you hear me? This is an experiment. I want to see if I can make you appear right now.*

Unnervingly, a deep voice spoke back to him. *I can hear you. I can do anything you need me to...within reason. I'm here to help.*

Reuben jolted with surprise. *Wow. You speak!*

Of course I do. I've been waiting for you to contact me properly. We need to talk about what you and I can do.

Okay. Reuben floundered for words. *Do you have a name?*

It's long and complicated. What would you like to call me?

This was not a question that Reuben had anticipated, and he said the first name that came to mind. The Lone Ranger's horse. *Silver.*

Then that's my name.

Reuben did a little mental whoop that he was now, in his eyes at least, the Lone Ranger. *That's cool. So, er, how do we do this? My friend needs to see what you can do. What I can do. He's—we're—new to this.*

Do not be afraid. I am on your side. But I need to know. Are you doing this to impress? Because that is not a good way to use my skills.

No. We need to understand this. Like I said, we're new to this. He wants to find his guide, too, and thinks seeing you will help.

That is a good reason.

Reuben felt a strange *whoosh* and heard Alex yell, "Holy shit!"

Reuben opened his eyes and his mouth fell open.

Silver was standing in the attic, pawing the ground, tossing his head, and shaking his mane. He was made of shimmering blue-green water, his mane a froth of seafoam. Reuben could even smell the strong, briny scent of deep ocean. He hadn't fully taken in his appearance the day before, or when he was surfing; it was all such a rush. *But now...*

"Herne's Horns!" he stammered out.

Alex stood, speechless, and left the circle to walk around the horse. He finally found his words and turned to Reuben. "This is more than I ever thought possible! It's amazing."

Silver spoke softly in Reuben's head. *Tell him thank you, and that it is possible for him, too.*

Reuben related his message. "I must admit, Alex, I'm pretty shocked. He says we need to talk, and I think he's right. I need to find out exactly what I can do with him." He corrected himself. "Actually, how we can work together."

"So, he's talking to you?"

"Sure. Right in here." He tapped his head. "This is going to take some getting used to."

"Can you ask him a question?"

"Of course."

"Is this connection forever, or can it change? From what Avery and I read, it seems your spirit guide can change, or you can have several, depending on what you need. The animals have different meanings."

Reuben didn't even need to ask Silver, because he answered immediately. "He says that it's up to you and what you need. Yes, a guide can change, and yes, they'll leave if you don't respect them. It's a two-way deal."

Alex's eyes gleamed with enthusiasm. "In that case, please thank your wonderful spirit guide, and let's try and find mine."

Chapter Twenty-Three

El was trying to complete some of her latest jewellery pieces in the back room of her shop, but it was proving difficult.

Aunt Oly, as she had promised, was working in her shop; she was a taxing presence—and that was being polite. She fussed over her customers, talked Zoe to death, and wouldn't stop fiddling with the displays. As much as she loved her aunt, she was exhausting.

El pushed her goggles onto her head and looked around as Oly burst into the room, yet again. "Don't mind me. I'm making tea, and getting some cake. It's such hard work being a shop owner!"

El urged herself to be patient. "Yes, it really is. It's fantastic you're here to help, though. It means I can spend more time making new jewellery. Are you busy?"

"So busy!" Oly flew to her side and kissed her cheek, enveloping her in a musky scent. "You're so talented. Your products just fly off the shelves. It's such a lovely atmosphere, too. The shop looks so beautiful with all the twinkly lights."

"Thank you." El smiled at her, unable to be cross with her aunt. "I have you to thank for everything. If you hadn't taken me under your wing, I would never have learned magic, and I wouldn't be here."

"I firmly believe that you would have found a way, regardless. Talent will always manifest itself one way or another." She clattered in the kitchen, filling the kettle and preparing the pot as she talked. She was wearing one of her voluminous cardigan cloaks over a bold red woollen skirt and jumper. Her flat leather boots were also red, setting off her white hair piled elegantly on her head. "Cake, darling?"

"Yes please." El gave in to the inevitable. She would get no work done for the next half an hour.

Oly's face lit up, and she handed her a slice and sat next to her. "Do you remember those weekends when we would snuggle up in my spell room and experiment? It was so much fun!"

"It really was. It always smelt of cinnamon and nutmeg. It used to make me so hungry. I think you gave me a lifelong addiction to cake."

Oly's spell room was a cavernous conservatory on the side of her ramshackle house. It was stiflingly hot in the summer, and needed heaters to keep it warm in winter. But it was glorious. It was full of light, plants, herbs, and shelves stacked with books, all on long tables. Oly loved to experiment. No spell was out of bounds.

Oly smiled. "Cake is an excellent addiction. I especially loved those afternoons when it was raining. Do you remember how the rain drowned out all other sounds? It was like being underwater."

"Of course I remember it. It was so cosy and safe. You made everything fun." El laughed at the memory, affection flooding through her for those halcyon weekends when magic took over her life. "And your strange chanting music. Do you still play that?"

"Oh yes, and my tribal drumming. It grounds me, you know. The beat is like the heartbeat to my house."

El was suddenly struck by how much older her aunt looked, and fear washed over her as she wondered how long Oly would have left. "I should have visited you more often. In fact, I *will* visit you more often. I can't believe I don't."

Oly squeezed her hand. "You're busy, with a full life here, and I'm so proud of you. Plus, you have that lovely Reuben. He's got such a good heart. He's more powerful than he knows. Still waters run deep, you know."

"I agree with you. I think he's just starting to see it, too."

"He's very proud of his horse familiar, isn't he?"

Reuben had been like a small child on Christmas morning after chasing away the mist. "Yes, he is, and rightly so. I was very impressed. I hate to think what might have happened to us. We could have gone missing, like Stan." The White Haven gossip had reached The Silver Bough earlier that morning, leaving El feeling horrified that their last conversation had been so strained.

Oly stood abruptly and headed to the kettle, which had just boiled. She busied herself putting water in the teapot as she said, "I've been thinking about my own familiar. I want to use Egberk. He is my spirit guide, after all."

Herne's hairy bollocks. "I'm not sure that would be a good idea."

"I don't see why not!" Oly whipped around to stare at her. "He's very good, and steered us in the right direction to Wyrd. Your vision and Alex's corroborate it, and that young Beth—who I would like to meet by the way."

"Of course, I'll arrange it with Briar. But Oly, he was quite aggressive the other night. You said yourself he could be hard to control. You have to keep him in a protection circle!"

"But I think, once he realises the gravity of the situation..."

"Aunt Oly!" El interrupted her. "He's too dangerous. Why can't you admit that? I know you've used him for years, but it worries me that he's using *you*."

Oly folded her arms across her chest, eyes flashing with annoyance. "Using me how?"

"To try and get out of the spirit realm. To use your magic! Your energy! Honestly, it's a terrible idea."

"You think I'm too weak to control him?"

The air was crackling between them with tension and magic, and El took a deep breath as she considered her next words carefully. "You are still a powerful witch, of course, but I'm only repeating what you said the other night. And what I saw! You need a protection circle around you to use him. You said that he tested his boundaries all the time! Please be rational."

"Oh! So now I'm an irrational old woman?"

"No! Yes! Oh, for the sake of the Goddess, will you calm down?" El's heart was pounding. She hated arguing with her aunt, but she had to make her see sense. "Aunt Oly, you should see this as an opportunity to find a new spirit guide who could be just as powerful, but far less threatening. This is a chance for all of us to learn something new and enhance our magic. We can do this together—just like the old days in your spell room." El stood and took her aunt's hands in her own. "This will be such a fun thing to do. Just think, we're working with our ancestors to defeat an ancient wizard with a vendetta. This is Samhain, the veils are thinning, and tonight's experience could change everything. This is the first stage in our battle. I want it to be positive, don't you?"

Oly was thin-lipped, but her eyes softened slowly. "Of course."

"And we certainly don't want to harm our ancestors in any way. What if Egberk lashes out at them? However that would work..." El hadn't quite worked out the logistics of all this yet.

"I certainly wouldn't want any harm to come to them. Or you. But I know him!"

"The familiar is comforting, Auntie, but it's not always the right path."

"Such wise words from one so young," she said loftily. "All right. I'll try to find a new guide. If he'll let me."

"What do you mean by that?"

"Well, he might not want me to have a new guide, that's all. Anyway. Let me pour the tea and you can get back to work."

She turned her back, discussion over, and El sank on to her stool, hoping Oly was very wrong about Egberk.

Ben watched the wolf leap, claws outstretched, jaw open, sharp teeth ready to rip his throat out, and hated the fact that this was how he was going to die. His family and friends would forever wonder where he was, and his bones would be spread through the forest, lost to time.

Suddenly, a piercing whistle and a harsh shout silenced the wolf. It fell short, snarl vanishing as it sat only feet away from Ben, its yellow eyes watching his every move. The other wolves stopped growling, sitting back on their haunches instead, and turned to face a group of slender figures wearing green and grey sweeping cloaks and leather boots. A mixture of male and female, they were tall, ethereal, sharp-eyed, and long-haired. They weren't dryads, and they weren't humans.

They were fey.

Stan whimpered, back pressed to the tree. *Not surprising, really.* Every single fey had a huge longbow, cocked and pointing at Ben and Stan.

Ben raised his hands in surrender, hoping that if they didn't understand his words, they would understand body language. "Please, don't shoot! We're harmless!"

"I can see that." A young man with long, dark hair woven through with feathers stepped forward and lowered his bow. He crouched and ruffled the head of the wolf closest to Ben, murmuring words of praise before addressing Ben again. "However, you have wondered far into our territory. You have crossed the borderlands, humans."

"The borderlands?" For a second Ben wondered what he meant, and then it struck him. *Shit.* "Oh! We're in the Otherworld. Your world." *No wonder everything felt so different.* "It was an accident, I swear!"

The fey looked amused. "It is easy to do, especially at night. You are lucky we found you. Not all are so welcoming to humans."

Ben was still eyeing the wolves, as was Stan, both still backed into the tree trunk. "Including your wolves."

"You have nothing to fear from them, as long as you are friends. If not, your death would be swift. They help us hunt—are as one with our tribe." His eyes narrowed as they swept over him and Stan. "Are you injured?"

"Cuts and bruises only." He looked at Stan, hoping he wasn't about to have a heart attack. His face was red and covered in sweat. "What about you, Stan?"

"I'm fine. I think."

Wrestling his emotions under control, Ben said, "Thank you so much for saving us. We were running from a powerful wizard who took us captive. He lives on the edge of the forest. We, er, got lost." Saying it out loud made Ben feel ridiculous. Like he was in a fairy tale.

The fey's eyes darkened. "I know who you mean. His name is Tiernan. Our people call him Weaver of the Dark Path. But why capture you?" His eyes swept over them. "Your clothes are strange, as is your language, but your companion...A Druid? He dresses as one, yet does not carry their power."

"He's a Druid in training." Ben shot Stan a look to shut him up. "We are not from Tiernan's world. We think we have been brought here from the future."

"How?"

"Tiernan used strong magic that I don't understand. However, I think we have friends here." Ben recalled the huge raven that swept overhead the other day, and how it had seemed to indicate where they should go, hoping he hadn't imagined it. "We need to reach them. Will you help us leave the Otherworld and find the edge of the wood? Is it even possible to leave? You see, in our time, we cannot cross to your world anymore. The way is closed."

"Is that so? Perhaps that is a good thing. For now, however, the gateways between worlds are many. We can take you to the edge of the forest. That is as far as we will go."

"That will be perfect! Thank you."

"Before then, you must eat and get warm, and we also need to eat." He gestured behind him to his companions. Ben had been so focussed on his conversation that he hadn't noticed them building a camp in the small clearing. "Take a seat by the fire. You can sample some of our local brew, and we have food to share." He shouted an unintelligible name, and a huge half-beast with a horned head and cloven feet stepped forward with a stoppered leather bag. Ben's mouth went dry as he realised he was looking at a satyr. The fey continued, "But I warn you. Don't have as much as he offers you! The brew is strong, and he is an expert drinker. You will *never* outdrink a satyr. Please, take a seat."

Without another word the fey joined his companions, and Ben said, "We better do as he says, Stan. I must admit, I'm starving."

"But is it safe?" Stan muttered as he sat on the tree trunk.

"It's safer than being eaten by wolves, or recaptured by a mad wizard." They accepted a drink from the satyr, and Ben raised his cup in thanks. The liquid had a thick, foamy head, and Ben sipped tentatively. "Wow! It's a dark beer. It's delicious, and definitely very strong."

The satyr sat across the fire, drinking out of a huge horn that he raised in salute. A strange expression crossed his face, and Ben realised it was a smile. He smiled back, his face feeling stiff. He really should relax and enjoy this...if he could bring his thoughts into focus. He was in shock, not surprisingly. He'd travelled back in time, been drugged, and was now in the Otherworld. Of course, the other option was that he'd travelled forward in time after civilisation had been utterly destroyed. *It was Planet of the Apes all over again.*

As anxious as he was to leave the wood and find a way home, he also knew he needed to rest and eat, as they had no idea what they would encounter next. *Besides*, Ben mused, *he was actually in the Otherworld! Shadow's world. This was an adventure he could not miss.*

In the end, Alex decided he did not need to link hands with Reuben. It was enough to have him in the circle with him. His familiar's energy signature was strong, and signalled what he should be looking for.

He huffed to himself. *Like he could even forget.* The water horse was stunning. It's ancient wisdom and power were more than he could ever have imagined, and he hoped his own spirit guide would be half as effective. He was pleased for Reuben. He'd battled for so long to find his magic and strength, and now it seemed to be magnifying rapidly.

It was time to focus on his own needs, and he stared into the candle flame, feeling the potion he had brewed taking effect. He knew that

Reuben hadn't needed one, but Alex always worked like this when he entered the spirit realm. If he was to truly relax and be open to the experience, he needed to use a way that was familiar to him.

The attic was dark, the blinds drawn to keep the grey skies at bay. The steady drumming of rain on the roof and the crackle of the fire cocooned the experience. The flames became larger and larger until they filled his whole vision, and the world slipped away as he sought the woman who had appeared to him.

No. Not the woman. The wolf. Alex remembered how Hunter looked in *his* wolf form. The size of his paws, his huge head, and powerful jaws. His thick fur, and the way his muscles moved. He thought of the wolf's scent, and the cunning in its eyes. The wolf took shape in front of him. But it wasn't *his* wolf. He felt no connection to it.

He thought of his ancestor's wolf. How it had growled its speech, its eyes boring into his. He let the image fill him up. Consume him. The beat of its heart replaced the sound of the rain, and the candle flame became the flame of intelligence in the wolf's eyes.

It felt so real, Alex's initial instinct was to retreat. He forced himself to stay calm and opened himself up to the experience. The wolf slipped inside him. Their heart beats fell into sync, and suddenly Alex felt its wild, distinct power flow through him.

He was so startled, his self-defence system kicked in. In seconds the wolf vanished, leaving an aching emptiness. The candle flame came into sharp focus, as did Reuben beyond it.

"Bollocks!" Alex was devastated. He'd come so close, but he'd lost it.

Chapter Twenty-Four

Briar asked Newton to drop her off in White Haven's square after they finished examining the mist at the castle. Being in the cold and wet on the clifftop had invigorated her, and she didn't want to go indoors just yet.

They hadn't spoken about her split with Hunter again, although she could tell he wanted to. She did not. Neither did she wish to encourage him in thinking they might have a future, because the honest answer was that she really wasn't sure one way or another.

What she needed to do was talk to one of her female friends, and seeing as she also wanted to talk to Avery about her latest spell idea, she decided to walk up the hill to her shop. Briar was guilty of avoiding the subject of her split, but she couldn't pretend it hadn't happened any longer. Plus, Eli could manage for another hour, and she wanted to see White Haven's Samhain decorations in all their splendour.

Briar set off up the hill, lifting her face to the fine drizzle as she slowed to appreciate the decorations. Pumpkins of all sizes lined the streets, and the shop fronts were filled with displays of fake skeletons, witches, jack o' lanterns, and spiderwebs, as well as more rustic, pagan displays. In the gloom, the fairy lights beckoned to the warm shop interiors, and the scents of coffee and cinnamon wafted from cafés.

She wasn't lying when she told Newton she couldn't leave White Haven. The idea horrified her. This place was in her blood, and she loved it. She paused outside Happenstance Books, admiring Sally's skilful display and preparing herself for the coming conversation. And then she giggled as she saw Avery cross in front of the window. *Herne's horns...*

As Briar entered the shop, the bells announcing her arrival, Avery turned to see who had arrived. The smile on her lips vanished. "Briar, don't say a word! It's all Dan's fault."

She couldn't help but ignore her plea. "Oh my, Avery. That really is an impressive costume." Her eyes drifted down the tight bodice and the voluminous layers of skirts. "It's very flattering!"

"Don't you start! Reuben virtually thrust his groin at me. Cheeky bastard!"

Briar threw her head back and laughed. "Of course he did! This is exactly what I need right now." She walked to the counter where Avery had retreated to, noting a few of the customers laughing, too. "Seriously, you look fantastic. Your shop is always fun. Maybe I should suggest costumes to Eli. I think he'd like that! I know I would."

Avery's keen ears, however, had not missed her earlier comment. "Why do you need *this* right now? Has something happened?"

"Nothing serious. I just need to chat to you about a couple of things."

Avery immediately raised her voice. "Dan! Sally! I need a favour!"

In a few moments, both arrived at the counter from opposite ends of the shop, Sally's huge skirts brushing the shelves as she passed.

Briar gaped. "Look at you two! You look great!"

Sally grinned. "Thanks. I like being a queen. I think I'll wear this at home. My kids love it—especially as it's a bit dark!"

"I'm rather fond of my raven," Dan added, patting it where it was perched on his shoulder. "I think it should have a place on the shelves when we're done."

"It's part of the costume," Avery pointed out. "You can't."

He poked his tongue out at her. "I'll buy one, then."

"Whatever." Avery clearly hadn't fully forgiven him for her costume. "I need to speak to Briar, and I may be gone some time—just so you know! In fact, I'll have lunch while I'm gone."

"No problem," Dan said. "No doubt you will foretell if we need help."

Briar stifled a giggle as Avery shot him a look of loathing, and flouncing her skirts, she led the way to the back room as Dan winked at Briar.

As soon as the door was shut, Briar said, "You're so lucky to have such lovely friends to work with, Avery."

"Lucky! I am surrounded by cheeky men." She was smiling, though, as she said it. "But, yes, you're right. Anyway, enough of them. Are you hungry? We could go upstairs. We've got loads of food."

"Is anyone up there?"

"Alex and Reuben, although they might be in the attic. Why?"

"Let's just a have a quick chat here first, and then we can go up."

Avery's shoulders dropped. "What's wrong?"

"I've split up with Hunter. That's all. Nothing terrible or dramatic. I should tell you all together." She rushed on, feeling a twit. "I think I'm making it more dramatic than it should be."

Avery rushed over and hugged her. "Oh, no! I'm so sorry. Of course it's a big deal." She pulled back to stare at Briar, eyes roving over her face. "What happened?"

Briar shrugged, tears threatening, until she lifted her chin and blinked them away. "Nothing. It's been on the cards for a while. We both knew it. It was absolutely the right decision. I hardly see him lately. It's a shame, because he was so lovely. Well," she giggled, "for a brawling, swaggering shifter."

"But he was good to you." Avery's expression was kind and gentle. "For the record, although I liked him a lot, I really did, I didn't see it lasting forever. But I think he came around at the right time. He was what you needed *then*."

"He was, actually. I only have great memories, but the distance proved too great."

"Now you have room for someone new. Or old."

Briar shook her head. "Newton is not an option at the moment. Maybe never. Right now, I need space. Healing time. And I'm enjoying spending time with my family."

"Excellent thinking, Briar! I will support whatever you choose, anyway, you know that."

Briar's heart already felt lighter. She didn't know why she'd been dreading it. "Thank you. So, now on to issue number two, and we can go upstairs for this if you want."

"Okay." Avery headed to the door that led to her flat, but then paused. "If you ever want to chat, or need a night with me and El, just say so. Or all the girls, even. Sally and Shadow? Maybe Caro, Dan's girlfriend? We can blow off steam and girl talk all night."

"I might well take you up on that! Thank you. I'll tell the others later, okay?"

Avery mimed zipping her lips. "I'll say nothing."

Briar smiled and followed Avery up the stairs, hearing Reuben and Alex talking above. The scent of bacon was wafting through the air, and as soon as they opened the door, the clatter of activity greeted them.

"Hellooo!" Avery shouted. "It's me and Briar!"

In a flash, Reuben emerged from the kitchen and leaned against the arched wall that divided it from the living room. "Ah, the wench and her dark-haired witch are here."

"If you call me a wench once more…"

"Go on. You'll do what?"

Briar decided to head off an argument. "Why are you here, Reuben?"

"Alex needed my wisdom, because I have found my familiar. Unfortunately…"

"Yeah, yeah." Alex joined them, a tea towel thrown over his shoulder. "I failed."

"Oh, no!" Avery headed to his side, reaching up to kiss his cheek. "What happened?"

"I think I was trying too hard." He looked tired and despondent, but forced a smile. "I'll try again later. Having found it once already, I know I can do it again. Anyway, do you two want lunch? Reuben insisted on cooking a mountain of bacon. Surprise!"

They both nodded, answering together. "Yes, please."

"Grab a seat. Bacon and egg sandwiches coming up."

For a few minutes, there was aimless chatter while they settled themselves, and when everyone was seated, Avery asked, "How can I help then, Briar?"

Briar summarised her trip with Newton and the discovery of the mist that had settled on the clifftop. "I want an early warning system for the town. I thought we could cast a spell on the bells at the Church of All Souls. When they ring, it means the town is threatened. But it means talking to James and getting his permission, and I don't know him."

"Bloody hell!" Reuben exclaimed. "While I admit I'm impressed, how do we tell the town about that without outing ourselves as witches?"

"I actually haven't fully reasoned that out yet. I was hoping that James would take some responsibility. However, I can modify my existing spell, and with your help, I'm confident that it will work." She repeated what she'd told Newton. "Being indoors has surely got to be better than being outside. We can get the council to make an announcement."

Alex huffed. "I can't see them doing that. It will terrify everyone."

Avery looked sneaky. "Maybe a bit of pressure from James will help. And even the lovely Sarah Rutherford."

"The news reporter?" Briar asked, not sure whether to hate the idea or love it. Visions of stampeding people running through the town filled her mind. "We're in danger of making this worse."

Reuben rolled his eyes. "All we need is glamour! Let me talk to the council. I know Judy, the mayor, quite well. I'll work my charms on her."

Avery nodded, resolute. "Okay. I'll get in touch with James. Do you want to meet him, Briar? He doesn't know that you're a witch. Certainly not El. If we're all to cast this spell, in his church…"

Briar nodded. "I'm fine with it. He's been supportive of us. We need to be honest with him. It's only fair."

"I agree," Reuben said, wiping crumbs from his chin. "He's a good bloke. Don't forget Caspian, though. I presume we need him, too?"

"Maybe not," Briar reflected, "but I'll have a think and chat to him about it later."

"All right. I'll arrange it for tomorrow," Avery agreed. "I think we should focus on our spirit animals tonight. Sorry, familiars. I'll work out the details with him and tell you later."

"I don't think we can wait another twenty-four hours!" Briar argued. "Can't we do both tonight?"

Avery exchanged an uneasy look with Alex and Reuben. "What do you two think?"

Reuben didn't hesitate. "Tonight for both. It could be days before we stop the attacks. Especially as we haven't got a clue how to do that yet."

"Agreed," Alex said.

Satisfied, Briar addressed Reuben and Alex, ready to tell them about Hunter. "Excellent. And now, I have news for you two."

After that, she would see El. Then it was done.

Cassie finished reviewing the data from the surveillance of Ravens' Wood and the castle, and promptly swore.

"Damn it, Dylan! There is nothing here that can tell us where Ben is! Or Stan! Or even if they're together. We have lots of pretty readings and footage, but it gives us bollocks all!"

It was Thursday afternoon, and they were both sitting in front of computers in their office that was filled with fuggy warm air and the scent of coffee and pizza. Her hair was still damp from tramping around the castle that morning in the rain, and disgruntled, she reached for another slice of pizza.

"That's not true. We need to be logical, Cas!" Dylan said. "It's a puzzle."

"Right now, I hate puzzles. I want answers! Where's Ben? It's been three bloody days!"

"I know. I'm as worried as you are." Dylan was studying his monitors, several video feeds on the screens. His earphones, as usual, were around his neck where he'd slipped them off. "We are making progress. The mist on the clifftop is definitely magical. You're detecting higher than normal energy readings, and the mist is red. It should be blue. It's a big bank of cold air. That's progress. And I've enhanced that face. Come and see it."

Taking the pizza box with her, Cassie sat next to him. "Go on then. Wow me."

Dylan gave her a cocky smile before hitting a button and bringing up the image. "Grizzly old fucker, isn't he?"

Cassie almost choked on her pizza. "Herne's horns! Is that for real?"

"Yes! I haven't doctored it. I just cleaned it up."

Cassie leaned forward, studying the intense eyes, sharp cheekbones, and thin lips. "How did you do that?"

"I focussed on the reddest parts. Sort of brought those forward and dulled the rest of the image. That's the man who's behind all this."

"What did Alex say he was called? Tiernan?"

"Yep." He pointed at the man's chin. "That's a bit fuzzy. I think it's a beard."

"Is it wrong to say I can feel his power? His malevolence?"

"No. What I really want to know, though, is why can't the mist enter the wood? I can't see any kind of protection spell around it. Maybe I need to try a different energy resonance."

"You can do that?"

"I can try. If I can see something, it might tell us the type of magic that's effective. *Might...*" He reached for a pizza slice and took a bite, mumbling while chewing. "It can't be fey magic. It's not a portal to the Otherworld."

"What about the dryads? They're fey creatures."

"They're not anywhere near the perimeter. They stick to the deepest parts of the wood. Is it a kind of tree magic?"

Cassie stared at him. "Tree magic?"

"They *are* ancient trees. They will have huge roots. You know, trees are said to be symbiotic. They connect to each other deep underground. They sense when another tree is ailing, and try to help it. I read that. Fascinating, isn't it? It's an underground, mycelium network involving fungi." He tapped the screen, showing a shot panning around the wood. The murky green light, a permanent fixture despite the mostly bare branches, illuminated the dust motes in the air, and the occasional leaf fall. "That place is a big, interconnected network. Supposedly, what happens on one side of a wood can be detected on the other. And Ravens' Wood, as we well know, is older and weirder than most. We may not remember it, but the witches swear the Green Man dragged it from the depths."

Cassie still had trouble wrapping her head around that. "You're suggesting it has its own defence mechanism? A magical one."

"Yes. The guys just need to work out how to replicate it." He took a deep breath and sighed. "Maybe. I might have gone mad."

Cassie stared at him with new appreciation. Dylan was smart, but this was something else. "Consider me impressed. Frankly, anything that helps us defeat this lunatic is brilliant. I'll call the witches. We need to crash their meeting later, because they will definitely want to hear this."

Chapter Twenty-Five

Rather than wait until later in the day, Avery decided to visit James as soon as Sally and Dan had eaten lunch. Although, she made sure to change out of her costume first.

It was almost two in the afternoon when she walked up the path to the vicarage, but the sound of a choir carried to her from the church, and mesmerised, she listened for a moment. Their voices were beautiful, and unable to resist, she tried the side door. Pleased to find it unlocked, she headed inside, hoping she would find James.

Once inside, the music swelled, lifting her spirits. They may not have the same beliefs, but the sound was lovely nonetheless. She hesitated at the entrance to the nave, hoping she wasn't intruding, but there were only a couple of people seated in the pews. All the activity was out of sight. James spotted her, and smiling, called her over. Once seated next to him, she could see the choir in the area beyond the altar, faces lifted as they sang.

He leaned in, voice low. "They're rehearsing a few Christmas carols, but also music for the All Saint's Day service."

"It's lovely. Very calming."

James nodded. "I always listen when I have time. Helps me to focus when I feel I'm becoming overwhelmed with work."

"You're busy?"

"Always, but Stan's disappearance has—not surprisingly—scared people." He huffed. "The usual doomsayers are saying that White Haven is cursed. As always, I deflect that. Have you come with good news?"

"No, but we do have an unusual plan. The only thing is, it involves this church."

"Go on."

Hoping James would be receptive, she outlined Briar's idea, keeping her name out of it until she'd seen James's reaction. "It's not a solution, by any means, but we know that the smaller version of the spell works. The only thing is, we're not sure if it will provoke more panic."

"Interesting."

He watched the choir again, and Avery allowed him time to think. At least he wasn't horrified by the idea. Her thoughts drifted to Helena. If she was to use her in a spell, and Avery was convinced she should, whose body was she to use? *Avery certainly wasn't about to let her in her own again.* It was in the hidden crypt below her feet that she'd battled for her life with Helena over twelve months ago.

She'd found a couple of spells that she thought could be adapted successfully for their current needs, incorporating her three tarot cards. The power of nine in the coven would be an excellent counter to Wyrd and her magic. The number kept cropping up in her readings, and like everything to do with the tarot, numbers had several meanings. Nine denoted compassion, and the ability to see the big picture. It also symbolised the end of a cycle, a time of completion. But to complete what? To end their ancestors' strife with a wizard from hundreds of years before? More importantly, nine symbolised the bridge between worlds—the material and the spiritual. *That was exactly what they needed right now. A path to their spirit guides. A plan to battle Wyrd and the wizard in a different way.*

James's response brought her back to the present. "I agree, Avery. In fact, I think it's an excellent idea. When the bell sounds, I could open the doors for those who wish to shelter in here. Or even leave them open all day. I don't normally, but in times such as these..."

"Shelter in here? I hadn't even considered that. Are you sure about the spell, though? It means using magic in your church."

He smiled, lines crinkling around his eyes. "I understand that casting a spell means magic, Avery. I trust you, and your friends. Our interests are the same. We want to protect White Haven. I also like the fact that we get to blend both pagan and Christian beliefs in one place. It's something the church has always done—I think we both know that."

Avery laughed. "Just don't expect us to convert."

"There's a place for both in this world. Can you do it tonight?"

"That's the plan, although we have something we need to do first. We'll only need you to open the church up. I'll introduce you to the others then. I should warn you that it might be late."

"I'm only next door. It's not a problem. So, I get to meet your coven?" He cocked an eyebrow, amused.

"Of course! Unless you don't want to."

"Oh, I want to. I'd like to know who I'm lining up with in the battle for White Haven. Deal?" He offered her his hand and they shook on it.

"Deal."

Reuben strolled into the council offices, looking like he belonged there. He found this was the easiest way to get in anywhere. No one questioned someone who looked like they knew what they were doing.

It helped that most people there knew him well. Greenlane Nurseries provided plants for the town's displays, and he contributed money to all sorts of projects. He didn't even need to glamour security to get through the screening. After a short, amiable chat, he headed upstairs to the mayor's offices, hoping she wasn't in the middle of a meeting, but prepared to wait anyway.

There was definitely an air of panic in the building, he noted, as he passed various offices. Huddles of people conferred in low voices, their expressions serious. Although a lot of people greeted him, it was clear their thoughts were elsewhere.

That was good news. It meant Judy would be more amenable to his suggestion.

Her secretary smiled when he knocked and entered her office. "Mr Jackson! What an unexpected pleasure!" She frowned at the computer monitor. "Do you have an appointment?"

"Lovely to see you, too, Janice," he declared with a big grin. "But it's just Reuben." Janice was a middle-aged woman with three kids, and Reuben had the feeling that the only control she had in life was in the office. Fortunately, she liked him, so he took advantage of it. "I'm being a bit cheeky. I haven't got an appointment, but I was hoping to have a quick word with the mayor."

Her face fell. "She's so busy today, especially because of Stan. We're all so worried about him! It's not like him not to come in, especially with Samhain around the corner. There're so many final things to organise! Judy is tearing her hair out! And the mist thing... It's all so worrying."

Interesting. Not everyone said Samhain instead of Halloween, even in White Haven. She also didn't seem to be in denial about the weird mist. He sensed a kindred, pagan spirit. "Did you see the mist?"

"Did I? I was right on the edge when it happened! One minute the harbour was there, and the next it had gone! Nothing but beach, cliffs, sea, and sky was left. The silence was uncanny."

Reuben pulled a chair up to her desk and sat down. "Fascinating. I wish I'd seen it. The thing is, some people say it didn't really happen. That it was a mass illusion."

"Then they're bloody idiots! I've had nightmares ever since." Her eyes stared into the distance and a hand settled over her heart. "For a moment, I couldn't breathe! I felt I'd fallen through time."

"How close were you, then?"

She pulled herself together. "By the warehouse conversion. Another step and I'd have been in it."

"Anyone with you?"

"No. I was heading to the chippy. The kids were out, and I was treating myself. I just don't understand why the others aren't remembering properly. I think they just don't want to." She lowered her voice and leaned across the desk. "Some people are scared of what they don't know. I embrace it. Maybe that's the difference."

Clearly, there were hidden depths to Janice. "I like that attitude. Me, too."

"But you're from one of the old families, Reuben. You know this place is different. We feel it more than others. I reckon that's the difference. We see what others don't."

Reuben mimicked her action and leaned forward too, so they were inches apart. "You're absolutely right. What do you think is happening?"

"It's the ancestors. It's their time, right? They are knocking on that door loudly this year. I swear I heard my old mum's voice, the Goddess bless her soul, last night. She told me to chuck my oldest out. She's right. I should do it. Lazy layabout. But then she said I should protect myself. I've got rosemary at my front and back door. I've even got a sprig in my bag now."

Reuben was suddenly filled with an overwhelming affection for Janice, and all the other residents like her. They were indeed kindred spirits. "Good. It will certainly help." He could feel Briar's amulet on his chest, and wished Janice had one, too. "Can I see it?"

"Of course!" She pulled a drawer open, extracted a huge leather bag, and plucked a healthy sprig bound with ribbon from the pocket.

Reuben took it from her, and under the guise of studying it, said a quick spell of protection over it before handing it back. "Nice strong plant, that. Keep it close, Janice."

"It won't leave my side. I can promise that." She put her bag away, eyeing him speculatively. "What do you want to see Judy about?"

"Keeping the town safe from our wayward ancestors."

"Go on. Best do it now. She's got a meeting in ten minutes." She buzzed through on the intercom, and not giving Judy a second to complain, said, "Mr Reuben Jackson to see you."

"Thanks, Janice." He headed to the door before there were any interruptions, knocked, and walked in.

Judy had a mass of wild red hair, and right now, it looked as if she'd just walked through a gale. "Reuben! You haven't got an appointment today. I don't know why Janice has let you in. I'm so busy!"

"Which is why I'm here to help!"

He sat on the chair in front of her desk. He'd been in here a few times since Gil had died. All of this schmoozing with the council, as Reuben liked to call it, was once Gil's job, but Reuben had now taken it on, and decided to do it his way. Judy had got used to his jeans and board shorts. He had a feeling she liked it, because it was completely different to what she was used to.

Before she could respond, he said, "I know about Stan's disappearance, and of course I've heard all about this weird mist. I think the town, and you, need a bit more support. I propose a sort of early warning system. We can have a few people watching out for mist, and if it appears, we will ring the church bells."

"Church bells! Are you insane? Who's going to watch? Who will ring? And what will people think? Or *do*?"

Reuben leaned forward, a waft of glamour floating between them, and started to explain the cover story he'd concocted in earnest. One way or another, Judy would agree and give her backing. She had to.

It was nearing dusk when the fey escorted Ben and Stan to the edge of the forest, and the undulating moors were filled with pockets of violet shadows.

Out there, the wizard could be lurking and watching. He might even have set traps to catch them. He would have known they couldn't go far. Plus, he was smart, and vindictive. They'd debated the best time for them to set off, but the fey had said that although it was easier to travel in the daylight, it would also make them easier to spot. The half-light of dusk was deemed the safest, even though it would be dark by the time they reached the settlement.

Fortunately, the fortified hillfort was on a distant rise, its stone walls just about visible in the thickening twilight. It may only be late afternoon, but night fell early at this time of year. Even now, the flare of torches sparked along the wall. Beacons in the dark.

"That's where we're going, Stan."

Stan shuffled next to him, drawing his cloak closer to his chin. "That looks a fair distance away, Ben."

"Only a few miles, but it will be hard going over rough ground, especially in the dark. Can you manage it?"

"I'm middle-aged, not decrepit."

Ben laughed, admiring his spirit, and then turned to thank Ninthalam, the fey who had met them. "Thank you, for everything. The fire, the food, the very strong beer... And for not letting your wolves eat us."

A huge, brown wolf sat next to them like an obedient dog; a large-pawed, wild-eyed, intensely predatory dog, and Ben eyed it nervously. Ninthalam, however, patted the wolf's head. "He wouldn't have eaten you. Maybe just taken a small bite."

"Funny."

Smiling, he gestured towards the settlement. "Sorry we can't accompany you. Fey are not always welcome there. Not like they once were."

Ben felt the sorrow behind his words. Even now, so many hundreds of years before his own time, the world was changing. Ben patted his rucksack. "It's okay. I still have a few tricks to use." He had told them about the bottled spells, and his friends who were witches. He hadn't even bothered to hide it from Stan, who had muttered, "I just knew it."

Ninthalam continued. "We will watch you over the first ridge, and then leave. I hope you are able to return home. If not, and you are in trouble once more, come find us."

Stan's eyes lit up. "Would you take us to your world again?"

"I would, but I think it better that you find your way home. Our world is dangerous, even to those who know it well."

With a few final farewells, Ben and Stan aimed for the hillfort, walking along a narrow track that might have been made by animals or humans. Maybe both. They kept alert for signs of the wizard, but only the distant sound of the surf and bird calls disturbed the silence. When Ben eventually looked behind him, all he could see was the black line that marked the edge of the wood, and there was no sign of the fey at all.

"Perhaps," Ben suggested as they walked, "we should use another spell. It will hide us from view, just in case the wizard is searching for us."

"What if the bird you talked about is looking for us? Won't that hide us from it?"

"Bollocks. That's a good point." Ben scanned the landscape. "What's worse? Being captured by him, or not meeting our potential rescuer?"

"The latter." Stan didn't hesitate. "As much as I'm excited to be on this mad adventure, I'm also beyond terrified to think we might actually be stuck here. I'm also worried about White Haven. Our only way of getting back is finding someone else to help us. Save your spells for when we really need them."

Ben studied Stan's determined stride and resigned expression. "You seem to have accepted all of this quite well. Witches in White Haven, spells, magical mist. Fey."

"I dress in Druid's robes and officiate at the town's pagan celebrations. I give libations to the Gods. What did you expect? That I'd scream and run for the hills?"

"Actually, yes. The celebrations are good for the town. They bring in money. I presumed you did all this for show."

Stan shot him a look of disdain. "While I admit that it is indeed lucrative, I love magic and witchcraft. It makes far more sense to me than many other things. I joke with Avery about her witchy past, but I have always wondered about her. I thought perhaps it was something far less powerful than it seems to be. Who *are* the witches in White Haven, anyway?"

"I'm not saying. I respect their privacy too much. Just know that they are good people."

"I know one of them is Avery. It has to be. She has this..." he wafted his hands around. "An air of old knowledge and power. I also think Briar is, from Charming Balms Apothecary. Her products are just too good. She looks like a piskie. And after the conversation I had with El who owns The Silver Bough, I reckon she is, too. I feel bad about that. Any more?"

"My lips are sealed. What happened with El?"

"We had an argument about the mist and cancelling the festival." He looked sheepish. "I was in denial. Thought the mist had been made up. I feel a right fool now."

Ben had managed to have a long chat with Stan around the fey fire, and had fully caught up with what had happened in White Haven during his absence. At least, as much as Stan knew. "Don't feel bad. It was a powerful spell. You were meant to forget."

They fell into an easy chat as they walked, and Ben was glad to learn more about Stan who he'd always liked, but presumed to be bumbling and affable. It seemed he was much more than that, and Ben was immensely grateful he wasn't alone.

It was getting darker now, and when they reached a shallow hollow, Stan paused to light the lantern given to them by the fey. It wouldn't give them much light, but it was better than nothing. Besides, too much light would be a bad idea. To keep out of the wind, Stan crouched, and Ben sat next to him on a rock, happy to rest his legs.

It was a good job they did, because out of nowhere, a sizzling bolt of magic whizzed over their heads, and they both dived for cover. Ben cursed himself. Too much chat meant he had paid less attention to their surroundings, lulled perhaps by the deep silence of the wild landscape that surrounded them.

Ben risked lifting his head, and saw a familiar dark figure on the rise, silhouetted against the bruised purple sky littered with grey clouds. Magic crackled around them, and Ben knew he would strike again. He reached into his pocket, grabbed the spell bottle he'd put there, pulled the cork, and hurled it at the wizard. He uttered the spell to break the glass, and although it fell short, it was effective.

A blast of magical energy exploded beneath the wizard's feet, throwing him to the ground. Ben grabbed Stan, hauled him to his feet, and ran in the opposite direction. They stumbled back down the path, tripped over bushes, and fell down the hill. Light exploded above them, and the air pulsed with magic again.

Regaining their feet, they ran in a half crouch, trying to put as much distance between the wizard and them as possible, all while keeping the torchlight of the hillfort in sight.

But something else was happening. Ben realised it wasn't just the wizard's magic he could see. Someone else was there. Then another figure reared up ahead of them, yelling something incomprehensible, and gesturing for them to stay down.

Shouts echoed around them, and a rumble of magic cracked above. They didn't need to be told twice. Ben scrambled beneath the shrubs, Stan next to him, his heart pounding.

The noise seemed to go on and on, until eventually a gentle voice murmured close by, and someone tugged on Ben's elbow. It was time to sit up.

Torchlight flared above him, illuminating an old woman with long, grey hair, braided with beads. She wore a thick cloak and a long dress, and she gripped a staff. She extended her hand and beckoned them. Ben hoped it was to safety.

Chapter Twenty-Six

Alex had been nervous about introducing his dad to Avery, but he knew he shouldn't have been. His dad was easy going, and Avery was charming and clever, and within a few minutes, they were chatting as if they had known each other for years.

It was just after seven in the evening, and everyone was at Reuben's house, gathering themselves for the ritual ahead. He left Avery and his dad chatting, and went to find Reuben who was in his kitchen preparing snacks.

Alex eyed his friend from the doorway, amused. Finding his spirit animal had definitely given a boost to his magical self-confidence. Reuben, always upbeat and fully confident in himself in many respects, had changed over the last year. He'd become more assertive about his business, too, and it was good to see. He was chatting animatedly to a casually dressed Caspian. El and Briar were seated at the kitchen table with Oly. Oly shot him a narrow-eyed look of suspicion, and Alex knew he'd upset her the other day. *That was fine.* She'd upset him, too. He just hoped Oly wasn't about to pull the same trick with Egberk that night.

He joined Reuben and Caspian. "Where are we doing this, Reuben?"

"In the garden, like you asked. Although, we're likely to freeze our arses off." He nodded to the illuminated patio. "I've set up a bonfire on the bottom lawn, in front of the copse. It will be a big blaze. Magic will keep it burning for hours."

"Thanks. I don't think we'll get the same effect inside. I think outside, in the elements, is the best way to summon our familiars."

Caspian nodded. "I agree. Inside is too tame. I half wondered if you wanted to use Ravens' Wood."

"Not bloody likely," Alex said with feeling. "Not at night, at least. I did consider Old Haven Wood, but here is good enough. It's private."

"We're not really going to get naked, are we?" Reuben's face wrinkled with concern as he nodded to his groin. "It's a bit cold for the old fella!"

Alex laughed. "Of course not, you tit. What we need are lots of rugs and blankets. I brewed a potion that will help relax us, too."

"I told you; I didn't need that."

"But some of us might." The sting of his failure earlier still made him cranky. "You were in the water. Your happy place. Everyone needs to feel comfortable and safe tonight. Some of us may want to sit, others may need to walk. I brought a drum with me, too."

"So have I," Caspian said. "I've been reading up on the various ways to find your guide, as have we all, I'm sure. Drumming sets a steady, calming beat."

"I also have one, if anyone else feels the need," Reuben added. "How long will this take?"

"Hard to say." Alex considered his own experience. "It could be minutes or hours. I'm hoping that our connectedness around the fire means that once someone connects, the others will feel it, too."

"We're going to link, mentally?" Reuben frowned. "Won't that confuse everyone?"

"It will be more of an emotional link. Loose, only."

"I get it. A shared experience." Caspian sipped tea, rather than beer. A herbal mixture, by its scent. "We'll enhance each other, but allow for individual experiences." He looked at Oly. "I presume Egberk will not return."

"He'd better bloody not."

Reuben laughed. "El has banned the Ouija board, but I warn you," he leaned in, lowering his voice, "Oly wanted him. Thought it would be good to use someone she was already used to. Said he was already her guide. I'll keep an eye on her. I'm confident my horse will appear quickly. I can keep an eye on everyone, actually."

"In theory, then," Caspian asked him, "once we connect with our animal, we'll be fully aware?"

"Yeah, but it does take a bit of getting used to," Reuben confessed. "I guess everyone will be different."

Alex knew that tonight would be tricky, but it had to work. His ancestor had suggested it was necessary for the next stage of their fight, and although Reuben had found his familiar, he wasn't a teacher. Alex knew that was his job. His familiar, the wolf, suggested it, too. That was what it designated—a teacher and pathfinder. *If* that's what his familiar ended up being. He had read enough over the last twenty-four hours to know that sometimes familiars changed, depending on need.

He took a deep breath and exhaled slowly. "Okay. Let's do this."

The atmosphere around the campfire was electric as El took her place within the circle of witches, illuminated by a ring of candle-filled lanterns. Reuben had spread tarpaulins on the damp ground, on top of which were layers of blankets, cushions, and rugs, and El felt almost cosy in her thick clothing as she extended her fingers to the fire.

They drank the prepared potion as Alex outlined the plan, but only Reuben looked relaxed. While Alex led them in a guided meditation, Caspian and Reuben beat a rhythm on the traditional skin drums they'd brought with them. The sound mingled with the crash of the surf and the wind in the trees. In a startlingly short time, El lost herself in the bright flames.

She closed her eyes. The firelight was bright behind her shut lids, her cheeks warm, but her back was cold as the icy fingers of autumn brushed past her. She stiffened as Oly shuffled next to her, but taking a deep breath, and hoping Oly would behave, she opened her mind to the night.

In seconds, another energy joined them, bringing with it the sharp scent of brine and the crisp cold of the deep ocean. Reuben's familiar had arrived. *Stay calm,* she urged herself, *everything is as it should be*. Elemental fire reached out to her, and her magic responded. The drumming resonated through her very core, connecting her to the water-soaked earth, and the wind tugging at her clothes. All the elements sang together, weaving their creation around her.

Something else nudged her thoughts. Something huge and earthy. Something powerful. Hardly daring to breathe, El waited, opening her mind more fully. She felt hot breath on her cheek, a nudge against her ribs, and the scent of something musky.

The nudging grew stronger, and El resisted, fearing she would be knocked over.

And then a face manifested in her mind and she jerked backwards. It was huge-jawed, black-eyed, and had thick fur.

It was a bear.

Caspian continued to drum, although his mind was travelling far over Reuben's garden.

The night sky wheeled above him, the vast expanse of the universe making him feel insignificant. So gradually that he almost didn't notice, he became aware that his mind was floating higher and higher. A screech and a rush of wings had him twisting around, desperate to see the creature causing the disturbance.

It was a predator; intelligent, patient, and fearless. He could feel its power filling him up. He opened his eyes, or thought he did. He was hallucinating; he must be. The ground was far below him, the fire only a pin prick in a vast ocean of darkness. He was flying. But it wasn't witch-flight. It was something far different.

With an unexpected sureness that Caspian couldn't explain, he knew exactly what he was. His familiar was an eagle, and they had somehow bonded together.

He also realised something else. An ache that was seated deep within him, so constant that he almost never noticed it, had vanished. He felt as light as a feather. As if he would drift on currents of air forever.

He welcomed the feeling, and leaned into it.

Avery was no longer seated around the circle. She was instead sitting in the branches of a tree, watching the others. She could even see herself sitting utterly motionless—her head sagged forward on to her chest, her breathing deep and even.

Her mind, however, was fully alert. Spectacularly so. Her tiredness and indecisiveness had fallen away as soon as her familiar found her. It had taken seconds, as if he was waiting. *Of course, he was waiting. They had all been waiting. What were they so worried about? Their ancestors had prepared this. Somehow...*

The rest of the circle looked the same as she did—except for Reuben. He had mounted his water horse that was a shimmer of blue and green, even in the darkness. Every now and then the firelight caught it, reflecting off its watery substance. Nevertheless, despite its seeming impossibility, Reuben was riding across the grounds, low to his familiar's back, as sure-seated as any experienced horseman.

Caspian's drum had fallen to the ground, his hands now in his lap. However, Avery could still hear drumming; complex, steady, rhythmical. A screech high above made her stare upwards through the bare branches. Her keen sight showed another bird in the sky, one with a huge wingspan and a razor-sharp beak. *An eagle had come to play.* Even from a distance she could tell it was Caspian's familiar.

A snort drew her attention to the ground where she saw a huge bear lumber through the undergrowth, its musky scent almost overpowering her senses. Surprised, she recognised El's spirit with it. Like El, her familiar was strong and self-confident, but if Avery had been asked to choose a familiar for El, she wouldn't have been sure it would be that.

Avery couldn't see any other familiars yet, but her own, she was pleased with. She stared at where it was perched next to her. It seemed as big as she was. *Or was she smaller?* Avery couldn't tell. It cocked its beady eye at her, and ruffled its dark, slick feathers. A raven. She looked back over Reuben's grounds, seeing through her familiar's eyes. Danger and power were gathering over White Haven, and the moors and fields surrounding it. A web of shimmering connections that sparkled like frost on spiderwebs. Connections that reached through time and space.

Skuld's Net, or Wyrd's weaving. Or maybe it was Tiernan, twisting fates. Whatever it was, the warp and weft of time was being knitted closer, and with startling clarity, Avery suddenly saw a way forward.

Briar found herself in a thicket of trees, walking alongside a large, liquid-eyed deer that trod surefooted on the uneven ground.

With every step, she felt the deer's heartbeat settle to beat with her own. The deer led her along narrow paths, speaking of the moonlight and the earth, the tree roots beneath them, the trees settling down for winter, the leaf fall underfoot, the birds sleeping in their nests, and the small mammals burrowed beneath the earth; although, to be honest, not a word was spoken aloud.

Briar's familiar was gentle, and she offered a quiet space to walk and reflect, a space for healing. Healing that she knew she was ready for. She carried so much guilt. Guilt about Hunter, about Newton, about not knowing about her family. Briar knew that she spent so much time healing others, she didn't allow herself time to heal. Her familiar chided her, telling her that she wasn't being fair to herself. Briar was good at finding balance, and that sometimes meant being selfish.

Nodding, Briar took a deep breath, rested her hand on her familiar's warm, soft neck, and walked onwards.

Alex had never felt such a huge rush of power and energy, and it bubbled up through him until it escaped as a howl.

He threw his head back, as Alex the man *and* the wolf. The wolf's vision was his vision, and the dark shadows of the night came into sharp focus. He bounded over the fire with one enormous leap, and raced across the mix of wild and cultivated grounds that made up Reuben's garden. For a while he ran free, unhindered by his responsibilities. Then he slowed, allowing his mind to wander far from his familiar. He sought out the other witches, knowing instinctively that his coven had connected with their familiars, too.

Not only could he feel their elemental magic, but he scented their familiars and detected the wild intelligence they carried. Their ancient wisdom, deeply rooted in the elements.

His father was close by. Watchful, agile, sensitive, wise. A lunar creature who embodied secrecy and mystery. He caught the long ears silhouetted against the dark sky before he bounded away. *Hare*. A creature who passed through realms with ease.

But Oly... Alex sat on a rise, staring down at the circle of silent witches, locked within their own experiences. *Why couldn't he feel Oly when he could feel everyone else?*

And then he knew why. A creature of fire and smoke was twisting in the flames in the centre of the circle. A creature wearing skins and carrying a staff, whose feral grin was exultant as he stepped from the flames and onto the earth.

Egberk, the ancient shaman, had arrived.

Alex lifted his head and howled again, summoning his coven, before racing across the grounds. However, he knew he would be too late, and locked deep within his body, Alex couldn't summon his magic.

Egberk was striding towards Oly, his staff lifted high, ready to swing at her. And he wouldn't stop there. He would kill them all to take his freedom.

Caspian had already spotted the shaman emerge from the fire when he heard Alex's howl. Wings tucked in, he arrowed towards Egberk with startling speed.

Not knowing whether Egberk was flesh and blood or a powerful illusion—or even whether his eagle was as solid-bodied as he felt—Caspian aimed at the object that would do the most damage. *The staff.*

His familiar shrieked as it drew close, the sound enough to distract Egberk, and have him search the night sky for his attacker. But Caspian was too close to stop, and extending his wings, he struck Egberk across the face, and with his powerful talons, gripped the staff and wrenched it from his grasp.

He wheeled away, carrying it far from Egberk's reach, wondering what he should do next, when a huge bear burst from the undergrowth with breath-taking speed, hit Egberk like a steam train, and smacked him into the ground.

El couldn't control herself. Her rage and predator instincts took over.

As soon as she saw that Egberk had returned, and was marching towards her aunt Oly's helpless body, the urge to kill exploded from her.

Only one thing was fixed in her mind, and that was the evil man who had manipulated her aunt, and toyed with her need for knowledge.

She bounded out of the copse, leapt across the bodies of her coven that were in her way, and struck Egberk on the chest, knocking him to the ground. Before she could even consider her next actions, her huge, powerful paws with their razor-sharp claws ripped into him. She tore into his chest, shredding flesh, bone and organs, and the roar of her vengeance was like a mighty wind.

The screech of the eagle broke her trance, and she sat back on her enormous haunches. Caspian, in his familiar's body, perched on Egberk's head, staring at her with unblinking eyes. She heard his voice in her head.

It's over, El.

She shuddered, gasping at the carnage of Egberk's body beneath her, as the rage ebbed away.

What had she done?

Chapter Twenty-Seven

Kendall sipped her pint, wishing she didn't have to drive home. Sitting in the comfortable warmth of The Wayward Son, chatting to the locals, Cassie and Dylan, and Zee, was a nice thing to do on a chilly winter's evening.

It had been a hard, long day of reviewing video footage of the town, and sifting through interviews. They'd also had many reports of 'odd mist' that suggested that not everyone had suffered the hazy memory of Monday night, including herself. Clearly Stan's disappearance had rejuvenated that problem. She was still furious with herself for even thinking she could have imagined it. Moore had tried to reassure her, telling her it was the nature of magic. It hadn't helped. Instead, she'd felt even more powerless at having her mind violated. However, she appreciated that he tried. Moore was a good man, and a very good detective. He and Newton had welcomed her into the team, and now she couldn't imagine doing anything else.

She was perched on a stool at the bar, half-listening to local gossip, hoping to pick up something of use, whilst also listening to Dylan describe how he'd enhanced the image of Tiernan. *The man who'd caused all this.* In between pulling pints, Zee listened carefully, asking pertinent questions. She knew what he and Eli were planning to do later that night, and she didn't like it one bit.

A blast of cold air announced the arrival of another customer, and Kendall saw Eli enter the bar. Immediately, most women did a double take. To be honest, so did the men. Eli was astonishingly good-looking. His olive skin spoke of his foreign origins, which added to his allure. His jeans skimmed his well-muscled legs, and his t-shirt clung to his chest in all the right places. He rode an old bike, she knew because she'd seen him on it, and he was wearing a biker's jacket, the zip open, and a scarf around his neck. But it was his eyes that sealed the deal. They were a soft brown that matched his tousled hair. Whenever he looked at Kendall, she felt that no one else existed.

Kendall often drank in Alex's pub, and she had never seen Eli there. In fact, other than meeting him a couple of times—one of them being when he rescued them from the hunters in Ravens' Wood—she hardly knew him at all. To be fair, that was true of all the Nephilim. It was only Zee that she really knew. She steeled herself not to giggle like a schoolgirl.

He leaned on the bar, nodding in greeting at them all, but as soon as he saw Cassie, he beamed. "Cas! I haven't seen you for a while. Miss you in the shop."

She groaned and pouted. "Miss you, too. We've been so busy, especially now, with Ben gone..."

"We'll get him back. Right, Zee?"

"We will if this hairbrained scheme of yours works." In the seconds that it had taken Eli to cross the pub, Zee had already poured his drink, and he placed it in front of him. A neat whiskey that smelled of peat and the moors. "Here you go, something to keep the chill away later."

Eli settled himself on a stool. "Cheers. But if we don't try, we won't know. Besides, the dryad told us to come back. That means there's something to tell."

Kendall stared at him. "For a price. I don't like it."

He dazzled her with his smile. "Are you worried about me? I promise I can look after myself."

"I've seen you fight, so I know that." The image of his flashing sword, and his wings outstretched as he hovered in the pale green light of Ravens' Wood, still visited her dreams sometimes. "But I don't think she's going to ask you to fight. It's what else they may want that worries me."

Dylan shook his head. "Never make deals with fey."

"I know." Eli shrugged, unconcerned. "Not a deal you can't afford the terms of. I'm familiar with the ways of the fey. I live with one. She's very trying."

"To be fair," Zee said, leaning across the counter, "Shadow is blisteringly honest. I don't think all fey are like that. For all we know, dryads are more slippery than most. Unfortunately," he said, addressing the question Kendall was about to ask, "Shadow is overseas with my brothers, so we can't use her tonight."

Eli sipped his drink, his eyes closing as he savoured the taste before he swivelled on his stool to face them all. "Despite our doubts, we need to know where Ben is. Zee, you're the one who saw the old guy up there. That place on the cliff is a hot spot. I know it wasn't where Ben went missing, but we can't ignore it." He focussed on Kendall. "Do you have any leads at all?"

"No. None. I mean, obviously, we have insight into what's going on. We know it's a magical mist that seems to transport things through time, and that Wyrd and a bloody madman are involved, but the details elude us. Our focus right now is on keeping people safe." She slumped, deflated, on the bar. "We're failing at that. Despite Stan's disappearance, the council is refusing to cancel the celebrations. Newton tried again today. Visitors are flooding into White Haven. It's insane."

Dylan nodded. "It's like *Jaws* without the shark."

"Exactly! And look what happened there!" Kendall was exasper-ated. "At least the witches will be working their charm spell on the church bells later tonight. That's something."

"Well, we," Eli said, including Zee in that, "need to do what we can do."

Deep misgivings filled Kendall, and she knew Cassie and Dylan felt the same. They both looked grim, but resigned. "What will you offer in exchange for information?"

Eli just smiled enigmatically. "I don't know yet. I have a few ideas. What I am good at, though, is knowing what women want, and de-livering it."

Many men made this cocky claim; most of them were wrong. How-ever, Kendall did not doubt that Eli would deliver every time. She blocked out the unbidden images that flooded her mind, and hoped she wasn't blushing. Instead, she just raised her glass. "Let's just hope she wants what you can give her. For Ben and Stan's sake."

Ben studied the low-ceilinged room they currently found themselves in, wondering how the day could get any weirder.

He and Stan were being looked after by five very different individ-uals. There was the old woman with long, grey hair who had urged them to take cover, a young, black-haired man with green eyes, a middle-aged woman with a mass of brown curls, a man who looked to be in his forties with piercing blue eyes, a shock of greying hair, and a thick beard, and a young woman with dazzlingly clear skin and hazel eyes that seemed to look straight into Ben's soul.

However, they weren't the only beings in the room. A raven was perched on the back of a chair, and a wolf was curled up next to the fire. Ben knew that a bear, a stag, and a horse were outside because they had accompanied them on their walk to the low-roofed, stone building they were now in. *A bloody bear...*

The old woman pressed a cup of a hot, herbal drink into their hands, urging them to drink it in an unknown language.

Stan sniffed it and asked, "Do you think it's safe?"

"I think if they wanted us dead, it would have happened by now." Ben took a tentative sip. It was sweet and earthy. "Strangely pleasant, actually, Stan." He smiled at the woman. "It's good."

She smiled back, her bony hand patting his shoulder, then spoke to the bearded man. He was stirring a huge pot suspended over the fire. A cauldron. It emitted the rich smells of cooking meat. A stew, Ben hoped. The man nodded, but indicated the young woman with far-seeing eyes, who was preparing something in the corner of the room with the other two people.

Ben sipped his drink and absorbed the details. The room was long, a fire at one end in a proper stone fireplace, and candles in niches and on tables. Rudimentary wooden chairs were dotted about the space, and a table was positioned close to a stone wall. There were spaces for windows, but they were shuttered against the dark and the cold. Every now and again the wind rattled them, and the rain spattered against the roof. The beaten earth floor was covered in a thick covering of sweet-smelling rushes. Woollen blankets and thick furs were stacked nearby, ready for use, but fortunately the room was warm. An enormous pile of firewood lay chopped neatly in a corner.

The room, however, smelled strongly of animals, no doubt because of the room next door. Ben could hear them shuffling and snuffling, kept inside to protect them at night. Two beds were at the back of the room. A simple configuration, but comfortable and warm. Ben was pretty sure it belonged to the old woman, just by the way she moved around it, and he thought the young woman lived there, too.

What really struck him, though, was the fact that dried herbs were hanging from the ceiling beams, and the room was lined with shelves filled with clay and wooden pots, bowls, and stoppered jars. It reminded him of Briar's herb-filled back room in her shop, and Avery's attic. There were also collections of stones, feathers, twigs, and all manner of strange, natural objects. He was sure it was a spell room, not just a living space.

As another gust of wind and rain struck the building, Stan shivered. "We're lucky they found us. We would have frozen to death out there. Or been killed or captured by the mad man, of course."

"But what does he want, Stan? And do these people know? They must be witches, from what we saw earlier."

"Then why didn't they stop that man before? Rescue you?"

"I think he was too strong." Ben considered the chain of events. How he was dragged here, through time and space, drugged repeatedly so that he was confused and weakened, and then his mind was violated almost beyond bearing as he fixated upon the White Haven witches. And the mist, of course, that heralded the appearance of White Haven Harbour, and the other pockets he'd conjured that fortunately no one but Stan had emerged from. "He's searching for our witches, I'm sure of it, but whether to drag them here, or just kill them, I don't know."

"The woman you said you saw him talking to one night. Who was she?"

Ben shuddered. "I think I imagined it. He'd drugged me, remember? It's hazy. She seemed to glow."

"Couldn't you read her with your instruments?"

"I wasn't thinking straight. I could barely open my eyes."

Stan nodded and changed tack. "Why aren't we in the hillfort? Surely that would be safer."

"I've been wondering that." This building was on the moors beyond the small, enclosed village, not the destination they had been expecting. "From what I've read of wise women and men, they would often live outside of settlements, but maybe the others live there. It's hard to know what's out there in the dark."

They were interrupted by the young woman who finished her preparations, summoning their attention with a click of her fingers. She gestured them to watch her, and she carried the bowl to the other witches, and daubed their brow and lips with a dark substance. Then she carried the bowl over to them. She showed them the thick paste that was in it, and dipping her finger in it, she smeared some along her own brow and over her lips, and then gestured to Ben and Stan that she wanted to do the same to them.

Stan edged back, clearly suspicious. "What's that?"

The woman gestured to her mouth and her ears, and then gestured between them.

Ben nodded with understanding. "It's to help us communicate." He leaned forward to indicate his willingness, and in a few deft movements, she had smeared the cool paste on his face. Immediately he felt a tingling sensation sweep over him, and heard a buzzing in his head as if a swarm of bees had taken residence in there. "Holy cow!"

"What? Have you been poisoned?" Stan asked, horrified.

"No! It's magic. It's weird." As he was talking to Stan, words emerged from the buzzing, and he focussed on the group around the fire, a smile spreading across his face. "Herne's hairy balls. I can understand them."

The young woman smiled at him. "You understand?"

"Yes! It's brilliant!"

"A mixture of our magic and fey magic. One of their herbs." She turned to Stan. "Your turn."

Stan didn't hesitate, and within moments, he exclaimed, "This is amazing!"

The raven squawked and spoke too, and this time they both nearly fell off their chairs. His words, however, a strangely guttural sound, were not encouraging. "This won't work. They have no magic. They will not help our passage to the others."

The old woman huffed at him. "You're supposed to be wise and helpful. Instead, you moan, old man."

The raven rustled his wings. "I say the truth. You should listen, for once."

Ben interrupted what sounded like the bickering of an old married couple. "We will do anything we can to help. *Anything*. But do you think someone could actually explain what is going on?"

The man who was stirring the pot straightened and wiped his hands on a cloth. "We'll explain later, when we eat, but now, there is no time. Tiernan will want retribution for tonight, and he will strike quickly. It won't be just us he'll strike at, either. It will be your friends. Our descendants."

"What if we fail?" Stan asked.

"Then your future will cease to exist."

Reuben leapt from his horse's back and raced into the chaos that had replaced the calm of the circle.

He had been seconds away from stopping Egberk, but he was annoyed with himself. He'd said he'd pay close attention, and he hadn't.

He hadn't really expected Egberk to appear, though. He'd seen everyone connect to their spirit animals, each in their own way, and presumed everything was fine.

However, nothing by the fire looked as he expected it to. Egberk's ravaged body wasn't there, and yet he'd seen the man emerge from the flames, and he'd seen Caspian and El attack him. He particularly remembered El's bear ripping into the man's body. But of course, it wasn't Egberk's body. It was his spirit.

Now, Reuben couldn't work out if what he'd seen was an illusion or real.

Caspian's eagle, however, landed on the ground next to Reuben, even as Caspian stood and stretched, cramped after a long period of sitting. In another few moments, Avery's raven and Alex's wolf arrived in the circle too, but there was no sign of El's bear, Briar's deer, or Finn's hare. Everyone was stirring as their spirits returned to their own body. Even Oly.

Caspian stared down at where Egberk should have been. "I don't understand what's happening. I saw him fall. I ripped the staff from his hand. Now he's gone?"

"You don't have to tell me! I should have been here quicker. I said I would keep watch."

Caspian clasped his shoulder. "I don't think any one of us really expected it. I'm just glad I saw him in time." He looked around the campfire. "No staff, either."

"All smoke and flames, like him. I guess it was Oly's spirit he was trying to kill." Reuben shook his head. "I'm struggling to understand, too."

Alex crossed the circle to join them. "How the fuck did that even happen? That should not have been possible!"

"It was my fault," a subdued voice said next to them, and Reuben looked down on Oly, her eyes huge in her pale face. "I should have listened to El." El was still seated next to her, and Oly glanced at her apologetically, but El didn't respond, and Reuben knew she was angry. "I thought connecting this way to him would be safe."

"You almost got us all killed!" Alex was furious. "If you couldn't control him in a circle before, what's the difference now?"

"I thought *you* would be." She stared at Alex, imploring him to understand. "You're so powerful. I can feel it. You move between the realms with ease. Linking with you, feeling how you do it, made me think I could manage him this time."

Alex took a deep breath, obviously trying to control his anger. "We were connecting to our familiars. That was the point."

By now everyone was fully awake, watching the exchange, but they stayed seated. Reuben crouched next to Oly, feeling that standing over her was intimidating. "Are you okay, Oly? You look terrified."

She took a deep, shuddering breath. "I was. I'm so sorry." She looked at El again. "Thank you for saving me."

El's expression softened. "I'm just pleased that you're okay." She studied her hands, turning them over. "I can still feel it. Where I ripped into his flesh. That was too real. It was horrific. But, it actually wasn't flesh, was it? I'm just glad I stopped him." She rolled her shoulders and her spark returned, a flash of fire in her eyes. "I've never felt so powerful in my life. I was a bear. An *actual* bear!"

The circle was in shock, it was obvious. Every single one of them. Reuben had made a joyful connection to his spirit animal and now felt fully grounded with him, but it wasn't the same for the others. Reuben was still crouched next to Oly, and he gestured for Caspian and Alex to sit again. Standing over her wasn't helping anyone.

He raised his voice to address them all. "Egberk's appearance was an unfortunate end to a great experience. You all connected to your familiars—except for Oly, who will eventually do so, I'm sure." He squeezed Oly's hand. "Take a moment to appreciate it. To enjoy it. We have just shared a powerful moment, and we're all safe." He smiled, unable to contain his pleasure at what they'd all achieved. "This is what we wanted, and thanks to Alex, we did it!"

"Thanks to our ancestors, too," Avery said. "They were waiting for us. It happened quickly."

Reuben shook his head. "Not as quickly as you might think. It took an hour for it to happen."

Avery's eyes widened with surprise, and the others murmured their disbelief. "Seriously?" she asked. "It felt like minutes."

"It wasn't. I was riding around for a while waiting for it to happen, and keeping an eye on you all." He checked his watch. "It's close to nine o'clock already. You had an hour with your familiars."

Alex raked his hand through his hair. "I shouldn't be surprised. I lose hours in my spirit state. I suggest we head inside, drink some restorative tea, and eat. Then we need to get to the church."

"I don't think so, not yet," Finn said. He was sitting cross-legged, elbows resting on his knees. "Like Reuben said, we achieved a great thing tonight. I would like to repeat it. Hopefully it will happen quicker this time. We need to get used to this, and it's safe to do this together. Communally. I like it. We should also help Oly find her familiar." He stared at Alex, appealing to him.

Oly looked uncertain. "I don't think that's a good idea. I'll leave you all to it."

"No." Alex stopped her. "My dad's right. We achieved something great tonight, and I know it was different for all of us, but I loved it. If we're to be truly successful, then you need to do this with us, Oly. I'll help. I'll sit next to you."

Avery spoke again. "I need a coven of nine to defeat Wyrd and the wizard. I suspected it before, but I know it for sure now. Our ancestors, through our familiars, will help us."

"Are we sure that Egberk has gone?" Caspian asked, staring at the fire, as if he would step out of it again.

"I am," El said. "Very sure."

Oly swallowed. "Oh yes, he's gone."

"Okay, then." Alex relaxed, and once again, he looked eager. "Let's do this again, but only for a short time. You'll wake us up, Rueben?"

"Sure." But this time, he'd stay seated in the circle so he wouldn't miss a thing.

Chapter Twenty-Eight

Zee had a very bad feeling about meeting with the dryads, but nevertheless, he accompanied Eli back to Ravens' Wood. Afterall, he could hardly let him go alone. Once they reached their designated meeting place, the wood nymphs slipped from the trees and surrounded them.

Zee doubted that they would hurt them, or even try to. Despite the fact that they were magical creatures, born in the heart of a tree and bonded to it for as long as the tree lived, from what Shadow had told them, they didn't cast spells or harm anyone. They were essentially elemental earth creatures, whose role was to care for the tree and the grove that it grew in. They didn't age either, no matter how old their tree might be. *However*, he thought as he studied them, *they were also beautiful women with an alluring sexuality*. One he was certainly not immune to.

Eli had opted to take the lead once more. "Thank you for meeting us again. You honour us with your presence." He swept low in a respectful bow, and Zee followed suit. "Have you found the information we require?"

"We have some news, but I fear it will not help you."

"Any news will be useful."

"You have a gift to offer?"

The others swayed and drew close, faces upturned, as Eli said, "I have been thinking about this, and about where you live. Your lands on this Earth are smaller than they once were. You are restricted to this wood, and only the centre of it. Once upon a time, your lands spread far and wide."

The dryad gave Eli a knowing smile. "We do not seek to acquire land. There are many forests in the Otherworld. Deep, dark forests with tangled hearts, mossy grounds, and clear streams that dance amongst our roots. Those glades are ancient beyond all reckoning."

"But," Eli said, not backing down, "I believe that your contact with the Otherworld is limited. Shadow, the fey warrior, says so. This is a borderland, full of fey magic, but you do not have full access to it. Isn't that right?"

"That is true, but nothing you can offer will change that. It was the Green Man's will that we should be here. A token of what once was. There are enough of us, and the other creatures, that we are not lonely." She stepped forward, laying her hand on Eli's chest again, but this time he was wearing a thick top. Both of them had decided that prowling around Ravens' Wood half naked was not a good idea. "Besides," she continued, "the great Goddess and her consort visit us. With every passing day, the Otherworld magic spreads a little farther here."

Zee's ears pricked up. *Did it?* That was news to him. *Alarming news.*

Eli continued, regardless. "What we propose is that, with your blessing, we will take young saplings, with dryads, from here, and plant them in old forests. It will give you a chance to repopulate our forests. Wouldn't that be something?" Eli's eyes sparkled with pleasure. "Dryads would once again dance under a moon that hasn't seen dryads in centuries. That would be a good thing. This Earth needs a little more magic."

She glanced at her companions, but she didn't look convinced. "You would do that?"

"We would," Zee said, deciding he should be more vocal in supporting Eli. "We could plant whole groves. We know it would take a while."

"A lifetime," she answered. "There would need to be many in one place. We dryads are social creatures. We care for each other."

"Excellent," Eli grinned. "It's a deal, then."

"It is a start." Her words drove them both to silence. *So much for Eli knowing what women wanted and delivering it.* "What we really want is your guarantee of guardianship."

"Guardianship?" The words were out before Zee could stop them. "What does that involve?"

"Looking after us."

Eli's face was pinched in confusion, his reassurance now vanished. "How? You caretake your own trees, you've just said so. Plus, the paths in and out of here are confusing. People get lost. You make it so, we know."

"But that is the limit of our power. If someone chooses to cut down our trees, our options are few. That is how the forests were destroyed before."

"You have the Goddess and the Green Man," Zee pointed out.

"They come, they go. We need surety in this world. You will provide it."

Shadow's words were ringing in Zee's ears, and he hoped they still were in Eli's. "We cannot make any promises, but we will do what we can to keep this place safe."

"There are no caveats. This is sacred forest, dedicated to the Goddess, and it must remain so. When we need you, we will call upon you." Her voice dropped to a silky whisper. "You are powerful. Sons of the fallen spirits who walked here long ago. You two and your brothers walk between worlds. Only you can understand what it means."

"We cannot make decisions for the others, but we," Eli said, eyes narrowing as he looked at Zee, "will do what we can when you call us."

"You promise?"

Zee jumped in. "We do not promise the fey. What are the consequences of failure?"

She spread her hands wide, and the trees rustled, seeming to close in. "We will take you into the earth. You will become one with us, our fates intertwined. There are worse fates."

A cold sweat broke out on Zee's forehead at the thought of being swallowed by the mossy groves of the dryads, but Eli was already answering. "You have my word. I am a Nephilim. I do not lie on matters such as this."

"And you?" She turned her liquid eyes on Zee.

He worded his answer carefully, wondering if Eli had lost his mind. "I will do what I can to protect you and your trees, if it is within my power."

She nodded. "Good enough. I take you at your word. Do not cross us."

Zee leaned in, over the negotiations and wanting answers. "Do not cross *us*. We can be dangerous, too. Tell us what you know of Ben and Stan."

"I have questioned our elders. They remembered Ben and his help with the hunters. They said that he came here with an old man, centuries ago. Maybe millennia. They crossed into our world. The veils were thin then. The paths many."

"They were here, but they crossed to your world?" Zee didn't actually believe they'd get an answer, and this certainly wasn't the one he wanted. "They are lost, then?"

"*Listen*. They escaped from the Weaver of Time. The one who dances with Wyrd as he changes fate. He messes with that which should not be changed. They were lost, confused, in fear of their life. They lost their way in the dark. Fortunately, they were found by the fey hunters and their wolves." Her eyes took on a distant focus. "All good fey, now lost to this forest. They saved them. Brought them back through the twilight paths and took them to the far end of the forest so they could cross the moors. The elders watched them leave. That is all we know."

Zee tried to take it all in. It was astonishing.

Eli answered instead, clearly incapable of constructing a proper sentence. "They were here? Both of them? Together? Alive? And went where?"

The dryad laughed. "Across the moors. They sought the wise ones, from what was heard whispered in the leaves. One had appeared to Ben, calling him. A raven."

"A raven?" It sounded like madness. "Did they find the wise ones?"

"What happened beyond here is unknown to us. They never returned."

Something struck Zee. "But the Weaver of Time who danced with Wyrd. What happened to him?"

"We do not know. He was forbidden to walk these paths. His magic was not welcome here. We had the power then to banish him."

Eli asked, "So, the ancient magic that banned him still works now? I mean, you have essentially said what we thought. That part of this wood was the original one that was here then."

"It is. As I have said, this place was drawn from the ghosts of the ancient roots, and the Green Man brought that ancient magic back, too."

Zee and Eli exchanged a victorious look. This trip and their uneasy vows might have been worth it after all.

Briar was still feeling the exaltation of having met her familiar when they arrived at The Church of All Souls. Newton was waiting at the church for them, stamping his feet in the cold by the side door, and after reassuring him that they had been successful at Reuben's house, Avery led them inside.

The deer's healing words and gentle gestures had done much to calm Briar's uneasy mind, and while she always felt connected to the Earth and her mysteries, in the last few hours that had deepened. Even now, in the centre of White Haven's night-time bustle, she carried stillness within her. The image of dappled woods and leaf fall was vivid in her mind, and when she closed her eyes, she returned to the grove. Not even the stone of the church could dispel it.

Avery's introduction to James made her focus, and Briar shook his outstretched hand. "James, so good to meet you. Thank you for letting us do this."

She had seen James around the town, but had never been physically close to him. In the vestry, lit only by a couple of lamps positioned over his desk, he looked tired, worried, and very curious.

His gaze swept over her, and then over the other witches gathered in the room. "As I'm sure Avery has told you, I am open-minded, and fully aware of the mysteries and magic of White Haven. Only now, however, am I appreciating the full nature of that."

Newton snorted. "Trust me. It's the gift that keeps on giving."

James gave a low, nervous laugh. "I am happy to help keep White Haven safe, but it goes without saying that this is between us. My superiors must never know."

Alex said, "It is as much in our interest to keep this quiet as yours, James. Thank you. How do we get to the bell tower?"

"The stairs are to the side of the nave. I'll take you there. Just be aware that the steps are narrow and winding, and the space in the bell tower isn't huge, either. There are more of you than I expected."

Avery smiled apologetically. "There are normally only five of us, but these are exceptional times."

"I'll wait with you," Newton told James. "I want to make sure it's done."

"I was planning on waiting in the vestry." He eyed the witches a little defiantly. "I trust that will be okay?"

"Of course. You and Newton are welcome to stay," Avery reassured him.

He nodded, and without another word, led them into the nave, already decorated for the upcoming All Saints' Day with seasonal flowers and candles, and then to the door to the bell tower. "Here you go. I'll leave you to it."

"Thank you," Avery said. "I'll find you when we're done."

He cast them all another nervous glance, and walked away with Newton.

Once they were alone, Reuben asked, "Now what, Briar?"

She ran through the spell again in her head. "I don't actually need all of you upstairs. The spell is essentially the same as I used to make the amulets, just on a bigger scale, but it will encompass the church, too. I want to offer some protection to the whole building, not just trigger the bells. I think four of us upstairs, four down should do it." She had already decided whose skills would be better placed where, and said, "Avery and Caspian, I want you with me. Your air magic will work well to spread the spell over the whole building. I also want Finn with me. His skills echo yours, Alex, and I hope your psychic skills mean that you can link together."

Finn nodded. "I think we can manage that."

"Good. The rest of you need to be split by the side entrance, main entrance, and nave. Utilise the cardinal signs according to your element, as much as possible. And take these." She handed out candles that she had specially prepared, spelled for protection and imbued with herbs and oils. "When the spell is done, these will light. Then we need to leave them burning on the altar. The flame will never die. If they do, the spell is broken."

"Does James know that?" Reuben asked.

"Not yet," Avery answered, "but I'll tell him. They will blend in with the rest of the display."

"Good." Briar checked her watch and addressed the team who would stay in the main church. "Give me ten minutes to set up, and then start the spell down here. Hopefully, by then, Alex and Finn will be connected. If for some reason that hasn't happened, I'll call one of you. Okay?"

Reuben winked. "You can count on us."

Caspian led the way upstairs, and with every step it grew colder and colder, the occasional window showing how far they had climbed. Eventually they reached a thick door. Pushing it open, they entered the room below the bell tower, and saw the ropes dangling down from above.

"Six ropes, six bells. That's a lot of noise!" Caspian observed.

Finn's brow wrinkled with concern. "Are we sure about this? We could cause a whole lot more worry."

"The attacks on White Haven aren't going to stop," Avery reasoned. "We still don't know what's really at stake here, or how bad it could get. I don't think we have a choice."

"I guess I'm not used to using my magic on such a scale, but it seems, from the conversations I've had with Alex, that this is quite normal for you."

Caspian grunted as he led the way up the final stairs to the belfry. "I wouldn't say normal, but it has been necessary."

A strong wind whipped through the room that was open on all four sides, exposing the six bells within to the elements, but the view was incredible. Four arches framed the views across White Haven, showing the sea, the town and the moors. Lights twinkled below them, but the sight of a wall of mist advancing from the sea tightened Briar's breathing.

"Look. Is that sea mist, or something else?"

Avery squeezed her arm. "With our amulets quiet so far, let's hope just a mist. Come on. Let's get on with it."

Briar searched her bag for the remaining candles, herbs, and other ingredients, positioned the witches on all four sides, and took a deep breath. "I'm ready."

Dylan was crossing White Haven's main square, on the way to the church with Cassie and Kendall, when a strange, prickling feeling washed over his skin.

He stopped, sniffing the air like a dog. "Can you feel that?"

Kendall shook her head. "Feel what?"

"The build-up of energy. It's like what you feel when a storm is gathering." He searched around him, studying the people leaving pubs and restaurants as they strolled back home or to hotels. There was no mist. No strange, hooded characters who looked like they'd stepped from a fantasy book.

"Getting spooked, Dylan?" Kendall asked, eyebrows raised.

"Trusting my instincts. Cas?"

Cassie tucked her scarf into her coat, and shivered. "I know what you mean. There's a sense of expectation."

Kendall frowned. "I don't feel anything. Are you sure you're not just sensing the crowd? With Samhain only days away, there's a holiday atmosphere here." Her sharp eyes took in the passers-by. "Just high spirits."

Dylan quickened his pace, and so did Cassie. "Nope. It's more than high spirits. Maybe it's the witches magic at the church we can feel. Let's get there and see what's going on. James is expecting us."

They weaved through the crowds that thinned as they left the centre, and Dylan looked up at the bell tower as it came into view, a huge finger of stone that stood proud above the huddle of buildings. A flicker of orange light revealed the curve of the arches, and he quickened his step. They were already there.

Before they had gone half a dozen steps, a piercing scream sounded from the square, quickly followed by shouts. Kendall froze. "Shit. You were right. I'm going back to investigate. You two go on ahead."

"No way!" Dylan was not about to abandon Kendall to some strange fate, or the rest of White Haven. "Cassie, go tell the others and open up the church. If this is magical-bollocking-time-mist-related, we need a safe place, and the church will be it. Go warn them!"

Without waiting for a reply, he sprinted after Kendall.

"I must admit," Newton said to James over a cup of tea that he wished was something much stronger, "I didn't think you'd consent to this." He pointed above him, his meaning clear.

"I trust Avery, and I want the best for White Haven. They have come to its aid too many times to turn down this request. It would have been unchristian not to help."

"Even so. Magic in the church?"

"The church is built on pagan traditions and the old Gods and Goddesses. After all, what really is the difference between magic and a miracle? Nothing, except what you attribute it to. The lines were blurred back in Medieval times. Men like me, but far more fluent in Latin than I am, admittedly, were responsible for creating circles to summon demons. In order to battle the pagans," his eyes sparkled with amusement, "we embraced some of their beliefs. It was the only way to win over the masses."

Newton laughed, too. He liked James. He wasn't prone to hysteria or doom-mongering, and fortunately, he had a good sense of humour. "So, you're just doing your part in the present. Cementing relationships between witches and the church."

"It is all one under God, and I believe that some witches are Christians, too. However, as I said, I doubt my superiors would think so."

James fell silent as he stared out of the window to the dark night, and Newton strained to hear any noise from the nave. The sound of chanting, perhaps, or the static-like feel of magic as it rippled across the church. It had been a hard day, spent reviewing footage, going over interviews for anything that may help them, and sealing off the castle. He'd had to leave a couple of PCs on the carpark to deter anyone, and he hated to think of them up there now. They were as vulnerable as anyone to attack by the mist. He rolled his eyes. It reminded him of the 1980s film called *The Fog* that contained vengeful sailors out to kill the locals. He'd enjoyed that as a kid. Maybe he wouldn't have if he'd have known his life was about to imitate art.

The sound of running feet and a gust of cold air had him standing and heading to the office door, but Cassie was already there, eyes wide in her pale face. "Newton! There are screams in the town. Kendall and Dylan have gone to investigate."

Newton pushed past Cassie and headed to the side door. "I'll join them. Is it the mist again?"

"I don't know. Dylan said to open the church, just in case." She appealed to James. "We might need it if people need shelter."

"I don't know if the spell is finished!" James was flustered, but tried to appear calm. "We could be in danger here as much as anywhere."

"Oly was sitting by the side door," Cassie said, "but I didn't disturb her."

"Wait here," Newton instructed. "I'll go and check."

Leaving Cassie and James talking, Newton strode down the passage, passing a candle that was positioned on a small table opposite the side entrance, as yet unlit, with a silent Oly sitting next to it. Her eyes were closed, but her lips moved, and he realised the spell hadn't been completed yet. He passed her, and halted at the entrance to the nave. Unlike Oly, all the witches there had their eyes open. Reuben was positioned by the doors to the main entrance, El was at the base of the tower, and Alex was pacing around the periphery of the building. If they saw Newton, they didn't acknowledge him. He could feel their power magnifying; he was familiar enough with it now to recognise it, and silently, he urged them on, torn between wanting to run out of the door and staying to see if they were successful. This was a big spell, and success wasn't guaranteed.

His thoughts drifted to Kendall. He had lost one new sergeant already this year, and he didn't want to lose another.

Suddenly, the candles they had placed around the church lit without human intervention. The flames shot high for a few brief moments, and a feeling of peace and safety shimmered around him, along with the strong scent of herbs. A cascade of bells that Briar had warned would happen on completion sounded above, and Newton sighed with relief. *It had worked, but would it be enough?*

He hurried over to the witches as the ringing faded. "It's done?"

Alex nodded. "Let's hope it works."

"We'll soon find out. Something is happening in the town. Reuben, open up the doors. We might need this sooner than we thought."

Reuben made a swift turning movement with his hand, and the inner door to the hall and then the outer doors both flew open as he announced, "I'll come with you."

He had barely finished speaking when the bells rang again, but differently this time, just two of them; doleful, funeral, even. There was no doubt now.

They were under attack.

Chapter Twenty-Nine

Avery held her hands over her ears as the two bells started tolling again. She stared across the town's rooftops, horrified to see a thick bank of the mist sweeping into the heart of the town.

Before it had been patchy, but now it moved like a predator, slowly and surely. White lights that flashed like tiny lightning strikes rippled through it, and the sounds of screaming carried to them.

"What the hell is in that mist?" Finn asked, horrified. "It looks like it's alive."

"I don't know, but we have to stop it," Avery said, instinctively summoning air, ready to fly. "Caspian? We can be there in seconds."

"No." Briar's hand shot out and clutched her arm. "Not that way. We work from here."

"How?" Avery was flustered, not thinking straight. "We've protected the church and sounded the alarm, but no one out there knows about it! They won't know to come here! Even if they did, they won't have time!"

"You going down there won't change that," Caspian said. "Briar is right. We have a great position up here. Let's see if we can stop its advance. The attacks are usually short. We just need to frustrate him long enough until he's exhausted."

"A defensive spell?"

He nodded. "If we work together, we can create it here, and push it forward, like a dam, using wind to really get behind it."

"He's right," Briar said. "You two are air witches. It's perfect."

"I like that suggestion." Finn started to look hopeful. "Battling your onslaught might exhaust him more. Like Alex, I also have strength with elemental fire. You can draw on that."

"And my earth magic," Briar added. "I can ground the spell."

Avery nodded, suddenly clearheaded as she remembered her earlier revelations in Reuben's garden. "I don't think we'll need either of you." She looked to Caspian for confirmation, and he murmured his agreement. "What would help are markers to create a boundary. Something to anchor our spell to. We are going to weave our own protection, like a net across the town. No, something better. A net to catch him with!"

"Now?" Finn asked, wide-eyed with confusion.

"No. Right now, we have to manage the threat. But later, I know what we need to do, and it will take all of us. Plus Helena, and my grandmother." Resolve flooded through her as she considered the necessary tools and ingredients. "Go and join the others, but be careful." Avery turned away to survey the mist, and standing next to Caspian, felt his magic already reaching out.

It was time to begin.

Eli headed towards the edge of Ravens' Wood with a spring in his step. They had valuable news about Ben and Stan, and had confirmed that the forest in some way offered protection. *Perhaps the witches could use*

that in a spell. The only downside was their promise of guardianship, but he was sure it was something they could achieve.

Zee was not as certain, and he was making his feelings about it very clear. "We have very likely sworn our futures away to those bloody dryads. Guardianship! I hate to think what Shadow will say."

"You worry too much."

"And you're nuts if you think this will be—" He fell silent as they stepped out of the trees and into the castle grounds. "Herne's steaming balls. Things have exacerbated."

A dense swathe of mist cloaked the cliff edge and the harbour below, and was advancing across the town. Lightning crackled within in it. Two figures down on the carpark were retreating, their car already lost in the mist.

Eli pointed them out. "The police officers. They're stuck! We need to bring them here."

"They won't like that."

"They'll prefer it to the alternative, I imagine."

"What if we fly into the mist? Do you think it would take us to Ben and Stan? We could help from that end."

"So the witches would have to find us, too?" Eli couldn't believe Zee had even suggested that. "What about what we've just found out? How would we tell them that? Is this an attempt to get out of guardianship?"

"No!"

"Stop making stupid suggestions, then. Besides, Gabe will kill you—if the mist doesn't."

"All right." Zee looked frustrated. "I don't feel like we're helping enough, that's all."

"We're helping plenty. Let's rescue the police, and then we'll see what else we can do."

El stood on the pavement outside the church, looking towards the town. The church was on a slightly elevated position, and from here she could see the crackling force of the mist advancing above the roofs, swallowing building after building in its wake.

This was far worse than it had been before. She sensed real malevolence within it. *What would it feel like to have it surround you? Would it hurt? Would she be displaced in time and place, carried far from her friends, like Ben and Stan? Or were they dead? Was it just wishful thinking to hope that they were alive somewhere, but in trouble?* So many questions. In such a few short days, their whole lives had been turned upside down, and White Haven was being threatened like it never had before.

A stream of people were fleeing ahead of the mist, some giggling, but most were scared, and Alex and Reuben urged them on from their position further down the road, pointing to the church. It was obvious, even to the most sceptical, that something very odd was happening. Newton was now lost to view, having headed into town after Kendall and Dylan.

James's voice jolted her out of her reverie as he shouted, "This way! The church is open."

She shouted too, urging people to come, while Oly stood at the door next to Finn, welcoming the growing crowd into the church. El was relieved that her aunt had found her familiar on their second session, an inquisitive fox that she was thrilled with. Briar was inside, her gentle manner and welcoming demeanour doing a lot to reassure everyone. The herbs and oils that burned in the candles, along with the protective magical spell, did much to create a sense of harmony and peace, and the setting itself helped.

Only the depressing tolling of the bell displaced that, as if already mourning the dead.

Alex pushed his way through the crowd, Reuben next to him, and in minutes, the advancing wall of mist was visible at the end of the road. The town square that lay beyond it had vanished.

By now, most people had already fled, with only a few stragglers emerging from the lanes to either side. Alex took the time to direct them to the church, and then spotted Newton, Kendall, and Dylan further down. *At least they were safe.*

"This is insanity, Reu. What the hell is happening inside it?"

"I'd rather not find out."

"Maybe we should. Maybe it would give us some real insight into what magic he's using." Alex voiced what he'd been thinking all day, and what his tiny, ringing amulet bells seemed to be telling him. "I feel like a coward for not going in there."

"You're not a coward. You're being sensible. You can't fight it if you're not here." Reuben glared at him. "And we need you, so don't give it another thought."

"An hour ago I felt fantastic because we'd connected with our spirit animals, but how can they help us here? I can't even feel my wolf anymore."

"They aren't meant to help in this way. They're spirit guides and helpers, not charging warriors!"

"So what was your horse doing yesterday?"

"Protecting me." Reuben studied the mist ahead. "That's too big for him to deal with now. I'm not in direct harm right now, either."

Suddenly, a strong blast of magic ripped through Alex, and he rocked on his feet. "Fuck! That's Caspian and Avery!"

Reuben didn't answer, too intent on watching. It was clear when the spell had reached the mist. It lit up as if it was electrified, throwing sparks and forks of lightning ahead of it. Without speaking, he and Reuben sprinted the short distance to reach Newton and the others.

"Get back!" Reuben shouted. "This could get messy!"

Kendall's eyes were wide, her mouth open in horror. "What's happening?"

"A meeting of magic," Alex explained, grabbing her arm and pulling her away. "Dylan, come on!"

While the others retreated up the street, Newton didn't budge. "It's taken the lower half of the town. All of it! Look!" His hand swept in front of him.

He was right. As far as they could see, the entirety of White Haven from this point had gone. His pub, El's flat, and even their house had disappeared. A jagged finger of lightning leapt out of the mist and struck mere inches from their feet.

Alex pulled Newton back. "Staying here will not stop it."

Newton allowed himself to pulled back a few feet, but then stopped again. "This isn't just about you witches. It's about all of this place. He wants to wipe it from the face of the Earth." He stared at Alex, eyes narrowing with suspicion. "What the hell did you do to make him hate you so much?"

Alex felt the accusation like a punch. "It wasn't *us*! It was our ancestors. And whatever they did, they must have had a good reason to do. Some people don't need much of an excuse to wreak havoc, Newton!"

Electricity was now crackling in the air between them and the wall of mist, and not all of it was caused by magic. Alex knew Newton was worried and scared. They all were, but accusing him was not helping. They retreated again, both furious with each other. And to make matters worse, the mist edged forward again.

Caspian and Avery's magic wasn't working.

A wild wind whipped around Caspian as he stood next to Avery in the bell tower, his attention focussed on Tiernan's magic that crept insidiously closer. They were failing, and the continually tolling bells with their mournful clang only reinforced that knowledge.

He drew even more power up through the stone beneath his feet, magic that had once been deep within the earth. Grounded, he then drew on more elemental air, feeling it fill his being so that he was as light as a feather in the vastness of the universe. Hands outstretched, he forced that energy out again. Avery wielded her power with just as much skill as him, and together they attempted to stem their enemy's advance. But something extra seemed to be powering it, and they were not making progress.

The sudden shriek of his eagle overhead broke his concentration. It appeared out of nowhere, arriving so swiftly that he hadn't felt its approach. It swooped down and landed on a roof near the advancing mist, and looked back towards him. Their eyes locked, and instinctively, Caspian knew exactly what he needed to do.

Focussing ahead, he said, "We need to change tack, Avery. Our dam isn't strong enough. We need to breach his wall. Bring the whole lot crashing down."

"Shatter it, you mean? Hit one spot?"

"Exactly. But we need to do it right. We'll have one chance at this for maximum damage. Once we breach it, we can get deeper, destroy it from within. That means I need to be closer."

"You mean *we* need to be closer."

"No." He glanced at her, seeing her face lifted towards him, a scowl marring her features. "You need to stay here, and funnel power to me. I will fly to the closest roof, and strike out from there. Agreed?"

"No, I do not agree! That's insane. You'll be too close."

He laughed, a feeling of exhilaration running through him, as well as amusement. Even though they were in a battle, she still argued. "It's a risk I'm prepared to take. We'll drop power for an instant when I fly. Can you cope? I'll be seconds only."

"Caspian! I haven't agreed to this!"

"Avery. You know that I'm right. We are failing. This is no longer a discussion. I'm going. And I know you won't let me down, because you never do."

"Caspian!"

"I'm counting down. Three, two, one…"

Chapter Thirty

It was so dark on the hilltop from the low clouds smothering all moon and starlight that Ben could barely see the witches gathered in the circle of which he would be a part. Stan was next to him, having agreed to take part in something they barely understood.

However, the implications for failure had been made clear. Already the first part of the older man's warning was apparent. What could only be described as a storm-filled fog was filling the valley that ran down to the sea, a valley that was now all too recognisable. Earlier, Ben was able to discern its shape clearly from their elevated position. It may look different with its wooded slopes, empty beaches, and winding river that ran through its heart, but he knew it was where White Haven was in the future. The river had either dried up or now ran underground, and the trees had been felled, but the shape of it, and the surrounding hills and moors, were unmistakable.

The crackling mist that Tiernan had been experimenting with for days filled the bottom half of the valley starting from the coast, and it was slowly advancing. Unfortunately, he was manipulating it all from some unknown, new location, and they were trying to find him. It would have taken him hours to get back to the house where Ben and Stan had been imprisoned, and the assault had started quickly.

"How are we going to stop him?" he asked the young woman with the far-seeing eyes next to him. He had yet to learn their names.

"With great difficulty. He draws on Wyrd's magic. A result of a pact we cannot break."

"I saw her, I think. She looked like a ghost." He recalled the woman's long, white gown and flowing hair. The threads that drifted around her in the wind. "They were arguing. Or that's what it seemed like."

"He has promised her his future in order to take ours."

"What? Why?"

"Because we frustrated him, and now he seeks revenge."

Ben hated vague explanations. He was a scientist. He liked reasons. "Frustrated him how? Something significant must have happened to trigger all this!"

She had been looking across the valley, but now she turned to him. "He served the tribe leader of this area, his magic earning him a place as his advisor. However, he fell from favour when he saved his own son. He manipulated events for his own ends, and other men died. It didn't help that we exposed him. There is more, but now is not the time."

It wasn't the level of detail that Ben really wanted, but he guessed it was better than nothing. To be cast out of a sheltered and protected position was bad enough at the best of times, but here, in this bleak world? And yet, the old woman lived outside of the hillfort, as perhaps the others did.

He still had more questions. "Why would she—Wyrd—make a pact with him? That seems mad!"

"Because he offered his life willingly when all this is over. The sisters weave all day and night, setting many paths for our possible futures, but *this* path was not written. To give up his life is bold, and it means he gives his power to her. Wyrd. She accepted that. But she does not offer to do all." Her lips twisted into a half smile. "That is not how Wyrd works. There are always choices, despite his manipulations. The question is, will we in the future make the right choices to set our path on track again? And how can we help them now?"

Ben's stomach was churning with the implications of her pronouncement. Her companions were frantically using their abilities to find the wizard, but she stood calmly looking on, her distant gaze unnerving and frightening.

"How can *we* help?" he asked. "I have no power, and neither does Stan. What are we even standing here with you for?"

"Because you carry the future. It is written in you. You are our link. Every time he tries to destroy it, he aids us a little more. See!" She pointed. "It is our connection. But it is also White Haven's doom."

Below, images of White Haven flashed in the mist. A roof, a row of houses, lights where the harbour was.

Suddenly, the young man with the black hair shouted. "I have found him!" He slammed his hand down into the earth, and a huge crack resounded beneath Ben's feet. Stan staggered and almost fell, but Ben's hand shot out and steadied him.

"Now!" the old woman commanded.

The witches joined hands, and Ben and Stan found themselves a part of it. What felt like electricity rocked through Ben's body. Fire, air, water, earth, all combined in a heady mix of magic that made him feel that every single part of him was composed of the universe. It was as if his skin had dissolved and Ben had vanished, his very core channelled to the young man with black hair who funnelled that power down into the earth.

Ben could barely hang on to conscious thought. *Was it working? Was it enough?*

Avery watched Caspian vanish with a mixture of fury and anguish, and then felt his power vanish, too.

All her thoughts turned to holding the wind ahead of her. *Why had she refused Finn and Briar's offer of help?* She was stupid and arrogant! Then again, she had no idea that Caspian would do such an insane thing.

In a flash, Caspian appeared on a roof close to the mist. It had surged ahead in the split second that his magic had ebbed, and he was silhouetted against the crackle of light. A black figure struggling to control the elements.

Not stopping to second guess herself, she funnelled the wind at him, sending as much of her magic as she could with it. She was shaking. She could barely hold on.

Caspian didn't hesitate. He threw everything he had forward, and with a deafening crash, a blast of power hit the mist, punching a hole through it. He followed it up with spell after spell, and Avery tried to support him, but she was just too far away. *Where was her coven?*

Reuben was halfway up the street with Kendall and Dylan when he heard the enormous crack, and saw the raw, jagged hole blasted into the mist wall.

The explosion had thrown Alex and Newton to the floor.

He had no idea who had caused the damage, but knew what he had to do now. He thrust Kendall and Dylan behind him. The air was saturated with water, and he pulled it to him, and then punched it forward. The first shot went wide, but the second found its mark. His magic surged through the ragged opening and split it further.

Alex regained his feet and he blasted it with power, too. Reuben ran to his side, yelling, "Fire and ice! Follow me!"

The gap in the mist wall revealed a swirling vortex within it. Glimpses of White Haven's buildings could be seen inside, and hopefully people were sheltering within them. They couldn't let the man behind this regroup.

He sent another jet of water through the opening, super-cooling it at the same time. The ice expanded as it entered the gap, mixing with water within the dense mist, and that also turned to ice.

Alex followed it up with a ball of fire and pure energy. It hit the ice like a cannon ball, and everything exploded. Chunks of ice shattered in all directions, the blast throwing all three of them into the closest building. They fell, crumpled on the ground.

However, it had worked. The mist shattered, ripples running through it, lightning popping and flashing as it petered out. Shops, flats, and roads finally came into view, but they were scarred. Black welts marked stone walls, and a few windows were shattered.

Then Reuben spotted something else. A figure was on the ground, on the edge of where the mist had been, unmoving. A figure that looked horribly familiar.

He gained his feet as if in a dream, aware that the mournful tolling had stopped, leaving an unearthly silence in its wake, and before he'd even reached the man's side, he knew it was Caspian.

Briar didn't know she could run so quickly, but as she rounded the corner into the lane and saw her friends crowded over a figure on the ground, she sprinted as if death itself was chasing her.

Perhaps it was.

She skidded to a halt next to Caspian's body. Reuben and Alex had already laid their hands upon him, Alex leading them in a healing spell, but it wasn't anywhere near powerful enough. She could feel Caspian's ebbing energy. His skin was pale, and blood was pouring from a wound on his head, but there was no obvious sign of broken bones.

Briar edged in next to Reuben. "Let me."

Briar had many healing spells at her disposal. She knew it was one of her roles in the coven. An important one. She placed her hand on Caspian's head, detecting the trauma within. She immediately cast her most appropriate healing spell to stem the bleeding and knit his flesh together, half listening to the conversation around her as she worked.

"Where did he come from?" Newton asked. "He wasn't here with us!"

"He wasn't with us, either," Kendall said.

Alex rocked back on his heels, watching Briar. "That's because he was with Avery, working on the spell to stop the mist advancing. I don't know why he's here."

"Because he was willing to sacrifice himself to save us," Avery said from behind them all. She had arrived in a whirl of witch-flight, and quickly joined Briar. "Is he alive?"

"Barely." Briar was too focussed on healing Caspian to say anything else.

"He left you?" Alex asked, confused.

"Yes. He flew to the roof above us. We were having no success with our spell. We were barely containing it." She took a deep, shuddering breath. "His plan was a good one, though, and you two helped him. I saw it all from the bell tower."

Reuben grunted. "Not good enough to stop him from getting injured."

Briar knew she had achieved as much as she could in the street. "I need to get him home. Avery?"

"I'll take him, and then I'll come back for you." In seconds, she and Caspian had vanished.

Reuben nudged Briar. "Do you need us?"

"Not yet. I'll work better alone, and I have my tools in my house. If I need you, I'll call. You need to go to the church. It's chaos there."

"It's chaos here, too," Dylan said, interrupting them. He pointed down the street to where a few people were exiting their flats and homes, clearly in shock. "I think we need to round a few people up."

Newton straightened, all business. "Let's get in there and see what's going on. Kendall, you're with me."

"Us too," Cassie said, speaking for her and Dylan.

Briar focussed on the damage for the first time since she'd arrived. Some of the buildings were blackened, windows shattered, and yet she couldn't concern herself with that yet. She had a long night ahead of her, looking after Caspian.

Avery returned in seconds, impervious to the fact that others might see her. Her face was all hard planes, etched with concern. "Briar. Let's go."

El moved amongst the people gathered in the church, offering reassurances, and feeling like she had just witnessed an apocalyptic event.

Oly, Finn, and James were similarly engaged, and although El knew it was important to make sure everyone was all right, her thoughts were filled with fear about her coven and the rest of White Haven.

As soon as she had heard the thunderous crash, she ran onto the street, witnessing the storm-filled mist breaking up. Briar had run past her, but El returned to the church, torn between wanting to help her coven and look after the people gathered within.

Fortunately, and in a typical White Haven manner, most people seemed more excited than terrified by the weird events. Once in a safe place and able to talk to others, fear had been replaced by curiosity. No doubt many visitors were here anyway because of their interest in the paranormal. The locals took it all in their stride. It was only a few that seemed genuinely distressed, and now that the bells had stopped tolling, word spread that whatever had occurred was now over. People drifted away, back to the streets, despite El urging them to stay a little longer.

She found Finn as he ended a conversation with an older local man, and he turned towards her. "Any news on the others?"

"No, but I'm heading out now. I'm worried sick."

Finn cast a worried glance around the church. "I don't feel I should leave James just yet. There are still too many here. Besides, he looks quite shook up, too."

"Thank you for staying, but I can't wait. Keep an eye on Oly?" She was in the middle of what looked like a very intense conversation with another woman.

"Of course. When you find Alex, will you call me?"

El left him with her reassurances, and hurried out into the street. She had only covered a short distance when something caught her eye up on the hill to the left of the town. A couple of the streets seemed to shimmer, and for a second, she couldn't work out why. And then she realised they were veiled in some of kind of net.

Part of the town appeared to be vanishing.

Zee stared, horrified, at the shimmering part of White Haven, all too obvious from their position by the castle.

"Bloody Hell, Eli. Look at that. We need to get down there."

Eli nodded. "So do the PCs. Newton will need all the help he can get."

For the last half an hour, they had sheltered at the edge of Raven's Wood, only emerging when the mist had vanished with a thunderous crack that sounded like White Haven had been swallowed into the earth. To see at least most of it still there had been an enormous relief.

PC Kevin Whitehall, now known as Kev after their enforced time spent together in the wood, said, "It's pointless for us to stay here now. The mist has vanished from the cliff."

Zee had been so transfixed by the town, he hadn't noticed. But Kev was right. Whatever had banished the mist in the town had banished all of it.

The other PC, Hamid Singh, was equally keen to leave. "Yeah, Kev, let's go. But what is *that*?" He pointed at the mirage of streets.

Zee stumbled to find an explanation. "Maybe a kind of power outage?"

"That does that?"

He shrugged. "Maybe."

Hamid looked at him with suspicion before addressing Kev. "Whatever it is, I imagine there's a fair degree of chaos down there. We need to be on the streets. We might find out more there than we can here." He cast an amused grin at Eli and Zee.

The PCs, both of them observant and resilient, had questioned him and Eli as to what was really going on while they sheltered in the wood, and neither could be put off. Zee found that he liked them, but even so, he and Eli lied—a lot.

"Can we offer you a lift?" Hamid nodded to the carpark. "How did you get here?"

"We parked on a back lane," Eli said quickly. "We enjoy a night-time walk."

Hamid just smirked. "Sure you do. Come on, Kev, before Newton gets all worked up."

Eli and Zee watched them leave, and Eli laughed. "He thinks we're gay and came up here for a tryst. Which, you know, is fine."

Zee rolled his eyes. "Anyone who knows you, knows that you keep a harem on call day and night. Let's give them a few minutes to get out of sight before we fly. I can do without those two knowing we're Nephilim!"

Newton stood in the middle of White Haven's main square feeling utterly dejected and defeated.

Most of the town might be still standing, but it looked battered around the edges. Worst of all, a patch of the town was shimmering like it had a force-field around it. He couldn't see it earlier, but in this spot, it was all too obvious.

"Can you stop it?" he asked Alex and Reuben next to him.

"Not right now, we can't." Alex looked as dejected as Newton felt. "Of course, we'll try, but we don't know what's causing it."

"What about the people who live there or work there?" Newton was suddenly furious. "What about them? Poor buggers! What if they're dead?"

"Let's not jump to conclusions," Reuben said. "I have a solution—short-term, admittedly. We can do a glamour spell. An illusion to make it appear normal. But you have to cordon it off."

"I don't want a bloody illusion! I want it back to normal!"

"And so do we!" Alex exploded. "Herne's fucking horns, Newton! *We* didn't cause this. If it wasn't for us, the whole fucking place might look like that."

"Because of something your bloody ancestors did!" Newton resisted poking Alex in the chest. In fact, he had to make a conscious effort to unclench his fists.

Cassie had been taking readings with her ever-present thermometer and EMF meter while Dylan filmed, but now she pushed between them. "Stop arguing like bloody school kids! I have had to deal with Ben being missing for days! We will solve this." She turned to Reuben. "Your suggestion is a good one. Do it quickly, before anyone else notices."

"Notices!" Newton thought he was hearing things. "It's *glowing*!

"People are shocked right now. They're focussing on their immediate surroundings. They'll think they were imagining things! Cordon it off! Say buildings were damaged, and then focus on the rest of the town."

"And the people who live there and who are now stranded in town?"

Cassie floundered. "Well, they will need other options."

Kendall stepped in. "I've called Moore and the PCs. They're on their way."

Newton had forgotten about his PCs. "Are the PCs okay?"

"They sheltered in Ravens' Wood with Eli and Zee, apparently."

"They were safe there?" Alex asked.

"Course they were," Dylan said, butting in. "And with luck, they'll have news from the dryads. We all need to meet to plan our strategy. Soon."

"Tomorrow," Reuben said. "Nothing else will happen here tonight. Our enemy will be licking his wounds, like us. Let's get this illusion done, Alex. Then we can work on the next plan."

Chapter Thirty-One

Caspian woke up feeling as if a vice were clamped around his head. He eased his eyes open and immediately wished he hadn't. The light was horribly bright, and he groaned.

A hand came to rest on his, and gave it a gentle squeeze. "You're back. Thank the Goddess."

He smiled, eyes still closed. "Thanks to you, you mean. Have you saved me, Briar?"

"Yes. *Again.* Can you please stop putting yourself in danger?"

He opened his eyes, squinting, but this time was relieved to find it didn't seem so bright after all. "Where am I?"

"In my spare bedroom. Sorry. The bed is a bit small for you."

He finally focussed on her. Dark shadows were beneath her eyes, and her hair was piled on top of her head in a crazy, tangled mess. "You haven't slept. Sorry."

"Oh, dear. It's that obvious?" She smiled, but palpable relief was already chasing away her furrowed frown. "I actually thought you wouldn't make it at one point. You hit your head quite badly. Actually, that's an understatement. You nearly bashed your brains in. What happened?"

"That's a good question." He fell silent and stared at the low-beamed ceiling, trying to recall the pattern of events. It slowly filtered back. *The storm mist, the advancing wall like a tidal wave waiting to break...* Alarm flooded through him, sending a piercing jolt of pain through his head, but he still tried to sit up. "Did it work?"

"Lie down!" Her tone brooked no argument and he flopped back, already exhausted. "Yes, it worked. Very well. How did you fall?"

"As I struck the mist, a powerful blast struck back at me. I fell heavily, smacking my head on the roof tiles. Then I started to roll off the roof, and I did the only thing I could. I used witch-flight to take me to the street. I don't even know what part. I just knew I needed to be on the ground. It's the last thing I remember."

Briar sighed and leaned in close, her hand resting on his head again. Her scent washed over him. A rich, earthy, woody smell that was wonderfully Briar. "That explains how you have no broken bones."

"How is everyone else? Avery?"

"Avery is fine, but worried about you. Everyone else is well, too. Newton is just steaming around being angry." She huffed. "Nothing new there."

He risked a smile. "I was right, though. Well, me and my familiar."

"*What*?" Her mouth fell open with surprise. "You saw your eagle? Avery didn't say she saw it."

"Perhaps she didn't. She was too focussed on the problem. It appeared above me, out of nowhere, and landed on the roof, just as I was floundering for a way forward. I knew immediately what I needed to do."

"It led you into danger!"

"It *guided* me, just as it's supposed to do."

"I suppose so, but you nearly died, so don't get cocky."

"I can be a little bit cocky, surely." She frowned, so he decided not to push it. "So, what's our next plan?"

"There is no new plan for you!" She cocked her head, assessing him. "Do you think you're strong enough to work a big spell? I don't think you are."

"Avery needs nine witches! I need to be there."

"There are other witches we can call on."

Caspian felt bereft at being left out, and he struggled to sit up. Briar helped lift him, plumping pillows behind him, until he finally settled upright, glaring at her. "I'll be fine in a few hours."

"We need a witch who can fully control his powers. This has to work, Caspian, whatever it is that Avery has planned. And before you ask, I do *not* know the details. I do know that we have one chance to get this right before the mad wizard rallies and attacks again. You helped us win this round. You don't want to help us fail the next."

He stared into her calm, soft brown eyes that were filled with sympathy. "No, I don't, but I'm pretty sure you'll need me—and my familiar."

"I'm worried you're being reckless, and that's very unlike you."

"It wasn't reckless. It was a calculated risk, although admittedly, it sometimes feels like a fine line between the two. You don't manage a multinational company without being willing to take risks, but I judge well. I did this time, aided by my familiar. I just got caught by a rogue blast of magic."

She smiled. "I will concede that you were right. In fact, you were brilliant. So were Alex and Reuben. They were the ones who saw what you were trying to achieve. They found you on the ground."

"I must thank them later. And White Haven? It's okay?"

"Battered and broken. Part of it has vanished behind a sort of force-field. It's hidden behind an illusion spell, for now." She stood up. "I'll make you tea and soup. Only then can you get up. I'll let everyone know you're okay."

"What about you?" he called after her. "Are you okay?"

"I've been better, but I'll tell you more later. For now, rest."

With that, she closed the door, leaving him to work out how he could help the others.

When Alex woke up on Friday morning after a horrible, fitful night's sleep, he felt as if the events of the night before had been a nightmare.

Curled around Avery's body, he listened to the rain, wondering if he could sleep all day and pretend the outside world didn't exist. Except he couldn't. His conscience wouldn't allow it, and there was far too much to do. He needed to assess the damage on his pub, although hopefully, like the house, their protection spells would have saved it from the worst effects of the magical storm. A higher priority, though, was his staff.

After he and Reuben had completed the spell of illusion on part of White Haven, he had gone to the pub to check on them, and that's where he'd found Zee. Unfortunately, there had been little time to chat. Instead, they had comforted their shocked colleagues.

Avery stirred next to him, breaking his thoughts, and he nuzzled her neck. "Morning, gorgeous. Are you okay?"

She stretched and twisted within his arms to face him. "I'm so-so. What about you?"

"Shattered, and hoping last night was a nightmare."

"Me too, except we know it was all too real."

"Perhaps things will look better in daylight."

She gave a short laugh. "They won't. All those scorched buildings and sizzled pumpkins..."

"You know what struck me last night after chatting to my staff? That they thought they'd been caught in an intense electrical storm. There was no mention of magic! No comparison to the harbour events. That will work in our favour."

"Really?" Avery settled against him more comfortably as they talked. "They didn't see anything odd in it? Or feel anything?"

"They felt plenty! Said the air crackled with electricity. The power went out, and they were in darkness for ages. They locked the doors and kept the last few customers inside with them. Apparently, all they could see outside the windows was intense lightning strikes in the darkness. Marie said it was terrifying."

Avery's expression softened, some of the dread leaving her eyes. "That's great! I mean, it doesn't solve our problem of the missing streets, but we can spread that idea. Reinforce the fact that it was a crazy local weather event! How much of the town is affected?"

Avery had spent some time at Briar's place helping with Caspian, so she hadn't seen as much as he had. "A couple of streets, which is terrible, but it could have been a lot worse."

"What type of spell did you use?"

"An illusion spell. Something to make people's eyes slide right off the area. It should mean they sort of see it, but don't." He propped himself on his elbow as he looked at her.

"Could you step into it? Did you even try?"

"No." Alex shook his head, recalling how odd it had looked. "Dylan and Cassie took a few readings that showed the magical energy was high, but to be honest, me and Reu could feel it. We kept well away from the boundary, and Newton cordoned it off. He's so angry with me! Like it's all my fault."

"He's mad at all of us, and for good reason, too. It's our ancestors' fault. We have to take some responsibility for this."

"No. It's that madman's fault! Even though we antagonised him in some way, it doesn't excuse this. Last night, with our familiars, it just felt so good!"

"But I didn't feel connected to my ancestor, though," Avery said, puzzled. "I thought that was the point! That they would be a conduit to the past."

"Maybe it was too soon. Maybe it needs to be quieter—mentally. Or maybe we just need more practice."

"We haven't got time! We need to stop this today. With luck, his exertions from last night's attack will leave him weak. If we strike today, we could have the advantage."

"What if time works differently here?" Alex had been puzzling over this. "What if all of this is happening in a short time frame for us, but long for him?"

"We can't worry about that. We just have to act on what we know now!"

"What spell have you got planned?" He knew she'd been working on it for days, but she hadn't revealed any details beyond the fact that she needed nine witches.

"It still needs some refining."

"I think you need to hear what Zee and Eli have to say first." He smiled as he recollected their good news. "The dryads remember Ben and Stan. They're alive! And Ravens' Wood is protected from the crazy guy by ancient magic. Magic we might be able to use."

Avery shot up in bed. "That's brilliant. I need to talk to them!"

"You will. They're coming over around midday. I'm going to spir-it-walk again before then. See what energy I can detect over the town."

"Great. I'll have time to check the shop, and reinforce my protection spells." A frown crossed her face. "You know, seeing through the eyes of my familiar last night, in our trance state, I saw a web over White Haven. It was very different to how I saw energy when I spirit-walked with you."

That was different. "A web? What did it look like? Energy wise, I mean."

"It sparkled, like frost on a spider's web. It was Wyrd's weaving, I know it was."

"Or Tiernan's. Maybe both."

She shrugged. "Perhaps. Anyway, it made me think about my spell. About us weaving a trap. It sounds weird, and a bit half-cocked at the moment, but I think it will work. We need to find the weak spots, or anchor points for us, or something..."

She trailed off, and Alex smiled, knowing her brain was firing through solutions and spells. *His brilliant girlfriend.* He waved a hand in front of her eyes, and pulled her down to him. "Earth to Avery. Come in." He grinned as she giggled. "There's time for one more thing first."

Right now, he needed her body, her lips, her gentleness, and her fire. In a world of uncertainty, Avery was his foundation.

Avery couldn't miss how uptight Sally was when she arrived in the back room of Happenstance Books.

She was slamming mugs on the counter as she made coffee, cursing anything and everyone. Then she fished a tissue from up her sleeve and dabbed at her eyes. "I can't believe how White Haven looks! Everything appears to be chargrilled. Even the pumpkins on the streets!" Sally shut the cupboard door with a thump and rounded on Avery. "Was it really an electrical storm, or was it that maniac?"

Dan was also there, trying to keep out of Sally's way. "I think it was more than just a storm, Sally!" He looked speculatively at Avery. "Although, a storm would be preferable to the alternative."

Avery wished she could lie to them, but she couldn't. "No. It wasn't a storm, but that's what we want everyone to think. I would appreciate you lying to anyone who comes in today, talking about it. Just...spread the word."

Sally slammed another mug down. "I hate lying to our friends and customers!"

"It will protect them! They'll be scared if they knew the truth. This is better!"

"Is it? Today will be a frenzy of questions and gossip. Some might believe the weather crap, but not everyone."

"Please try. They trust us."

"Which is why I don't want to lie." Sally stared at her, jaw clenched. "Are you going to stop him?"

Dan answered for her. "Of course she will, Sally. When has she ever let us down?"

She glared at him. "When has it *ever* been this bad?"

"I can assure you both," Avery cut in, "that this is what I am focussing on today. In fact, it is the only thing I am doing today. I've popped in just to check on you, but then I'm going upstairs. Well, after I have renewed my protection spells."

Dan gave her a mournful smile. "I think that's why this place looks better than most."

Avery had to concede that he was right. Compared to most buildings, they were relatively unscathed. She was just grateful that Dan and Sally both lived at the edge of town. "Yes, we're lucky. Is Caro okay?"

"Shaken up, but otherwise fine. Actually, I was at her flat last night. We saw everything. Well, maybe not *everything*. A good part of it. We'd only just got home, after the pub." His eyes darkened. "I hate to think what would have happened if we had been caught in it. Was that real lightning? It looked like it. It's damaged buildings like it was."

"It did seem that way, didn't it?" Avery mused. "I think it was, but made by magic. Highly charged, and very powerful magic. Potentially, it could have killed someone." Just the thought strengthened her resolve. "I'm going into the shop to reinforce my spells, and then I'll leave you to it."

Dan reached for his costume. "Great. I'll get dressed, and be in soon." He tapped the shoulder where the raven should be, and winked. "I left him in the shop, keeping an eye on things."

"You're still dressing up?"

"Of course." Dan shook his head. "I will not let this spoil our Samhain celebrations. That's our gift to our customers. The rest of White Haven will do the same. It was just a storm last night, and hardly anyone remembers the harbour disappearing, either. We carry on as normal. Right, Sally?"

Sally squared her shoulders. "Right. I have a box full of cakes, and I *will* enjoy Samhain!"

Avery smiled. "What would I do without you two? If I can, I'll join you later. In costume!"

"Only if you have time. Other things are more important right now," Sally said.

Avery left them to change and headed into her shop. It was gloomy without lights, and in the silence, the rain sounded even louder as it pounded the pavement and lashed against the windows. She spelled the fairy lights on, relieved to see that everything looked as it normally did. Until she heard the squawk of a bird, and the flutter of wings.

Alarmed, she raised her hands in self-defence, walking slowly between the stacks as she looked around. When she rounded the final bookshelf and saw the counter, a raven was sitting there, preening itself. *Dan's raven.*

It fluttered its feathers and fixed its beady eyes on her. "*There you are. We have work to do.*"

"Herne's horns. I've finally gone mad," Avery murmured.

Words resounded in her head. "*Foolish girl. We're here to help, or did you forget that?*"

"No. I just..." she faltered. "I didn't know what to expect." She stared at the large bird and its glossy, black feathers. "You're supposed to be a toy."

"*I am. This is an illusion. Are you a witch or an idiot?*"

Avery recoiled as if she'd been slapped. "A witch! Are you always this cranky?"

"*I am when we're busy. Finish your spell and see me upstairs. We have much to do.*" The raven puffed up, feathers rippling again as it extended its wings and flew around the shop. In seconds, it had vanished.

Avery blinked, and with a shock, saw Dan's fake raven still on the counter. But there was no time to contemplate the strange turn of events. She'd been given an order from a very impatient familiar. *Or was that ancestor?* No matter. She'd better get on with it.

Chapter Thirty-Two

"O kay," Ben said decisively as he stared at the mysterious witches gathered inside the stone bothy. He had finally found out their names that morning, but was still baffled by what was happening. "Stan and I cannot wait any longer. You need to tell us what's going on."

Stan echoed his sentiments. "Yes, please explain. This is all very bewildering. And take it slowly. I didn't sleep very well." He massaged his back as if to emphasise the point.

It was the morning after the battle above the valley, and they hadn't been awake long. After stopping Tiernan's attack the night before, it seemed he had escaped. Rather than pursue him, they had retreated to the hut, cast spells of protection, banked the fire, and slept, most of them on the floor wrapped in woollen blankets and animal furs. There had been no discussion, no explanation of events. Last night, Ben accepted it. He was exhausted, and so was Stan. This morning, however, was a different matter.

After a simple breakfast, the witches started preparing potions and grinding herbs again. They talked amongst themselves, casting Ben and Stan speculative glances, and it was clear they were being discussed. Kendra had said that he and Stan carried the future, and could help. *But how?*

"I also want to know," Ben added, "why the five of you are unable to stop one man! Is he a super-witch or something?"

The young woman called Kendra who he had discerned had Alex's psychic skills said, "I explained last night."

"You gave me half a story. None of it made sense. I need more."

Twyla, the old, grey-haired elder, nodded. "It is only fair, seeing as you have been brought here and must help us. It is not a pretty tale."

"We don't care. Kendra, you said that Tiernan was the tribe leader's..." he fumbled for the right word as he recalled the conversation. "Magician? His advisor. But that men died because he tried to advance his own son's cause, and he was thrown out of the court or whatever you called it. You also said that you helped expose him. Why has that led to all of this? His pact with Wyrd. His attempt to destroy White Haven. And how does he even know that White Haven exists?"

The middle-aged man called Clesek spoke up next. "All good questions. Wyrd's weaving means that all futures are available for those who know how to see them."

"But that doesn't make sense, either!" Ben looked desperately at Kendra. "You said there are many possible paths. Many possible futures. How does he know what that future actually is?"

Stan nodded. "So far into the future, too."

Kendra placed down the bowl she had been grinding herbs in, looking at both of them as if they were idiots. "You are thinking about this all wrong. It is not the place that he sees, but the people, our descendants—of which there are many. However, some threads shine more brightly than others. Some weave more tightly. He follows them. He sees where they are tight, like a knot, and, in your world, in your time, is where the threads are most tightly enmeshed. The strongest they have been for a long time."

Kendra clenched her fist, her gaze distant as if she too could see the knots. Then she slowly opened her hand and actual, silvery threads unwound from her palm, snaking up and around. Some trailed away into nothingness, but others wound together like a ball of wool. She touched it with the index finger of her other hand, sending it spinning. "This is what he sees. This is what he seeks to destroy. I know, because I have seen it, too."

Edlin, the young man with the black hair who seemed to be an earth witch like Briar, said, "Fortunately, he has set himself a challenge. A knot like that is hard to break. You cannot weaken it by pulling one thread, you must find the way to release them all at once. This is why he uses such strong magic."

"So why not pick a time when they are weaker?" Stan asked, taking the spinning magical threads in his stride. "He sounds like an idiot."

"Because to destroy something so tight," Twyla said, "proves his power. To us, to himself, and to Wyrd. It would shred the weaving—well, for us, at least."

"And the many others who live in White Haven, too," Stan pointed out, rounding on her. "It's not all about witches and wizards. There are lots of people there, who all have futures, all have threads they could choose to be something different—for better or worse. The fate of children, whose lives have barely begun!"

"We know that," Ellette said, the woman with curly brown hair whose magic Ben hadn't discerned yet. Her faced was etched with sadness. "This is why we try so hard to stop him. Unfortunately, his pact with Wyrd makes him stronger."

Ben was mesmerised by the spinning ball of threads. *Was that how the Fates saw their lives? These tiny silver threads spilling across time and place.* He shivered. *So delicate. So fragile. Alone, at least.* He thought of his knot of friendships, especially with Ghost OPS, and smiled. Family and friendships made a person stronger. He saw that now more than he ever had before.

Ben roused himself as if from a dream as Kendra made the threads disappear. He still had more questions. "The fey we ran into call him the Weaver of the Dark Path. Is that his magic? It sounds dangerous. Godlike."

All the witches exchanged nervous glances, and Twyla said, "It is a skill that he uses to manipulate small events. He can see the end results of paths chosen—years into the future. A great skill, and one he uses wisely when he chooses to apply it, and part of the reason he gained his position. We call him the Twister of Fates. But then he foresaw a death, and in the course of trying to stop that death, he advised a choice. The consequences would have meant the death of many others. Kendra saw it all."

"You're psychic," Ben said, turning to her. "I thought as much."

"Not like Tiernan," Kendra explained. "I see things in flashes. However, I saw enough that we intervened. In doing so, we saved many lives, except the one he had originally foreseen and tried to stop. A death that he reversed. A broken thread that he wove anew."

Stan's hands shook. "Are you saying he brought someone back from the dead?"

Ben wondered if the translation spell was failing. "I don't understand. That's impossible."

"Not with the right words, the right magic. It was an act of desperation. A line that all witches know not to cross."

Kendra's words from the night before flooded back to Ben. "He saved his son! I thought you meant saved him from an accident, not actually brought him back from the dead."

Clesek rubbed his face with his hands, the wrinkles around his eyes deepening as he frowned. "As it turned out, we did not need to intervene. His son died in a hunting accident, making a choice of self-sacrifice in order that others should live. He was a good man. Our paths are many, to choose our fate as we decide, but all choices eventually lead to death. That was his time."

"You intervened. You can't possibly know what he might or might not have done," Ben said, appalled. "I presume you told him that many men would die. He might have felt compelled to sacrifice himself for them. *You* could have changed his fate!"

Kendra glared at him. "He made his choice."

"You revealed the future to him. You skewed his choice."

"No! Tiernan foresaw it. He was the one that tried to change it."

"But that's bollocks! There are choices, you said so yourself! Nothing is written until it happens." Ben was suddenly furious. "No wonder Tiernan wants revenge. His son is dead because you told him the consequences of an action, and possibly changed his decision."

"But you are forgetting," Clesek pointed out forcefully, "that he brought him back from the dead."

"A decision he felt compelled to make out of grief and anger!"

Twyla crashed her staff on to the ground, shaking the building. "Which is no excuse! There were consequences."

"Yes, I'm sure there would be when you use magic to thwart death," Ben said, trying to rein in his anger.

An awkward silence fell, as everyone tried to maintain civility. Eventually, Kendra said, "Men died, because Wyrd demanded an exchange. The men who should have died in exchange for his son's life. And then she wanted more. Tiernan's death, too. That was to be his gift of self-sacrifice."

Stan was sitting in a wooden chair, arms folded across his chest, eyes darting around the room as he listened to the conversation. "So, why isn't he dead?"

Ellette gave a hollow laugh. "Because he asked for one final act of revenge before then. To sabotage *our* future, because he blames us for everything. He has been cast out of the settlement, his position gone. Regrettably, his son killed himself anyway, out of shame for his father's actions. And of course, Tiernan's life is forfeit. He is furious and grief-stricken, and I doubt he has any reason left at all. I'm not sure why Wyrd allowed this ridiculous challenge. Perhaps she thought he would fail, and it would be another level of punishment that would show how weak he is in the face of her power. His final hubris before death. Or," she said, thoughtfully, "perhaps she felt sorry for him. His magic is closely aligned with her own abilities. They are kindred spirits in many ways."

"But he is stronger than she thought," Stan mused, his jaw tightening with fury. "Meanwhile, we suffer, and she lets him continue because of a pact. Like it's all a game."

Ben rubbed his eyes and his cheeks, aware now of the thick stubble on his jaw. He was suddenly exhausted and wanted to go home, but to do that made him a hypocrite. "In order to get home, we have to mess with the Fates, too, don't we? Stop him from destroying the threads that will destroy so much more than just your descendants. In reality, we should just let this play out. What is meant to be, will be." Even if that meant he and Stan would be stranded there forever. That was his choice. His thread.

Kendra fixed her eyes on him, and again he felt that uncanny sense she was peering into his soul. "But it is *not* meant to be. That's the point. It was *never* meant! This is a whole new weaving that Wyrd is powerless to stop, and so are we. We must connect with our descendants to stop Tiernan."

"How?"

"Through our animal guides," Kendra explained. "They are old, wise spirits that transcend time. The flashes we see of the future have actually helped us link to them. But it's tenuous."

"Your guides walk in the spirit world," Ben said, sounding more knowledgeable than he really was. He'd heard Alex talk about it often enough. "The raven, the wolf, the bear, and the others. I heard them speak!"

Edlin nodded. "Because of us. The good news is that our guides connected to your witches, our descendants, last night. Now we have to consider a way to help them. We haven't much time. You saw what he did last night."

"You don't know?" Stan asked, aghast. "I thought you had it all planned. All these potions and pastes, the magic and silvery threads you conjure. The circle last night! Isn't that enough?"

"*No!*" Twyla snapped her fingers, and the candle flame next to her snuffed out. "One more attack like that, and the threads will snap, White Haven will unravel, and all will cease to exist."

Ben snorted with derision. "If I know my friends, they will have a plan. They are very smart! Especially Avery."

Twyla smiled and patted his arm. "And that is how you can help. You know them well. Where were you when you came here?"

"At Old Haven Church. Actually, in Reuben's mausoleum. A place where the dead are interred for generations."

"Reuben is a witch?"

"Yes. One of the five."

Clesek turned from where he was tending the fire. "The water witch. He bonded well with his guide. *My* guide."

Ellette spoke as if she hadn't heard Clesek. "A burial place has great power. Another knot. Tiernan would have seen that." She studied Ben, eyes narrowed. "A clever move on his behalf, but instead he found you. Somehow, he pulled you through time. And you..." She turned to Stan. "We need to work out how that happened, so that we can send you back."

"It was an accident, I'm sure of it!" Stan protested.

Ben backed him up. "That's true. Tiernan did not expect him."

"Very well," Ellette said, sitting upright, suddenly decisive. "Something to consider. But in the meantime, Kendra was right. You can help. You look and smell of the future. You must tell us everything you know." She wagged a finger. "Not a detail missed. If he succeeds, it is all over. If he fails, I think Wyrd will kill him. She grows impatient, and wants her debt paid. We have to find a way to send you home before either of those eventualities occur."

"Or we'll be stuck here?" Stan asked.

"Forever."

Chapter Thirty-Three

A lex spirit-walked over White Haven, surprised at the details he could see. Even more surprising was the fact that his wolf was with him. In fact, not *his* wolf, just Wolf. He couldn't see him, but he felt him, and their connection was even stronger than it was the previous night.

"*I am unnerving you,*" Wolf said. "*Forget about me. Focus on the web.*"

"*That's very easy for you to say. You're used to this. I'm not used to hearing things.*"

"*Not true. You talk to spirits. And communicate with Avery.*"

"*That's different.*"

"*Perhaps.*" Wolf was growing impatient. "*Focus. You see the web?*"

"*Unfortunately, I do. I couldn't see it the other day. I saw energy, of course. Connections, colours, and magic, which has its own resonance. But not this.*"

"*Tiernan has grown stronger.*"

"*Or you have enhanced my abilities.*"

Alex knew now what Avery had seen when Raven was perched next to her. Spread over White Haven and the surrounding hills was a vast spiderweb of threads. Some pulsed stronger than others, with a silver or gold light. Other threads were darker, glowing purple, red, green, and black. They sparked where they connected, some bright, others dark. And there were knots. Clusters of threads bound together. In general, though, he had to say, White Haven was one big knot. That wasn't surprising, really. All towns would look the same. Lives bound together by events and geography.

The threads didn't just connect people, either. They connected buildings and landmarks. The castle, the sea, churches, graveyards. It was bewildering. Some threads were so tiny, he could barely discern them. One blink, and they vanished.

"*Actually,*" Alex continued, after a sudden insight, "*that's exactly what has happened. These threads have always been here. I've just never seen them before. I normally see swirls of elemental energy—wind, waves, etcetera. The big brushstrokes. I'm not sure I like seeing this much detail. Or the destruction Tiernan has caused.*"

Unfortunately, those knots were fraying, and over the town where the streets had vanished, they were barely visible.

"*Focus on the points that will help your spell. Our spell,*" Wolf said. "*Your ancestors will work with you. I can communicate that.*"

"*You're saying that our ancestors will cast a spell at the same time as us? Have I got that right?*"

"*Yes. You cannot fight Tiernan alone.*"

"*A pincer movement. Smart.*" While the other witches may have questioned that, Alex didn't. As he knew only too well, and Egbert had told them emphatically, time had no meaning in the spirit world. An animal guide that could move between their ancestors was a brilliant way to connect. "*Did you nudge my dad to come? And El's aunt?*"

"*Not I. As far as I am aware, they came of their own accord.*"

"*My dad said he was summoned.*"

"*Perhaps the thread that connects you pulled him. Tiernan's actions must have triggered something.*"

"*Why is he doing this, Wolf? What did we do?*"

"*There is no time for that now. Focus only on your actions. Believe me when I say his motivations will not change what you must do.*"

That was something Alex needed to think on later; for now, he considered Avery's instructions. "*Avery wants to weave her own web, somehow. A trap. I need anchor points—however that will work.*"

"*He is strongest at his base. The clifftop.*"

"*Which would suggest that is where we should avoid, and yet...*" Alex manoeuvred himself towards the castle. "*If this is where he is, this is where we should attack him. But he is everywhere when he starts.*" A flash of inspiration struck Alex. "*Surely he will attack the areas that are already weak. We have to defend those. The weakest part is where the town has almost disappeared.*"

"*But that doesn't constitute a trap.*"

Fuck it! Alex studied the threads below him. What should he do?

Another thought suddenly struck him. Something he should have thought to ask earlier. "*Have you seen Ben and Stan? Our missing friends?*"

"*The young man and the old man? Yes. They escaped, and your ancestors found them. They are well.*"

Relief swept through Alex—for a second, anyway. "*Excellent. And the affected streets? Are they visible in your time?*"

Wolf hesitated. "*That I do not know.*"

"*You need to find out and tell me. If they are, and Stan and Ben can get to them, that could be their way home. Although, that is another problem for us. We not only have to stop Tiernan, we have to repair the broken web.*"

Even as he was saying it in his mind, Alex knew how insane that sounded. Repair Wyrd's web? Return the shimmering streets to the normality? Insanity. And yet, they had to find a way.

Raven perched on the highest bookshelf in the attic spell room, watching Avery as she spread out the grimoires and tarot cards. Every now and then, he ruffled his feathers in a distinctly and audibly realistic manner, and she glanced up at him, unnerved.

Just as unnerving was Wolf who lay curled at Alex's side as he spirit-walked over White Haven. Avery couldn't see him so clearly, though. He was only visible in a certain light, or as the flames shifted within the fireplace. Their lives had taken a very weird turn lately.

Avery tried to focus on her plans, but her thoughts were chaotic, fragmented. She was worried about Caspian, the town itself, and what they would remember about these events—if they even survived, and she was concerned about Ben and Stan. And more importantly, she stressed about how to connect to their ancestors effectively.

Raven squawked and spoke, his voice not in her head, but instead coming very clearly from his body that should not exist. "Stop it! This is not helping."

"And neither are you!" she shot back. "I thought you were supposed to impart wisdom!"

"You're the witch, not I. I am a conduit, so get used to it. Ellette is far easier to get along with than you."

She ignored his spiky, barbed tone. "Ellette? My ancestor?"

"Yes."

"An air witch?"

"Amongst other skills. But she works differently to you. She has no books, or cards."

Avery leaned back in her chair. "I suppose they live in a time well before the common use of books and the written word, and tarot cards are a more recent invention. What about runes, though? They have been in use for millennia."

"Yes, she uses those, although not as much as Twyla. But it is useless to compare. Times are different, and so is your magic. Focus on what you can do now. What are your strengths?"

"Elemental air, the tarot, and making new spells."

"A type of weaving."

"*What*?" Avery thought she'd misheard him.

"You weave spells, the old with the new. New words, new actions. It is a great skill."

Avery was embarrassed. "Well, it depends how well they turn out."

"Stop doubting yourself." Raven flew down to the table, and at the same time, Helena manifested next to the bird, sitting in the chair opposite Avery. She smiled enigmatically, in her usual way. "See," Raven said, "another ancestor is here to support you. You are not alone. Especially now, when the veils are thinning. You must draw on that power and support."

"Which means Gil can help, too," Avery mused. "Particularly Reuben. As far as my skills go, I hadn't thought of making new spells as a type of weaving, but I suppose you're right. Which should stand me in good stead for facing Wyrd."

"It is less Wyrd that should concern you, than Tiernan. The Twister of Fates."

Avery shuddered at hearing his name again. "He's the danger, then? More than Wyrd?"

"Far more. One of his skills is that he sees far into the future. Can see which thread will bring the most success."

"Oh, great. And you've only just thought to tell me that now?"

Raven bristled. "We have only just connected."

"I suppose that's true. I guess that explains why he has been able to manipulate us so effectively."

Helena tapped the cards, as if to remind her of the spell, and Raven asked, "What will you use those for?"

Avery stared at the three cards she had already selected—The Nine of Wands, The Magician, and The Hermit. "They represent what we're facing. The rune called Skuld's Net, otherwise known as Wyrd, had nine strokes. Nine wands. That's why I wanted nine witches. Tiernan is The Magician. And you, our guides, are represented in the Hermit. Which also..." she trailed off as she stared at Alex and Wolf. "Wow. The hermit represents Alex, too. He's our guide when it comes to the spirit world." In a flash, the way forward became clearer. "I need nine cards, including these three. One to represent each of the witches. Or do I need more?"

She picked the pack up, shuffling through the cards, knowing instinctively what she needed. The King of Wands would be Finn. Like Alex, he had fire skills, and the fire element was represented by the wand suit. Swords represented air, so the King of Swords would be Caspian, although, she wasn't sure if he would be strong enough to help after his accident. Briar was the Queen of Pentacles. El the Queen of Wands. Reuben the King of Cups. Avery was the Queen of Swords. That made nine cards. *But what about Oly and Helena? And whose body could Helena use? Cassie, perhaps. Or Dylan?* She knew they would volunteer to help. *But could she risk them?* Besides, they had no magical abilities. Her thoughts drifted again to Clea, her grandmother. She had a wealth of magic, all lost now because of her Alzheimer's. *No, not lost. It was still there.* Her conversation with Finn last night had confirmed that. He said he sensed it when he went to see Clea, and said that she had also recognised him. *Could she subject her grandmother to Helena's possession?* She needed to consent to such an intrusion. *Could*

she do that, when she wasn't even fully cognizant of what was happening?
But if she didn't use her...

Avery stared at Helena. "If you're to help, I have only one option,
and I think I have to do it. I need to use Clea."

Raven put in, "She would do it. You know she would."

"You don't know that."

"But I know you, and you are sure."

"I am far from sure." Avery held the Queen of Swords card in her
hand. "I'm not sure about this, either. It's me, but I think the Queen
of Swords has to be you and Clea, Helena."

Helena regarded her silently, a smile playing on her lips as if she had
a secret. It was unnerving.

Avery turned her attention back to the cards. The Magician could
only be Tiernan. Their quarry. He needed to be in the centre of their
net. That left one card out of nine, and there were two witches left. Oly
and herself. And then she realised her error. "Herne's hairy bollocks!
I need *ten* cards! Nine for the witches, plus The Magician. We are the
nine, and he is not part of that!" She shuffled through the pack again.
"I am the weaver in this scenario. It is my spell. Oly must be the Nine
of Wands. She wields her magic like the rest of us. I am another card
entirely." The card she required slid into her hand, and she held it up
triumphantly. "The Wheel of Fortune!"

Helena beamed, but Raven asked, "What is its relevance?"

"The wheel represents change and destiny. It marks events that are
set in motion. This card," she wagged it at Raven, "means you must
accept what is happening, but it also means you should attune yourself
to the forces that effect those events. Even more important, it is linked
to the three Fates—a reminder of the Wheel of Life – or even the
Wheel of the Year. Life, death, and rebirth. This card represents me."

Excited, she cleared space on the table, arranging the cards in front of her, assigning her coven their respective positions. She also knew what spell she needed to cast, using these cards. A map was behind her on the wall, one she and Alex had used before when working out Helena and their other ancestors' binding spell.

"Helena, I am taking inspiration from you. Your binding spell all of those years ago used a pentagram, the five points positioned around the town, the centre of which was All Souls Church. That's what I need to do again, but not using a pentagram."

She turned to stare at Alex, willing him to return to his body, and then checked her watch. She still had so much to do. Eli and Zee would arrive at midday with valuable information, so she should gather everyone quickly. She reached for her phone.

Time to summon a meeting.

Chapter Thirty-Four

S ick of being cooped up inside the one-roomed building, Ben stepped outside to reacquaint himself with his surroundings in the daylight.

The ancient witches were preparing to support his friends at some far, distant point in the future, and were waiting for news of a plan. They also wanted to undermine Tiernan in some way in their own time, but were debating how best to do that. Stan, fascinated by everything, was listening to their discussions.

Ben drank in the view of the sea and the familiar shoreline, finding comfort in the ebb and flow of the tide. Now up on higher ground, he saw that the land was more cultivated than he first realised. There were hedges and the evidence of crops, even though it was so late in the year, as well as herds of sheep and cows. Twyla had her own smallholding, where animals grazed, a pig snuffled in its pen, and vegetables and herbs grew in a well-maintained plot.

He could also see the vast expanse of the original Ravens' Wood, the march of its trees covering a far larger area than it did in his own time. No wonder they had got lost.

Unexpectedly, there was a higgledy-piggledy couple of streets low down on the hillside above the valley, almost obscured by a line of trees. *Odd*. He hadn't spotted that before. They looked almost modern, and seemed to fade in and out of his vision. A mixture of hope and horror filled him. It wasn't an old settlement. It was part of modern White Haven.

Home.

He whirled around and threw the door open. "White Haven is here! In the valley. Well, some of it, at least! It must have happened last night." In seconds, the witches and Stan had abandoned their plans and were standing next to him. "We have to get down there."

Stan was already gathering his cloak about him, ready for the trek. "If there are people there, they must be terrified."

"While I hate to sound selfish," Ben admitted, "this could be our way home!"

"Slow down." Clesek studied the area, a restraining hand on Stan's arm. "I'm not sure that place is really here. It shimmers in a strange way. And Tiernan could be there."

"I don't care," Ben said. "It's White Haven, and if Tiernan is there, that's an even bigger reason to get down there."

"Absolutely. What if he's hurting people?" Stan's hands rested on his portly hips as he glared at the witches. "If we can't get home, they'll need comforting, and help acclimatising. And we," he stared at Ben, "can live there, too."

"Stop being a doom-monger! We are going home!"

"Slow down!" Twyla snapped her fingers. Her magic magnified the noise, making it sound like a clap of thunder. She addressed the other witches. "They are right. We have to see what's happening. If people are there, but have wandered from the area, they need to be found and herded back."

"They're not cows!" Ben pointed out.

Twyla ignored him. "He has partially succeeded in his task. White Haven is part here, part in its normal time. If we are to return it, then they must be in it, and Ben is right—so must they."

"That is our solution," Kendra agreed, eyes closed. "It is a place of weakness, because the spell is incomplete. It was interrupted. It offers us a window—a connection to your future." She opened her eyes again, hope shining within them. "We must gather there, while your witches focus on Tiernan himself. He will be focussing on his next actions, feeling he is at his strongest now. We must do it before anyone from the settlement sees it, or they will interfere with all our plans."

A thought struck Ben. "Why haven't *they* waged war on Tiernan?"

"They tried and failed," Twyla said, "and instead tasked it to us. Kendra has taken Tiernan's place. A great honour for one so young."

"Which explains how you know so much," Stan said, nodding. He shuffled, impatient to be off. "Come on! We need to go."

Ben headed into the hut to gather his belongings, and took a long last look around the inside. With luck, he wouldn't see this place again. If he did, it would mean they had failed.

Newton listened to the back and forth of conversation, his attention mainly on the map spread across Avery and Alex's large wooden table in their attic, and the tarot cards scattered across its surface.

The attic was full, and consequently hot and stuffy. A fire burned low in the fireplace, and what seemed like a million candles blazed on every surface. He and his sergeants had joined Cassie, Dylan, Zee, Eli, and the extended coven—including an injured Caspian who had a large bandage wrapped around his head—to plan what they hoped was their final battle with Tiernan.

This was one of their oddest meetings, mainly because of the raven perched on a book shelf, the barely visible wolf curled by the fire with the cats, and Avery's white-haired grandmother who sat on the sofa with a ghostly Helena by her side. Avery had collected her from the care home to assist with the spell.

There was an air of expectation and tension as Avery outlined her plan to use nine witches to combat Wyrd and Tiernan, worried Caspian wouldn't be well enough to help.

Caspian shrugged. "I have a headache, that's all."

Avery pursed her lips. "It is a big spell. Are you sure? I could ask Eve, or Nate."

"But what about needing a familiar?" El asked. "If they don't have one..."

"I've been thinking about that," Avery said. "From what I've gathered from Raven, there are only five ancestors. That means that only five of our familiars are really needed—just ours, the White Haven Coven."

Reuben shook his head. "I disagree. We bonded last night when we all connected to our familiars. We could tell where each of us were, and what our familiars were. It was a very strong connection—more than I've ever had before with you guys, even when joined in a circle." His gaze encompassed his coven. "If this spell is to spread across all of White Haven, we need to know what everyone is doing. Our familiars will allow us to do that."

El was looking through the tarot cards, but she nodded in agreement with Reuben. "He's right. To stop Tiernan, we have to use our ancestors *and* our family. Finn and Oly felt compelled to come here, and you want to use Helena."

"True," Briar said, "and you haven't actually explained how you'll do that." She looked at Avery's grandmother. "I presume it has something to do with Clea."

Avery leaned on the table, staring at the map for a moment, before looking at them all again. A range of emotions played across her face, predominantly worry. "You make a good point, Reuben. Our familiars are an excellent way of communicating. As for Helena, this is going to sound mad, but we know she needs a body to inhabit in order to use magic. It will have to be my grandmother. Finn, what you said to me last night supports that. That's why she's here."

Newton turned to stare at Clea. She still had her back to them, taking no part in the conversation. She did, however, appear to be talking to Helena. "I thought your grandmother was senile?"

"She is." Avery watched her, worry in her eyes. "I just hope I'm doing the right thing."

"You are," Finn said, smiling. "Her magic is not being utilised now, not liked it used to be, but of course she still has it. It's just dormant. She seems pretty friendly with Helena, too. I suspect she visits her."

Avery's mouth gaped open, but before she could comment, Oly huffed, clearly still smarting about ageism. "Of course she still has magic. Age does not make you stupid or magically weak."

"Exactly," Finn continued, but far less aggressively than Oly. "Helena can manipulate that. It might even help Clea mentally."

"It also might make her worse, and then I'd hate myself," Avery said. She shuddered. "I also remember how *that* felt. I was squashed beneath Helena, like I was suffocating."

"If Clea is not fully cognisant, she might not even notice. And you'll hate yourself even more if we lose without her," Dylan pointed out, speaking for the first time since Newton had arrived. "Or if we win and still fail to find Ben and Stan."

Cassie nodded. "Agreed. But what about their familiars?"

Avery pointed to the raven. "He will work between us."

"And Gil?" Reuben asked Alex. "Have you heard from him?"

"Very briefly, after I spirit-walked. He confirmed that he has heard nothing in the spirit world. He has said, however, that he will help if he can. With the approach of Samhain, and the thinning of the veils, he believes he can connect to you—especially if we cast the spell at a crossing time."

"Crossing time?" Kendall asked, confused.

"Dawn, twilight, midnight or midday," Newton explained, to the apparent surprise of the group.

Oly intervened. "Are you sure about needing nine of us? It seems an abstract notion to me. Does it matter if there are only eight?"

"Yes. I know it, down to my bones," Avery said. "*I feel it*. Skuld's Net has nine strokes. To counteract that I see the Nine of Wands. If you're unfamiliar with the tarot it makes no sense, but that card designates us defending our territory. We are that nine. Tiernan is The Magician." She picked up the card for them to see. "He is the tenth card that I will weave into the spell. He even looks like that image of him in the mist you showed us, Dylan! Trust me. I need nine witches."

Her coven stared back at her, all of them nodding their agreement, but not all looked convinced of the wisdom of her suggestion.

"What about the other piece of information we discovered," Eli said, turning to Briar, "about the tree magic. Do you think you can work out what that is? Does the Green Man know?"

Briar was silent for a moment, chin resting on her fingertips, her eyes on the map. Eventually, she said, "Perhaps. The Green Man sleeps, and it was not his magic, but if I position myself there, it might be possible. I'll be honest, it's unlikely that I can replicate it because it's fey magic, but if I find it, I might be able to draw on it, and add it to our spell. My familiar will help. She is of the woods and the earth."

Avery slid her hand to the Queen of Pentacles and placed it over Ravens' Wood on the map. "Good. That's where you will be, then."

Newton frowned. "The cards represent you?"

Avery's fingers grazed them, almost a caress. "Yes. We need to decide where exactly to place them based on Alex's experience. But, they're not just placeholders. They're part of the spell. I don't often use them in that way, but they can be effective."

It sounded like mumbo-jumbo to Newton, but he trusted that Avery would know what she was doing.

Alex tapped the map. "This is where the two affected streets are. The threads were very faint here. I'm wondering if that means this is a weak point. I'm just not sure if that's to Tiernan's advantage, or ours."

Now Newton was even more confused. "They've faded? But I thought these threads represented Wyrd's weavings, and our choices. The fact that they've faded suggests a kind of unmaking."

Alex sighed. "Newton, I'm working my way through this, just like everyone else. I don't understand it all, not really. What I'm suggesting is a theory."

"Whatever it means, we still want to return the streets to normal, correct?" Moore asked. "We've confirmed that there were people there. A few of the buildings were shops, and one was a gallery. They were empty. But the rest were houses, flats, and a couple of Bed and Breakfasts. It's hard to be sure, but we think there are a dozen people missing."

The witches exchanged worried glances, and it was obvious that the news would make their jobs harder. Avery stirred first. "We'll do our best. I'm hoping that Ben and Stan will find a way there. Raven, can you ask about that?"

Raven cawed, ruffled its feathers, and its head sank on its chest.

Kendall studied it, eyes narrowed. "Shouldn't it be flying off somewhere?"

Avery smiled. "He's not really here, he's just manifested very strongly. Mentally, it travels between us. But it's not easy. It's like trying to phone someone when you're going through a tunnel, or are in cave."

"Patchy reception," Dylan said, nodding. "It's still cool."

Newton was exhausted and desperate to get back on the streets of White Haven where he could keep an eye on things. "Can we please get moving so we can leave? What's the general plan?"

"Our spell has several functions, part of which is a protection spell. To protect the whole town for a long time would be unsustainable. We need to stop him for good. You see, what I realised is that the threads are our choices—well, we all know that. The Fates weave our beginning, middle, and end. How we get from one point to another is our choice. Our choices have led us here!" Avery's eyes kindled with fire and intent as she banged on the table. "Even to this room. Some of us are bound by friendship, some by family, but now we are all knitted together. Bound. The more that are bound, the stronger we are."

Alex's nodded, eyes on Avery in admiration. "You're right. I saw how tightly some of those threads were. They flashed like lightning where they met."

"Exactly!" She banged on the table again. "The lightning we saw in the storm mist was his attempt to break those connections. But Tiernan is alone! One thread trying to sever thousands. He's tried to compensate for that by weaving new threads across White Haven. I sensed a spider's web, and Alex saw it."

"I did." His fingers darted over the map. "I saw lots of dark green and red threads between all of them when I spirit-walked. Initially I thought they could belong to anyone, representing illness, anger, or bad relationships. But then I realised there was a pattern. They were everywhere. His recurrent attacks were an attempt to thread weakness into our connections."

Avery became more animated. "My original idea was to trap him in a web of our making, but actually, it's simpler than that. I just need to cut his threads. Or narrow his choices so much that he has nowhere to go."

Zee folded his arms across his chest, watching her. "That's all very nice in the abstract. How does it work in reality?"

Avery picked up The Wheel of Fortune card. "I am number ten. I am the ending and the beginning. This card represents the Wheel of the Year, and a link to the forces that are operating, and right now, that is Samhain and the thinning of the veils. A time when our ancestors are honoured and come to join us. Supported by your energies and theirs, I will search for him using his own threads. When he attacks, I will follow it. I will chase him and cut it, and then keep cutting until he has nowhere left. I just have to hope that the Fates are not so far on his side that Wyrd helps him weave his own thread anew. In fact, that should be beyond him."

"Wow." El stared at Avery, her manicured eyebrows raised. "That's actually quite brilliant. So, while we prevent his advance, using a protection spell that is hopefully strengthened by Briar, we also attack, pushing him back."

"Yes, distracting him while I destroy his threads. Well, me and Alex." She smiled at him. "You are The Hermit. My guide."

Newton had no comment on any of that. It sounded bewildering and beyond what he could understand. And yet, it did make a weird kind of sense. He liked the idea of them being connected, all of them helping each other. *But...* "If he can't make new threads, how can you? How can you restore the faded part of White Haven?"

Her face fell. "I don't know that yet."

Cassie stuttered. "So, there's a chance we might not find Ben?"

"A chance, yes." Avery leaned forward, reaching for Cassie's hand across the table. "I promise you that we will do what we can." Avery squeezed her fingers then leaned back, studying the others. "The thing is, I will be spirit-walking, with Alex. That's the only way I can see the threads. We can get a head start and destroy some of them now, but I know once we start, he will attack straight away."

"So we have to be in position first," Reuben said. "Makes sense. And we shouldn't wait. He might still be weak from last night. Let's time it for twilight. That's only hours away."

"Woah!" Newton held up his hand, alarmed. "People will be on the streets then. It will be barely five in the evening."

Avery stared at him unflinchingly. "Which means *you* need to keep them safe. Use Eli and Zee, the PCs, Cassie and Dylan, James. Anyone! The witches will be around White Haven. Some of us near the affected streets."

"We should use the church bells," Reuben reminded them. "Get James to ring them at twilight—or Briar could set them off magically. Judy has made the announcement now. People know to stay indoors when they sound."

It was a sign that Newton was shattered. He should have thought of that. "Thanks, Reuben. That's a great suggestion."

Avery sighed with obvious relief. "Yes, brilliant. Finn, I think you should be with Beth."

"My Beth?" Briar asked, looking alarmed. "Why?"

"Finn has psychic skills, and Beth seems attuned to our current predicament. It could be a useful link. Plus, they're on the hill, on the other side of White Haven. We witches need to spread out."

A squawk interrupted them. "*No!*"

Everyone looked up at Raven as Avery asked, "What?"

"You must focus on stopping his attack. Your ancestors will focus on mending the threads of your streets. Kendra has said so."

Newton's head was reeling. "You have just talked to the ancestors?"

"Yes! You doubt me?"

"It was just a question!" *Bloody cranky bird. Good grief. And now I'm talking to a raven.*

Avery took it all in her stride. "Okay. A change of plan."

Newton stood, chair scraping back, unwilling to stay any longer. "You finish your arrangements, and I'll make ours. Moore, Kendall, come with me. You four," he pointed at Cassie, Dylan, Eli, and Zee, "keep your phones close in case I need you. I wish all of you good luck. And be careful!"

Newton strode downstairs without a backward glance, especially towards Briar. Everything sounded huge and deadly. He needed to focus on his own role in all this, and distractions weren't going to help.

Chapter Thirty-Five

After Newton and his sergeants left, Avery made swift adjustments to her plan and explained it to the others, hoping the witches would agree.

"I suggest we have Reuben, El, and Briar fighting Tiernan on the ground, to repel any attack that Alex and I may trigger. Helena, Oly, Finn, and Caspian will support our ancestors in repairing the affected streets. It's too important not to assist them." She addressed Caspian. "I know you want to join us, but I want you out of the direct firing line because you're injured."

Caspian looked as if he was about to argue, and then just nodded. "Fine."

"Thank you. First, however, I'll cast the spell I've devised that incorporates the tarot. I know it's unusual, but it's the best way to defend against Tiernan's attacks. Our unity is our strength."

"I agree," Finn said, nodding confidently. "A spell using the tarot cards, each signifying us, or our strengths, acts as a binding spell, connecting us together."

"Like glue," Dylan added. "I like it."

Avery nodded, relieved that they agreed. "It means that whatever is happening, we can all draw on each other, and know what everyone else is doing. Hopefully, it will mean you can follow me and Alex, too, as we spirit-walk and corner Tiernan." She looked at her grandmother.

"But to do that, I need to put Helena in Clea's body. I'd better do that now."

Alex squeezed her hand. "I trust you. Do you want me to do the spell with Clea?"

"No. It's my responsibility. Just give me a few minutes."

Leaving the others talking, she crossed the room and sat next to Clea.

Clea and Helena were knitting, sitting close, and Clea was nodding and looking at Helena as if they were conversing. She hoped they were. Seeing Clea being looked after by Helena made her feel less guilty about not visiting her as often as she should. Something she must rectify after all of this. Clea seemed settled and relaxed now, which was also good. When she'd first brought her here, she had been agitated and confused, and then had talked about the place as if she was still living there.

Avery rested her hand on Clea's arm. "Gran. I need to ask you a question."

"Sorry, Diana. I was miles away." She thought Avery was her daughter, and she didn't correct her. Clea lifted her pale blue eyes to Avery's, leaned over, and patted her cheek. "It's so nice to be here again. I better open the shop up soon, or the customers will complain."

"No, don't worry about that. We have something better to do. I need your help in a spell."

Clea's face flushed with pleasure, her eyes widening with delight. "Of course! What are we doing?"

"Actually, I need to ask you a big favour. Helena, our ancestor, needs to use your body. She needs to possess you to..."

"That's fine, dear. She told me all about it."

Avery glanced at Helena who continued to knit, a smug smile on her face. Exasperated, Avery focussed on Clea again. "She did?"

"Oh, yes. We chat a lot lately."

"How?"

"Just as anyone does. Just like this." Clea's face clouded with confusion. "Such an odd question."

Avery sighed, but there was no time to pursue it now. "Are you sure you're okay with it? It will just be for a few hours." She shot Helena a warning glance. "Then she will leave your body."

Helena rolled her eyes, but Clea nodded. "That's fine, dear. It's Bingo night, though, so I have to get back home for that."

Avery laughed. Clea was just gorgeous. She lifted the chalice containing the potion that Alex had prepared. "You need to drink this, and then say a spell."

Clea drank it quickly, no doubt used to taking her pills at the home. She shuddered. "Potions always taste horrible."

Avery hated this, but there was no turning back now. She passed Clea the spell written on paper, and adjusting her glasses, she read it out faultlessly. Her grandmother was still a pro when it came to spellcasting.

Helena vanished, and after a few seconds during which Clea's face wrinkled with alarm, she finally smiled.

A stone settled in the pit of Avery's stomach. "Helena?"

Clea gave a beaming smile, a calculating gleam in her usually guileless blue eyes. "Avery. How lovely to be back."

Reuben stared across the harbour from his position at El's window, hoping this would be the first place to be attacked like it had been before. Their plans were based on that fact. If it was, and he couldn't hold it back, he would need to retreat quickly.

As he was a water witch, with his water horse as a familiar, it was an easy decision for him to be positioned near the water. At the moment, he was undecided as to whether he should stay in El's flat where he could work his magic without anyone seeing, or whether he needed to be in the sea.

He eyed his wetsuit that he had close by, just in case. His surfboard was strapped to his car roof next to the harbour. *Being stranded in the water in a possible lightning storm sounded like suicide, but if that's where he needed to be...*

He thought back to their meeting. Once Helena had possessed Clea, she sat at the table, greeting them all with a cool reserve. She appeared completely at ease, self-contained, and yet there was an uncertainty behind her eyes. Perhaps she felt as bad about possessing Clea as they all did. Or maybe she was just disappointed that she was inhabiting an old body. Avery had warned her to treat Clea gently. Helena had retorted, "I'm neither a fool nor a monster." Avery had then cast the spell that linked them all.

Reuben pressed his hands to his eyes, suddenly overwhelmed. This whole ancestor thing was getting to him. *And if Gil turned up...* He'd barely seen him when the pirates had attacked, but now he might actually be able to cast spells and fight with him. That would be something.

He took a deep breath, and turned to study the town, placing everyone in position in his mind. Avery and Alex were at their home, getting ready to spirit-walk and finalising their spells. Helena, Oly, Finn, and Caspian, were positioned by the affected streets, ready to support their ancestors. El was in Alex's apartment. Briar was in Ravens' Wood. They would communicate through their familiars, both with each other and their ancestors. Eli and Zee would patrol the town, as would Cassie and Dylan.

At least, that was the plan. *Who knew how it would end up?* He pulled his tarot card from his pocket. The King of Cups. This was taken from another pack, not Avery's own. She knew they might be damaged, and she was right. This one was already rumpled. This was unfamiliar magic to Reuben, but they had started with a type of binding spell, but not a binding of restriction; instead, it was of strength. They combined their magic together, binding it into the cards and onto the map. It reinforced their connections, and even now, Reuben could feel the others' magic flowing through him; the familiar magic of his coven, and the newcomers'.

Reuben stared at his wetsuit again, and then back at his tarot card. He was the King of Cups. He commanded water. His familiar was a water horse. *Time to suit up, get on his board, and get in the sea.*

Briar walked inside the perimeter of Ravens' Wood, comforted by its ancient trees and fertile ground. She always enjoyed her time there, foraging for herbs and roots. She suspected that she was more connected to it than the other witches, purely because she was an earth witch. Not to mention she had the presence of the Green Man within her. She hoped that would stand her in good stead now.

She had debated whether she should move further into the interior, where the ancient magic was stronger, but she also needed to see the castle and the cliff edge, as it was likely to be where Tiernan would first manifest. She slipped her shoes off, wiggled her toes, and buried her feet in the rich loam. The earth should have been cold, but not to her. Her magic responded to the magic within the earth, warming her skin. Placing her pack on the ground, she stretched her arms out and touched the trees on either side. Now she could feel magic flooding through all of her limbs. She opened up to it, filling herself with wild, primal energy.

As her breathing settled, she searched for her familiar. Briar felt her before she saw her. Deer's gentle spirit, intuition, and hidden strength. In seconds she nuzzled her ribs, and Briar smiled as her connection to the forest intensified. She felt the wind rustle branches, heard the birds in their nests, the mammals in their burrows, and even the dryads within the trees.

Briar stared into the beautiful creature's deep brown eyes. "Can you help me find the fey magic?"

"*I can try,*" she answered, her voice in Briar's head.

Deer nestled at her feet, her warm body resting against Briar's legs. Connected, they searched for the magic that would help protect White Haven.

Alex's spirit body floated out of their attic room for the second time that day, Avery at his side.

He pointed to the mesh of threads around them. "*See what I mean?*"

Avery gasped. "*This is more than I expected! More complex. How can we search all of these?*"

"*We need to be higher.*" He glanced behind them to the silver cords that linked them to their bodies. They looked different to the threads that twisted around them. More substantial. Perhaps because they were life lines, rather than being choices and paths that might or might not be chosen. "*It's odd though, Avery. I can see the colours better than I could before. Maybe because I'm more used to it. Or maybe because Wolf and our ancestors are helping us.*"

He could feel Avery's panic rising. "*What is the difference between a true connection and a possibility? Everything looks the same. There are aura colours, too! It's bewildering.*"

"*We don't need to understand it all. We just need to find Tiernan. Look!*" He twisted to show her the dark threads woven between the silver and gold ones, and then pointed towards the castle. "*That's where you can see a nexus of lines spiralling out. They're dark green and mottled red. Jealousy and anger. A horrible combination. Tiernan.*"

"*But there's no way to tell for sure. What if we cut a thread and harm the wrong person?*"

Alex didn't answer straight away. He studied the coast, the area that was shimmering in and out of the present, and where the fog had advanced to. "*It has to be those ones. Look where they stop! Right where the wall reached the other day.*"

Avery had turned to study the other direction. "*Some of them are over there, too. That's either someone else, or he's been attacking a few areas that we never even knew about. I guess there's only one way to find out.*"

He nodded. "*Do it.*"

She drifted lower, hovering over a thread of dark red and green. It pulsed, like it was breathing. She took one long look at Alex, and then directed her fingers at the thread and cast a cutting spell. The thread fizzed and popped, and then shattered. It was like igniting a fuse in a cartoon. Light travelled down the thread on either side until it burned out.

For a few moments, nothing happened. Then the network of lines flashed and shimmered, and a dark cloud manifested on the cliff top.

Wolf sounded in Alex's mind. "*He knows what you're doing!*"

"*Avery, we were right! Cut more!*"

In a frenzy they cut lines, shattering connections. But Tiernan had responded quickly, and a huge ball of energy rolled at them, sending them flying.

A thunderclap resounded across the valley, making Newton jump.

He cursed his jangling nerves, and studied the witches positioned in a line a short distance away. The illusion spell had been removed, and they all faced the faded streets of White Haven, trapped behind a shimmering wall. In the twilight, they looked even more ghostly. Nothing moved on the other side. It was eerie.

The town felt eerie, too. After liaising with Judy, the mayor, and James, the church bells had rung only fifteen minutes before. Most people were now doing as they were asked and sheltering inside, but not all. Newton could only hope than when the battle started, they would see sense and find shelter.

A second clap echoed across the town.

"What the hell?" He stared up at the castle that was almost invisible in the twilight and heavy cloud cover. "Is this it? It's starting?"

Moore squinted at the cliff. "Hard to say. It could be mist. Oh, no, it definitely is."

The crackle of distant light illuminated the dark band of fog that rolled down the hill at alarming speed. But it wasn't just rolling down to the harbour, it was heading inland across the hills, different to its last approach.

Newton braced himself. "This is quick! *Too* quick." As if to emphasise his point, the church bells started their mournful tone. "Better join Kendall in the centre—"

And then he stopped speaking as the mist ground to a sudden halt, and a huge spout of water erupted from the harbour.

Reuben.

Chapter Thirty-Six

B en stopped at the threshold of the tarmacked road that ran between the houses, the others lined up next to him, staring at the shimmering wall where old met new—the present butting up against the future.

"What do you think will happen if we cross it?" he asked.

Stan picked up a stone and threw it. It hit the magical wall and exploded. The blast knocked them off their feet.

"Well, I guess that answers that," Stan wheezed, winded. "We die."

Clesek grunted as he staggered to his feet. "If you had asked for my suggestion, I would have cautioned against that."

"You could have said so, anyway!" Ben stood and brushed himself off. The barrier ahead had returned to its shimmering state, reminding him of the spell that Alex had cast around Stormcrossed Manor, and the way that the banshee had strengthened it so that no one could cross it. "I've seen something like this before." He explained what had happened and how El's knife had cut through it.

Stan looked hopeful. "Have you got her knife now?"

"Unfortunately not."

Clesek ran his hand inches from the barrier, and Ben wished his thermal camera still had a functioning battery. "I doubt this is a protection spell. Twyla?"

The old woman mimicked Clesek's actions before stepping back to study the whole barrier. "I agree. This is something to do with time and energy. The place is trapped between here and there, on a knife's edge of existence."

"Which means what?" Ben asked, heart sinking.

"It is impossible to cross."

"But there has to be a way! You told Raven to tell them that you would do this! They are busy with Tiernan." He trusted his friends to complete their end of the spell, but he wasn't sure what to think about these people. They exchanged worried glances and then drew close in deep discussion.

"We're stuck here, aren't we?" Stan asked, resigned.

"I refuse to believe that." Although, even as Ben was saying it, he doubted himself, and from the look in Stan's eye, he knew it, too.

Ellette crossed to their side, leaving the other witches to make their preparations, all sitting in a circle, draping their furs and pelts over themselves. "We have a possible solution. In order to allow you to cross this barrier, it must align with here. That means we have to temporarily align ourselves with Tiernan."

Stan and Ben answered together. "*What*?"

"It is the only way. You will see the barrier start to disappear, and then you must cross—quickly! Raven will tell you when. After that, we reverse everything. It is the only way."

"And if we miss the timing?" Stan asked, jaw tight.

"You will die. Or of course, you can choose to remain here forever. No risk in that. We don't support Tiernan, and instead focus on returning this place to its own time." Her expression was grim. "I realise both of these options are hard. If you stop here, of course we will support you."

Ben groaned, clutching his head. "If we cross, *can* you reverse it?"

"There are no guarantees."

"Fine. It's a chance I accept. Stan?"

"It feels like a horribly selfish decision, because of whoever may be in there…" Stan looked at the deserted White Haven street beyond the barrier. "*If* there's anyone there. But yes. I accept the risks."

"Then we must begin. Once we start, none of us can break the circle. We will not speak to you again. I hope. Good luck."

Without another word, Ellette joined the others, and Ben shouted, "Thank you. Thank you all. You'd better tell your descendants what's happening, too!"

She nodded, already distracted as she took her place in the circle. The air was charging around them as they drew on the power of their spirit animals. On the walk, Clesek had explained about some of their magic, and using totem animals was a big part of it.

Ben marched to the boundary. "Come on, Stan. We have to be ready."

"If they get it wrong, I just hope it's a quick death."

"Stan!"

He shrugged, apologetic. "Sorry. It's been fun, though, despite everything." He looked around at their surroundings. "What a trip!"

Ben couldn't give two hoots about their surroundings. Instead, he focussed on the barrier and their future, until a prickle of growing power made him glance behind him. Then he had the shock of his life. The witches had vanished. Only their totem animals remained.

Bear was restless. El could feel that he needed to roam the streets of White Haven, but for now, she reined him in.

She spoke out loud, even though he talked in her head. She preferred it that way. "Settle down. If I need to cast big spells, it's easier in here."

"*The elements are where we best connect. Not contained by walls.*"

"Yeah well, this is the modern world. Magic is not common. Well, it is, but it isn't talked about by everyone."

"*Sad.*"

She ignored him, staring out of the window and onto the street below. She should have stayed with Reuben. She knew he'd gone into the water, because she could feel where everyone was. This was so weird. Her senses were warring with each other. She could hear Bear, buzzing with both impatience and his ancient wisdom. She could even feel a hint of her ancestor, the old woman with the grey hair. She felt full of everything, and she didn't know what to focus on first.

"I'll open the windows. That's a connection to the outside." She flung the windows wide, allowing the cold wind to blow inside.

"*Good. Now sit quietly. Your magic is best served mentally rather than physically.*"

"It is? It feels odd."

"*That's because you like blasting things with fire. Twyla is the same. This is different.*"

"From the animal that ripped Egberk to shreds."

"*You did that, not me.*"

El was just about to argue with him when a clap of thunder silenced her. She leaned out of the window, and saw the mist rolling down the hill.

"Avery? Alex?" El shouted their names, looking up as if she would see them in the sky above. "What's happening."

"*Focus! You must do as we did around the fire. Connect mentally.*"

"But the mist is coming!"

"*Do it!*"

Bear's presence, which had been casual up until now, exploded within her. She felt his fierce intent, and knew the truth of his words. Beyond that she sensed Twyla, her ancestor. El closed her eyes, opening her senses up.

The shock of what she saw drove her to her knees. The impression of everyone's energies was so strong, she saw the world around her completely differently. Reuben was close, his energy rampant. A plume of water exploded a short distance ahead of her, and she knew the sea was raging.

The thunder of hooves pounded within her, along with Bear's roar, Wolf's howl, and the screech of Raven and Eagle. *But where was Briar's Deer, Oly's Fox, and Finn's Hare?* El had barely time to consider that when Bear pounded out of the window and onto the street below, and she was with him. No one saw them. They were an invisible force. The pavement pounded beneath her strong, huge paws, his muscles rolled, and his thick fur meant she was impervious to the cold.

In seconds they were at the harbour, and she saw Reuben riding his water horse, directing all of his power toward the mist. Rearing back on huge haunches, she did the same.

Alex recovered from the onslaught of Tiernan's power quickly. Avery, however, was not as adept at spirit-walking as he was.

She was spinning end over end, the silvery cord that was her life line, tangling below. He soared across to her, ignoring the angry red threads firing below him, but Raven appeared out of nowhere, reaching her first.

Avery slowed and steadied. "*I'm okay. Keep destroying his threads!*"

Alex zeroed in on Tiernan's web. The threads pulsed and popped with power, and following them to the coast, he saw the mass of red and green power rolling down the hill. *So, this is what the mist looked like in energy form.* It was ugly, domineering. They had definitely summoned his attention. Everything the mist touched ignited, and once again, lightning flashed within it.

Alex felt Wolf's power magnify within him, and drawing it in, and his ancestor's power, he blasted more of Tiernan's threads. A short distance away, Avery continued her assault.

But there were so many that Alex felt despair creeping in. Especially when he sensed the balance of power shift toward Tiernan. He twisted to look at the weak threads over the missing White Haven, and with horror saw them fading even more. *They were losing!*

"*Wait,*" Wolf commanded. "*Your ancestors must do this to get your friends home. Trust us.*"

Ben watched White Haven become more visible as the barrier weakened.

His heart was pounding, his mouth was dry, and he wasn't sure if it was anxiety or magic putting him off-balance. *Probably both.* He could hear distant claps of thunder, and he couldn't work out if it was his present or his future. When Raven finally screeched, he thought he was imagining it.

"Now!" Stan yelled, and he grabbed Ben's elbow, propelling them both through the now barely-there barrier.

A tingle erupted across his skin like a burn, and he yelled as he fell on the ground. Instantly, the familiarity of modern White Haven came into clear focus. "Holy shit! We made it! Stan, are you okay?"

Stan groaned next to him, his face contorted with pain. "What was that? It felt like an electric shock."

"Magic—of some sort." The barrier was already strengthening again, the witches in their familiar form becoming harder and harder to see. "Herne's horns. They actually did it. We're here!" Ben patted the ground, feeling its solidity. It felt so good.

Stan groaned as he rolled to his feet. "I suspect that was the easier part, supporting Tiernan. Reversing it will be harder. Let's hope our witches have things well in hand. And let's hope if there are people here, that they are still alive. Start door-knocking." He strode to the nearest one. "This is no time to be dainty."

Ben and Stan worked methodically down the street, shouting and rattling door handles. If people were here, they'd be hiding. However, no one responded, until they entered the street that intersected the main one.

Ben pointed up to a window. "I see movement."

"Let me! They know me." Stan raised his voice. "It's me! Stan from the council! We come in peace!"

"Seriously? The peace thing?"

Stan smirked. "It seems the right thing to say, and I love saying it."

"We're not alien invaders." Ben pounded on the door, reflecting on Stan's unexpected humour. Then again, he was the town's Druid. "It's Stan and Ben—the ghost hunter! Friends."

He heard the thump of footsteps, and then the door was thrown open. A young man with a shaved head and a pierced nose answered the door. He was wearing old jeans, a worn sweatshirt, and looked like he hadn't slept in a week. "The ghost hunter! Are you for real?"

"Of course!" Stan shuffled into view and Ben introduced him. "Are you from White Haven?"

"No! I'm here visiting with my girlfriend. We came because of you and your videos. We expected a fun Samhain. We did not expect *this*!" He pointed to the magical wall. "That should not be there. Is this a White Haven trick? Is there a camera behind you?"

"No!" *Why was everyone so obsessed with TV?* "Anyone else in there with you?"

"Oh, yeah. We're all upstairs. No one is risking going out there again."

Ben glanced at Stan, uneasy. "Did something happen?"

The man looked at him like he'd gone mad. "Dude. We are *somewhere else*. We heard wolves last night! I mean, I love your shit, but this? Can we ever go home?"

"Ah, that. Can we come in? We should talk."

The earth trembled beneath Briar's feet, and she knew Tiernan had resumed his attack. She could also feel the other witches as they responded. For now, she blocked them out.

She focussed instead on the earth beneath her feet, and the trees around her. She could feel their connectedness. It ran far across the forest. Dylan was right. All the trees were connected, and ancient magic ran through their sap. She sensed Deer running through them, pausing every now and again, searching as Briar was for fey magic. But it was hard. Ravens' Wood was full of the Green Man's magic, and it overpowered most other things.

Briar reminded herself of Shadow and how her magic felt. She felt the dryads murmur around her, and appealed to them, too. "*Show me.*"

Suddenly, the tree trunks warmed beneath her hands, and a wild singing erupted around her. It was eerie. Her skin broke out in goose bumps, and a vision of the Beltane night spent here filled her senses. A night spent with Hunter, when the Green Man and the Goddess walked these woods, along with the wild wedding party.

She took a sharp intake of breath. *Of course. That was them! The fey.* She had seen an echo of their presence. She focussed on that feeling, and then suddenly she sensed the net of fey protective magic that stopped Tiernan.

It was pure, filled with love, a shining light that would repel all evil intent.

She inhaled, drawing it within her, filling herself up so that she was almost drunk with it.

Then she opened her mind to Tiernan and her coven.

They raged and fought, the land trembling. It wasn't Avery and Alex who would need this, it was Reuben and El. She found them, and sent the fey spell their way, before attacking Tiernan, too.

Caspian knew where the other witches were, thanks to the connection fostered by Avery's spell. Now, he needed to play his part.

He, Helena, Finn, and Oly had waited for the ancestors to work their magic, horrified as the streets faded away to the point of non-existence. Caspian itched to intervene, but knew he had to wait. Helena, Oly, and Finn, had fallen silent a while ago, all of them connected to their ancestors, all lending them their magic. Caspian, joined to them, had given them as much as he could, but more acutely than ever, he felt his inherent disconnection from them—and their families.

All the while, the crashes of thunder resounded overhead, and the battle raged by the harbour.

But now, the missing streets were becoming more visible again, and even through his distant connection, Caspian knew Ben and Stan had crossed the barrier.

Helena had assumed a leadership position, and she shouted, "Call the elements! Weave them anew. Air, Water, Fire, Earth. Ground White Haven in our present. The streets straddle time, but they belong here. The threads tie it here, and they are weak—not broken. Tiernan is too distracted to stop us."

Caspian's headache intensified. Briar was right. He really wasn't strong enough for this, but he was needed, and he would do what he could. He just hoped it was enough.

Cassie was sheltering in a doorway with Dylan, refusing to retreat any further. The ebbing and flowing of the missing streets was nightmarish.

"Are you still happy to stay, Cass?" Dylan asked her, his eyes on the shimmering wall.

"Of course! Aren't you?"

He pulled her into his side, a hug of reassurance. "Of course. But if the whole thing explodes, we're very close to the epicentre."

"I know, but we have to be here if he returns—and there's nothing else we can do."

Newton had urged them to leave the area, as no one knew what might happen, but they refused. She eyed the flickering lightning over the harbour. It wasn't advancing, but she had no idea what that meant. They weren't telepathically connected like the others.

She returned her focus to the missing streets, and waited.

Avery was like a whirlwind as she destroyed every one of Tiernan's poisonous threads, watching them shrivel to nothing. With each cut, the remaining ones became more apparent. They darkened and distended like engorged snakes as his power retreated.

Tiernan was pinned down, and couldn't respond, and with every thread they severed, they weakened him even more. Alex had already destroyed the ones that choked the streets caught between past and present, and they could see the natural threads growing in strength. But they hadn't the time to watch.

Raven appeared beside her. "*Leave the smaller ones now. Aim for the biggest. Cut those. Without them, he cannot make more.*"

She looked across the twinkling network of threads and saw the ones he meant. He was right. They were his lifeline.

"*Alex! Join me over there!*"

In seconds they reached the sinewy ropes that laid the foundation of Tiernan's attack.

"*Take my hand,*" she instructed Alex. "*We'll work together.*"

As they joined hands, she opened up to the others, too. She drew on her coven's magic, and together they tackled the slithery ropes that he used to twist fate. Raven pecked and pulled, while they wrestled to cut them. When one finally snapped, it ricocheted like a whip, and everything of Tiernan's began to unravel.

Alex squeezed Avery's hand. *"We need to get out of here, Avery, before our own cords are severed."*

"But—"

"No buts. Time to go."

Zee felt as if he was witnessing an apocalypse—again. One in which this time, he didn't die.

He hoped.

The clouds that amassed over White Haven's harbour were mottled with black and green, and lightning crashed within them. A wall of water rose beyond the harbour, and at the top, lit by lightning, was a figure on a huge, rearing horse. But in seconds it had vanished beneath the surf as the wave rolled and crashed onto the beach road.

Anyone who was still out on the streets—and there weren't many, because they had all made sure of that—screamed and ran for the nearest building to seek cover.

Behind him, Eli and Kendall were urging people through the door of The Wayward Son, while other shops and pubs offered shelter, too.

This was not the lightning-filled mist of the previous night. This was in a much smaller area, restricted to the harbour and the cliffs, but it was as if it contained the wrath of God. He had seen that up close and personally, and did not want to experience it again.

Just as Zee was thinking that the clouds could not contain the power that had gathered within them, they started to disperse. Ragged whisps were caught by the wind, carrying them far out to sea, or rolling up beyond the headland to disperse over the castle. Stars began to appear as the crackle of energy that had threatened to swallow White Haven petered out.

Kendall appeared at his side. "Is it over?"

"It seems so." He twisted to look at the hill where the streets had almost vanished, wondering what was happening there.

Ben thought he might be sick. A very peculiar sensation was ripping through the time-suspended streets of White Haven. The pressure kept changing, and his ears were popping. It was like being on a plane when it hit turbulence.

He was sheltering with Stan and about ten other people in the first floor living room of a rented flat. They were a mixture of locals and visitors. Ben's nose was pressed to the window, and Stan and the young man with the shaved hair called Morgan were beside him. Some people were at the next window, others were on the living room floor, braced as if for impact. They were all obsessed with the notion of crashing. Ben wished he had kept his thoughts about turbulence to himself, especially as some equated this idea with alien aircrafts. That was Marjorie Bishop, owner of the gallery, and Sci-Fi obsessive. Give him a pagan any day.

"Ben!" Stan tapped the glass and pointed above the opposite roof. "I see White Haven! It's coming back."

"We're *going* back, Stan."

"This is no time to correct me!"

"Sorry." He grinned at him. "I think we might actually make it."

Morgan summoned their attention. "Do you think we need to go outside? Gather on the border? We might have to make a run for it." He shrugged. "I mean, what if it only lasts for seconds?"

Ben knew magic, better than anyone else here. To go outside now could be dangerous, but Morgan made a good point. He nodded. "All right. Let's do it."

Newton sheltered within the closest doorway, Moore next to him, watching the shadowed streets of White Haven slowly crispen and sharpen.

The thunder had finally ceased, and the church bells had stopped tolling.

Moore eased his head around the porch, looking up. "The cloud has gone. Bloody hell, Guv. I think it's over."

Newton was too busy watching the witches. They had finally dropped their hands, and all sank to their knees. Beyond them, a ragged group of people were making their way down the street.

Newton ran, and the PCs sheltering nearby joined them. "Get them all of out there! Moore—pull the witches back!" He didn't trust the streets not to vanish into some other dimension again.

But before he could even get close to any of them, Cassie bolted out of a side street, yelling, "*Ben!*"

She plunged into the crowd as if she had laser sight, and threw herself on Ben. Despite the tension, Newton laughed.

Ben and Stan were home.

Briar lowered her arms and opened her eyes as the fey magic faded away, and the Green Man stirred and then settled again.

It was dark now, and stars were appearing overhead. The storm mist conjured by Tiernan had gone. *But had he? Had they really defeated him?*

She left the wood and walked across the castle ruins, Deer next to her, wary of attack. But everything was silent. There wasn't even a breath of wind.

A shimmer of light ahead caught her attention, but Deer nudged her on. "*It's safe. She comes to apologise.*"

Briar didn't need to ask who. Hand resting on Deer, she walked onwards, and the white-clad form of Wyrd appeared before her, threads streaming around her. She was ageless and beautiful, but her eyes were haunted as she said, "I have done you a great disservice."

"You have. You almost killed us."

"Not I."

"You didn't stop him."

"He was like a brother to me, and I made a pact."

"That doesn't excuse it."

"He carried great grief."

"That is also not an excuse. You bargained with our lives." Briar would not back down, not even to Wyrd. Perhaps the Green Man and the fey magic had emboldened her. Mostly, she was just tired and heartsick.

Wyrd regarded her silently for a moment, stars shining in her fathomless eyes as the threads continued to weave around her. "You chose well today."

"I know. I chose good friends."

Wyrd smiled. "Your future is bright, Briar. Go safely."

She vanished, leaving Briar alone with Deer. "*Where now?*"

"*The Wayward Son for you. Celebrations await.*"

Briar laughed. "*Will I see you again?*"

"*Any time you choose.*"

"*That's a yes, then.*" And with a light heart, Briar walked down the hill to her car and her friends.

Chapter Thirty-Seven

The noise emanating from The Wayward Son was deafening as Alex opened the door and stepped inside.

He and Avery were the last of his friends to arrive. He could see them crowded around the far end of the bar. Well, everyone except Newton, Moore, and Kendall, and he knew from the conversation that he'd had with Newton on the phone that they were with the people who'd been caught in the weird time warp in the missing streets. Ben, however, was sitting next to Stan, surrounded by everyone else, being bombarded with questions by the look of it. Both of them had a pint and looked victorious, besides being grizzled and unkempt.

Alex paused just inside the door, preparing himself for what was to come.

Avery nudged him, a broad grin on her face. "I can't believe we did it. Look at them!"

"Perhaps fate was on our side after all."

"I remain convinced that we make our own fate!"

He kissed her. "After everything that happened tonight, I can't disagree with you. I'm just glad that the town looks more or less intact."

"It will survive a few lightning blasts."

"Magic blasts, you mean!"

"*Lightning storm*, remember?" She winked. "We can also lend a healing, helping hand."

"I still feel as if I'm half in the past." Their walk through the town had shown that White Haven had survived, and the locals seemed to have taken the battle in their stride as they emerged from their shelters. The walk had also served to ground them in normality, almost dispelling the strange sense of displacement that their spirit-walk had caused. *Almost.*

"Can you still feel Wolf?" Avery asked, looking up at him.

"He's faint, but I need time to process it all. Raven?"

"Faint too, and that's good. He's exhausting!" She grinned and pulled him to the bar. "Come on. I need a drink."

Eli saw their approach, and shuffled to make room for them. Avery headed to Ben's side, but Alex stayed with Eli as he said, "I'm glad to see that you two look okay."

"You, too. Thanks for all your help." Eli leaned against the bar, relaxed but alert; a typical Nephilim trait. "I had one of the easy jobs for a change, helping keep people off the streets."

"You made a trade with dryads. That was a big deal. I won't forget that."

"And neither will they," Zee said, passing him a pint. His lips twisted with worry. "Not sure what we've got ourselves embroiled in there."

Eli shrugged. "We didn't promise anything we couldn't do."

"We have long lives, Eli, and we've just tied ourselves to Ravens' Wood and its future."

Alex had a horrible feeling that Zee had a far more realistic outlook on this than Eli, but before he could answer, his father hugged him and pulled him aside. "I'm glad to see you. What you two did was insane."

Alex studied him. He looked tired, drawn around the eyes. "No more than you and everyone else. Thank you for coming. We couldn't have done this without you."

"I'm talking about *you*! Fighting while spirit-walking was risky."

"I've done it before, and no doubt I'll do it again. Hopefully not with some fate-twisting, time-changer though."

Finn glanced over his shoulder, his gaze encompassing his friends. "I have a feeling you do this kind of thing more often than I know."

Alex laughed. "I can't deny that. White Haven has turned into a hot spot of paranormal activity. We do have some breaks from it, fortunately."

"Even so, you're playing with fire."

"Not playing, Dad. We don't do this for a laugh! You saw that, surely?"

"Of course, but you know what I mean!"

"No, I don't, but I'm not about to argue. White Haven is my home. I stayed, you left. I do what I have to do."

His father stared at the floor, a sigh escaping his lips, before he looked up. "I can't help how I feel."

"I know, and I won't judge you for it, but equally, you can't judge me for my choices, either."

Finn squeezed his shoulder. "I'm your father, and I can't stop worrying."

"Best you're not here to see what we get up to more often, then. Having said that, I really hope you'll stick around for a few more days. At least until Samhain. I think you'd like White Haven without the drama, and you'll love the celebrations." Alex desperately hoped he'd say yes. It was good to have his father visit, and he really wanted to show off his home's best side, and wanted him to get to know his friends properly.

"Of course I will."

Alex grinned, but then Clea caught his attention. A very animated, lively Clea with a gleam in her eye. "Great. So, tell me. How is Helena?"

"Ah! She's an interesting one, isn't she?"

El studied Reuben, noting that his exuberance was tinged with sadness, and when he finally stopped joking with Ben, she placed herself between them.

"Reuben! What's going on? Something's bothering you."

"I'm fine! Did you see me on top of that wave? On Silver. Wow! Best feeling ever."

She rolled her eyes. Trust him to name his horse Silver. "I not only saw you on it, I experienced it, too, with our connection—which, by the way, I do not wish to repeat again. I felt as if I was in a million places at once, and I did *not* like it. Anyway, you were brilliant, but something's not right. And don't you dare lie to me!"

He fixed her with his bright blue eyes. "I had hoped to see Gil. I didn't. I'm gutted."

She had suspected this would be the issue, and she hugged him. "Maybe Gil found it harder than he thought. Maybe you being in the water made it tricky. Plus, the tarot spell connected us all. That probably made it even more confusing." She knew she was gabbling, so she stopped.

"I know all that, but still...I'm disappointed."

"It's Samhain. You're stronger than you've ever been, and I sense Gil is, too. Why don't you try to connect over the next few nights? Just you, a fire, and a quiet place. You'll find each other." El didn't dare show too much emotion; Reuben wouldn't want it. Not here, anyway, but she hated seeing him so vulnerable. "If you want me to help, I will, but you don't need me. If there's one thing I've seen this year, Reu, one thing I really know to be true, it's that you have finally stepped into your power, and I'm so happy for you."

A familiar twinkle returned to his eye. "Do you think so?"

"I know so. Don't you?"

"Well, I did rock it out there." He winked. "I'll rock your world later, too."

"Did you really just say that horribly cheesy line?"

"You know it, babes."

"Okay. I am officially not worried about you anymore. Pint?"

"Yes, please. Skulduggery Ale."

"Of course it is!"

Avery headed to Helena's side, reassured that Ben and Stan were okay, but desperately wanting to talk to them privately to hear more details. Helena was in animated conversation with Caspian, and flirting too, which was very disconcerting in her grandmother's body.

"Helena, Caspian. How are you both?"

Caspian winced and rubbed the bandage on his head. "I've been better."

"Avery!" Helena stepped in and enveloped her in a hug. "I, however, have never felt better—well, not for centuries. Your grandmother is a wonderful woman. And," she stepped back and nodded at Caspian, her eyes raking over him, "it's been very interesting getting to know Thaddeus's descendant. It's quite the season for it."

By the Goddess. "Are you drunk?"

"I have had a glass or two of wine. I hardly think that constitutes *drunk*."

"Clea probably hasn't drunk alcohol in years."

"She has a sherry every night! You should know that."

"Don't you dare guilt trip me!"

"Ladies! I have a headache, remember?" Caspian reminded them. "And I am only drinking Coke. Can we please not do dramas?" Both of them swung around to glare at him, and Caspian froze. "Carry on! Ignore me."

Avery wrestled her emotions under control. "Sorry, Caspian. Look, I just wanted to thank both of you for tonight. We couldn't have done it without you."

Caspian sighed. "I'm not sure I was equal to it. Helena and Clea, however, were brilliant, as were Oly and Finn. I was the odd man out."

"No, you were not," Helena said briskly. "You added your own blend of knowledge, plus knowledge of *their* magic. I could feel it through the tarot card spell that connected us. You've been spellcasting with them for a while."

Avery smiled. "He's Team White Haven now."

"Sort of," he confessed, "although Oswald reminded me the other night, I have my own coven to sort out. He's right. I'm planning on getting us together. "

Avery wasn't sure how she felt about that, but Helena answered, "Never neglect your coven. They're worth their weight in gold. Even if you have disconnected, you'll work it out. Especially family." A smug smile crossed her lips. "The Favershams have always been very close."

"Not recently," he shot back. "How long are you sticking around for, Helena?"

She stared at Avery. "I suggest a week, until Samhain."

Avery was flabbergasted. "I cannot justify keeping Clea—er, you—from the home that long! Besides, she's old, and I know what it feels like to have you in my body. It's horrible!"

Helena pouted. "Spoilsport. Clea is older, and confused. She won't notice like you did. And wouldn't it be nice to chat? You could ask me all those questions that you really want to know the answers to. My past? Our magic? What I get up to in the spirit world?"

Caspian laughed. "She's got you there, Avery."

Damn it. That was exactly what she'd love to do. "All right. But I suggest a compromise. Two days."

"Three."

Alex was going to kill her. "Deal."

Briar inhaled the scent of her mulled cider, sighed with pleasure, and sipped it. *This was perfect—almost.* Hunter's presence seemed to haunt her, and in danger of becoming maudlin, she butted into Oly's conversation with Stan.

Stan had a few days of stubble on his face that actually suited him, and it seemed Oly thought so too, from the way she was teasing him. Unfortunately, his Druid's cloak was looking a little worn. Mud splatters coated the bottom of it, and it was torn in a few places.

"I have a spell for that," Oly told him, pointing at the tears in his cloak. "It will save you from having to sew them all."

"Really? But a spell for that seems so mundane compared to what you do!"

"No spell is mundane, Stan. Magic is a wonder. A joy!"

"You don't have to tell me. You saved my life!" He spotted Briar and grinned. "I always knew there was something different about you. Does he know?" He pointed at Eli.

"Yes, he knows, and is happy to keep our secrets." *And some of his own*. "I hope you are, too."

"Of course! I love being in on the secrets of White Haven. But, you know, there's a few who suspect..." He raised an eyebrow and tapped his nose.

"Let's keep them guessing, then! A little mystery is always a good thing."

"Of course it is!" Oly proclaimed. "You can never really tell who won't approve, either. Some people appear open-minded but actually aren't, whereas, some who you think will hate what you do, will be incredibly supportive!" She lowered her voice, leaned in, and gave a faint, almost imperceptible nod to Clea. "No one wants to be at the wrong end of a witch hunt. Helena will attest to that."

Stan frowned. "That's not Helena. That's Avery's grandmother. Delightful woman, although I must admit, her memory is better than..." And then he gasped. "No! Is it?"

"I'm afraid it is, Stan," Briar said quickly. "Perhaps you could keep that little secret, too. It won't be for long."

"Oh!" His eyebrows shot up. "I didn't even know you could do such a thing! But what am I saying? I saw your ancestors become animals! Actual animals! Such wonders. Such sights! I will never forget it."

Another thought struck Briar as she saw Rupert, the owner of the occult tour guide group, across the pub, shooting them curious glances every now and again. "Speaking of people who shouldn't know our secret, Rupert is on that list."

"Really! But he runs the tour group. He loves the occult."

Oly huffed. "I can feel his aura from here. Nasty little man. It's like he's carrying his own storm clouds. Oh no, Stan. He must *never* know."

"Really?" Stan stared at Rupert, eyes narrowed as if evaluating him. "My lips are sealed."

"Thank you."

"Now," he shuffled and leaned closer, "I'd like you two to tell me a little more about your magic. I am thirsty for knowledge!"

"I still can't believe you're back," Cassie told Ben. "I had nightmares you'd be lost forever, especially when we heard where you were."

He raked his hand through his hair. "I can barely believe it myself. Me and Stan were preparing ourselves for the worst. Well, it wouldn't have been awful, the ancestors were good people, but blimey…"

"Primitive?" Dylan asked.

"And then some. I'll tell you all about it when we're somewhere quieter. It was amazing, and terrifying. And I met the fey. Shadow's people. That was something. And ancient Ravens' Wood…" He trailed off, eyes distant. "We think it's odd now, but back then, in the Otherworld, well, that's agelessness. It was uncanny."

It was clear that Ben's experience had changed him, even though he'd only been there for days. He looked older, wiser. Cassie exchanged a glance with Dylan, and it was obvious he thought the same.

Dylan joked to make light of it. "Well, mate, as glad as I am to see you home, you really need a shower. You stink."

Ben laughed and ran his hand across his face. "Yep, and I need a shave. We need to top up our spell kit, too. I used some of it to escape from the mad bastard. I have to tell the witches that. I still don't understand most of it. I mean, I know my half."

"Don't worry. It looks like Alex is already rounding us up," Cassie said, noticing him having a chat with the others and pointing upstairs. "Have you got enough energy for it?"

"I am *so* looking forward to my own bed, but it can wait. I'm far too buzzed to sleep now, and I want to hear all your news, too. Wait until I tell you about Stan. He was brilliant!"

Cassie smiled. He may have changed, but he was back home and in one piece, and that was all that mattered.

Newton watched the last of the people caught in the spell leave the Community Policing Centre in White Haven, sighed, leaned back in his seat, and put his feet up on the table. He wished he still smoked.

"Good job, team. That was tricky. You handled it well."

"Cheers, Guv," Moore said as he took a seat. "I'm not sure the whole electrical storm thing will wash with those guys, though. I mean, I don't think I'd believe that a power grid had blown and sealed off the area."

"Yeah! What if Sarah Rutherford interviews them? Alien abduction was mentioned!" Kendall said while she put the kettle on.

"Good! Alien abduction always rules people out as nutters." In fact, Newton welcomed that. *Let's see how Sarah handles that one...*

"Doesn't magic?" Hamid asked, looking at each of them in turn. "You three are skirting around that topic, and yet me and Kev saw it, too. The witches chanting spells in a line. The streets returning from wherever they had been. The weird mist."

"Yeah." Kev nodded. "And the giant wall of water in the harbour. And what's with Zee and Eli? There's something funny about them."

Newton wondered how much to say. They both worked in White Haven, and were well known to the community. Kev was newer than Hamid, having replaced Joe earlier in the year, a local who had moved to Devon. Both had seen some of the odder happenings here, and yet neither had said a word or compromised them in any way.

Moore cleared his throat. "Might be wise, Guv."

Newton nodded. "All right. But I'm not doing this over tea! Is there some kind of alcohol here? Beer, whiskey? Just one, mind, because then you're back on patrol for a few hours, just to make sure we're all settled down."

Kev grinned, and headed to the corner cupboard. "Christmas supplies. Whiskey, bourbon, I think there's some port. And there may be some beer in the fridge for Hamid. He hates spirits."

Hamid feigned choking. "Disgusting."

"That'll be one for both of us then," Kendall said, reaching into the fridge.

"Right. Settle in," Newton instructed them. "This may take a while."

Chapter Thirty-Eight

Avery leaned on the counter at Happenstance Books and reached for a Halloween cupcake decorated with pumpkin-shaped icing. "That's the last time someone crosses my palm with silver this morning."

"Looks like it's going well, though," Sally said, adjusting her elaborate costume. "The shop has quite the buzz this morning. Must be because you banished that gloomy cloud and mizzle last night!"

It was Saturday morning, and outside was a crisp, clear autumn day that promised a frosty night. Already, shop owners were cleaning up their paintwork and replacing their sizzled pumpkins with fresh ones.

Avery finished chewing her mouthful of cake before she answered. "Let's hope we have a similar day for the Samhain celebrations. Stan will be thrilled."

"He's all right, then?"

"Better than all right. He's bouncing. No doubt he'll be in here later."

Dan joined them, the toy Raven perched on his shoulder, and Avery eyed it suspiciously. He was too busy reaching for a cake to notice. "He's in on all this, then?"

"If you mean magic, yes he is. He had a twinkle in his eyes every time he looked at me last night." Avery had already told them most of what had happened the night before.

Sally grinned. "I think it's fantastic. I love Stan. It's only right that he knows. Ben will be fine too, I'm sure."

Avery considered his expression from the night before. "It affected him more, for some reason. Not in a bad way, I think, just hit him a bit deeper. Probably didn't help that Tiernan was drugging him with some weird, powdered concoction."

They had spent a good couple of hours in Alex's flat the night before, exchanging news with everyone. Newton, Kendall and Moore had finally joined them, and it had been a relief to see that Newton had shed his grumpiness.

"By the way," Avery continued, "Kev and Hamid, the two constables, know about us too, just in case they pop in."

"Ah!" Dan said through a mouthful of cake. "Interesting. That's a good thing. They're around too much not to know."

"That's what Newton's team thought, too. They also all know to keep it a secret, especially from Rupert."

Sally grunted. "I'm glad we haven't seen much of him lately! Anyway, what are you going to do about your familiars."

"Excellent question. I'm not sure. I quite liked mine, although I'd like him to be a little quieter. He's very opinionated."

"Does he still link you to your ancestors?" Dan asked.

"No. The link was always faint, but has vanished completely now. They have done it deliberately, from what Raven said to me, and I can understand why."

"Something about disrupting the space-time continuum," Dan said, smirking. "Very wise."

Avery laughed. "You're as bad as Stan. Star Trek obsessed. I believe the explanation was that they didn't want to interfere any further in our future. It's a shame, though. I would have liked to talk some more. Even through Raven. At least Ben can tell us about them. Our coven has decided to honour them over Samhain. One night next week, in Reuben's garden where we first found our spirit animals, we're having a bonfire. I'd like to think I have one last chance to say goodbye. In fact, I'll have a fire in my garden later. Twilight was when we first felt the connection last week. It really was quite magical. I'd like to recapture that."

Sally squeezed her hand. "Sounds lovely. Of course, in the meantime, we all have Helena to enjoy." She nodded behind Avery.

Avery could already feel her approach, and turning, she saw Helena in Clea's body emerge from the bookshelves with a stack of books and a mischievous glint in her eye. She laid the books on the counter. "Some for me, and some for Clea. I thought you'd like to make a note of the ones I've chosen, Sally. Clea likes murder mysteries and has requested a few more for when she returns to her body." She stared reprovingly at Avery. "Something to bear in mind—especially Miss Marple. I, meanwhile, am refreshing my knowledge of modern witchcraft. I plan on returning, too."

"*What*?" Avery shouted, and then lowered her voice as customers stared. "What do you mean, return?"

"I have told some old friends who have expressed interest in my apparent mental recovery that I am trialling a new drug and will be here more often."

"Oh, really? And how do you propose that?"

"A little possession, of course. Just once every couple of months." She beamed at her, and then at Sally and Dan, who looked as shocked as Avery felt. "We have mentally shaken on it."

"I think you'll find you need me to help with that, and I have *not* agreed."

"There are other ways, my dear Avery. Now, let's not bicker. I presume these books are a gift?"

Sally sniggered. "Of course. Would you like them wrapped?"

"No. Just as they are is perfect. By the way, I'm heading out for lunch with Oly. Lovely woman. We have so much to share."

Helena picked up the books and headed to the backroom, leaving Avery dumbfounded.

"Has Beth said anything else about our ancestors?" Briar asked Tamsyn on Saturday evening. She had headed to Stormcrossed Manor as soon as she closed the shop, and they were in Tamsyn's kitchen.

Tamsyn shook her head. "No. She seemed to brush it off once the storm vanished. Rosa has taken her and Max out. They've gone to the cinema to watch a film. They won't be long, if you want to see them."

"No, it's fine. I'm just glad she's okay." She accepted a cup of herbal tea from her grandmother. "It's you I wanted to see."

Tamsyn's face wrinkled with pleasure, and she kissed her on the cheek. "Walk with me, then. There's a fire burning in the garden, and I want to bank it down for the night."

"The last of the leaves and old wood?"

"Almost. One pile left."

Tamsyn led her outside and along the already dark paths, using a torch to navigate their way. "I'd like some lighting out here once we've finished tidying. It would be nice to illuminate the paths."

"I'm sure we can arrange that." As Briar's eyes adjusted to the evening darkness, she took in the shapes of the surrounding hedges and gardens, and a feeling of peace swept over her. "This is such a beautiful place. I'm so glad we're bringing it back to life."

"It had plenty of life. It needed order!" Tamsyn chuckled as the smouldering fire came into view in the centre of the courtyard. "I want lights in the potting sheds, too. Some new shelving. Get the plumbing fixed for the sink."

"Ready for some spring planting?"

"Yes!" She picked up the garden fork, prodded the fire, and then threw another branch on. "Time for one more, I reckon."

"Did you keep some for the house?"

"Of course. That lovely Zee came and chopped me a huge pile. Should be enough to keep us going until spring."

Briar smiled and took a deep breath of cold, sharp air, delicious wood smoke, and rich earth. The stars wheeled overhead, and once again that feeling of timelessness crept over her. "Our ancestors would have done exactly this, Gran. Burned old wood, prepared the ground for the spring, looked to our past and our future." Her gaze shifted to the horizon. "Do you still see the stag?"

"I saw him this morning, at dawn, just as the early mist was rising. He's beautiful."

"I thought he'd play a part in everything that happened, and yet he didn't. What does he mean? What's he here for?"

"I don't know, other than what I said last week. Support, change." Her eyes sparkled as she looked at Briar. "Maybe some things are meant to remain a mystery."

"Or maybe the meaning isn't yet clear."

"Maybe. How were your friends when you told them about Hunter?"

"Lovely, as always."

"And Newton."

"Surprisingly lovely, too. But I warned him not to expect anything. I'm in no rush right now."

"Good, because I have a feeling someone else is coming your way."

Voice laced with scepticism, Briar said, "Really?"

"Really. Don't forget your old gran sees the future, too."

"Sounds more like wishful thinking."

"Cheeky. Just you wait and see."

On Saturday night, close to midnight, Reuben shut the snug door behind him, and settled into the large cane chair lined with cushions and blankets.

At his side was a small round table with two glasses and a bottle of whiskey. In front of him was a brazier filled with branches. With a word of power, he ignited the wood and watched the flames leap high, carrying heat towards him. He raised his glass of whiskey, downed his shot in one gulp, then topped it up and threw one at the fire. The alcohol ignited with a flash of brighter flames before settling again. He then poured two more shots, one in his glass and one for Gil.

The night settled around him. The surf crashed on the beach below his garden, and an owl screeched across the fields. Even from here the water called to him, and Silver's pounding hooves matched his heartbeat. He could wait. Reuben had other things to do.

He cleared his mind, thinking of Gil and the times they had spent together, especially remembering how he had tried to teach him magic, and Reuben had brushed it off. He sighed, and spoke out loud. "I was a fool. I should have paid more attention."

"Rubbish. You weren't ready."

Reuben whipped his head around, staring at the figure in the chair next to him. "You came!"

"You asked." Gil smiled and nodded at the glass. "I wish I could join you in that."

Reuben felt so overwhelmed that for a moment he couldn't speak. His throat felt thick, and his vision blurred. He fought to control his emotions. "I've looked for you before."

"It's not easy for me to be here. Helena made it seem so, but the time of year helps."

Reuben studied him from his head to his toes. "You haven't changed."

"It's timeless where I am."

"So I hear." Reuben swallowed a mouthful of whiskey, the fierce burn of the liquid steadying him. "I'd hoped to see you yesterday. Get your help."

Gil laughed. "You didn't need my help. I considered it, but I'd have only been a distraction. Wow, little brother! Your magic is very impressive."

"Not as…"

"Shut up. It's great. And your spirit animal. That's really something else. You're hanging on to him, I hope?"

"Absolutely."

"And what about our ancestor? Is he around?"

"I'm not sure. I barely connected to him. I just had the sense of him." Reuben lifted his head as if he would feel him. "I think he's gone. What about you? You don't see him? Or any of them?"

"There are millions of us in there, Reu. Too many to single out."

Reuben had so many questions, so many things he wanted to say, that he didn't know where to start.

"It's fine. Take your time." Gil read his mind just as easily as he always had. He settled himself in the chair and stretched his legs towards the fire as if this was just any other evening. "I'm not going anywhere for a few hours."

Reuben took a deep shuddering breath to steady himself, and leaned back, too. There was no rush. He could savour this moment. Just him and Gil talking into the night, and there was nothing that he wanted more.

Thanks for reading *Wyrd Magic.* Please make an author happy and leave a review. There will be another book in this series, released in September 2023.

Storm Moon Rising, Storm Moon Shifters book 1, is on pre-order now, out in April 2023. This is part of the White Haven world, so if you love shifters, you can order it here.

If you enjoyed this book and would like to read more of my stories, please subscribe at tjgreenauthor.com. You will get two free short stories, *Excalibur Rises* and *Jack's Encounter*, and will also receive free character sheets for all of the main White Haven Witches and White Haven Hunters characters.

By staying on my mailing list you'll receive free excerpts of my new books, as well as short stories, news of giveaways, and a chance to join my launch team. I'll also be sharing information about other books in this genre you might enjoy.

Read on for a list of my other books.

Author's Note

Thank you for reading *Wyrd Magic*, the eleventh book in the White Haven Witches series.

I knew I wanted to write another book set at Samhain and explore the witches' ancestors. I wasn't quite sure how that would go, but it certainly took turns I wasn't expecting. I hope you enjoyed it. I've left a few fun things to explore in the next book.

I must thank the members of TJ's Inner Circle, my Facebook group. I asked them to suggest Halloween costumes for Avery, Sally, and Dan, and they had some wonderful ideas. Thanks to Lisa Jordan for suggesting Gypsy Rose for Avery, Michelle Taylor for the Queen of Hearts, and Jan Shelton for Edgar Allen Poe.

It's also my biggest book to date, and my twentieth book in total. I can't quite believe I've written so many, but I've enjoyed writing every single book so far, and can't wait to write more. I'm starting on *Storm Moon Rising*, the first book in my next spinoff called Storm Moon Shifters, very soon.

There are more White Haven Witches stories to come, and although I'm not exactly sure what the next one will be about yet, there are still plenty more English and Cornish myths to explore. The next book should be released in September 2023.

If you'd like to read a bit more background on the stories, please head to my website, www.tjgreenauthor.com, where I blog about the books I've read and the research I've done for the series. In fact, there's lots of stuff on there about my other two series, Rise of the King and White Haven Hunters, as well.

Thanks again to Fiona Jayde Media for my awesome cover, and thanks to Kyla Stein at Missed Period Editing for applying her fabulous editing skills.

Thanks also to my beta readers—Terri and my mother. I'm glad you enjoyed it; your feedback, as always, is very helpful! Thanks also to Jase, my fabulously helpful other half. You do so much to support me, and I am immensely grateful for your support.

Finally, thank you to my launch team, who give valuable feedback on typos and are happy to review upon release. It's lovely to hear from them—you know who you are! You're amazing! I also love hearing from all of my readers, so I welcome you to get in touch.

If you'd like to read more of my writing, please join my mailing list at www.tjgreenauthor.com. You can get a free short story called *Jack's Encounter*, describing how Jack met Fahey—a longer version of the prologue in *Call of the King*—by subscribing to my newsletter. You'll also get a free copy of *Excalibur Rises*, a short story prequel. Additionally you will receive free character sheets on all of my main characters in White Haven Witches series—exclusive to my email list!

By staying on my mailing list, you'll receive free excerpts of my new books and updates on new releases, as well as short stories and news of giveaways. I'll also be sharing information about other books in this genre you might enjoy.

I encourage you to follow my Facebook page, T J Green. I post there reasonably frequently. In addition, I have a Facebook group called TJ's

Inner Circle. It's a fab little group where I run giveaways and post teasers, so come and join us.

About the Author

I was born in England, in the Black Country, but moved to New Zealand in 2006. I lived near Wellington with my partner, Jase, and my cats, Sacha and Leia. However, in April 2022 we moved again! Yes, I like making my life complicated... I'm now living in the Algarve in Portugal, and loving the fabulous weather and people. When I'm not busy writing I read lots, indulge in gardening and shopping, and I love yoga.

Confession time! I'm a Star Trek geek—old and new—and love urban fantasy and detective shows. Secret passion—Columbo! Favourite Star Trek film is the Wrath of Khan, the original! Other top films—Predator, the original, and Aliens.

In a previous life I was a singer in a band, and used to do some acting with a theatre company. For more on me, check out a couple of my blog posts. I'm an old grunge queen, so you can read about my love of that on my blog: https://tjgreenauthor.com/blog/

Why magic and mystery?

I've always loved the weird, the wonderful, and the inexplicable. Favourite stories are those of magic and mystery, set on the edges of the known, particularly tales of folklore, faerie, and legend—all the narratives that try to explain our reality.

The King Arthur stories are fascinating because they sit between reality and myth. They encompass real life concerns, but also cross boundaries with the world of faerie—or the Other, as I call it. There are green knights, witches, wizards, and dragons, and that's what I find particularly fascinating. They're stories that have intrigued people for generations, and like many others, I'm adding my own interpretation.

I love witches and magic, hence my second series set in beautiful Cornwall. There are witches, missing grimoires, supernatural threats, and ghosts, and as the series progresses, weirder stuff happens. The spinoff, White Haven Hunters, allows me to indulge my love of alchemy, as well as other myths and legends. Think Indiana Jones meets Supernatural!

Have a poke around in my blog posts and you'll find all sorts of posts about my series and my characters, and quite a few book reviews.

If you'd like to follow me on social media, you'll find me here:

facebook.com/tjgreenauthor/

pinterest.com/Mount0live/

tiktok.com/@tjgreenauthor

youtube.com/@tjgreenauthor

goodreads.com/author/show/15099365.T_J_Green

instagram.com/tjgreenauthor/

bookbub.com/authors/tj-green

Other Books by T J Green

Rise of the King Series

A Young Adult series about a teen called Tom who is summoned to wake King Arthur in the Otherworld.

Call of the King #1
The Silver Tower #2
The Cursed Sword #3

White Haven Hunters

The fun-filled spinoff to the White Haven Witches series! Featuring Fey, Nephilim, and the hunt for the occult.

Spirit of the Fallen #1
Shadow's Edge #2
Dark Star #3
Hunter's Dawn #4
Midnight Fire #5

Storm Moon Shifters

Storm Moon Rising #1

Made in United States
North Haven, CT
20 February 2023

32924674R00232